STACY M. JONES

Close Killer

For Michael

Acknowledgement

Thank you to the detectives and forensics teams I've had the pleasure of working with through the years and the knowledge and expertise shared with me. Special thanks to 17 Studio Book Design for bringing my stories to life with amazing covers. Thank you to Dj Hendrickson for your insightful editing and Liza Wood for proofreading and revisions. Thanks to my family and friends who are always a source of support and encouragement and to my early readers whose feedback was invaluable. I am so fortune to work with the best people and have the most amazing readers. Thank you!

A special thanks to all of the wonderful people I met and who shared stories with me during my research in Edinburgh, Scotland. I enjoyed my month in your city. Thanks to Cluny for his fabulous apartment and for the wonderful tour guides at Rabbie's Tours. The sights and history you shared with me made the trip so special. I apologize for any logistical revisions to your wonderful city. I tried my best to make it all work with the city landscape. You gave me so much to work with. It was hard to fit it all in!

CHAPTER 1

FBI Agent Kate Walsh stood in the middle of her living room in Boston's Back Bay surrounded by Christmas decorations – mementos from her childhood spent in this brownstone. She inherited the house when her parents were killed in an Embassy bombing two weeks before she was to graduate from Harvard.

The Christmas before their deaths was the last time the decorations had seen the light of day. Her parents, Ambassador Joseph Walsh and Madeline, had arrived home for the holidays that year filled with praise for Kate's hard work at college. They stayed through the New Year and then returned to Kenya. That holiday season was the last time Kate saw her parents alive. It was the last time Kate celebrated the holiday season and the last time she had a feeling of wholeness – which she had never spoken aloud to anyone.

Her work in a specialized unit of the FBI had been the perfect cover for not decorating or celebrating Christmas. She was home so infrequently she never had to make excuses to the neighbors whose homes were lit up magically each year. Her block on Marlborough Street was a Christmas spectacular except for her brownstone, which remained sadly unadorned. Kate was never home to witness the disappointed look on the faces of those checking out the Christmas lights but she imagined the people stopping and wondering about the residents of her home.

This season life changed in all the best ways.

Kate was sharing her brownstone with her best friend and FBI partner, Agent Declan James, and the FBI had no major cases that needed her attention. After the last in Martha's Vineyard, their boss, Martin Spade, seemed to be giving them an unspoken reprieve.

Kate consulted on a few cases from her home office and Declan pitched in at the Boston field office. They had settled into a nice routine working during the day and sharing a late dinner in the evening. It was nice, domestic even.

Kate spent Thanksgiving with Declan's huge family in the south part of Boston. She even managed to make pleasant conversation with Declan's slew of brothers, all involved one way or the other with criminal activity. She set that aside for the holidays and felt like part of the family.

When Declan suggested they decorate, Kate couldn't come up with a reason to say no. Not only was there no reason not to, but there was a part of her looking forward to it. They had gone to a local shopping center and bought new greens and outdoor lights for the front of the house and even splurged on a front door Christmas wreath. Declan had argued for a real tree, but that's where Kate drew the line. They compromised on a new fake tree with pre-lit white lights that looked the part enough to be real. She didn't want to spend time watering it and picking up the needles.

Earlier that morning, Declan helped her pull the decoration boxes from the attic and carry them to the living room where they sat stacked waiting for the tree to be ready. Kate stood amid the mess in the living room while Declan arranged the branches. He wanted it perfect before the first ornament touched a branch. She had already decorated the mantel with her mother's silver reindeer, colorful trees, and nutcrackers.

With each piece she unwrapped, she thought of her parents. She had been waiting for the grief to wash over her, but instead, she relived some lovely memories.

If anyone looked in the windows that December evening, they might assume Kate and Declan were a happily married couple. Kate had to admit their relationship was… complicated. It was only recently, after more than a decade of working together, that they had admitted their attraction for each other after Declan's divorce. They shared a few hot stolen kisses while working cases when the heat between them reached a boiling point.

To Kate's concern, the heat had cooled when they returned to Boston. She wasn't sure why because they had come so close to sleeping together in Martha's Vineyard. Declan might have changed his mind and she wasn't sure how she felt about that. For weeks, she had pushed her feelings for him aside and focused on work. Now though, standing in the middle of the living room amid all the memories of her past, the swell of emotion for him surged again.

Declan stood to his nearly six-foot-two height, stretched his muscular arms overhead showing a thin strip of skin when his gray Boston College tee-shirt pulled up, and declared victory over the tree. He turned his seafoam green eyes, which always carried a hint of mischief, to Kate as she laughed.

"What?" he feigned confusion. "That's the worst part of having a fake tree. It takes sheer willpower to get all those branches in the perfect spot." He flexed a thick bicep. "I deserve a beer for that."

"Real trees aren't perfect. They are messy and have spaces between the branches. Besides, I like it a little asymmetrical. We aren't aiming for the cover of a magazine." Kate stood back and appraised it. She had to admit he did an excellent job.

As Declan headed toward the kitchen, he stopped to throw another log on the fire then disappeared down the hallway. He returned with a bag of chips in his teeth and two opened beers in hand. He handed her one and pulled the chip bag from his mouth. "Before you yell that you have a stew in the crockpot, I'm hungry."

Kate took a sip. "I'm not your mother or your wife. I'm not going to yell at you for eating before dinner."

He tipped the beer bottle back to his lips and side-eyed her. After he swallowed, he grinned. "If you were my wife, you'd yell at me?"

Kate rolled her eyes at him and set the bottle down on the floor. She opened the first box of tree decorations while she ignored the heat that ran through her at the mention of being Declan's wife. She had gone from barely being attracted to him to blushing at the most inopportune time.

The other night while she'd lain awake tossing and turning, Kate convinced herself that her crush on Declan was only due to proximity and even a Catholic nun would admit he was attractive. It was probably the reason he didn't get in so much trouble in school. He had probably charmed every one of them.

"What are you stewing about?" Declan said, suddenly standing over her. She could feel the bristle of his leg hair against her arm. He crouched down until he was right next to her and then sat cross-legged on the floor. "I haven't even stopped to ask if this has been difficult for you. I know you haven't gone through this stuff since you lost your parents."

Kate turned to look at him. "How do you know that?"

He took another sip of beer. "You mentioned it like ten years ago when I asked you why you never decorated for Christmas. You gave me some lame excuse about travel, and when I asked when you had decorated last, you didn't answer me. I assumed. Am I wrong?"

Kate shook her head. "I can't believe you remember that."

He reached out his hand and squeezed her shoulder. "I remember everything you tell me, Katie. If this is too much for today, we can finish another day. I'd be happy to sit on the couch and do nothing."

Kate turned her attention back to the box, hiding her smile. "You're not getting out of this. You're the one who convinced me we needed Christmas decorations. Now that we've made a mess, you're going to sit on the couch? No way."

"What's wrong then?"

"Nothing," Kate said, not wanting to tell him. If he wasn't going to talk about what she thought was their mutual crush, then neither was she. "I'm just anxious to get the ornaments up."

"Okay then," he said and got up from the floor. He headed for one of the boxes while she unpacked the other.

For the next hour, they slowly decorated the tree. Kate stopped every few ornaments to tell Declan a story about it. There were several from her parents' travels around the globe that had special meaning or stories attached. Some were from before Kate was born, but her parents had told her the story of each one every Christmas.

When they were finally done and the boxes stacked to the side of the living room, Kate pulled out the silver star her father put on top of the tree each year. When she got big enough, he'd lift her and she'd put it on top of the tree. The star was tarnished in spots and dull from sitting in the box over the years, but it was special, nonetheless. After this Christmas, Kate promised herself she'd find someone to restore it if they could.

Declan must have been thinking the same thing. "I can stop at the hardware store and fix that for you."

Kate thanked him. "I'll put it on the tree for now." She pulled the small stepladder over to the tree and climbed the few steps to the top. She reached up, careful not to hit any of the ornaments, and placed the star in position. While she stood there, Declan went to the outlet and plugged in the tree. Kate climbed down and stood with him. They admired their work.

"We did a pretty good job for our first Christmas tree," Declan said and looped an arm over her shoulders. He had the beer in his other hand and took another sip. "I feel like we should sing a Christmas carol or something to commemorate the moment."

Kate tried not to laugh at him. "I don't sing," she said, pushing herself out from under his arm. She surveyed the room and had to admit to herself she liked what she saw. "My neighbors are going to think I've lost my mind. I appreciate you talking me into it. It will be nice to have almost a full month of enjoying this."

"I knew you'd be happy you did it." Declan set his beer down and grabbed some of the empty boxes. He carried them up the stairs with Kate right behind him carrying the rest. He went to the far end of the hall and then up the few steps to the attic. When he got to the attic landing and realized she wasn't behind him, he called to her.

Kate didn't follow him up. She tossed the boxes down on the floor and stood there taking loud audible breaths with her hands on her hips, fighting herself. She knew she shouldn't say what she was about to, but she couldn't help it. "Why haven't you kissed me since we got back?" she asked, shouting up the stairs.

Declan bounded down the steps, his footfalls heavy. "What?" he asked, confused. "You haven't kissed me. I didn't think you wanted to. I figured you changed your mind."

"I thought you changed your mind."

Declan raked a hand through his dark messy waves. "Katie, nothing has changed for me. I guess I was waiting for you given this is your house. I didn't want to start something here neither of us was ready to finish." He took a few tentative steps toward her. "You're not some girl I picked up at the bar. Once we cross the line, it's crossed. We might have a lot of weirdness and questions for each other."

"That you're not ready for," she said with anger tinging her voice.

"Stop right there before you get yourself all worked up over nothing." Declan closed the distance between them. "I never said I wasn't ready.

You're reading into what I said. We work together and live together. If we add sleeping together, how is all of that going to work? Maybe I should move out first."

Kate didn't want that. "Do you want to move out?"

"No." He locked his gaze on her. "I don't want to overwhelm you."

Before Kate could respond, her work cellphone rang from the floor below. "I need to get that." She jogged back toward the stairs and down to the first floor. She answered before it went to voicemail then climbed the stairs back to her second-floor office with Declan following right behind her.

"Spade, I'm here," she said as she sat.

"Is Declan there?" Martin Spade asked and Kate put the call on speaker.

Declan perched on the edge of her desk. "I'm here too. What's going on?"

"I have a case for you in Scotland," Spade said in a tone that meant all business.

Kate looked up at Declan and frowned – so much for holiday fun. "Has there been a murder of an American?"

"Three."

"Over what period?" Kate asked.

"The last year is what I've been told but details are still a little fuzzy," Spade said and then cursed. "I'm not sure why we are hearing about this now. We should have been notified with the first. I got a call from Chief Inspector Cameron Fraser with Police Scotland. He's been working the investigations and wants our expertise. He believes all three cases are connected. It's similar circumstances with all three victims, particularly where and how they were killed."

"Where were they killed?" Declan asked, leaning toward the phone.

"Three American women, all solo travelers, were found in Edinburgh off the Royal Mile. They were strangled and have bruising on their faces and necks. There is possible bite mark evidence."

Kate winced. "Any signs of sexual assault?"

"Not that I'm aware of but you can sort it out when you get there. Pack your bags. You're heading to Edinburgh. I'll have briefing documents for you before your flight and I'll take care of the mountain of paperwork to ensure you can carry your guns."

"Merry Christmas to us," Declan said sarcastically when the call ended, echoing her disappointment.

CHAPTER 2

"How on Earth does this heater work?" Declan asked, standing in the kitchen with the wall panel open. The apartment rental Spade's travel assistant secured was on Jeffrey Street right off the Royal Mile. They were on the third floor, really fourth if counting like Americans. They learned as they dragged their luggage up the steep winding staircase that the first floor didn't count as a floor.

The bone-chilling cold was unlike any Kate had felt in a long time. It was far worse than Boston winters. "It's radiator heat," she said, noting that each room had a radiator box and exposed piping in the kitchen. She had gone through each room and made sure the radiators were turned on as high as they could go.

Declan said he'd tackle the heating unit in the kitchen but so far hadn't made much progress. "It seems to be set on a timer but not by a temperature like ours at home but by time. Like we are only going to get heat a few times a day." He turned to her. "I can't go without heat."

"There's a fireplace in the living room. I saw some wood piled downstairs. Maybe we can just start a fire while we discuss the case." Kate headed for the door without waiting for a response. She figured carrying wood up all those stairs would at least warm her up.

Kate had only been to Edinburgh once, when she was a teen. It was a trip she had taken with her parents. Kate and her mother explored all the major sights while her father was in meetings for most of the trip. It had been late spring though, so she had missed the biting cold.

When Kate got to the bottom of the stairs, she looked for signs that the wood belonged to someone. With no signs and no one in sight, she grabbed as many logs as she could carry and climbed the stairs back to the top. She and Declan made a few more trips. He made sure the fireplace was in working order and set out to warm the small apartment.

Once they were settled and warm enough to take off their coats, Kate relaxed back on the small two-seater couch. They hadn't talked much about the case on the flight to Edinburgh. The documents had come later than planned and they hadn't had a chance to go through everything. Once in the air, they read through the documents Spade had provided about the first two cases. Information was still pending on the third. The investigations were thorough but yielded no suspects.

It turned out the murders happened in Edinburgh's many closes.

"Do you know what a close is?" Kate asked Declan. When he shook his head, she explained, "It's the Scottish word for alleyway, which was common in Old Town where we are right now. The Royal Mile is a succession of streets forming the main thoroughfare of Old Town. High Street, which we are off, is the most popular. Closes are alleyways that lead north and south, some of which lead to open courtyards. Centuries ago, most led to private property and were closed to the public. They are narrow, at the time crime-ridden, and have steep stairs. I think I read there were nearly two hundred and fifty at one time."

"How many remain?" Declan asked as he settled on the couch next to her. He stretched an arm behind her on the couch and kicked his legs out in front of him. Kate knew he was tired. They both were.

"I'd have to look it up, but I think about seventy." Kate reached for the box on the floor that had all the files including crime scene photos. "It's believed the killer attacked the victims in the closes and murdered them right there. The newspaper has started calling him the Close Killer, both in reference to where the murders took place and the close personal nature of the crimes. It's believed he was right in their face as he was strangling the life out of them. As we saw in the forensic pathologist reports, there were what looked like bite marks but not deep enough to leave impressions. Needless to say, these attacks were sadistic."

Declan nodded his head. "There wasn't much of a crime scene left. It's why they are having such a hard time finding him. The pathologist indicated their faces had been wiped clean after death. The same for their hands and fingernails. There was nothing under them which is uncommon just as a matter of daily use."

"He knows what we are looking for." More than anything it told Kate this killer was organized and planned. These weren't crimes of passion in the heat of the moment. He planned to kill these women. That brought her directly to something she hadn't agreed with in the file.

Declan tapped Kate on the back of her head. "Something is swimming around in there."

He knew her too well. "I was thinking about what I read in the report. It was speculated by the Police Scotland detective they were surprise attacks. He speculated these women were walking through the closes at night and he attacked. He indicated it was random and unplanned."

"You don't think that's what happened?"

Kate shook her head. "This is an organized killer. He had materials with him to wipe down the victims' faces, hands, and nails. He spent time with them after the murder. Also, if this was random then how come no one other than single American women were targeted? We are in the middle of tourist central here – all nationalities, colors, and creeds. But all the victims were Caucasian American women – solo travelers as well. This was planned and targeted. I wouldn't be surprised if he had contact with them before the murders."

Declan considered that. "That would certainly explain the clean crime scenes and the lack of video surveillance. The Royal Mile has excellent video surveillance on the street. The victims were seen walking into the closes and then never seen again. The odd thing though is no offender was ever seen. The report says they went through all the footage. He must have been waiting in the close for them and then left without being noted."

"He knows the area," Kate said, surer than ever this had been targeted.

Declan pulled another document from the box and opened it on the coffee table. "It wasn't the year that Spade said. There was a six-month cooling-off period between the first and second victims but only a month between victims two and three. It's not quite a year from the first."

Kate had noted that too when reading the file "The murders were in three different closes. We know he doesn't have a particular attachment to the location other than here in Old Town – the Royal Mile in particular."

"That seems like a prime hunting ground if he's looking for an American."

Kate agreed with that. "I'm struck by his victim choice. All the women I know who are solo travelers are on guard. They pride themselves on being safe. Some even wear wedding rings or pretend they are traveling with a husband or friends. They lie to give themselves cover. Certainly not all women do this, but the experienced ones have occasionally resorted to those tactics to avoid saying they are alone. He's getting around their defenses."

"Maybe they aren't experienced, Kate. We also need to consider where we are. Edinburgh, Scotland, is by far one of the safest places to travel to, even as a solo traveler. I'm sure their guard wouldn't be up as much here as someplace else. Especially some places in the states."

That was true. "You may have a point. There were fifty-two homicides in all of Scotland last year. There are small cities in the United States with double that. Gun violence isn't the problem here it is in the states. It's generally safe and it might cause people to let their guard down even if they otherwise wouldn't."

"Let's talk about the victims," Declan said, grabbing another file. "Viola Hinson was thirty-two and had been in Edinburgh for a week before she was murdered. She was staying in an apartment on the Royal Mile not far from where she was killed. She arrived here from London where she had spent the previous week. She was traveling for a few weeks stopping at different places in the United Kingdom. She was an experienced solo traveler and had traveled extensively on her own over the years. Not married and no kids. She was from Wisconsin. Her parents were notified and her sister came over to identify her body and bring her back home."

"Where was she found?"

"Advocate's Close. A local shopkeeper found her body in the morning when he went to open his shop. He thought she was drunk and passed out. When he tried to wake her, he saw the marks on her face and realized she was dead. It caused quite a stir when the case broke. To have this happen in an area that is supposed to be safe is going to stir up a lot of chatter. Chief Inspector Cameron Fraser was on the scene and did everything right. If there was evidence to be found, he and his team would have found it. They spoke to everyone around the area but no one saw anything. They were able to trace her steps earlier in the evening. Viola was seen leaving her apartment at close to two that morning and went right to Advocate's Close. There was nothing on her cellphone to indicate she was meeting anyone."

Someone or something had lured Viola out of the safety of her apartment in the middle of the night. She asked Declan to grab the next victim's information.

Declan closed Viola's file and pulled another from the box. He flipped through a few pages until he had the information. "Rose Dillard was twenty-nine and was on a solo trip exploring Edinburgh. She had arrived in Scotland two weeks prior and had been traveling around. She had gone up to the Isle of Skye and Inverness as well as a few other stops. She had a full week planned in Edinburgh before she was to fly back home to South Carolina. She was staying in a rental apartment like ours. We don't have any video surveillance of her. We know she was seen entering Fleshmarket Close at midnight. She was found by two guys walking home from a pub at one-thirty that morning. They were thoroughly questioned and provided alibis. Cellphone data does show she was texting with someone and had planned to meet up with them at the entrance to Waverly Train Station, which isn't far from the bottom of the steps of the close. The assumption is she was heading to meet that person and he caught up with her in the close."

Kate hadn't read the full transcript of those texts but noted Rose had saved the texter as Knox in her phone. The phone number was registered to a tourist from Paris who said his phone had been stolen in Scotland weeks prior. That was a dead end, but at least the transcript would provide some information about the guy.

"What do you think, Kate?"

"I think we have an organized killer hunting the Royal Mile for victims."

"According to Spade, the third victim was staying in a rented apartment," Declan explained. "She was here in Edinburgh for two weeks. She was using the apartment as a home base while she traveled to different areas of the country. That's about all I know from Spade.

He said he couldn't get that file to us. Det. Fraser should have it when we meet."

Kate yawned. "When is that again?"

"Later today at five," Declan said. It was four in the morning Scotland time. "We can get a few hours of sleep and then get something to eat before we head out to meet him. He wanted to meet after dark so we'd get a sense of the crime scene and how easy it would be to kill someone undetected."

Kate pushed herself up off the couch. Their sleep would be a mess until they settled in. If the meeting wasn't so late in the day, she might have tried to stay awake until then. Declan was right though, they needed sleep. She offered her hand to him and tugged him up from the couch. "Let's go figure out where we are sleeping."

There was one small room off the living room that had what looked like a child's cot in a space that was also being used as a large walk-in closet. The other room, off the short hallway near the front door, had a bed and armoire but no closet.

"You take the bedroom and I'll go in the little room," Kate said and started to walk out of the living room to get her suitcase in the hall. She didn't make it far as Declan reached for her hand and pulled her back. He leaned down and kissed her, a sweet press of lips.

"I've been wanting to do that since we talked earlier." He raked a hand through his hair. "That's a lie. I've been wanting to do that since we got back from Martha's Vineyard. Sleep in the bedroom with me."

Kate raised her eyes to him and for as much as she wanted him, she pulled out of his grasp. "Not like this."

Declan shook his head. "I only meant sleep. That other bed won't fit anyone bigger than a child. You'll be uncomfortable."

His bed was more inviting. "As long as you stay on your side."

Declan seemed satisfied with that answer.

CHAPTER 3

After a long nap and dinner at a local pub, Kate and Declan walked the distance to the top of Advocate's Close. It started on the Royal Mile across the street from St. Giles Cathedral. The uneven cobblestone ground took some adjusting. It wasn't like in Boston where for the most part it was even and walkable. The way these stones were laid out seemed haphazard and uneven. Some were shorter than others and some were even broken in places. She had to remind herself that the roads were laid hundreds of years before Boston was even settled. But she'd need to remember to watch her step, especially if the weather got any colder. Kate assumed it might get slippery.

Even though they had slept nearly seven hours, Kate still didn't feel rested. She was sure it was just jet lag and stress from the case. She always felt this way at the start, not grounded in the information yet. Taking a case outside of the United States was something their specialized unit did all the time, but it didn't mean it got any easier. The biggest hurdle was always working with law enforcement in other countries and the push-back they'd sometimes receive about taking over cases. Kate and Declan tried to go out of their way to stress the local team was important and they were simply a part of that. She was prepared for the confrontation that sometimes happened, wearing the stress in her neck and across her shoulders.

As they stood at the top of the close, Kate pulled her coat tighter around her and shivered against the air, which had grown considerably colder as night fell.

"You'll get used to it eventually," said a man with a thick Scottish accent. He stood about six-foot-three, an inch taller than Declan, but had the same build and wave of messy dark hair. He had a kind smile and dark eyes like Kate. It was obvious despite his coat that he lifted weights and was fit. He was handsome in a rugged outdoorsy way and Kate didn't see a wedding ring on his finger. She assumed he couldn't have been much older than them, maybe early forties.

"Agents Walsh and James?" he said as he extended a large, calloused hand.

Her hand felt small and childlike in his. "Please call us by our first names. I like to get the formality out of the way if we are going to be working together."

"Fraser then," he said with a grin. "No one calls me Cameron other than my mother." He jutted his chin toward the entrance to the close. "I wanted to meet you here to give you a sense of the Royal Mile at night. I also figured you might have needed some sleep when you got in this morning. Settling in okay?"

"Getting used to your heating system," Declan said. "Other than that, had a good rest and a decent dinner. We are ready to get down to work. We don't have any information about the most recent case."

"I'll get to that but first let me explain. I called for help," Fraser admitted. "With three American women dead, I figured the FBI would want to be involved. I've seen a few news reports about the kinds of cases you've solved in the states, and I figured you'd be perfect for this too. The FBI office at the American Embassy in London made the connection for me. Kate, your work is well known. I'm sure you might have some thoughts already."

"I try to leave my full judgment until I have all the information." Kate didn't want to tell him a few minutes after meeting him she thought he had made a mistake. "Can we head down and see where Viola Hinson's body was found?"

"Certainly," he said and led the way. "If you walked to the end of the close, you'd end up on Market Street at the foot of Cockburn Street. I don't think Viola was going quite that far that night."

The feeling of dread hung heavy as they walked deeper into the close. It was a bit like stepping back in time. While the close once provided access to prominent families' homes, as those with money moved out of the Old Town and into what's considered New Town Edinburgh along Princess Street, the closes became tenements riddled with disease and crime.

The weight of history was palpable. Kate's father had been an American history professor. If she hadn't gone into the FBI, she might have been a history professor too. Learning history from textbooks was one thing. This was something different. This was like stepping back in time.

Kate wasn't claustrophobic but the walkway narrowed and seemed to close in on her. Small lamps were the only illumination. They cast shadows along the close, making even the bravest stand on alert. It was not an area she'd venture into alone at night.

Halfway down, noise from the pub, Devil's Advocate, spilled into the close. Kate stopped for a moment hoping to read a sign with their hours of operation. She didn't want a drink but she wanted to understand if the pub might have been open when Viola was murdered.

"They closed at one on the night of the murder," Fraser said and pointed just past the pub's set of double large barn doors. "Those are open in better weather but would have been closed by the time Viola made her way down here. We heard from her landlord that she was spending time with a guy but we haven't been able to find him. I suspected she might have been meeting him for a drink that night but the killer got to her first. I was told pubs stay open sometimes as late as four in the morning back in the U.S."

"In some states," Declan said. "It's a reasonable assumption. What do you know about the guy you suspect she was meeting?"

"Nothing. I don't have a name or anything. She was seen on the street speaking to a man a few times. I've not been able to confirm anything. I don't know for sure that's who she was meeting. It made sense they saw each other earlier in the day and made a plan for later. Given we have no cellphone data indicating someone contacted her. He could have shown up at her place too and asked her."

"Do you consider him a suspect?"

Fraser shrugged. "I don't have information on him one way or the other. Just speculation on my part."

"Were any of the staff around at the time?"

Fraser shook his head. "We questioned them. There were two staff people in the back cleaning up from the night, but they didn't hear or see anything." He pointed to a rounded part of the building just after the doors to the pub. "It's just on the other side of this."

Kate walked past the pub and down a few steps. The rounded brick structure had three small windows and a door. On the other side of it was a small crevice that made a cutout between the next building that jutted out in a box-like shape. Kate wasn't sure how two people would fit but it was enough for one person.

"It happened here?" she asked, examining the area. The photos hadn't done justice to how small and dark the area was. Kate glanced up and looked at Declan. She was sure he was thinking the same thing. The area was small enough the killer could have backed Viola into it then killed her right there. It was out of sight enough that someone looking up or down the close might have missed them in the small cubby area. If they saw them, unless Viola was screaming out, one might have assumed they caught two people in a lover's embrace.

The whole thing had Jack the Ripper vibes.

Kate wobbled slightly on her feet and stepped back into the more open area of the close.

Declan reached out to steady her. "Are you okay?"

"I'm fine," she said, brushing him off. She didn't like showing weakness in front of Fraser or any new cops they were working with. "It's probably a bit of jet lag."

"No," Fraser said, shaking his head. "The closes will do that to you. The ground is uneven and the buildings jut out every which way. It's sometimes hard to get your bearings. You'll adjust eventually," he said with a smile. He was trying to comfort her and normalize it and for that Kate was grateful.

Kate wanted to focus back on the case. "We read a shopkeeper found Viola the next morning."

"William is his name. He came up the close steps toward the Royal Mile at five that morning. He was headed to his shop to do inventory before the day started. He saw her feet sticking out and stopped. He thought she might have been drunk and passed out. He quickly realized she was deceased and called for help. Everything he told me went into his statement."

Kate was sure it did. "My understanding is there are no witnesses and no evidence left here at the scene. Is that correct?"

"Correct on all counts." Fraser stepped back and looked down at where Viola's body was found. "It's a shame, a young woman like that. We don't see this kind of crime here, not currently anyway. All kinds of criminal activity including murder took place in these closes back in the 17th and 18th centuries. But not today." He glanced back up the close the way they had come. "If there's nothing else you want to see here, let's go to the site of the second murder." When Kate and Declan agreed they had seen enough, Fraser turned and headed back up the close.

Kate lagged, still trying to get a sense of what the victim might have seen and heard that night. Tonight, the pub was open and people were coming and going up and down the close. It was dark but the people made the area seem livelier.

Kate caught up to Declan just as he was asking about Knox. "Fraser, does the name mean anything to you? I know you couldn't find the person and the cellphone information indicated the phone had been stolen."

He didn't stop to answer the question. He continued his quick jog up the rest of the steps back to the Royal Mile. When Kate and Declan caught up and joined him on the sidewalk, he cocked his head to the side. "Let's walk and talk. I'll give you a little history lesson."

Fraser pointed out different buildings and gave some historical facts as they made their way back down High Street. While his depth of knowledge about the area was fascinating, Kate wanted to know the details of the case more than anything. She listened patiently and figured maybe the historical facts would matter later during the investigation.

Fraser reached the top of Fleshmarket Close, named for the butcher's market, where meat would hang along the alley, dripping blood down the steep incline to the lake in the valley. The stairs were steeper than they were in Advocate's Close or at least that's how it appeared to Kate. This close also led down to Market Street, steps from Waverly Station.

Fraser regaled them with tales of the close as he jogged down the steep steps. He was used to navigating them and while agile, Kate was still afraid if she went too fast, she'd tumble to the bottom. When he reached a flat area below one flight of steps he stopped and stepped out of the way as people walked up.

"This is the area where Rose was found. As you can see it's much more open than the area where he attacked Viola. The murder also took place earlier so it was a more brazen attack."

"What's that there?" Kate asked, pointing to a small building on the right side of the close just a few feet from them. The black paint stood out from the brown drab brick that surrounded them.

"Halfway House Pub," Fraser said. "There were staff there when the attack happened but no one heard or saw anything. The pub had just closed and their staff was busy. Given the distance to the front door though, I'm assuming Rose didn't call out for help because she would have been heard."

The landing between the staircases wasn't big – a few feet in either direction. There were a few more steps to the front door of the pub. Help wasn't far off if Rose had been able to scream or get away. There wasn't much to see though, not that long after the murder. This area was a little more well-lit than Advocate's Close but not by much.

Kate was confused about some reporting in the file. She wanted to address it first before asking again about Knox. "It was noted in the file that these were surprise attacks. Someone had indicated it was random. But you also acknowledged Viola was seen previously with a guy and might have been meeting someone at Devil's Advocate. Those facts don't add up to me. Either it was random or planned. It can't be both."

Fraser leaned back against the brick wall. "We don't know what we don't know. We've not been able to identify who Viola and Rose were planning to meet. Those people may have nothing to do with this. It certainly looks like random attacks to me. Otherwise..." His voice trailed off and Kate understood.

He didn't want to be the one to admit a serial killer might be at work in the heart of Old Town Edinburgh. It wouldn't be good for tourism and it certainly wouldn't be good for the country's safe reputation. It was also difficult for local cops to admit a serial killer could be working in their city. One crime could be dismissed, the second could be a coincidence but a third meant it was time to take the connections seriously. That's why he had called them in. He didn't necessarily need the help investigating – he didn't want to be the one to publicly call it what it was.

Better to leave that to the outsiders, the FBI. These were American women who were murdered. If he got lucky, the killer would be American too. If not, then another outsider. As long as they weren't Scottish, it wasn't a Scotland problem. It made it an American violence problem that spilled over to Scotland. The optics would look much better for them.

Kate wasn't afraid to speak the truth aloud. "Otherwise, you have a serial killer on your hands," she said finishing what he couldn't. She waited a beat to see if he'd agree with her. When he didn't, she said, "Please tell us about Knox. You have a name but I didn't see much in the file. When I asked you before, your eye twitched and you told us to wait. Here we are."

Fraser looked at Declan. "Is she always so quick?"

"Not much gets past Kate. To be fair, I've noticed the eye twitch too. It happens when you're not ready to answer the question or when you're being evasive. It's a tell."

"Yanks," he said with a shake of his head and a hearty laugh. "They told me you were on top of your game." He pushed himself off the wall and took a breath. "Knox was a name associated with Edinburgh's most infamous serial killers."

"Serial killer in Edinburgh?" Declan asked, turning to Kate.

"Burke and Hare?" Kate asked, trying to remember the history.

"The very same." Fraser pointed to the pub. "I'll buy you a beer and tell you all about them."

CHAPTER 4

raser must have planned it this way because there was a small
table set up for them inside one of the smallest pubs Kate had
ever seen. He shook hands with the bartender, who brought
them over some Tennent's Lager. "That's the national beer of Scotland
right there," the affable bartender said with a broad grin.

Kate thanked him and took a sip of the pale ale even though drinking
alcohol was the last thing she wanted. It had a lemon taste with a
slightly bitter finish. "It's good," she said and meant it. "Let's get back
to Burke and Hare. One of us is going to have to catch Declan up to
speed."

Fraser sipped his beer as he turned to Declan. "William Burke and
William Hare murdered sixteen people over ten months in 1828 in
Edinburgh. They sold the corpses for dissection at anatomy lectures.
Most of the victims were those in poverty living in what is now the
South Street Vaults."

It didn't seem to make sense to Declan. "Sold for dissection? Weren't
there questions about how these two were getting bodies? I've heard of
graverobbing but killing people for the sake of dissection is something
else."

"You have to understand the times. Edinburgh was a leading
European center of anatomical study back in the early 19th century.
There was a need for cadavers. Scottish law required that corpses

used for medical research should only come from those who had died in prison, suicide victims, or orphans. There was a shortage of bodies and this initially led to grave robbing."

"How did the two start killing people?" Declan asked.

"It started with Hare who had a lodger die. He asked Burke what they should do and they ended up selling the corpse. They made money and it seemed lucrative enough." Fraser took another sip of beer. "There was a good deal of poverty in the city. People living in tenements were sick and it was easy for them to kill those on the edges of society. It was other lodgers who eventually found one victim who was thought to have been suffocated. There wasn't much evidence and Hare eventually turned on his friend, getting immunity from prosecution. He admitted to all sixteen murders and implicated Burke, who was found guilty of one murder and sentenced to death. Burke was hanged shortly afterward. Want to know the irony?"

Declan's eyes were wide as he took in the tale. "This has got to be good."

Fraser smiled as he finished. "Burke's corpse was dissected and his skeleton is still on display at the Anatomical Museum of Edinburgh Medical School."

"Are you kidding me?" Kate asked, not hiding her shock. She had known all the details of the case, except Burke's dissection and the fate of his skeletal remains.

"Not kidding you," Fraser said and took another sip of beer. "Now, you're probably asking yourself how Knox fits into all of this."

Declan looked over at Kate. "Do you know?"

Kate nodded but yielded to Fraser who seemed to be enjoying telling the story.

"The doctor who was getting the corpses from Burke and Hare was none other than Robert Knox, who was a Scottish anatomist. It was Knox's methods of obtaining cadavers for dissection that led to the passage of the Anatomy Act of 1832. After being involved with Burke and Hare, his reputation was ruined and he eventually went to London, not teaching or practicing again."

Declan shifted in his seat, leaning forward on the table. "He never killed anyone though?"

"No," Fraser said with a sigh. "But I couldn't help but immediately think of Robert Knox when I heard that's who Rose was texting. There is another famous Knox here too – John Knox. He lived during the 1500s. You've passed by his house as you walked up High Street. He was a Scottish minister and writer who led the country's Reformation. He was the founder of the Presbyterian Church of Scotland. The murders don't seem to have any religious component to them so I dismissed John Knox of any connection."

Kate studied his face as he was speaking. She was sure he'd known possibly after the second murder that there was a serial killer. "Your assessment makes sense to me. I can't say for certain there is a connection to the Burke and Hare case. It's not like he made it that obvious by calling himself that. But the assumption is solid. When did you first start to suspect you might have a serial killer on your hands?"

Fraser stalled by taking another sip of beer. When he was done, he arched an eyebrow. "I've never voiced this to anyone but after the first case." He saw the surprise on Kate's face. "I didn't know anything then but it seemed like such a horrific murder, it made me wonder. When the second happened, I knew. That's when I called the FBI office in London. I wanted them to review the case file and tell me what they suspected. They confirmed my suspicion and offered assistance, but we didn't have much to go on. Now, we have a third murder and I knew you by reputation. There wasn't even two months between the last two."

"Can you tell us about that one?" Kate asked. As he gestured toward the bar for the check, Kate stopped him. "I don't need to see the scene right now. Just tell us what you know. You seem hesitant to discuss it."

"It's not hesitancy," he confirmed. He seemed to struggle to find the words. When he was comfortable, his shoulders relaxed. "I'm overwhelmed by it. I have no leads or suspects. I'm concerned because the first two murders were six months apart and now it's two months. Believe it or not, even with this cold weather, the holidays are a prime tourist season. We have the Christmas market and huge Hogmanay celebration."

Declan looked at Kate. "Hogmanay?"

"New Year's celebration that lasts for a few days," Kate said in response. "We agree with your assessment and concern. I made a preliminary assessment, but I need to know about the most recent murder to know if I'm on track."

"Understood," Fraser said and gestured toward the bartender for another beer. Kate had only had a few sips of hers and Declan's beer was still full. Kate wasn't sure if he didn't like it or just didn't want to drink.

When the bartender brought Fraser another, he took a large gulp and rested his glass on the table. "Mable Reney's body was found in Mary King's Close by a woman who works as part of the tour. The worker was in early and went through the close turning on lights and getting things ready. She discovered Mable and called the police. The forensic pathologist indicated Mable was manually strangled and she had what were probably bite marks on her face. It was the same as the other cases, not deep enough or full enough to do bite mark impressions. It was more like nips. The only thing different this time is I couldn't locate her cellphone. We haven't had much luck getting cellphone data yet. I can only assume she was there to meet someone. Her body didn't show other signs of a struggle as if she'd been kidnapped or something like that. We believe she was killed where she was found like the others."

Kate wanted the background on the victim but figured fast-forwarding to her death might be a better place to start. "What were the circumstances of her death?"

Fraser paused for a moment and took another sip of beer. "This close is a bit different than the others in that it's only accessible by tour and most of the close is underground. Let me give you some background first so you understand the context." He looked at Kate and Declan and neither disagreed. Kate didn't care what path he took to get them the information, just that he got them there.

When Fraser spoke next his voice was low. "I'm not someone who believes in ghosts and all of that. Well, I try not to. That said, Mary King's Close is probably one of the spookiest places I've been. Maybe second to the South Street Vaults. The close was named after Mary King, who was a merchant who resided on the close in the 17th century. The close was partially demolished and buried when the Royal Exchange was built in the 18th century. It was closed to the public for many years and became shrouded in myths and urban legends. There are stories about murders and hauntings."

"Have people died there?" Kate asked.

Fraser nodded. "The Black Plague hit Edinburgh in 1645. The narrow streets and overcrowding at the time created the perfect storm for the plague to sweep through the city. Mary King's Close was used as a place to keep those infected quarantined. The close was bricked off and people remained there suffering and dying. That's part of where the lore comes from but I'm sure there were murders there too over its history. The tour that's run is both historical and a ghost tour. We've had several ghost shows feature Mary King's Close. It's not the kind of place a young woman would wander alone at night or meet up with someone. Then there is the other question of access. It's only accessible via the tour. As you can see, this one presents some challenges the others haven't."

"There's an escalation here," Kate said and wasn't surprised when Fraser asked her to explain. "The first murder is hidden from the close. It's late, at two in the morning after the pubs have closed. Her body is left in that small crevice. The next murder is more in the open and earlier, around midnight. There were still people in the Halfway House Pub. He could have been caught. Now, he's breaking into a well-known attraction. He's looking for the same thrill he got the first time."

"Thrill?" Fraser asked wrapping his hand around his pint.

Kate would have to explain how Fraser was wrong in his earlier assessment to explain what she was seeing now with the case. "When I first read the case file, there was one thing you noted that struck me as incorrect. I don't believe this killer is picking women at random. He's not attacking at random. You said yourself that someone lured these women to the locations. There's no mysterious date these women were meeting and the killer got to them first. The killer knows these women at least for a brief time before the murder. They aren't strangers to one another. It's not a crime of opportunity for him."

Fraser's face was expressionless. "How can you know that?"

"It's too coincidental that three women were all meeting mystery dates and then were intercepted by the killer. Plus, the killer seems to be targeting solo women travelers. I don't think that's a coincidence either. He's getting to know them in some capacity before they are murdered. Then he's luring them to their deaths."

Fraser looked over at Declan who had been quiet so far. "Is this what you believe?"

"I do," he said with force in his tone. "You also must consider what the pathologist said. The victims' faces, hands, and nails were cleaned. As Kate told me earlier, this is an organized killer. It's not a frenzied attack. He's planned and controlled and he hasn't gotten caught yet. He hasn't even left behind any evidence." He looked over at Kate before he said what was on his mind. Kate didn't need to give him permission but he seemed to be looking for it. She gestured for him to continue.

Declan turned back to Fraser. "I don't think this is the first time this killer has struck. I'd venture to guess he's been doing this for a long time and no one is connecting the cases."

What he said didn't surprise Kate. She had been thinking along the same lines. "Have you had other murders here in Scotland that are similar?"

"I didn't even think to look," Fraser admitted. "They were so unique that there's nothing in my history of more than twenty years with Police Scotland that comes to mind. Not here and not anywhere across the country."

"Then we need to look at other countries," Declan said, surprising both Kate and Fraser. He saw their faces and finally took a sip of his beer. The tension in his body seemed to relax too. It was as if he had been holding that in for a while. "I know what I said is surprising, but I believe it. There was nothing left at the scenes and he's killing out in the open in public. Yes, it's at night. That's not the marker of an inexperienced killer. If he had left evidence behind or maybe narrowly missed being caught. If he hadn't washed away evidence on the victim's bodies, I might have thought differently. Given all the factors together, this isn't his first time. It might be his first time killing three times in the same city or choosing the same kinds of victims. As you both said, you're seeing escalation. The thrill for him is wearing off and that doesn't happen with only three murders."

"What kind of thrill are we talking about?" Fraser asked with some hesitation in his voice.

For that, Declan turned to Kate. She said slowly, "I wouldn't put this in a report or create a profile on him yet, but if I had to say, it's a sexual thrill. He's getting off on these murders, it's why they are so up close and personal."

"He's not raping them," Fraser reminded her.

"There doesn't have to be a sexual assault in a case for a killer to have a sexual release. The crime itself is what turns him on. The thrill of the chase, overpowering the victim, and then the murder itself. I'm sure either at the murder site or back at his residence later, he's reliving the fantasy of it and getting sexual gratification from it."

Fraser shook his head in disgust. "That's unbelievable to me."

Kate could honestly say nothing was unbelievable to her anymore. She was no longer shocked by the depravity of the human mind and some people's willingness to act it out. "I'm not giving you a classification of this killer yet. I want us to keep this in the back of our minds as we proceed forward. It will help us narrow suspects and hopefully predict further crimes."

"You think he'll kill again."

Kate had no doubt. By the look on his face, neither did Declan. "Fraser, if this killer is still in Edinburgh or nearby, he's in the process of seeking out his next victim. If he's moving to another country, then he's going to start this all over again there. Declan is right. We should start looking to see if there are similar crimes in other countries."

"I can start that search," Fraser offered. He finished off the last of his beer and then went to the bar to pay the check. He refused Declan's offer to pay. When he came back to the table, he asked, "Are you ready to see one of the scariest places in Edinburgh?"

Kate was about as ready as she was going to get. "Lead the way."

CHAPTER 5

Seeing Mary King's Close firsthand was something to behold. If Kate thought she had stepped back in time while walking the other closes, she hadn't seen anything yet. Mary King's Close was a labyrinth of underground streets and low-ceiling rooms.

They met with Fiona, the young woman who found Mable's body. She couldn't have been more than five-foot-two with shoulder-length blonde hair. She was unassuming and quiet and it was obvious the murder had shaken her.

"Fiona, will you retrace your steps that morning for Agents Walsh and James," Fraser instructed the young woman. The attraction hadn't been reopened for tours yet. Fraser had explained on the walk over that they were eager to get back in business and didn't think a recent murder would curtail tourist traffic – if anything it might draw more of a crowd.

Kate couldn't fault them for wanting to get back to business. "We appreciate you meeting with us this evening. I'm sure there are other things you'd rather be doing."

Fiona offered her a shy smile. "It's fine. I don't mind. I don't know how they got in though. The door to this building was locked and there is no other entrance. They had to come through here and the door was locked when I came in that morning."

"Do you lock the door from the inside and then pull it closed on your way out?" Kate asked as she glanced back at the entrance to the small building. It was the start of the tour where people bought tickets and learned a little about Mary King's Close. She didn't think more than ten people would fit comfortably in the space.

"Yes, you could. Does that matter?"

"I was wondering if maybe someone hid out after a tour and you locked them in. They'd have access that way. All they'd have to do is lock up when they left. They wouldn't need a key to leave."

Fiona shook her head. "All the guests are accounted for after each tour. Nothing like that could have happened." Her tone was firm with a hint of concern.

Kate would table it for now. She sensed Fiona felt personally responsible for it and she didn't want the young woman to blame herself. After Kate let it go, Fiona explained how she had come in that morning, flipped on the lights, and then did a walkthrough of the rest of the close once another employee arrived.

"Is that something that's done every morning?" Declan asked, glancing to her side, at the doorway Kate assumed led to the close.

"Every day at the start of the day and every night before we leave. Follow me and I'll show you the path I took to where I found her." Fiona turned around and went out the doorway where Declan had been staring. Kate and Declan followed right behind her and Fraser took up the rear. Kate assumed he had walked the area many times, possibly before the murder but certainly after.

They followed the maze of underground streets and Kate could have sworn eyes were watching them as the hair on her arms stood on end. She wasn't easily scared, but this was one place she didn't want to be alone. "Does it ever spook you to work here?"

"All the time," Fiona said, looking up at Kate with big eyes. "I hated it when I first started because I thought I was always being watched. Once I realized it wasn't just a feeling and I was being watched, I kind of settled into it. That sounds a bit backward but it's what happened. None of the ghosts here have ever hurt me and nothing bad has happened." She paused and raised her shoulders slightly. "Until now, that is."

They continued to follow her down a few steps, across an alleyway, turning right and left, and came to a wide-open room with wood floors and brick walls. There was no furniture in the room but portraits hung on the wall. Kate assumed a history lesson took place in the room during the guided tour.

Fiona pointed to a spot on the floor. "I found her here. The lighting was low the way it is now, but I knew right away she was dead. She had her head turned facing the doorway and her eyes were open. She had her arms stretched out as if asking for help."

Kate was sure the victim had been posed to scare whoever found her. She didn't want to ask any leading questions, but she needed to know more. "How was she dressed when you found her?"

"Fully clothed in a shirt and jeans. She didn't have a coat, which I thought was odd given the weather. I called the police right away. I don't think anyone found a coat though." Fiona stood back as Kate and Declan walked over to where Mable was found. There was no evidence now. Any that might have been here had been collected.

Kate wasn't looking at anything other than the wood floor. Still, she was drawn to it. "Fraser, what if any evidence did you find with the body?"

"Nothing," he said with an air of annoyance. "It was another case with no evidence left behind."

Kate looked over at Fiona. "Did anyone on your staff touch the body or anything in this room?" When she looked startled, Kate clarified. "I'm just trying to figure out if anyone checked for a pulse or to see if she was still breathing. This room is empty so I didn't know if anything was moved out to make room for the police."

"Nothing like that. As I said, I didn't even make it that far into the room. As soon as I saw her, I knew she was dead." She gestured around the room. "We don't even have furniture or anything else in here. What you're seeing now is how it's always been."

Fraser took a step toward Kate. "Do you have concerns?"

Kate wouldn't call it a concern. This scene was just so different from the others. "I'm just trying to make sense of what I'm seeing." She glanced over at Fiona and didn't want to speak in front of her. "We can discuss the case particulars later. I have a few questions about the autopsy."

Fiona winced and backed up toward the door. "If you can find your way back, I can leave you here to discuss."

Kate thanked her and promised they wouldn't take too much time. When Fiona was gone, she said, "The killer would have had a lot more time down here than with the other victims. I'm curious if there was any other damage to the victim other than bites on the face. Any signs of sexual assault?"

"Not that was determined," Fraser said, agreeing with Kate it was a concern. "She was found fully clothed and it didn't appear to me or the pathologist that she had been undressed and then redressed. It looked to us as if she had been strangled and left here much like the others."

"It sounded to me like she was posed," Declan said, taking the words out of Kate's mouth. "With the way she was positioned with her head toward the door and eyes open and arms outstretched, it seems like the killer might have done that on purpose. We'll need photos of the scene."

"I'll get you them." He glanced around the room. "Is there anything you want to know or see before we go?"

Kate took a breath and let it out slowly. She felt like she was missing something. "Did you ever figure out how they got down here?"

"I had the same speculation as you. That he was here on a tour and stayed. The staff insisted, as Fiona did today, that was impossible. I don't see any other way though."

"There's no other entrance or exit?" Declan asked.

"Not that I'm aware of. You are free to look around if you like."

Declan looked at Kate and he sensed correctly she wanted to get out of there. "I think it's best if Kate and I head back to our apartment and process what you've shown us tonight. What time tomorrow would you like to meet?"

"Let's meet at ten. This will give you some time in the morning."

Kate took one last look at the room and followed Fraser and Declan down the narrow corridors. She had the same sense of being watched as she did when she first entered. The hair on the back of her neck and her arms stood on end. Kate kept her eyes focused on the back of Declan and didn't look to either side. She worried if she did she'd see something she couldn't explain.

As they turned right down another tight alleyway, something brushed up against Kate's hand. She jerked her arm up and away from whatever it was. "Can we stop for a moment?" she called out. Kate looked back at the area she had just passed, expecting to see a spider web or something jutting out from the brick wall. Her hand had brushed up against something but there was nothing there.

"Are you okay, Kate?" Declan asked, turning to her with concern on his face. He stepped toward her. "Did something happen?"

Kate held up her right hand and turned it over, looking to see if there was anything on her hand. There was nothing. "Something brushed up against my hand but there is nothing there. It was the weirdest sensation like passing it through a spider web."

Up ahead, Fraser laughed. "It's the ghosts, Kate. That's what they feel like when they touch you." He turned back and walked toward her. He sensed quickly she didn't find any of it funny. "Remember how

I said I don't believe in ghosts? Well, there are a few places around Edinburgh where I do believe there is something unexplainable. I'm sorry if it scared you."

Scare wasn't the right word. It had startled her and Kate didn't like things that didn't have logical and rational explanations. She shoved her hands in her pants pockets. "I'm fine. Let's go."

Declan arched an eyebrow in an unspoken question.

Kate shrugged it off. "It just took me by surprise. It's fine."

Fraser thankfully didn't press the issue. He turned his back to her and led them out of the close. When they reached the top and were back inside the small building, he left them with Fiona while he went to grab the file. It gave Kate a chance to ask her more questions.

"Is this your first time in Scotland?" Fiona asked, looking between them both.

"Kate has been here before, but it's my first time," Declan said. When she inquired about his name, he explained. "It's Irish. My grandparents on both sides were born in Ireland. The same with Kate's family. They immigrated to Boston as many had."

Fiona seemed satisfied with that response. "I assume you've seen lots of creepy and gory stuff in your line of work."

Kate nodded but didn't go into it. "Have you had trouble processing what you saw? It would be normal if you did. Most people go through their whole lives and never have to see a murder victim like that." She saw the way Fiona's shoulders tensed. "Are you afraid to be back in this building?"

"We haven't reopened since the murder but we have permission to now. I don't know if I want to work here anymore." Fiona stepped out from behind the counter. "I didn't want to admit this earlier, but it's probably important. What I told you about doing a walkthrough is true and we normally do one in the evening too. Sometimes we don't though. If the tour guide counts off as everyone leaves and reports in, whoever is closing might not walk through the whole close again. It's creepy here alone in the evening. Sometimes I feel too scared to do it."

Kate wouldn't want the job so she couldn't blame Fiona. What Kate saw tonight was enough for her. She didn't want to have to come back. "Did you skip the final walkthrough the night before you found Mable?"

"I did," Fiona admitted. "I'm sorry I did that. I had no way of knowing what was going to happen. Am I in trouble?"

"Of course not," Declan said. "It's important you told us though. This way we can figure out what might have happened. Has anyone asked for your receipts for that day? Do you have video cameras around?"

"There are no recordings of the close because we are under a government building. That's why photos aren't allowed either. I can look into pulling receipts for that day. Most people pay by card but we do have a few who pay in cash."

"He'd probably pay in cash," Kate said and Declan agreed. "Hold off on pulling those records. We might need them but there might be an easier way. There's no point for you to do all that work yet. Did anything happen during the day that raised any concerns?"

"Nothing unusual at all," Fiona said and then paused to think about it.

Kate walked over to her. She wanted the physical closeness between them. Kate wanted to show her she was a safe person to share information with. Kate knew the FBI could be intimidating and that's the last thing she wanted. "Anything you can think of might be important. Even if you don't think it relates, we might think it's relevant."

Fiona scrunched up her nose and pursed her lips. "It wasn't that day but about two weeks before there was a man here on the tour. He was alone and kept asking questions about the close and access. Were there other doors? Did any of the buildings provide access? Those kinds of questions. We didn't think much of it at first but he kept interrupting the tour guide."

"Did you see him?" Declan asked.

"Briefly. The tour guide pointed him out to me when she told me he had annoyed her throughout the tour." When Kate asked her to describe him, she said, "He wasn't Scottish. He was British and sounded posh like he was from an upscale part of London. He was about five-foot-eleven and probably in his late thirties or early forties. He was dressed nicely, probably more nicely than most people who take the tour. He had glasses and dark hair. He was good-looking but not intimidating looking by any means. He wasn't a big guy."

Kate thought it sounded like a lead. "Did anyone ask him his name?"

"That is the odd thing. Even when the whole group did introductions, he never said his name. Just that he was from London."

Kate looked over at Declan and knew he was thinking the same thing. If this was the guy, the killer had been planning at least two weeks before the murder.

CHAPTER 6

After taking a walk to the top of the Royal Mile to see Edinburgh Castle and then back down again, Declan stopped in a small shop on the corner of High and Jeffrey Streets to grab a few things for the morning. Kate waited on the corner in front of the High Street Pub and watched as a stream of people walked past. The sidewalks were still bustling in the evening.

Kate held tightly to the thick file Fraser had given them before they parted ways. Given the thickness of the file, he had done a good deal of investigative work for a murder that was barely seventy-two hours old.

Kate glanced up at the windows of the apartments above the shops across the street and noticed a few people had started to decorate for the holidays. Two people had lit Christmas trees in their windows and others had bright Christmas lights in theirs.

Disappointment washed over Kate realizing there was a chance she might not make it home for Christmas. It was a new feeling and one she'd have to sit with for a while to fully understand. Maybe she was getting older and just wanted to be more settled. She pushed aside the thought as Declan waited for the light to change and slowly jogged across the street.

He shook the bags. "They had everything we need if you want breakfast in the morning. Not a lot of coffee options so I grabbed some tea. There is a coffee shop right down the road and one around the corner if you want me to grab you coffee in the morning."

Kate looked up at him with a curious expression on her face. "You don't have to take care of me. The way you said it made it sound as if you were my assistant or handler." Kate tried to take one of the bags from him to make his load lighter but he refused.

"I'm returning the favor after years of you taking care of me when I was drinking too much." He hitched his chin toward the door. "Unlock it and I'll be right behind you."

Kate kept forgetting the number of the building but she didn't forget the bright blue color it was painted. It was hard to miss on the street. She slipped the key out, unlocked the door, and held it open for him. "What did you think of Fraser?" she asked as they climbed the stairs to their apartment.

Once they got to the top, Declan finally responded. "He seemed competent and he was right to call us in. I was surprised he thought it was a random attack. He might just be overwhelmed."

"He doesn't see the crime we see. Maybe it's our experience telling us better," Kate said as she unlocked the apartment door and flipped the light switch inside. The hall lit up and they kicked off their wet shoes in the foyer.

Kate headed into the large open dining and kitchen area with Declan right behind her. She tossed the keys on the table and offered to help him put the groceries away, but he refused as she assumed he would. She sat down in the large window seat that overlooked the courtyard behind the building.

Declan finished putting the groceries away then pulled a beer from the fridge and offered one to Kate. She declined and he twisted the cap and drank it. "I wanted the beer in that pub, but I can't drink and work."

"I wondered what was wrong with you. I thought maybe you didn't like it."

Declan took another sip. "I didn't know where he was taking us next and I wanted to be alert. I can't focus on crime scene details with a fuzzy head." He pointed over at the file still in her hand. "What does it say about the victim?"

Kate flipped it open to a photo of Mable Reney. She was a pretty woman only a few years younger than Kate. She had shoulder-length auburn hair and blue eyes the color of the ocean in the Caribbean. It was a striking contrast but fit perfectly with her full lips and high cheekbones.

Kate read the details. "She was a travel writer with more than fifteen years of experience. Her father told Fraser she traveled extensively for work and hadn't been home in more than a year. Mable had back-to-back trips planned and he didn't understand how something like this could happen. He said she was never careless and had traveled to far more dangerous places than Scotland. He assured Fraser that Mable would never have broken into anything and if she ended up there it wasn't by her own volition. She had a reputation to uphold and had written for several travel magazines."

"That's a little different than the other victims," Declan said, pulling a chair from the dining table over to the window seat. He leaned back and kicked his feet up. "The other two women were on vacation alone. Mable was a solo traveler but this was her work. It sounded like this was a lifestyle for her and she worked as she traveled. It means she was far more experienced than the other women, so it would have taken something compelling for her to explore Mary King's Close at night. If you were Mable, what would have gotten you down there?"

Kate wasn't sure she'd want to do the tour in the middle of the day, let alone go there at night. "It had to be about getting access. She was getting to see something or experience something she wouldn't have been able to during the day or on an official tour. That tells us she had to have trusted whoever was giving her access. She trusted herself to be safe with them and that they were allowed in Mary King's Close after hours."

Declan nodded as she spoke. "He was in some official capacity or said he was officially allowed to be there."

"The brochure indicated the tours are run by character actors who dress up as they did back then. Do you think he was one of them?"

Declan took another sip of his beer. "I assumed he was the person on the tour asking all those questions Fiona mentioned and then he faked having access."

"Either way, it indicates what we suspected – he's planning." Kate looked down at the file again and combed through the information. As she turned the page, something caught her eye.

"What do you see, Kate?"

She shifted her eyes up to him. "How'd you know I saw something?"

"Your cheeks get red and you've got a little sneaky smile on your face. That happens all the time when you think you've hit on something."

Kate hadn't realized he watched her that closely. "There was a note in Mable's apartment that she had a date with someone she met on TravelShip."

"It sounds familiar. What's that?"

"I remember reading it in the other files but didn't think much of it." Kate reached for her cellphone and did a quick search. "It's a travel dating app. It's for people who like to travel and meet either locals where they are visiting or other travelers."

Declan furrowed his brow. "You think all three of them were looking to date here in Edinburgh?"

"It's possible." Kate looked up from her phone. "Mable was in her thirties and traveled extensively for work. She was single according to her father and had no kids. Maybe she got lonely traveling so much and was looking to meet someone. I'm sure it was difficult to carry on a relationship with her job."

"Could have just been casual sex," Declan said and waited for her reaction.

"It could have been," Kate conceded, not sure why she felt so uncomfortable saying that. "Do women go looking for casual sex on dating apps?"

"You don't but I'm sure a lot of women do. There's nothing wrong with it."

"I didn't say there was anything wrong with it. I was thinking from a safety standpoint. They were all traveling here alone. I think it's common knowledge that there are people who use the apps to prey on women. I was wondering if they would have risked it here alone in another country."

Declan shrugged. "People have needs, Kate. We don't know what they were seeking. It might not have been sex but someone to have dinner with."

"I'll have to double-check what it said in the other files to be sure."

"You should download the app." Declan took another sip of the beer while Kate didn't look convinced. "You can change your name and use one of the photos from when we were undercover. Your hair looks different. We should get a sense of the app and how it works in case we need it."

Kate hated the one time they had gone undercover. But he was right, she should download the app. Kate searched the app store, found it, and downloaded it. "I'm too tired tonight to set up the profile. I'll do that in the morning."

Declan watched her carefully as she placed her phone down on the window seat and snuggled into the pillows. "You haven't said much of anything about what I said earlier tonight."

"What did you say?" she asked, her throat suddenly dry. She wondered if he was going to approach the conversation they hadn't finished before Spade called.

"I said these murders weren't the killer's first. I suggested he might have done this in other countries," Declan reminded her. "Did you think I meant something else?"

"I didn't know what you meant," Kate responded, trying to hide the disappointment in her voice. "You took a big swing with that. I don't disagree with you. I couldn't get a good read on Fraser, but he said he'd search. Don't you think we should have heard about other Americans being targeted?"

"Would we?" The look on his face said it was doubtful.

"I would hope so." Kate pushed herself off the window seat and crossed the kitchen back out into the hallway. She went to her luggage and pulled out her laptop. She sat down on the living room couch, put it on the coffee table, and connected to the internet. "Let's search right now," she called out to him.

While she waited for him to join her, Kate pulled up the FBI database and plugged in varying search terms including the bite marks on the victims' faces. That was the kind of detail the database tracked. It was a good way to connect cases that might not otherwise connect, especially across geographic locations. Her search came back with three cases with bite marks. The details didn't match anything else including the victim type.

"We can ask Spade to search for us," Declan suggested, sitting down next to her. "It's possible he didn't only target Americans. Spade can reach out to the other European offices and see if he finds anything. Did you search for solo women travelers?"

Kate was doing that now and still coming up empty. She closed the database and searched the internet for murdered solo travelers. Kate waited as the pages loaded and then pulled back from her laptop in surprise. "There are so many cases, Declan. More than I would have ever thought. Both murdered and women still missing. This can't all be from this killer. I don't know that zeroing in on solo travelers as the search term will get us what we need."

Declan pulled the phone from his pocket. "I'm calling Spade."

Kate was too tired to calculate the time change. She was sure he'd still be in his office. The truth was she didn't know Spade that well. None of them did. She didn't know if he was married or had kids or even where he lived. When she pictured him, it was in the basement office of the FBI headquarters in Washington, D.C. He had been in military intelligence in Vietnam and then had a long history in intelligence before starting up the specialized unit in the FBI. He was a bit of an enigma to most – even to Kate and Declan who had worked with him for their entire careers.

Spade answered on the first ring as he did so frequently. "Have you been given a briefing on the cases?"

Declan put the call on speakerphone and confirmed they had as he went over the details. Kate offered her assessment as well. Together, they gave Spade the full story. When they were done, Declan asked, "Is there anyone you have available who could help with some research?"

"There are always people I can call in. What do you need?"

"Fraser is doing some research too and Kate searched the database. We believe these murders are not the killer's first. As Kate explained, they are too clean and organized. He's left nothing behind for us. I suggested and Kate agrees this isn't the first time he's committed murder. There might be more victims in other countries."

"Americans?" Spade asked.

"We can't rule it out, but we think the killer is smart enough not to target too many Americans. Targeting them here might have been his worst mistake."

Kate agreed. "I searched the internet for solo women travelers and came back with so many search results. I can send you an email with some details about the victims here. We also found that all of the victims have a connection to TravelShip, which is a dating app. We are going to explore that tomorrow."

"You think this guy might be traveling country to country killing women?"

"It's possible, sir," Declan confirmed but not looking too confident. She assumed he was a little nervous because it was usually Kate who took the big swings like this on cases.

"Do you agree, Kate?"

"I do. I would have come to the same conclusion with more time. Declan saw it right away." She smiled up at him and his shoulders relaxed.

"I'll put someone on this right away," Spade said and ended the call.

"Thanks for backing me up," Declan said.

"Always." Kate stood and offered her hand to him to pull him up. "We're a team, Declan. Besides, you are right. Let's go get some sleep."

"Where are you sleeping?" he asked with a hint of a smile.

Kate had been thinking about it fleetingly for most of the evening. "We are going to be sharing a bed on this trip. No one is sleeping in the closet." She walked off toward the bedroom without looking back.

CHAPTER 7

The next morning, Kate felt more rested. The jet lag had worn off after more sleep and their schedules seemed to have adjusted to Scotland. While she was getting ready for the day, Declan had left the apartment and went to a bakery around the corner. He came back with coffee and pastries. It wasn't the healthy breakfast Kate usually had but it hit the spot.

It was so good she stopped at the shop for another Americano on the way to the meeting. Fraser had explained to them the night before that the police had a sub-station just down the road from them on the Royal Mile in the direction of Holyrood Palace. It wasn't more than a five-minute walk.

They arrived at the office with ten minutes to spare. Declan had been unusually quiet that morning. "Are you okay?"

"I couldn't sleep well," Declan said, his voice constrained.

"I'm sorry. Was I tossing and turning?"

Declan shook his head but didn't explain. He jutted his chin toward the building. "Are you ready to meet with him?"

Kate didn't want to go inside yet. There was something he wasn't telling her. "What's the matter, Declan? If you don't tell me, it's going to bother me all day." She wasn't lying about that. The few times Declan was in a bad mood, he was difficult to deal with during the case. He'd brood, remain quiet, and Kate would be hard-pressed to focus on the task at hand.

Declan licked his lower lip and looked down at her. He held her gaze for several seconds before he finally relented. "Sleeping next to you all night and not touching you was difficult. It didn't matter that you were in pajamas and those silly fuzzy socks. I still wanted you. You barely moved all night. I was the one tossing and turning."

"Oh," Kate said, warmth rushing to her cheeks. She felt bad he hadn't gotten any sleep, but she couldn't lie and say the reasoning didn't make her happy. She looked up at him. "I didn't realize you felt that way."

"How could you not know?" he started to ask as the door to the police station opened and Fraser stepped out. "All I ever think about is—"

He looked between them and raised an eyebrow. "Am I interrupting something?"

Kate remained focused on Declan while he turned his head to acknowledge Fraser. "Nothing that can't hold until later."

Fraser didn't hold back the smirk. "Okay, then let's get on with it. I have some information you might find interesting." He gestured toward the door and Declan led the way. Kate didn't want to let the conversation go, but she had no choice but to follow. It would once again have to wait.

Once inside, the constant hum of chatter drowned out Kate's thoughts of Declan and what he was about to tell her. Her mind easily retreated to work. She followed Declan and Fraser to his office and took a seat at a four-seater square table.

Fraser went behind his desk and grabbed a small stack of printed pages and carried them to the table. As he sat, he explained, "Late last night, I spoke to a colleague in London. He has five murdered women from England who were murdered in France and Belgium. There are some similarities to our cases."

Kate wasn't surprised by the news, only that he had confirmed

Declan's theory so quickly. "Did your colleague work on all the cases?"

"He was given some details but getting information from France and Belgium hasn't been easy," Fraser said and handed Kate the top three pages from the stack. "These are his main findings. As you'll see, the women were solo travelers from England in their late twenties to early thirties. All of them were killed near tourist locations. One of them was even found right near the Eiffel Tower. The cases span two years, a few months apart. No evidence was found at the scenes. For each case, it was ruled homicide by manual strangulation and there was similar bruising around the face. Similar nip marks too but not full bite marks, just like in these cases here."

Kate lowered her eyes to the documents she was provided. She scanned through the list not seeing anything about the TravelShip app. There was no cellphone data provided at all. She raised her eyes to Fraser. "I found a curious connection last night. I noticed all three of the victims here were using an app known as TravelShip. Did you explore any leads related to that?"

Fraser furrowed his brow. "I noticed the victims had been on the app but didn't explore it. Isn't almost everyone on one dating app or another? Do you think it's significant?"

Kate rested the pages on the table. "I don't know what's significant or not yet. I find it curious all three victims were using it. Do we have cellphone data on these victims killed in France and Belgium?"

"I'm sure they do but it wasn't sent to me." He didn't look convinced or even interested in the app.

"We need to see if that's a common denominator," Kate explained. "Do you understand why I'm looking for a common denominator?"

"I guess it's to see if the cases are connected." Fraser stared over at her waiting for the response. He glanced over at Declan a few times to see if he'd chime in. "Is there more?"

Kate didn't fault him for what he didn't know. Cases like these were complex. "Part of what we need to do is discover if the cases are connected. We can tell that by who the victims were and how they were killed. It sounds like the cases in France and Belgium might be connected. What I'm looking for though is his access to the victims. I know you initially thought he was choosing them at random. I don't see that. I'm convinced these are planned in advance and an app like TravelShip might be the key to how he's finding the victims."

Fraser's expression softened. "Say more, please."

Kate could tell he was coming around. "Let's take Mable Reney. She travels extensively for work. She's not some starry-eyed kid on her first trip alone. She's gone to dangerous locations before and she knows how to keep herself safe. As her father said, Mable wouldn't take risks. I looked up a few of her travel articles and she seems like a professional. She has a solid reputation and I don't think she'd risk breaking into Mary King's Close at night. That tells me she went with someone she thought had access. Now it could mean he works there or had in the past. More likely, he was the person asking questions to the tour guide about after-hours access then faked having access. It means it was thoroughly researched and planned. Now that tells me he's searching out these women someplace. He knows enough to know they are solo travelers and they are American. If this is the same guy, then in France and Belgium, he knew they were English."

Fraser cracked a sly smile. "Your boss said you were logical beyond all reason. He told me that when you get a hold of something you don't let go and that you'd see what everyone else missed." He glanced over at Declan. "He also told me you'd understand a crime scene better than anyone I'd ever met."

"He didn't leave me much of a crime scene," Declan said evenly. "He knows the area well though. That much I know."

Kate was glad Fraser wasn't annoyed or embarrassed they had seen things he missed. It was why they were often called in. Local law enforcement was sometimes too close to the cases. "Can we have a conversation with your contact in London?"

"Sam Harris with the National Crime Agency, which is like your FBI. The NCA has the powers of police, customs, and immigration officers. Sam was called into the case because he's successfully investigated several homicides. He knew immediately the cases were connected but didn't have much cooperation with France and Belgium to access the evidence. By the time he got it all, any chance of finding the killer was long passed. He said he'd be more than happy to offer his assistance. The cases have been haunting him."

Without asking, Fraser got up from the table and pulled his phone off his desk. He tugged the cord and stretched it over to the table. He dropped it down with a clang and punched in a few numbers. He hit the speakerphone button and ringing echoed through his office.

A man with a British accent answered the phone. Kate thought he sounded like someone far more likely to be teaching at Oxford than someone working a homicide. She liked the accent but she was having trouble picturing the man attached to it. "Fraser, it's good to hear from you so soon."

"I have Kate and Declan here with me from the FBI. They made some discoveries in the short time they've been on the case. It was Declan who suggested there might be more cases outside of Scotland, which is what prompted my call to you as I said last night. Today, Kate is wondering if your victims were on a dating app."

"What's the name of the app?"

Kate leaned onto the table and introduced herself. "It's good to connect with you, Sam. I discovered an app called TravelShip in the files. The latest victim, Mable Reney, had a note in her apartment that she was going on a date with someone she met on TravelShip. We don't know if that's what she was doing the night she was killed but it was an interesting find noted in the evidence. We are still waiting for her cellphone data. We have the data of the other two victims and know they were also using TravelShip. We have no information if they matched with anyone or went on dates in Scotland. It's one of the things the victims had in common and I thought I'd explore it. Learning you have a few cases, I'd like to see if it's something the victims in your cases used."

"That's a solid observation," Sam said. The sounds of shuffling papers echoed through the phone. "I won't give you a total overview of the five victims because I don't want to overwhelm you. Three were killed in Paris over nine months. Then two more were killed in Bruges about three months. Then it stopped and we didn't have another murder, that I'm aware of anyway, until the ones there in Scotland."

"Were they all solo travelers?"

"They were and they were killed in high tourist areas." Sam detailed the locations including the Eiffel Tower, near the Louvre, and along the beautiful canals in Bruges. "The cases didn't make much of a splash in the news for obvious reasons – protecting tourism. It was the Belgian authorities who reached out to us. When I went digging, I found the cases in Paris and connected them."

Declan leaned forward in his chair. "How did you connect them?"

"I went first to see if there were other deaths of English women. When I found them, I looked at the manner and method of death and the victim type. All the victims were manually strangled and had marks on their faces including bruising and tiny bite marks. Not deep but enough to leave an imprint. I saw the photos and I don't know if he was intentionally biting them or kissing them hard enough to leave marks and teeth scrapes. It was aggressive. We also noted the murders were exactly three months apart and we thought that was curious too."

Kate could tell by his process that he was an experienced detective.

"It sounds like you did a good job connecting them. What other similarities were there, Sam?"

"We all know manual strangulation doesn't leave a lot of evidence behind. Based on the reports I read and the crime scene photos I saw, there was no evidence left at the scene. What was most striking was what the pathologist in Paris told me. He said the victims' faces and hands were wiped down with alcohol pads as if cleaning a wound. The victims had no trace of anything under their fingernails. They were cleaned. I checked with the pathologist in Belgium and the same was true. I knew then the cases were connected. It was too much of a coincidence for them not to be."

Declan caught Kate's eyes and they shared a look. There was no way this wasn't the same killer. Kate wasn't sure how much Fraser had shared with him. She saw no reason to hold anything back. "We are dealing with the same thing here. All those similarities you found there, we have here."

"Then he didn't stop killing," Sam said with sadness in his voice. "I had been hoping he was caught for doing something else and was locked up or he stopped killing after the five. I've not been able to generate any leads on the cases. I've gotten nowhere with them. I even went to Paris and Bruges to investigate but didn't find anything. Because the victims were alone and I didn't get access to the cases until later, there weren't many people to interview."

Kate could hear the frustration in his voice. "What about the app?" she asked again, bringing him back to her original question.

Sam apologized for not answering the question sooner. "Two of the victims used TravelShip. I contacted the company but they didn't have the data for me. They said it's only kept for so long. The three other victims didn't use the app. At least, I never found that among their mobile records."

Kate was disappointed but not surprised. It didn't mean they could rule it out completely.

As she was considering what to ask next, Declan asked, "Did you have any theory about where he was meeting the victims?"

"I have a theory. All the victims took guided tours for checking out some of the sights. It wasn't the same company though, so I thought it might be someone joining the tours like them rather than working at a tour company. None of the employees matched up but it's certainly an avenue to find tourists."

Once he said it, Kate was surprised she hadn't thought of it sooner. She suddenly didn't want to be talking to Sam over the phone. She wanted him right in front of her. "Sam, is there any way you can come to Scotland for a few days and discuss these cases? I think it would be helpful if you were in front of us to discuss."

"I'd be happy to. I can be there this afternoon." A phone rang in the distance. "Let me take this call. It's my contact in Italy. When Fraser told me you thought there might be more, I called a few of my colleagues in Italy and Germany. I'll let you know what they say when I see you."

"I'll see you soon, Sam," Kate said, satisfied he was willing to help.

CHAPTER 8

When the call disconnected, Fraser stared at her across the table. "Don't you think that was something we should have discussed first?"

Kate noticed the anger in his voice. "I don't understand the issue. We often create task forces when crimes hit other jurisdictions. Sam has more than a year of investigating his cases under his belt. He might know far more than he realizes. I thought it would only expedite our investigations. I thought he was someone you trusted."

"You're here at my request. It just would have been nice to discuss bringing in others." Fraser folded his arms across his chest.

Kate wasn't sure what was wrong, but Declan picked up the clues faster than she did.

"Fraser, are you concerned about how it will look to your superiors needing to call in both the FBI and the NCA?"

"It's not going to look good. It's going to look like Police Scotland can't handle the investigations."

Kate apologized. "Please let me speak to your boss. That wasn't the intent at all. I wasn't calling in Sam to investigate the cases here. I was calling him in to help us because he's been investigating his cases long before we even knew a serial killer was at work. I can make a public announcement that we are creating a task force, which is common in these cases."

Fraser shook his head. "You can't make a public statement that a serial killer is murdering solo travelers across Europe. Do you know the kind of panic that would bring? Not to mention the impact on tourism."

Kate started to speak but Declan uncharacteristically spoke over her. "We don't have a choice. We have to let the public know what is happening. Now that we know, we can't keep this secret. This can't be hidden," Declan said with the kind of force she hadn't heard in a long time. When Fraser didn't seem moved by Declan's passion, he stressed, "If you continue to allow tourists to come here without warning them and someone else is murdered, it's going to look much worse for you and the police department. We should warn the public."

"Won't it make him run and just move onto the next country?" Fraser asked.

Kate thought it was a reasonable question. "That's always the risk we run with going public. At the same time, he needs to know we know what he's doing. Once we speak to Sam and wait for other information to come in, we can make a judgment call about how much we will say. It might be as simple as saying that all three cases here are connected to other cases we've discovered in France and Belgium and we've started a task force between the FBI, NCA, and Police Scotland. That's a real show of strength and that you're taking it seriously."

"I understand." Fraser excused himself from the table and promised to be right back.

When he was gone, Declan looked over at Kate. "I didn't mean to speak over you. He trusts us, but I needed him to understand that we don't have a choice but to go public. We can't wait, Kate."

"You don't need to apologize for doing your job, Declan. We talk over each other all the time accidentally. You sent him a strong message, probably stronger than I could have. I appreciate you doing that and for being sorry you interrupted me." She reached over and took his hand in hers and squeezed it. "I'm also sorry you didn't sleep well last night. I didn't know."

Declan raised his eyes to hers and cleared his throat. Whatever he started to say, he thought better of it. After a moment of steady eye contact, he let out a nervous laugh. "Stop looking at me like that with those big eyes unless your goal is for me to take you right here on this table." He pulled his hand back from hers and she pouted. "I think Fraser knows."

She was only teasing him with the pout. "I think he knows too. Does that bother you?"

Declan shook his head. "It doesn't bother me, but I don't want him to think we are distracted. We have his respect and I don't want to lose it."

"I'm not distracted. I know exactly what I'm doing." Kate hoped the double meaning was understood.

"You're killing me, Katie," Declan said with a grin.

She let the subject drop. "Do you think I should have discussed asking Sam to join us?"

"You did what you had to do. I wouldn't have thought twice about it. As you said, he has been investigating this a lot longer than we have." Declan ran a hand through his messy hair. "Let's face it, Kate. Neither one of us are good at playing politics when lives are at stake."

Kate was glad she had Declan on her side. For a moment, she thought she had overstepped. Not that she would have done anything differently. She didn't want anything to hamper their progress. Before she could say anything else, Fraser returned. His posture seemed looser than it had before he left the room.

"We are good with Sam Harris and to make a public statement." Fraser didn't elaborate about where he went or who he might have spoken to and they didn't ask.

Kate said and looked over at Declan. "Where do we want to get started?"

Declan had practicality in mind. "Fraser, do you have a secure war room we can use?"

"War room?"

"Someplace where we can hang the victims' photos and dry-erase boards we can take notes on. We are going to want to put up details about the case for a visual as we work. We can include Sam's cases. It will be easier to have the visual once we have all the cases. Too much to keep track of otherwise."

"Ah," he said with a smile. "We have such a place." Fraser grabbed all the case files off the desk and gestured toward the door. They followed him down a narrow hallway to the elevator and then down into the basement.

As they stepped off into the dark hallway, a musty smell wafted through the air. Kate assumed they probably didn't use the space often or it didn't have the best ventilation system. Fraser flicked on the light, allowing them to see the space. There were beige walls and a gray industrial carpet. It looked like every other police department basement Kate had seen. She wondered if this was where they kept the evidence locker.

They followed Fraser down the hall. He passed by several doors and finally stopped at one at the end. He took out a key from his pocket, unlocked it, and stepped inside. He hit the light as he held the door open for her.

Kate was surprised by the size of the conference room. There was a phone in the middle of the table, a row of televisions on the back wall, and several cork and dry-erase boards. "This space is perfect."

"It's a command center of sorts," Fraser said as he walked to the table and set down the files. "There was nothing down here for the longest time. Then the rise of terrorist attacks after 9/11 and the London bombing we figured we needed a place where we could all gather. The basement was the only place with enough space." He glanced over at Declan. "I'm happy to say we never needed it."

They made themselves busy setting up the case files on the board and Kate wrote notes under each of the victims' photos including biographical data, where they were murdered, and when. She also added any information she thought was relevant.

When they were done, Declan stood back and appraised their work. His cellphone rang before he had a chance to comment. "It's Spade," he said, holding up the screen to show Kate. He answered, informed him they were with Fraser, and then they all gathered around the phone to listen.

"I couldn't find any similar cases here in the states or Canada. I found two similar ones in Brazil and then three each in Spain, Portugal, and Greece. I was also in touch with Sam Harris who informed me you've spoken to him. He said he had three cases in France and two in Belgium. He also let me know he found three each in Italy and Germany." Spade didn't say anything for a moment while they absorbed the devastating news. "The cases go back ten years. Looking at the dates, it seems to me he stays in one place for a period, kills, and then flees before he's caught. All the women were solo travelers and were not native to the country where they were killed. Like choosing Americans in Scotland. In Germany, he chose travelers from Greece."

"He hasn't killed in the United States, England, or Canada," Kate said, repeating back the information. It was more telling where he chose not to murder women than the countries where he chose to kill. "He didn't target North America or England, Spade."

"That stood out to me too. Do you have a theory?"

Kate wasn't sure she would call it a theory. "I would assume he figured he might get caught more easily in those three locations. It could also be that he's from the United States or England. He chose Scotland to murder women instead of England. Not that the police force is any stronger in England than Scotland," Kate added not wanting Fraser to be put on the defensive. To be fair, it wasn't as if any of the other places had poor police support or weren't as highly skilled as the FBI.

"It's perceived to be," Fraser filled in Kate's thought. "It might be part of the reason I got defensive at the thought of bringing Sam Harris into the investigation. We are all part of the United Kingdom but we don't like the comparison. It makes sense though as his last victims were from England. I was surprised he started targeting Americans because anyone with half a brain knows that will bring in the FBI."

"He's upping his risk," Declan said. "Kate said it last night. The killer is upping his thrill. If this is all the same killer, and we'll need to do some work to confirm, then he probably needed more risk to get the same satisfaction so he chose part of the United Kingdom to commit the murders and chose Americans to call in the FBI."

Kate agreed with him. "That could be it, Declan. Do we believe the killer is American?"

Spade wasn't sure. "I don't think you have enough to speculate, Kate. Whoever he is, he can travel extensively and has the money to live under the radar."

Kate relayed the information Sam had told them about the travel tours. "It might be an avenue to explore. I also have some questions about a dating app all the victims here were using." Kate rarely speculated this early in the case, but they'd never had a case quite like this. "What do you want us to do, Spade? Should we call in the other police departments and form a task force? I already asked Sam Harris to join us."

"No, don't call them all in," Spade said to Kate's relief. "I'll work to confirm more of the details so we can say with more confidence the cases are connected, but let's keep the information locked down for now. You can always call the investigators in charge of the cases if you need more information."

Kate agreed with Spade's plan. She wanted a team but would rather it be small and manageable. Too big ended up with too many cooks in the kitchen and she'd spend more time managing than investigating. "We considered going to the media with a statement. Should we hold off?"

"Hold off only long enough for me to get more confirmation on these other cases. This way when you inform the public, you can connect them all." He paused for a moment and added, "The most he's ever killed in a country is three. You have three victims. He might have already left Scotland."

Kate didn't want to say what she was thinking aloud. It was a risk but so was everything in a case like this. "Spade," she said with hesitancy in her voice, "given we know he came to Scotland to target Americans and it signals he's upping his thrill, do you think going public with just the Scotland cases right now to let him know the FBI is here and involved might keep him here?"

"You're willing to put Americans at risk?" Fraser asked his tone incredulous.

Kate knew that's exactly what she'd be doing as well as putting the whole area of Old Town Edinburgh on high alert. "If he leaves, he'll only kill someplace else. We have a chance now to catch him."

"You've got some balls on you, Kate." Fraser was looking at her with newfound respect. He turned to Declan. "Is she always this risky?"

"Calculated," Declan said. "I agree with Kate. We have the chance now. We have to take it. Either way, someone is going to be at risk. If the killer stays or he goes, someone will probably be murdered. Here, we have a chance to stop him."

Spade didn't even hesitate. "I agree. Set up a press conference and inform the public with the strongest warning you can give. Let this killer know we are on to him and more information will follow when it's available."

Fraser was the only one who hadn't agreed. "You know you're going to completely blow up our Christmas tourist season and create chaos?"

Kate was aware but she also knew it had to be done. "Let's blow it up."

When everyone agreed, Kate's only thought was that she hoped she didn't just gamble her career away.

CHAPTER 9

After hanging up with Spade, the three of them worked for more than an hour on the statement to be delivered. Fraser had worked with the public affairs office at Police Scotland to put out a notice for the press conference that afternoon. They'd be putting the statement out before Sam Harris arrived. His information and that of the cases in the other countries would follow later. All they were focused on now was that the FBI was there in Scotland and had connected the three cases with dead American women.

In planning for the press conference, Kate figured she'd be the one to deliver the statement. About an hour before she was to be on live television, Spade called her privately. He wanted to know more about the dating app. While he didn't have any information about the app being used in other cases, he focused on the fact that all three Americans and two English women were using the app. He cautioned her about making the public statement in case she needed to go undercover later.

Kate argued she wouldn't need to be undercover and she had no plans to meet men from the app. Still, Spade wasn't sure given the limited information. He said it was better to be safe than sorry and he sidelined her from making the statement.

Spade was the boss and his call won out. Kate knew he was right, but it didn't mean accepting the news was easy. The one part of her job she hated was going undercover. In this instance, she'd be going undercover alone.

Kate prepped Declan to do the statement for her.

"Are you sure, Kate?" he asked right before he was about to go on. They were still in the basement conference room where Kate would remain while the press conference was held. She fixed his tie and the cuffs of his jacket while she gave him a pep talk.

As Kate fixed the knot on his tie, she said, "Spade doesn't want my face in public right now. He is concerned I might need to go undercover at some point. I think it's silly as people will see me walking around with you. But I guess he's right that I shouldn't be the public face of the investigation."

Declan stopped her fussing with the tie and put his hands on her arms. "I don't like the idea of you sitting down to meet with this killer. I said to download the app to figure out how to use it. Maybe look at some profiles. I don't want you meeting the killer alone."

"We'll cross that bridge if we come to it. Are you worried about the statement?"

"I've given them before, Kate. I'll be fine." Declan said the words but the beads of sweat forming at his hairline gave him away. He had never liked public speaking and he wasn't a fan of the media. He looked down at her and knew right away from her expression she didn't believe him. "Fraser will be there and we aren't taking a lot of questions. The only part I'm concerned about is the end."

The end of the statement had been the trickiest part to write. The goal was to taunt the killer into staying while not alerting the media that's what they were doing. Those few sentences took many rewrites until they were all comfortable with it.

"You'll be fine," Kate assured him. "You're good at sounding tough. That's the only image you have to project. That the FBI is in control with the support from Police Scotland and that you're close to finding him. You've uncovered his pattern and you know he might flee. You need to convince him sticking around is the bigger thrill. Use those words exactly – he must feel challenged to stay. Then you look right at the camera and tell him to turn himself in. You need to do that to cover us. Otherwise, we could be accused of urging on a serial killer, which we are essentially doing."

Declan smiled down at her. "You would have made a heck of a prosecutor." He saluted her. "I have my marching orders and won't let you down."

"You never do." He hugged her and then left her alone in the conference room. She was trying her best to feel confident about the decision they had made. They were egging on a killer and she was terrified it would blow up in their faces. She knew there'd be another victim before they could stop him. This was a death sentence for someone, but it was either one potentially dead here in Edinburgh or countless more in other countries. She hoped they could catch him before he struck again, but she had to face the reality that it might not be possible.

Alone in the room, Kate sat down at the conference table and turned on the television to one of the local news stations. While she waited for Declan and Fraser to take the podium, she pulled up the TravelShip app she had downloaded earlier. She typed in fake biographical data, making herself a few years younger, highlighted some recent trips, and put up the older photo of herself Declan had suggested.

She normally wore her dark hair past her shoulders. For the last undercover assignment, she cut her hair shorter and put blond highlights in to lighten it up. She wore heavier makeup and carried herself differently. Some agents were a natural fit for undercover work. That wasn't Kate's strength. She was much better behind the scenes putting the cases together and then interrogating the suspect. Regardless, she had taken an oath to do whatever had to be done.

Kate turned up the volume on the television when Declan tapped on the microphone once and started the press conference. He spoke clearly and his tone conveyed strength and power. She was reminded once again why they made such good partners in the field and how she was still surprised there was a time when no one wanted to work with him. At one point in his career, Declan tended to go rogue and do his own thing. It was bad for partnerships but often got the job done.

Kate was able to harness his energy differently. Once they were paired together, their weaknesses were diminished and they were stronger as a team. She listened quietly as Declan gave the first half of the statement and then stepped aside so Fraser would add in his part. Then, when it was time for Declan to speak again, he focused on one camera and threw down the challenge to the killer. When he was done, the crowd of reporters erupted in questions, one shouting over the other to the degree no one could hear anything other than a din of shouting.

Declan only took a handful of questions, expertly dodging most of them. One reporter asked if there were other cases elsewhere. Declan's response was simple and clear – nothing was off the table and they'd be exploring every angle and all evidence that came their way. He encouraged the reporter that if he knew of any cases that should be considered he should contact the tipline that had been set up. It was being manned by Police Scotland staff with the help of the FBI.

Another reporter asked if they were asking all tourists to stay away from Edinburgh this holiday season. Fraser handled that question, letting the crowd know that all city activities were still scheduled and that tourists were still welcome. He stressed, however, that all safety precautions should be taken, especially for solo women travelers. He also indicated there would be increased patrols and additional video surveillance monitoring during this time. Kate thought he did a good job of addressing the threat without panicking locals or tourists in the city.

Declan and Fraser came across as strong, in command, and ready to take down a killer. Kate couldn't ask for anything more from the press conference. As far as she was concerned that was one more check off the list of things to be done. When it was over, she clicked off the television and checked her phone.

She noted she had missed a call from Spade. She called him back and then listened as he explained that as far as he could tell, they were safe to connect all twenty-five cases.

Kate had never heard Spade's tone so heavy. "I don't know how the world missed it, Kate. Not all the victims had bite marks but all of them were manually strangled. This killer likes to be up close and personal with his victims. The most compelling evidence for me that they are all connected is how clean the victims were when they were found. Their faces, hands, and fingernails had been wiped down with alcohol pads and were clean of any potential evidence. We assume at least a few of the victims tried to fight him and he knew their fingernails could hold evidence. I don't know if this is something he perfected long ago or if he knows what cops search for on bodies. Either way, he came prepared."

"Did you see any sloppiness or mistakes on the first cases?" By date, the first time the killer struck was in Italy more than ten years prior.

"The investigations were sloppy, Kate. Only one of the crime scenes had photos. The women were initially accused of being prostitutes and nothing was done. If he was sloppy, we'd never know because the police were sloppy. Those first cases probably couldn't even be prosecuted at this point."

Kate cursed loudly and wasn't even embarrassed. She didn't often have a foul mouth and certainly not in front of her boss, but all bets were off in this case. "What about the second series?"

"Investigated better but still no evidence," Spade said matter-of-factly. "This killer might just be good at leaving no evidence, Kate. He kills them outside where evidence can be blown away, disturbed, or overlooked. Manual strangulation doesn't leave much evidence behind unless it's under the victim's fingernails as she's fighting for her life and he knew to take care of that. There's not a lot to go on and because he kills and moves on, he's been impossible to catch. Plus, not only are you dealing with different jurisdictions like in the states, but you're also dealing with entirely different countries and their unique policing systems – crime scene, pathology, evidence storing, investigations, and such. It's as if he created the perfect storm."

Kate knew for Spade to speak that way he was frustrated too. If there was anyone better than she and Declan, it was Spade. She needed to find a positive. "He is leaving clues behind to his identity though, Spade. He's organized, well-planned, understands what evidence cops will look for on the body and at the scene, meets the victims in advance, he's luring them out in the evening, and he's targeting solo travelers. I'm sure there is more evidence of his identity we haven't found yet. Here in Scotland, I suspect he's using the name Knox, which if you know your history..."

"John or Robert?"

"Robert," Kate said not surprised Spade knew. She had rarely come across a subject in which he wasn't well-versed. "We think he knew the story of Burke and Hare and was using that with the victims to possibly taunt the police. We still don't have the most recent victim's cellphone. It hadn't been found."

"Have you been able to get cellphone data yet?"

"Not all of it."

"I'll push that along. In the meantime, reach out to the last victim's family to see if she was known to post photos in the cloud or had a backup for her phone. Most journalists have several ways to back up their information, particularly if they are working on a story."

"We can do that. I haven't had much of a chance to explore the background of the victims. I know Fraser has spoken to the families but I'd like to do that too."

Spade agreed. "I know it's early and not a fair question, but what's your take on this, Kate?"

"All in all, I think he's trying to take more risks. Knowing he's been killing the same way this many years on, I'm more sure than ever that's what's happening. With Mable, the last victim, he posed her to terrorize the person who found her body. He's never done that before. He also broke into a location to kill her. The second victim, he killed in a heavily trafficked close with an open bar feet away from him. He's taking unnecessary risks and that tells me the thrill is wearing off for him. He needs more excitement now with each kill."

"That makes him liable to slip up."

"Exactly, Spade. It's why I was so adamant we keep him here." Kate wanted to see the evidence from the previous cases firsthand. "Do you think you'd be able to get me reports from all the previous victims? I'd like to create a timeline to see if there are any other similarities or evidence we are missing." She knew it would take a lot of political wrangling to get the information. She also knew no one said no to Spade.

"I'll follow up and get everything they are willing to give."

They talked for a few more minutes about the case then ended the call. Kate checked the time on her phone and wondered what was taking Declan and Fraser so long to get back. They had told her they'd head right back to the conference room after speaking to the media. She turned the news channel back on, but another program was playing.

Kate texted Declan and received a text right back that he was on his way down. There were no windows for her to look out and the door was closed. She stood in the middle of the room and waited.

A few moments later, the door flew open and Declan rushed toward her. Red burned his cheeks and his breathing was uneven as if he had run. He had a crumpled-up note in his gloved hand he thrust toward Kate.

"What is it?" she said and told him to catch his breath.

"We found this on the podium after the press conference. We were standing to the side answering a last few questions for some print reporters. When I went back to the podium to get my notes, this was on top. Do you think the killer left this for us?"

"What does it say?" Kate didn't have gloves and didn't want to contaminate it further. She glanced around the room and didn't see any.

Instead of reading it to her, Declan laid the note out flat on the table. "It was left crumpled like this. I didn't see anyone leave it and neither did Fraser. He's out there now interviewing the few media that remain."

Kate peered over it. In block-style writing, the simple, straightforward note said: *Catch me if you can.*

CHAPTER 10

atch me if you can. Kate read the note aloud a few times but was having trouble understanding how the killer walked right up to the podium and left it without anyone noticing. The area had been staged for media only and there were two cops checking media credentials.

She raised her head from the note. "I'm not sure I believe this is from the killer. It would mean he was with the media or has a fake media credential. All the media knew was we were giving a briefing on the last murder and that the FBI had arrived. We didn't even send the notice out in enough time for word to spread. How would the killer have even known?"

Declan didn't know.

"What do you think about the note?" she asked.

Declan considered. "It seems too risky for it to be the killer. When I first saw it, because of the message, I thought it might be him. Given what you said, I'm not sure."

Kate glanced down at the note again. She noted the hesitation lines in the printing and the generic statement. *Catch me if you can.* It had been a movie title. The crumpled paper looked like it had been in someone's pocket and they pulled it out and wrote on it in haste.

It didn't add up for her. "He wouldn't be this generic or write it on crumpled paper like this. He's organized and would take time if he were going to communicate with us. This was sloppy."

Fraser poked his head into the conference room. "I got a description of the guy. I think I know who it is." His eyes met Kate's. "He's probably not the killer, but it doesn't mean he might not have something to offer us."

Kate was glad he was on the same page. "Let's go interview him."

Fraser drove them five miles outside of Old Town. Kate couldn't keep up with the left and right turns. They arrived at a nondescript four-story brick building with a small grocer on the bottom floor. Fraser parked along the side street and then went into the grocery and pointed to the back of the shop. He flashed his badge at the clerk and pointed to Kate and Declan. "FBI," he said with a nod and the man let them go through.

Fraser hadn't given them any details about who they were going to see. He had only said it would be clear once they arrived. He climbed a narrow back staircase with Kate right behind him. Declan remained a few steps behind watching their backs.

Fraser got to the small landing and rapped his knuckles against the door. The flimsy wood shook under his weight.

"I'm coming! I'm coming. You don't have to pound," a male voice shrieked from inside. His voice was high-pitched and English. There was no trace of a Scottish accent. The door pulled open and there stood a man about five-foot-five with a balding head and round glasses. He had a small frame and a pointed nose. "I thought you were lunch. Do you have a tip for me?"

"Tip?" Kate asked, assessing him.

He raised his head to Kate but then thought better of speaking when he saw Fraser to her left and then Declan standing behind her off to her right. Then he smiled. "That was quick." He left the door open but turned his back to them and went inside.

Kate led the way into what she assumed was going to be a residence but it was an office. She introduced the three of them as she followed him. She assumed he knew who they were from the press conference but didn't want to be accused later of entering without identifying themselves.

She stopped in the middle of the room and turned. There were tacky printed tabloid covers framed all over the walls with the name Daily Morrow splashed in red at the top. The floor was littered with stacks of newspapers and other documents leaving only a small trail to the desk covered in debris and papers in front of a floor-to-ceiling window.

Kate had heard about the ruthless tabloid journalism in London. She knew there were more than a few in the states that usually lined the aisle of registers of any grocery store, but she had never spoken to someone who generated that kind of news.

"Are you a reporter?" Kate asked, choking a bit on the word. Tabloids made up news more frequently than they wrote about anything real. It seemed a disservice to the profession to call him a reporter.

He proudly held out his hand. "Billy Turnbull. I'm a reporter, photographer, and owner of this great newspaper. You name it and I do it."

"Like leave notes for the cops pretending to be the killer," Declan said as he stepped into the room. When Billy didn't say anything, Declan stepped toward him. The size difference between them was a sight. Declan towered over him and was twice the size in width. "I remember seeing you there. You were standing among the other reporters waiting to ask a question. You didn't stick around for long though. Why was that?"

"I had somewhere to be." Billy casually went to his desk and sat down. "I don't have anything else to say to you. The FBI has no jurisdiction over me."

"But I do," Fraser said, brushing past Kate and going to the man's desk. "What do you think you're doing, Billy? You're wasting police resources. I know it was you who left the note. I'm just not sure why."

He flicked his eyelashes up. "What note?" his tone and the smirk on his face gave him away.

Fraser pounded his fist down on the man's desk and made all of them jump. "There is a real killer out there, Billy, targeting women. Probably targeting another woman as we speak. Do you know anything about that?"

Kate needed to reduce the anger in the room. "When we came in, you said that was fast. You were trying to get us here. Why is that?"

Billy watched the three of them. As he folded his hands on his desk, Kate saw a slight tremor. He feared Fraser and probably Declan. She took a few steps toward him. "We aren't here to fight with you, Billy. We want to understand why you'd leave that note."

"You're the smart one," he said and stood. He gestured for her to follow him. "I know you all think I'm just a hack, a tabloid reporter who doesn't write about real news. It doesn't mean I don't follow the news. I find it interesting you found me so quickly after leaving that note but these murders have been going on for more than a decade and none of you figured it out."

Declan's hand went to the gun on his hip. Kate shot him a warning look and he withdrew his hand.

Billy wasn't the killer but he knew something. "How do you know the cases have been going on for a decade?" she asked, stepping closer to him as he moved one box after another out of the way of a door.

"I'll show you. It's easier that way." He tugged open the door, scraping the bottom along the old hardwoods. "I tried telling the police long before this but no one took me seriously. There were never any Americans involved. I called the FBI tipline but no one did anything. Do you have any idea how frustrating this has been?"

Kate followed him into a small rectangular room stacked with boxes on one side. If she stood in the middle and held her hands out, her fingertips would touch each wall. The back wall was filled with photos and newspaper clippings. Billy had created a murder board far bigger than their own. He had information for many more cases. "When did you first figure out the cases were connected?"

Billy angled his head to look at her. "Almost a decade ago when they first started. It was the third case in Italy," he said, pointing to news clippings of the cases. "There was almost no investigation done. I couldn't understand it – the first woman was found in an alley in Rome not far from the Trevi Fountain. The second woman was near the Colosseum and the third was near the entrance to the Vatican. It seemed curious to me so I called one of the reporters I know in Italy and he said the news reports were wrong. The first woman's body wasn't found in an alley but rather *in* the fountain. He tried to get the cops to tell him why they were lying in the news but he never got a response. They weren't sharing any information at all."

"What first alerted you to the murders?"

"My sister Lillian was traveling in Rome for a few weeks and she called me concerned for her safety. She was there for the first murder. The cops said the victim was a prostitute but that wasn't the rumor on the street. My sister heard the victim was traveling alone and so was my sister. She asked me if I thought she should cut the trip short. I didn't take it seriously and told her she'd be fine. I didn't even give it a second thought until she called me months later and told me two more women had been murdered. At that point, she was safely in London. I had already forgotten about the first murdered woman and her trip. Anyway, she called to tell me that she had reason to worry and that I should have taken it more seriously."

They were all stunned into silence.

Billy stared up at Kate. "When she told me the locations where the bodies were found and that all the women were solo travelers, I don't know, something struck me as odd. It was even more odd when my reporter friend said the police lied about where the first woman's body was found. The police had no suspects. They were adamant the cases weren't connected even though people suspected."

Kate stepped closer to the board and read the short clips from the paper. They couldn't have been more than two-hundred-word announcements. "Is this all the newspapers there wrote?"

"Sadly, yes." Billy stepped closer to her. "After that, I started scouring the newspapers in all the European countries looking for solo female travelers who'd been murdered. It wasn't easy to find but I relied on a network of reporters who were just as interested in the cases. I've counted twenty-two in all with the three that have happened in Edinburgh."

"There are twenty-five in total. There are three in Brazil you missed," Kate said not sure why she was sharing information with him. She didn't trust him – there was something odd and quirky about him she couldn't quite pin down. But he had done all this work and had been the first to connect all the cases. "Have you shared this with anyone?"

Billy shook his head. "I tried with various police departments but no one took me seriously. I'm a tabloid reporter and they thought I was making up a story and trying to get a quote from them."

"Did you send them any of this?"

"I didn't. I figured they'd send someone out to speak to me and I'd show them then. No one ever came. Then Americans were killed and the FBI showed up."

Kate was so focused on the newspaper clippings and seeing photos of the victims' faces, she absently asked, "Is that why you showed up at the press conference and wrote the note? You were trying to draw us here?" There were so many women. This was the first time Kate was seeing them all. Billy didn't have all the victims but he had enough. She ran her finger over some of the clippings and felt the weight of the case hang heavy on her. The trail of destruction from this killer was almost too much to bear.

"I needed you to see this," Billy said quietly.

Kate stepped back from the board. "Didn't any of the families create an uproar or push for an investigation?"

"Some but they didn't get far."

"Why not?" Kate asked even though she had a fairly good idea.

"The families are from countries other than where the victims were murdered, Agent Walsh. They didn't know the lay of the land or the legal system. The media wasn't connecting these cases and the cops didn't have much to say. Most were focused on shielding the information so panic wouldn't erupt. I was surprised to see Police Scotland standing side by side with the FBI willing to come out and say the three cases here are connected. I had no idea if you knew about the others."

Kate looked down at him. "We are only now in the process of connecting them. We weren't ready to make a statement."

Billy leaned down to a file on top of a stack of boxes. "Before you go public with it, you might want to see this." He righted himself and handed the file to her.

Kate opened it and stared down at composite sketches of three men – one of whom looked familiar. "Who are these men?" she asked, her voice catching in her throat.

"Suspects," he said and then left her standing there.

Kate lowered her eyes back to the sketches as shock seized her.

CHAPTER 11

Kate held the file in her hand and wasn't sure what to make of it. She turned to see Declan and Fraser standing at the edge of the doorway to the small closet-like room. They hadn't followed her in because there wasn't enough space for all of them. She held up the folder. "It seems Billy was the only one tracking these cases from the start. He only missed the cases in Brazil." She moved out of the small room so they could enter and look at the board.

They stood there as mesmerized as Kate had been.

When Declan was done looking it over, he moved out of the room to give Fraser time to look at the board. He pointed to the file in her hands. "He said he had suspects."

Kate handed it to him without saying a word, wondering if he'd see what she saw.

Declan flipped open the folder and looked over each of the three images. He raised his eyes to her in a question. "Is that who I think it is?"

"I thought so too. It might be a coincidence."

"I don't think so, Kate." Declan walked to Billy's desk where the man had retreated. "Where did you get these composite sketches?"

"They are potential suspects." He took the file back and laid it on his desk. "This first man with dark hair and cap was seen with one of the victims in Rome and Paris. He was also spotted again in Munich. The second sketch is of a man who looks like the first but with a shaved head. He was with a victim in Bruges, Belgium."

"What about this man?" Declan asked, pointing to the one who looked familiar.

"He was spotted with a victim in Paris and then later at the locations where bodies were found both in Paris and Bruges. A few people speculated he might be an investigator but no one has been able to positively identify him. I heard some killers will go back to the scene after the body is found. Is that true?"

"It's true but he's not an investigator," Kate said, trying to make sense of the information.

"You know him?" Billy asked, his tone rising in surprise.

"I wouldn't say I know him. He was involved in one of our previous investigations." She saw the question on his face. "I'm not at liberty to discuss the details."

Billy pushed the sketch toward her. "He's my prime suspect. We have the best witnesses tying him to one of the victims. It's clear-cut evidence."

"How did you get these?" Declan asked.

"I'm a journalist, Agent James. I work my sources on the ground both with other journalists and witnesses. Law enforcement has been unhelpful not because they are keeping their investigations quiet but because it seems like there haven't been any investigations at all. Someone had to work on this. I couldn't know this was happening and do nothing."

Kate still didn't understand why no law enforcement agency took him seriously. "If I'm understanding you, these sketches were derived from journalists on the ground speaking to potential witnesses?"

"That's correct."

"Is there a reason you never ran this story in your paper?" Declan asked, looking around at the framed covers around the room. "It seems like if you wanted to get the story out, you had the perfect medium to do that."

Billy stared at him but didn't say a word.

Kate knew exactly why he hadn't and she was grateful for his decision. "You print gossip. Because of that, you didn't want to sensationalize a real story. You know if you print the story in your paper, no one would ever take you seriously. Is that the reason?"

He gave a curt nod of his head. "I tried to give the story to more credible journalists, but no one would run the story without confirmation from law enforcement and no one would confirm a serial killer was targeting solo female travelers in Europe. I didn't bother trying any newspapers in the United States because it hadn't impacted them – yet."

Declan folded his arms across his chest. "Who were these journalists on the ground then?"

"They were like me – either wrote for or ran papers like mine." Billy stood and put his hands on his narrow hips and looked up at Declan. "You may not agree with what goes in my paper. You may not like the gossip and the speculation I print, but there's a business for it and I make a good living. It may not seem like a respectable career to you but I enjoy it."

Kate and Declan remained quiet as Billy continued with anger in his voice. She didn't want to interrupt him because he had a lot to say and she knew he had been holding it in for a while.

Billy cast his eyes toward the small room where he had kept the case information. "That doesn't mean I don't have a real sense of journalism and ethics when it comes to serious matters. I used my network to gather as much information as possible in the hopes someone would take this seriously. We flew under the radar for the very reason you might not be taking me seriously now – because of the kind of gossip papers we run. I care deeply about what's happening to these women and that's why I left the note I did this morning. I knew if I went to you directly, you wouldn't take me seriously. I had to do something to get you here. If that means you arrest me for it, I can live with that."

Declan let his arms hang at his sides and he raised his eyebrows. "Are you done?"

"I'm done."

Declan looked over at Kate but she gestured for him to continue. She wasn't sure what he was going to say, but she trusted him to speak his mind. What he did next surprised and pleased her.

He put a hand on Billy's shoulder. "We believe you. Fraser isn't going to arrest you for leaving that note. You've done some exceptional work with limited means. I'll be honest, if we had not already known the cases were happening in other countries, this might have been a little hard to believe. Your evidence is compelling and you did what law enforcement should have been doing for a decade. We are going to do everything we can to stop this guy."

"I second that," Kate said as she watched Billy lean back against his desk. He took a deep breath then let it out slowly, the stress releasing from his body. "I know you've gone it alone for a long time. This is too much stress for one person. I don't approve of the way you got our attention, but I understand why you did it. Is there any information we can take with us?"

Kate was asking but she knew it was probably within their legal jurisdiction to take it anyway. She wanted to play nice with Billy in case he had information he wasn't sharing. She also meant it when she said this was too much for anyone to take on alone. Kate felt bad for the guy.

Thankfully, Billy said, "You can take it all. Anything you want that I have, please take it. I have a whole box with witness statements that journalists I know took for me and then wrote up. Of course, they aren't official and most of the people wanted to stay off the record so there are no names or contact information. Regardless, the witness statements do have some relevant information about what the victims were doing in the days leading up to their murders, who they were seen with, and that sort of thing. There are only a few statements from people who thought they might have witnessed the killer either before or after the murders. No one saw the murders take place. Of course, if there were, this might have ended a long time ago."

Declan pointed to the file with the suspect sketches. "Can we take that as well?"

"Yes, that's why I showed it to you. Unfortunately, I don't have the names of the men. None of the witnesses knew who they were."

Fraser came out of the small room with his eyes wide. He had a shellshocked expression that Kate felt when she first saw the board. She thought Fraser might be feeling the full weight of what was at hand for the first time.

"Are you okay?" Kate asked, walking over to him.

He ran a hand down his face and shook his head. "I can't believe this has been going on undetected for this long." He looked past Kate at Billy. "Well, not completely undetected. Why did no one take him seriously?"

"We can talk about it later. He's going to provide us with his evidence and there is a whole box of witness statements we can have. I think that will be most valuable to us right now. There are also suspect sketches."

Billy directed them to the boxes of evidence he had collected over the years. Declan put the sketches into the witness statement box. Billy also gave Kate a timeline document with the names of each victim with biographical data and when and where she was killed including the location of her body. He had given each victim a code that was then used on witness statements and photographs. Kate couldn't believe how organized he had kept everything. It would save them hours of work.

"What about all the news clippings?" Billy asked. "Do you need them?"

Kate looked at the timeline one last time. "You can keep that. If we need anything else, we'll be in touch."

As they were leaving, Billy stood by the door. "Is it too much to ask to be kept up to date about what's happening?"

Kate understood his question. He had invested so much time, it was probably hard now to let it go. "We will share what we can," she said even though she knew they wouldn't share much of anything significant. "We appreciate the information. You've saved us so much time investigating. Please know you did all of us a valuable service, especially the victims."

Billy simply nodded and closed the door as they left.

"He seemed sad," Fraser said as they got back to the car. He opened the trunk so they could put in the boxes of information. When he closed it, he looked back at the building. "Do you think we can trust him?"

"I don't trust anyone," Declan said, looking back too. "He seemed trustworthy enough for now though. He certainly did a lot of work when no one else was paying attention. I'm willing to give him the benefit of the doubt until he proves otherwise."

"Fair enough then." Fraser got in the driver's seat.

Kate opted for the back. She kept thinking back to the sketches Billy had shown them. There was no real evidence yet to suggest it was any of the three men, but it's possible the witness statements could explain more.

Declan turned around to look at her. "Do you want to talk about it now or back at the police station?"

"Back at the station," Kate said softly and stared out the window as she took in parts of Edinburgh she'd possibly never see again. She was trying to make sense of the sketch before she had to discuss it with Fraser. If the man in the sketch was the killer, it meant he had slipped through their hands before and she wasn't going to let that happen again. A wave of sadness washed over her and she swallowed back the emotion.

Once they were back in the conference room, they found Sam Harris sitting at the table. Kate was surprised he had arrived so quickly. He was younger than he sounded on the phone and had handsome features, blue eyes, and an affable smile. He and Declan shared the same height and build. Sam's hair was a shade lighter than Declan's though and it looked like he at least attempted to run a brush through it.

Sam took a box from Kate and placed it on the table. "What's all of this?"

"Evidence from the only person who tracked the cases from the beginning," Kate said and then extended her hand and reintroduced herself and Declan. His hand was warm to the touch and strong. "Glad to have you working with us, Sam."

CHAPTER 12

Kate opened the lid to the witness statement box and pulled out the file with the sketches. She had explained to Sam everything they knew about Billy and how he had obtained the information. She needed to address the sketch of the man who looked familiar to her before she did anything else.

Kate sat down at the table and pulled out the sketch. She showed it to Sam and then to Fraser. "Does this man look familiar to either of you?"

Neither had seen the man before. Sam asked, "Should he look familiar to us?"

"How much do you follow global art theft?"

"Not very much," he replied and looked over at Fraser who said the same.

"We don't know this man's name," Kate started. "The Central Directorate of the Judicial Police and Interpol call him Le Fantôme. The Phantom in English. He is the leader of an international art theft ring known as The Curators."

Sam snapped his fingers in recognition "I've heard of them, but I didn't know anyone had ever seen the man's face."

"Kate did when he took her hostage," Declan said with emphasis.

Sam raised his eyebrows. "I find it hard to believe he got away from you."

Kate released a breath she didn't realize she had been holding. Now that the news was out and no one panicked, she felt calmer. "He didn't get away unscathed. I scratched him when he held me and I got his DNA under my fingernails. It was enough to run some analysis but he's not been arrested for anything. He's not in any law enforcement database. We know by ancestry DNA, he's Bulgarian. Although he speaks many languages fluently. The case we consulted on in Paris didn't end up being committed by the Curators, but we chased him for a while. Then he went off the grid and there hasn't been much heard about him since. No other major art thefts either at least from museums. We don't know what's happening in private collections. They rarely report when there's been a theft, depending on how they came in possession of the item that was stolen."

Fraser pointed to the sketch. "You think he's the head of the Curators?"

"I'm positive. I knew right away when I saw this sketch," Kate explained with conviction in her voice. "I didn't want to let Billy know his identity. That said, I'm honestly having trouble believing he could be a suspect. I know he's been operating in Europe for years stealing art and antiquities. But murder? I just don't know. He could have killed me when he had the chance and he did everything possible to make sure I wasn't harmed." She turned and looked at Declan. "What are your thoughts?"

Declan didn't hold back. "He's well organized, never been caught. We don't even know his identity. He's calculating and precise. He's been committing crimes in all the countries where these victims have been killed. I don't think we can rule him out, Kate."

It wasn't what Kate wanted to hear but Declan made a compelling argument. She stood from the table and took the three sketches over to the board. She tacked up each one. "These two men look enough alike they could be the same person and then there is the Phantom.

This killer, as Declan said, is well organized and has gone this long keeping his identity a secret. He is familiar with law enforcement procedures too and cleans the victims' faces, hands, and fingernails. We know the Phantom but we have no idea who the other man or men are and no idea how any relate to the murders. We can't go public with any of them unless we have some solid evidence to back it up."

Sam looked up at her. "Kate, you mentioned you scratched the Phantom. Is there a chance he learned from what happened with you to clean the victims' fingernails?"

Kate didn't think that was a factor. "The first murder predates my encounter with him. That was only a couple of years ago and this killer had been operating long before that." Kate stared at the man's face in the sketch. Declan had made a compelling argument but she still had a hard time believing he was the killer. "The Phantom is making millions of dollars each year in stolen antiquities and art. I can't imagine he'd risk a lucrative business to start killing women."

"He doesn't steal for the money, Kate," Declan said reminding her. "If you remember what he said to you, he does it because he can. Maybe the thrill wasn't getting him off as much as he claimed it did and he needed a little side hustle."

Kate shook her head. "This killer is sexually motivated." She thought back to the way the Phantom had held her, spoken softly in her ear, and even flirted with her. He was aroused by her when he was holding her. He might have taken her right there on the rooftop had the situation been different. He was charming and handsome with a roguish quality that attracted women. She wasn't sure now if she was talking herself into or out of him being a suspect.

"I don't know," Kate said and then realized how they were all staring at her. "Sorry, I was thinking back to when he held me hostage and trying to remember how he'd been and if he said anything that could indicate he had this propensity for murder."

Sam got up and went to the side of the room. "Fraser asked me if I could find any information on any of the other cases. There isn't much information out there from law enforcement. I was told I was going on a fool's errand even connecting the cases. The French won't even concede that all three of their cases are connected. I'm sure they are and so are the ones in Belgium."

He put five thick case files on the conference room table. "You said you have some witness statements and information from earlier cases. I've brought everything I've been able to gather on my cases. Where do you want to start?"

It was Fraser who spoke first. "I don't want to speak out of line, Kate, but you seem to be dismissive of the idea this murderer could be the Phantom. Before we take a deep dive into the victims and the cases, is it possible to match his art theft crimes against these crimes and see if they match up?"

The last thing Kate wanted to do was waste time on suspects when they didn't even fully understand each of the cases. It wasn't the worst idea. "Why don't the three of you start on the case files and read through the witness statements Billy was able to gather and I'll track down the cases thought to be connected to the Phantom. This way we aren't all focusing on one thing." She turned to Declan. "Not that we have many photos from the crime scenes, but could you see what we can gather related to that? Spade said he was also going to try to gather information from the other scenes. You might want to check to see if he's gotten anywhere with that."

Before any of them could agree or disagree, she dug through one of the boxes and pulled out the handy timeline Billy had created for them. She should probably check the data they had to make sure what he created was correct. Not that she fully trusted him, but she didn't doubt him either. With that in hand, Kate raised her eyes to each of them. "Are you on board with the plan?"

All three of them agreed and she grabbed her cellphone and laptop off the table and went to the far end of the room. The room remained eerily quiet as each of them grabbed a box and started going through the evidence. Kate would raise her head from the laptop every once in a while to see heads bent low over files or Declan adding to their timeline board.

Since being held hostage, Kate had kept a file on the crimes thought to be connected to the Phantom. She went back to the first theft thought to be connected to the Phantom and created a full dossier on the man including a timeline of his crimes. It galled her he had gotten away and she had vowed then that if given the chance, she'd catch him and bring him to justice next time. Neither Declan nor Spade knew she had been building an entire dossier on his crimes starting back with the very first theft thought to be connected to him more than twenty years ago. It was why she volunteered to take on the task. Fraser had no idea when he asked how accessible the information was and Kate didn't want to explain why she had become obsessed with stopping him.

Kate scanned through his earlier crimes and then went right to the dates Billy indicated for the first series of murders in Rome, Italy. She glanced from the sheet Billy provided to the timeline on her laptop. The dates matched. The Phantom had stolen a painting from the National Gallery of Modern and Contemporary Art two days before the first murder and then again at the Borghese Gallery and Museum five days after the last murder. It didn't mean that he was in Rome the entire time but the dates were undeniable. Kate's stomach rolled.

She moved on to the next country and victims and then the next, each of the dates matching. She grew increasingly more uncomfortable with each set of dates. Perspiration pooled at her lower back, making her shirt feel two sizes two small. When she got to the dates in Paris, she couldn't believe what she was seeing.

She and Declan were there in the city during one of the murders.

They heard nothing about it at the time. The last murder in Paris happened two nights before he held her hostage. Then the Phantom was gone and the murders started in Bruges, Belgium. A week after the first murder, a painting was stolen from the Groeninge Museum in Bruges. Kate had been back home in Boston by the time that theft had occurred.

Kate let out an audible breath. There was no denying what she was seeing even if she couldn't wrap her mind around it. Evidence was evidence. She only had one question to ask before she let the team know what she found. Kate did a quick internet search but came up empty. There had been no art thefts in Edinburgh or all of Scotland recently.

She couldn't say the Phantom was there, but she certainly couldn't rule it out.

Kate needed to make a phone call. If anyone would confirm or deny her suspicions it was one person – the man who had once been arrested for being the Phantom. Jax Talbert. She hadn't spoken to him in more than two years. It was easier that way. Their relationship was complicated and spanned years. They shared intimate dinners and strolls through museums followed by hot passionate nights when they could both find the time or happened to be in the same cities.

Their lives kept them moving in different directions. It didn't help that Declan hated him. She and Jax had reconnected in Paris when he had been arrested and accused of being the Phantom. Kate had known immediately the cops had the wrong man. They spent a night together and she had paid for it for days with Declan's brooding mood. She understood why now, but then his jealousy hadn't made any sense at all.

While Jax wasn't the Phantom, he'd been following the thefts longer than she had. He ran in the art world as a broker. She was sure not everything he did was legal. If anyone would have an opinion about the Phantom, it would be Jax.

Before she could talk herself out of it, Kate grabbed her cellphone and pushed back from the table. "I need to make a phone call and get some fresh air. When I come back, I can give you an update about what I found." She didn't wait for comment before she headed for the door.

Once on the street and a block away from the police station, she called him. "Jax, it's Kate," she said when he answered.

"I know who this is," he said in his familiar Australian accent. "I can't believe you're calling me. What's it been…two years?"

Twenty-seven months. Not that she was counting. Kate didn't say it aloud. She didn't need him to know she had been keeping track like that. "I'm in Edinburgh and I need your opinion on something."

"I'm in London finishing up some work," Jax said with excitement in his voice. "How about I take the train up and we can spend some time together."

"No," Kate said a little too forcefully and then laughed it off. "I'm in the middle of a challenging case and don't have time for fun. Have you heard much about the Phantom lately?"

"You're not getting away with dismissing me that easily," he said and waited. Kate remained quiet though. Finally, he answered her question. "The Phantom has been quiet lately. Are you after him again?"

"Have you seen the news about the murders of three American tourists in Edinburgh?"

"Haven't heard a thing, love. Is that why you're over here?"

Kate confirmed it was and then explained they had connected several other cases to the same killer. "One witness spoke to a reporter and there was a composite sketch done of the man she thought might be responsible. It was the Phantom."

"Kate," Jax said her name with confusion in his voice. "That can't be."

"I felt the same, Jax. It gets weirder. I just went through the dates of all the murders and it matches thefts in those same European cities. Even Paris. They are days apart. At most a week. I can't explain it. I was hoping you might have some thoughts. He was there. There's no denying that. There are many similarities in the crimes as far as organization and leaving no evidence behind."

Jax cursed softly under his breath. He matched Kate's disbelief and that made her feel better. "It can't be him."

"That's what I said, but now I'm not so convinced."

"He's an art thief. His crimes are as much art as the paintings and artifacts he steals. There is no way he's running around murdering women."

"There's evidence to suggest otherwise. I'm working with a team here and they already think it's odd that I'm not going after him full force. I just don't think it's him."

"Were you hoping I was going to tell you it was?"

"I wasn't hoping for anything, Jax. You hear things. I thought if anyone might know it was you."

Jax spoke to someone on the other end of the phone. "Let me ask around and I'll call you back."

Kate thanked him and ended the call. She stared back in the direction of the police station, knowing she'd have to go in and tell them all the Phantom might very well be the killer. The only problem was that she didn't believe it herself.

CHAPTER 13

Kate stood outside the conference room door for a moment to see if she'd catch any discussion but all was quiet. When she pushed open the door, all eyes turned to her.

"You okay, Kate?" Declan asked, standing. When she didn't respond, he explained, "Most of these witness statements don't add up to much, but there's one you should see."

"I'll do that in a moment." Kate wanted to get this over with. She went to the table and sat. Declan sat next to her across from Sam and Fraser. "I cross-referenced all the Phantom's possible crimes with the dates of the murders and they match. He was in each of the cities around the time of the murders. I can't say for certain it's him, but we can't rule him out."

"You'll need to see this then." Declan pulled a file from a folder and handed her the documents. He gave an overview so she didn't have to read through the whole statement immediately. "The Phantom was seen with the victim the evening she was murdered. They were eating dinner at a restaurant with a large outdoor eating area. The witness said they seemed to be having a good time. The woman said when the meal was over, they started to argue. She explained the young woman got up from the table, shouted at him, and then left. He had to pay the check so remained behind but then left in the same direction she went. The witness said he seemed agitated and angry. She's the one who provided the composite sketch."

"She had a good look at him?" Kate asked but it wasn't a question. Of course, she had a good look at him if she was only a table away.

Declan cleared his throat. "She wasn't the only one who saw him, Kate."

"We were in Paris at the time of the last murder, Declan. We were right there. I never heard anything about a woman from the U.K. being murdered in Paris, did you? She was left at the Eiffel Tower. Don't you think it should have made the news?"

"We were there?" he asked, the confusion on his face evident. He was feeling the same blow she had felt when she noticed the dates. "We were consumed with that case, but I think we would have heard that."

"It barely made the news," Sam said, drawing their attention. "I'm not surprised you didn't see mention of it. The French did everything they could to hide the cases from the media. Word of it spread online before it hit the mainstream news."

Neither of them followed social media unless they had to for a case. "We have to consider him a suspect," Kate said even though she still didn't feel it was the right course of action. It wouldn't be the final word on it but she still had another focus. "Is there anything in the other case files about the TravelShip app?"

"About half of the cases," Fraser said. "I was looking for that as I was going through the information. Billy circled it several times and underlined it. He thought it was important. Do you think this is how he's getting his victims?"

"I still think it's a possibility. He might be using other means as well. I downloaded the app earlier and started to set up a profile."

Declan didn't look happy with the decision. "If this is the Phantom, don't you think he'll recognize you?"

"I don't know. It was a few years ago and the photos I have don't look like how I looked then. If he is going to target solo female travelers, then I'm a good target."

Declan expelled a frustrated breath. "Are you sure you want to take the risk? I'm sure there are other ways we can draw him out."

When he looked deep into her eyes like that, it was easy to forget there were others in the room. "I'll be fine. I thought you said this was a good idea. You're the one who encouraged me to download the app."

"That was before I knew how many victims there are, Kate. This guy is highly skilled and dangerous. If it is the Phantom, he spared your life once. I don't know if you'll have luck on your side again."

Kate knew it wasn't luck that spared her. He hadn't wanted to kill her. She flashed back to the roof. At any point, he could have given the signal and she would have been shot. Instead, he had cautioned her about the snipers watching them. He didn't want to hurt her. He had only wanted his freedom.

"I'll be fine," she assured Declan. Then she turned to Sam. "I want to hear about your cases first before we go any further. It doesn't seem like we are going to have any cooperation from the other investigations and I want to hear about those victims firsthand."

"I'll tell you everything I know."

Declan slipped his hand into Kate's lap and took her hand in his. It was a sweet gesture no one else would notice. It steadied Kate when she was feeling nervous and unsure. He had sensed that and his touch was reassuring.

Sam pointed to the stack of case files in front of him. "For some reason, he killed five women from England while he's only ever targeted three from a particular country. He could have moved on to a different nationality while he was in Belgium but he kept targeting English tourists. I don't know why, but it's what he did. I couldn't access all the cellphone data. Mostly because the cases were so old by the time of my involvement. I found in my notes, three of the women used the app. The two women whose cellphone data I couldn't access are the ones I have no information about the app. Friends and family of the victim did not know either."

"Can you tell us a little about the victims and circumstances of each case?" Kate asked and looked to Declan and Fraser to see if it would be helpful. They nodded in agreement.

Sam didn't need the case files. He had been living and breathing the cases since he started. "Cindy was twenty-eight when she was killed in an alley near the Louvre. She had traveled to France a few times but this was her first time in Paris. She had what looked to me like teeth scrape marks on her neck and cheek but the pathologist thought it could be scratches. There was no sexual assault, but there was bruising on her face and she had petechiae and marks on her neck. Her cause of death was homicide by strangulation. The investigator on the case said it was a robbery gone wrong even though she had her wallet and cellphone still in her purse. The second victim, Mary Ellen, was thirty. She was found along the Seine. Again, all the same circumstances. This time the police speculated she had been buying drugs and got mixed up with the wrong people. There was no indication she had ever done drugs and no drugs or paraphernalia were found near her body or on her person. The toxicology didn't indicate any drugs in her system."

Declan leaned forward and zeroed in on Sam "How could they conclude that then? How could you let them?"

Sam held up his hand to stop him. "I didn't *let* them do anything. By the time I got involved, the cases had been closed. The family didn't call us. The French police didn't call us. No one asked for our help. We weren't even aware of the cases. You're right though, the police got it wrong. If you don't like that, you're not going to like this last case."

Kate could only imagine. It sounded like the police in Paris did everything they could to make it seem as if the deaths were caused by risks the women took rather than some element in the city that caused them harm. It was good spin and a way to keep it under the radar.

Sam waited to see if anyone else had a comment and then continued. "Amelia was twenty-two and was found at the base of the Eiffel Tower. This is the only case where video surveillance was captured if you can call it that."

"You have an image of him?" Kate asked with hope in her voice. Until now, the man had completely evaded cameras. "We've been hoping for a break like this."

Sam shook his head. "It's grainy and you can't make it out. It's why I didn't bring this up before. If we had a good image of him, I would have plastered it all over the news and internet long before now. I can show it to you, but first, let me tell you about the case because it sounds like Amelia DeBecker was with the man you call the Phantom."

Kate wanted to see the footage, but it could wait.

Sam continued. "The French police detailed Amelia's visit to the Louvre earlier in the day. There was a window from six until about midnight when she was spotted on the surveillance video that had remained unaccounted for until we went through Billy's files. It seems she was at dinner with this man sometime around eight that night. The witness saw her leave close to ten."

"What time was she seen on the video?" Declan asked.

"A few minutes after midnight. Her time of death was put between twelve and twelve-thirty, which lines up with what I saw. She walked below the Eiffel Tower with a man who is considerably taller than she is. He had a dark jacket on and a cap pulled low over his head even though the evening was warm. We never see his face or even a profile of it. We put his height around five-eleven. They briefly kiss and then she takes his hand and pulls him out of frame. She is comfortable with him and she doesn't seem to be afraid at all. We don't see him leave the way he came in. He walks around to the other side of the Eiffel Tower and exits that way. His back is always to the cameras as if he knows they are there."

Regardless, Kate was eager to see the footage. "Do you have the surveillance video with you?"

Sam held up his cellphone. He hit play once and showed it to Fraser and then passed the phone across the table for Declan and Kate to see. Declan hit play and the screen jumped to life. It was grainy, not good quality. The area wasn't well-lit. It seemed like the closer they were under the Eiffel Tower, the darker it was.

A few seconds into the video, two figures walked into the frame. As Sam said, the video showed their backs. Amelia is dressed in cuffed jeans, a white tee shirt, and sneakers. They pause for a moment and then the man takes her hand in his. Amelia leans into him and then rises on tiptoes and kisses him. His face is positioned in such a way that Kate can only see a little side profile of his hat, the bill of which blocks his face. After the kiss, Amelia takes his hand and pulls him out of the frame. The video changes to another view of the man walking away alone about thirty minutes later.

The video confirmed a few things she had suspected. He was engaging with these women long before the murder and getting them to let down their guard and feel comfortable. He was romancing them, which meant he had to be reasonably good-looking, charming, and could put a woman at ease even while alone in a foreign country. It was not an easy feat.

Fraser looked over at her. "What do you think, Kate? Is it the Phantom?"

"I have no idea. He fits the build but this guy is wearing a bulky jacket which could add weight to him. He's dressed all in black and I can't see his face. He could be anyone. I'm not even sure if he matches any of the three sketches we have."

"Is there anything you learned from it?"

"I think what we all knew – he took his time with her." He had thirty minutes with the victim before he walked out of the frame. Kate had no idea how quickly he killed her, but it was certainly plenty of time for him to wash her face, clean her hands, and scrape under her fingernails. Knowing the information before and seeing it now were two vastly different experiences.

She was also chilled to the bone with how calm he appeared after the fact.

The rest of the day went in a frantic blur of activity. Spade finally called her back at close to six and indicated he wasn't having much luck with any of the other investigators. Kate assured him they had enough information with what Billy had provided them. It occurred to her when she mentioned Billy, she hadn't given Spade an update about him, so she gave him the rundown.

Before the call ended, Spade had one final question for her. He asked if she was ready to go public connecting all the cases. Kate had remained quiet on the phone for far too long and then said she was. She had thought of every reason not to and none seemed compelling enough to keep quiet. It was time to let the world know exactly what was happening.

The murders stayed in the shadows for far too long, which is why they had been allowed to continue. Kate informed him she'd set up another press conference for the following day and would let Declan deliver the message. It would look like they had made progress overnight.

Kate thought the call would be over then, but Spade was perceptive. "Kate, is there something wrong? You don't sound like yourself."

She had not told him about the Phantom yet. If she held back the information any longer, she would have been hiding it. "One of the potential suspect's composite sketch looks like the Phantom from the

Curators. I assume you remember that case in Paris."

"I do," Spade said slowly. His tone was even and deliberate. "Someone believes he is connected to the murders?"

"He was seen with one of the victims at dinner a few hours before her death. That's not all, Spade." Kate recounted how all the dates of the murders matched up to art thefts. She couldn't even rule him out based on the grainy surveillance video. "It could be him. If it is, it means he slipped through our fingers in Paris and killed again."

"Hold on now, Kate. Don't get ahead of yourself," Spade cautioned her. "Do you think it's him?"

"I didn't at first, but there is a lot of evidence pointing that way."

"You still don't sound sure."

Kate wasn't sure. What was bothering her the most was why she wasn't sure. "I don't know if I don't want it to be him because it would mean Declan and I missed something huge or if I don't think it's him because it doesn't fit the profile. I can argue myself into thinking of him as a suspect and then as easily talk myself out of it."

"Don't put pressure on yourself then. If the evidence fits, it will become clear enough when everything else is eliminated."

That wasn't the only reason Kate was worried. "Spade, if it is the Phantom, no one has been able to catch him. He has hundreds of art thefts under his belt. I don't know that we'd ever be able to stop him." Once Kate said the words, the rush of anxiety that had been filling her since the Phantom's name was first mentioned diminished. That's why she had been so resistant to the idea. She couldn't conceive of a way to stop the Phantom.

"You sound like you're getting too far ahead of yourself. What does Declan think about this?"

"I'm not exactly sure. He seemed like he might be on board with the idea. We haven't had much time alone to discuss the events of the day."

"Take dinner and process," Spade suggested. "You don't have to decide now if the evidence isn't there. A dinner with the victim a few hours before a murder doesn't mean he's the killer. Being in all those cities certainly is suspicious, but you don't have him there on the exact dates and times."

That much was true – everything was circumstantial. "I think we are about ready to break for the evening. Fraser needs to get home to his family and Sam needs to check into his hotel. If Declan and I have any breakthroughs tonight, I'll let you know."

"Call me tomorrow with an update. Don't stress about it now."

Kate let her boss go and then went back to the conference room to gather her things. There were a handful of witness statements Declan wanted her to read. He had them ready in a file and she took them with her when they left.

When they were out on the street, they said goodbye to Sam.

Fraser stopped Kate before they left. "If you're still conflicted about the Phantom, it's okay. I know you seem a bit conflicted about it and I don't want to pressure you."

Kate decided to be honest. "There were a lot of reasons I didn't want to consider him. This case will be easier if it's not the Phantom. He's committed so many art thefts completely undetected for so long. No one has even gotten close to catching him."

Fraser looked down at her with sympathy on his face. "You did, Kate. You and Declan came closer than anyone. I was reading up on some of his cases today. Before the two of you, no one even knew what he looked like or what country he originated from. You can catch him."

"It's not as easy as it sounds. I think we had a lot of dumb luck on our side last time." They fell into conversation about the Phantom's many thefts and the famous paintings he'd taken. "Most have never been seen again. We assume they are with private collectors or in a warehouse someplace."

"You said he's Bulgarian. Do you have any idea where he has residences?"

Kate didn't even know if it was plural. "We don't know anything about him. His DNA told us his ancestry but that's all we could get from it. We were hoping for a relative hit or something like that. We've had nothing. He's a ghost, which is why it would be so much easier if he wasn't a suspect."

Fraser put a hand on her back. "It's been a good day and we've made considerable progress. Don't sell yourself short." He said goodbye and headed towards his car.

When he was out of sight, Kate leaned against Declan. "Are you feeling as badly as I do?"

Declan looped an arm around her shoulders. "You're probably just hungry and tired. Let's walk up High Street and find a pub. We can talk about the day."

That had been Spade's advice. She followed a few steps behind him as she pulled her coat tighter around her. The night had a chill to the air. She tried to keep a straight line as she walked behind Declan up the hill, but Kate found quickly that the Royal Mile wasn't like walking down the street in Manhattan where those going up stuck to one side and those going down stuck to the other. There was a flow for those sharing the sidewalk. Here people walked every which way. Twice she had to stop as she encountered families walking five or six people across, no one willing to step out of the way for her.

She laughed at the confusion of it all and called Declan's name for him to wait for her. He turned back and rolled his eyes. He reached his hand out for her. "It's like an obstacle course," he said, agreeing with her. "Just one more thing to get used to while we are here."

"Where are we going?"

"There's a pub called Whiskey Bar I want to try. I could use a drink." They walked the short distance and at the pub, Declan opened the door to a wave of chatter. The lights were dimmed enough for people to see but weren't so harsh she had to shield her eyes from the glare. It was perfect for Kate. There was no hostess there to seat them. Declan quickly found an open two-seater table. He ordered a whiskey neat while Kate ordered a Thistly Cross elderberry cider. She wasn't familiar with the brand but it sounded good and not too heavy. They ordered and then stared at one another across the small table.

Dark circles had formed under Declan's eyes. He looked as tired as she felt.

After a few moments of total quiet, they both laughed at how they felt. Declan leaned onto the table which made the whole thing wobble. "What did you think of today?"

"I like Sam and Fraser. I think the four of us will work well together. I was a little surprised Sam hadn't mentioned the surveillance video sooner. After seeing it, I can see why. It doesn't tell us anything."

"He's a good investigator. He was telling Fraser and me how he first got involved in the investigation and then took it over. He was as aghast as we were that not more had been done." Declan paused and considered something. "I don't think he would have held back evidence intentionally. He probably wanted to show it to us in person. As you said, it doesn't show much and his explanation helped us understand what we were seeing."

Kate agreed with him. "I can't imagine looking at that surveillance video and not trying to find that guy. I don't know what the French authorities were thinking."

The server dropped off their drinks. Declan took a long sip. "They were thinking they didn't want to have to admit they had a serial killer lurking in their city. Look at the places he's started and go cross-reference that with any list of safe places for female solo travelers. Sam gave us a list of groups on social media that are teaming with solo women travelers sharing photos, their trip itineraries, and tips.

He had created a fake profile of a woman and joined some of them thinking the killer might have done the same thing. He didn't find anything though. He even mentioned crime and most of the women gave him several travel safety tips."

Kate hadn't considered social media might be a way he's finding his victims. That seemed like a long path to take but it was possible. "I didn't know there were groups for female solo travelers. I know the cities this is happening in are high on the list for safety. None of them, except maybe Brazil, ever have travel warnings or restrictions. If I were a young woman traveling solo they are cities I'd explore."

Declan agreed with her and then changed the subject. "I want to stop talking about work to give ourselves a break. First though, when you walked out, you said you were calling someone. Who did you call earlier today?"

There was no point in lying. "Jax Talbert."

Declan nodded. "He's probably somewhere in Europe. You're here. Did you want to see him?"

Kate laughed at his jealousy that he wasn't even trying to hide. "I don't want to see him, Declan. I thought he might have heard something recently about the Phantom. Jax is in the art world. People talk about art theft. I figured he might know something."

Declan raised an eyebrow. "Did he?"

"No. He didn't think the Phantom made sense as the killer."

"Well, as you said, he's in the art world. He doesn't know anything about criminals. You know other than the fact that he is one."

Kate watched him across the table. "I don't want to talk about Jax. It was a brief phone call, nothing more."

"He asked to see you though." Declan took another sip of his whiskey.

"He did and I said no." She leaned back in her chair. "I thought we were…" She didn't know what they were doing, so she couldn't finish her thought. They were back to the conversation they hadn't been able to finish. "As I said earlier, if you change your mind, let me know."

Declan looked over at the couple next to them. They were in their sixties and still holding hands on the table. They were laughing, talking, and looked very much in love. He turned back to Kate. "I want that, Kate. I jumped from woman to woman in my twenties. I did all of that already. As much as my ex would disagree with this statement, I loved being married. I want that kind of relationship."

Kate wasn't sure what he was trying to say. The uncomfortable feeling in her stomach grew. "You don't see that as possible with me. Is that what you're saying?"

Declan groaned in annoyance. "That's most definitely *not* what I'm saying, Kate." He leaned forward, took her hand, and stared deep into her eyes. "I'm saying I don't know how to do this with you. I live in your house and don't want to seem like I'm taking advantage. I can't even take you on a proper date because you sleep down the hall and we are always at work. What I'm trying so badly to say is that I don't *just* want to sleep with you and I have no idea how you feel about me."

"Oh," Kate said and sucked in a breath.

He wasn't finished. "Trust me, Kate. I can't tell you the nights I lay awake hoping you'd come to my room. When you didn't, I wanted to walk down the hall to your bedroom, knock on the door, and…well… use your imagination because that's all I've been doing."

Kate blushed as his gaze roamed over her face settling on her mouth. "I had no idea. I thought you had changed your mind."

Declan made a low guttural sound and shook his head. "It's all I've been thinking about. But I don't know how to do this with you and not mess up everything we have." He swallowed hard. "I can't lose what we have. It's about the only good thing in my life. More important than the job and even my family."

Kate wanted to get up and hug him right there. There was something so innocent about the way he was looking at her. "If it makes you feel better, I don't know how to do this either. I didn't even know what we were doing."

"I think we need to go slow and talk about this more. I want to know what you want, but I want you to think about it. You have to believe though – I want you, all of you."

The server chose that moment to place their meals in front of them. Kate was glad he hadn't put her on the spot to share her feelings. He knew her better than that.

Declan let go of her hand and pointed to her plate. "Eat up, Kate. All this can wait…as long as Jax isn't coming to see you."

"He's not coming to see me," Kate reassured him and hoped it was true. Jax had a way of doing whatever he wanted whenever he wanted.

CHAPTER 15

The next morning Kate sat at the kitchen table going through the witness statements Declan had given her. She had read them briefly when they got home from dinner. She was too tired to process the information and had set it aside until morning. She had quickly fallen asleep and woke feeling rested and ready to take on the day. Declan seemed to have gotten a better night of sleep too. She wasn't sure she should tell him that in the middle of the night, he had rolled over and laid his hand on her stomach. She hadn't wanted to move it.

Focused back on work now, the first order of business was the witness statements. She had two stacks of statements – one from Sam's cases and one from Fraser's. She started with Sam's first. A few of the victims were seen in the days leading up to the murders with a man about five-eleven with dark hair, a handsome face with a strong jawline, and dark eyes. That could certainly be one of the men in the sketches. It could also be the Phantom.

When she was done with Sam's cases, she moved on to Fraser's. Unlike Sam, Fraser had no witness details in the hours before the victims' deaths. There were only statements from people who had seen the victims in the days before the murders. There was one man Viola was seen with and the description on the file matched the sketches of the man with dark hair.

The man who provided the description was the shop owner under the apartment Viola had rented. Kate jotted down his name. It would be their first stop that morning. They were also going to check a few tour companies and speak to the hotel staff where the second victim, Rose Dillard, had been staying.

Kate considered the sketches again. She studied all three side by side. Removing the one of the Phantom, the other two looked so similar they could be the same man with altered appearances or brothers.

"What did you think of those statements?" Declan asked, stepping into the kitchen as he fixed the belt on his pants. He was half-dressed and his damp hair stuck up all over the place.

"It's interesting. I want to speak to people here and see what more detail we can find. The description fits the sketch of the man who isn't the Phantom." That's what Kate was leaning towards anyway. She sighed. "I'm still having trouble believing he's our suspect."

Declan looked at her with curiosity. "I'm not sure why you keep defending him."

Kate shook her head. "I'm not. It's overwhelming to think it's him. We don't even have a photo of him to circulate to the media. He's a ghost, Declan. If he's him, it only means more women will die before we can stop him. That's even *if* we can stop him. Besides, these descriptions fit the other men."

"Keep an open mind." Declan walked out of the kitchen before she could say anything else.

Kate refocused her attention on the witness statements until her phone rang. She grabbed it and looked at the screen. Jax. She debated not answering but the pull for information was too great. "Hello," she said in a crisp formal tone.

"Are you around a bunch of people, Kate? I thought I would have caught you before you started your day."

Kate relaxed back in her chair. "I'm fine to talk. Did you find out something?"

Jax didn't waste any time. "There's been a rumble of speculation that the Phantom has been laying low in the last year. People are speculating that he might be slowing down or out of the game."

"That's just the last year though?" Kate asked.

Jax confirmed, then continued. "From what I'm hearing. I also haven't heard any information about recent thefts by the Curators, so the story checks out. No artwork from them has hit the black market."

"Would people admit they had works of art stolen? I thought the Phantom was getting away with this because no one was reporting, except for the big galleries and museums."

With his voice constrained, Jax said, "I hear things, Kate. You know how this works. I can't give you my sources and methods."

Kate knew he wasn't going to admit criminal activity or rat out anyone else. "Let me ask you a question. I know no one has ever seen the Phantom other than his crew, a few cops, me in Paris, and a handful of people in the underground art world. Has he always had thick dark hair?"

"I don't know. Why?"

"We have three descriptions of men seen with victims. One man looks identical to the Phantom. Another man with dark hair but his face doesn't resemble the Phantom. Then the third man has a shaved head. I was wondering if the Phantom might be changing up his appearance."

"I don't think he'd shave his head," Jax said quickly, piquing Kate's interest.

"Why is that?"

"There's been a long-standing rumor the Phantom had an injury from when he was a kid. Some rumors indicate it happened at boarding school, others say he had a brother who hurt him, and other rumors say it was his father. I don't know what's true. Regardless of how it happened, he's rumored to have a huge scar on his head that's covered by his hair. He's self-conscious about it, so I can't imagine he's shaving his head."

Kate couldn't believe what she was hearing. "You heard he's self-conscious? Help me to understand how it became a rumor."

Jax shared in her disbelief. "I know it sounds like I'm making this up. The story goes that there is a place on the back of his head where his hair separates from time to time because of the scar. One of his crew asked him about it one day and the guy was told to never ask again. The Phantom is known to fidget with his hair or wear a cap. That's all I know, Kate. It's all rumor and speculation, but there's got to be some truth to it for it to persist this long. Apparently, you can see the scar on his temple. That's where it starts."

Kate didn't recall seeing any scar on the man's face, not that she got a good look at him. "You said a few things that interest me. You mentioned boarding school and a potential brother and father. Do you know more about his upbringing?"

"You've asked me this before." Jax sighed deeply and heavily. No one liked talking about the Phantom. "His origins are unknown, but there are rumors he comes from a wealthy family, possibly with ties to the aristocracy. His upbringing is why he's rumored to know so many languages and so much about art."

Kate had heard those rumors before. They had never been substantiated – of course, nothing had been other than his Bulgarian ancestry, which Jax didn't know the FBI had obtained. "What about family?"

"Other than potentially a brother and father, I don't know. People have been speculating about this man for decades. I don't know what more to tell you."

Kate knew there was something more. "Are you sure that's all the rumors you heard? He's been laying low this year and hasn't pulled as many jobs. That's it?"

Jax hesitated. "Kate, it's all rumors."

She blew out a frustrated breath. "You've said that about fifteen times. I know you've not been able to substantiate anything. That's not what I'm asking. I'm asking what you've heard, even the rumors."

Jax cursed in frustration. "He's gotten paranoid. Jumpy and is not acting himself. Something is going on with him and no one seems to know what it is. It's why people think he's lying low. Maybe the pressure finally got to him. One of his crew broke ranks and told someone. This is how the information got out. His crew is stuck with no work and not sure what to do. The Phantom's loyal guys are seeing it through but there's a few dissenters in the bunch."

The only way the Phantom had been able to get away with his crimes for so long was because he had a small but loyal crew who kept his identity, and theirs, a secret. If one or even two were breaking ranks and talking, that could spell a break for Kate. "Do you know any of these crew members who are talking?"

"I don't but I might be able to get a message to them."

"I want to speak to one of them."

"No, Kate. No one is going to speak to the FBI."

Kate knew that would be his response. "He doesn't have to tell me his identity or anything like that. They can use an untraceable burner phone. I just need an in, a conversation about this unrelated matter."

"I don't know," Jax said slowly, dragging out his words.

Kate was wearing him down and they both knew it. "Just try, please. This isn't about art anymore. Women are being murdered across Europe. If I can rule out the Phantom, then we can focus on other suspects."

"You're talking about bringing down the greatest, most elusive art thief the world has ever known."

"Possibly the worst serial killer Europe has ever seen." Kate laid the guilt on thick. "You can be on the right side of this, Jax. We need your help."

He groaned loudly. "I'll do what I can. When can I see you?"

Kate should have known that was going to be the next question. If she didn't have this *thing* with Declan, she would have happily met up with him. "It's not a good time. Let's leave it at that."

"Are you seeing someone?"

Kate stared at the doorway waiting for Declan to walk through. She wasn't sure where they had left things last night. They had stopped talking about it at the pub. "Something like that," she said softly.

"I get it. Let me see if someone will be willing to speak to you. It may take a while. I'm not in direct communication with anyone close to the Phantom. I'll send a message through my channels and see what I can do. I doubt if they will be willing, Kate, but I'll try."

That's all she could ask from him. Kate ended the call and stared down at the phone, happy it had gone about as well as she had expected. She was processing what Jax had told her about the Phantom laying low for the last year. He was right in that she hadn't heard of any major art thefts over the last year. Kate assumed he was solely focused on private collectors. They were easier to hit than a gallery or museum anyway and they rarely publicly reported. She hadn't considered he'd stopped.

Declan knocked once on the frame of the doorway. "You ready to go, Kate? We have a meeting at nine. We've got about fifteen minutes to get there."

Kate stood and stacked the statements in a pile and slid them back into the folders. "Have you spoken with Sam or Fraser this morning?"

"They are running down some other leads. Fraser is going back to Billy's to see if he has anything to add from yesterday."

Kate cocked her head to the side, surprised by that. "Does Fraser think Billy is hiding something?"

"He didn't say. He told me he was going to swing by there today and ask a few follow-up questions. I think he was confused by a few of the statements. He wanted more information about how those were obtained and if we could speak to the journalists in his network." Declan glanced over at her. "Do you have a concern about that?"

"Not at all. When you say how they were obtained, what do you mean? He told us journalists asked the questions and the witnesses provided a statement. What more does he need to know?"

Declan shrugged. "It sounded to me like Fraser wanted to know how the questions were asked." With that settled, they left the apartment and started to walk up High Street.

They walked in silence for a few minutes before Declan asked, "Are you going to tell me about your phone call with Jax?" He was smiling so Kate knew he had overheard most of it.

"Why would I tell you something you already know?" Kate asked sarcastically.

Declan nodded his head and laughed. He was trying to get a rise out of her and it worked.

CHAPTER 16

After Kate realized he was teasing her, she told him about the call with Jax. "Ultimately, it sounds like the Phantom is dealing with something that's taking him out of the game."

"Killing women will do that."

Kate rolled her eyes. "It could be anything, Declan. A health issue, possibly. Anything. We don't know."

"Does Jax think he'll be able to set up a call with one of the members of the Curators?"

"Jax isn't connected like that, Declan. He said he has channels to get messages out there, but it didn't sound like he had anything direct. Most everything he knew was speculation and rumors."

Declan stopped in the middle of the hill and turned to her. "Do you trust this guy, Kate?" He held his hand up to stop her. "Before you say anything, I know you've known him a long time. I know you're going to tell me he's never lied to you and you don't have a reason not to trust him."

"That wasn't what I was going to say at all." When Declan gave her a blank stare, she added, "I was going to say that I don't believe everything he tells me, but I don't believe he'd hide information as important as this. He called me back after he got the information. I trust him enough."

Declan conceded. "If you say so."

Kate appreciated that. They chatted while they walked the rest of the way to the shop. When they arrived, Kate looked directly across the street and noted Advocate's Close was right there. "Declan, where Viola died is right there," she said, pointing across the street to the close. It was a straight shot.

"That may be why she was willing to go out so late that night. She wasn't going far," Declan speculated. He turned back and gestured toward the shop, which sold fine wool garments. "Kenneth Scott is the man's name. Fraser mentioned he's also the landlord of the apartment Viola rented."

Kate and Declan found Kenneth in the back of the shop, helping a woman find a scarf for her husband. She watched the short, white-haired man as he worked. He had an affable smile and an abundance of patience with his customer. When he was done, he pointed back to the register where she could pay and then approached them.

"Can I help you?" he asked with a smile. He started to tell them about the sales when Declan stopped him and introduced them both.

"Yes, that's right I remember now. Let's head upstairs to the apartment and you can see where Viola stayed if you like."

"That would be great," Kate said, glad she didn't have to ask. "Do you not have a renter right now?"

"Not for the holidays. I have family who come to Edinburgh and that's where they stay, so I don't rent it out." Kenneth yelled to a young woman in the back of the shop to take care of the customers while he was gone. He grabbed a ring of keys from behind a counter and then left through the front door and stepped to the side door Kate and Declan noticed earlier. "She was on the floor above the shop," he explained as he unlocked the downstairs door and then they ascended the narrow stairs. These were a straight shot up, unlike the stairs in Kate's apartment where they ascended in a spiral to the top.

Kenneth unlocked the apartment door and pushed it open, standing back and allowing them to enter first. A chill ran up Kate's arms as she entered. It seemed as if it had been some time since the heat had been turned on. Cold air permeated the space.

They stood in a small foyer and took in the layout. There was a bedroom and bathroom straight ahead while the living room was off to the left and the small eat-in kitchen was off to the right. It wasn't as big a space as their apartment but it was perfect for one person. Kate immediately went into the living room and pulled back the long curtains. Advocate's Close sat directly across the street. As Declan said, it made sense why Viola would have left so late at night to meet someone. She wasn't going more than one hundred feet. The distance would have limited the danger in anyone's mind, especially if she was leaving to meet someone she trusted.

As Kate stared out the window wondering what Viola was thinking about that night, Declan asked, "Did you get to know Viola while she was here?"

Kenneth shook his head. "Not any more than any of those who rent with me. She asked me several questions before she rented about safety. I assured her it was a safe building and the street was as safe as can be. There's a long-term tenant on the top floor but he travels for work all the time. Below that are three girls who go to college locally and this one I keep for tourists. Viola was quiet and didn't need much. She only stopped in the shop once to ask me how to get the light to work in the kitchen. It has a tricky switch."

"While she was here did you see her with anyone?"

"A man. I told the other investigator." Kenneth leaned back against the wall. "If I had thought he was dangerous, I would have told her to stay away. I don't get involved in the lives of people who rent from me. I assumed she knew this person. They seemed comfortable with each other. He never came upstairs with her that I saw. They'd stand out in front of the shop and talk. I saw them together at least twice before she was murdered." He lowered his head. "That poor girl. I can't even imagine what her family is going through. Her father came here to get her things. It was terrible. No parent should lose a child, no matter how old that child is."

His sympathy was genuine.

Kate turned her back to the window and faced him. "Did the man look familiar to you?"

Kenneth raised his eyes back to Kate. "It's hard to say. I see so many people come through here that all their faces start to look the same after a while. I don't think he worked in any of the shops or pubs right near here if that's what you're asking. I tend to know the locals. He might have worked farther up in the Grassmarket near the castle or down lower near Holyrood Palace. I only know the people right in this area."

Declan asked, "What about in the tourism industry? I heard there are several walking tours and tour operators who take people to other parts of Scotland. Would you know if he was connected to any of them?"

"I wouldn't know." He hitched his thumb over his shoulder. "There's a lovely young woman by the name of Vivian who runs many of the walking tours. You can usually find her in front of St. Giles around seven in the evening. The tours fill up fast." He gave them the website address and suggested taking the tour. He didn't know how to reach her otherwise.

Kate thought a walking tour at night might be a good idea. "Could you describe the man for me?"

"Five-eleven, dark hair, strong jaw, and medium build. He looked like so many other young guys you see out there on the street. I didn't think twice. Viola didn't seem afraid of him or worried. She acted like she knew him and was having a good time. Do you think he was the one who killed her?"

"We don't know," Kate said honestly. "There's still a lot of information we have to sort through. We can say for certain that the three murders are all connected so if you see this man again please call us."

"I will, Agent Walsh, you can be sure of that. I haven't seen him around since Viola. It didn't occur to me he might have had something to do with her murder. After it happened, I hoped to run into him because I wanted to direct him to Chief Inspector Fraser but I haven't seen him since."

Kate pulled out her phone and scrolled through her photos until she found the photos of the three sketches Billy had provided them. She had snapped a photo of each so she'd always have them with her. She showed her phone to Kenneth. "Do any of these men look familiar to you?"

He took her phone and Kate directed him to scroll through the three photos. When he was done, he looked back up at her. "Two of these men look familiar."

"Which ones?" Declan asked with concern in his voice. He leaned over Kenneth's shoulder as the man pointed them out. "Are you sure?"

"Yes, I'm sure." Kenneth pointed down at the photo of the dark-haired man. "This was the guy with Viola and this other man was in my shop just the other day. He was looking for a new cap as his was torn. He said he was going to be staying longer in Edinburgh and with the weather getting colder he needed a new cap. He was a nice enough man, very kind to a woman with a young child. The baby was fussing and this man helped a woman with her packages while she got the baby settled. Who are these men?"

Kate wasn't sure what to call them – persons of interest, suspects. Both seemed too strong a word for now. "They were men seen with the victims. We are just looking for them to get more information."

"If that first man comes back in my shop, do you want me to tell him to contact you?"

"No," Kate said a little too quickly and loudly. She smiled and apologized. "You know how people can get when they think the cops want to speak to them. I don't want him to take off and not speak to us. I'm sure if he's been around I'll be able to find him."

Kenneth looked at her curiously but didn't press the issues. "I'm happy to help in any way I can. As I said, Viola's father came and picked up her belongings. Chief Inspector Fraser said that would be fine. I didn't realize the FBI would be involved."

"It's fine," Declan assured him. "Let me just take a quick walk through the rest of the rooms and we can let you go back to the shop."

Kenneth handed Declan the key. "Take your time. Just drop them off at the shop when you're done."

Kate wasn't sure what good it would do them now this long after the murder. It wasn't as if they could fingerprint the place or gather any evidence. But when Kenneth was gone and the door closed behind them, Kate felt the stillness of the space.

"What are you thinking?" she asked Declan as she followed him to the small bedroom.

He checked on one side of the bed and then got down on his knees to check under the bed. "I wanted to see if there was anything left behind. I didn't think there would be, but you never know." While he was looking under the bed, Kate opened a closet door but it was empty.

Declan stood upright and checked the nightstand drawer. "There's nothing," he said and moved past Kate.

She knew he was frustrated with getting access to the victims' dwellings so late after the fact. Kate followed him to the kitchen and watched as he pulled out drawer after drawer and then went through each cabinet. He went to the small white microwave and stood there for a moment while he went through the basket filled with brochures. "These are all from two different tour companies, Kate.

One for night walking tours and the other for day tours. I think we should choose the night one first."

"Let's sign up for a walking tour tomorrow night and we can see the city. It will give us a chance to speak to Vivian. We might learn a few things mingling among the tourists." Kate reached out for the tour brochures and tucked them into her pocket. "What did you think about the two identifications he made?"

Declan stood with his hands on his hips. "It was interesting he didn't identify the Phantom as the one with Viola. It doesn't rule him out though, Kate. He was seen with the victim in Paris. It's not enough either way for us to do anything with."

"Are you at all concerned about the press conference this afternoon?" At three, Declan was going to stand in front of the media again with Fraser and Sam to announce that the Edinburgh murders were likely connected to murders across Europe and Brazil. They had called the other law enforcement agencies as a courtesy to let them know. None of them seemed interested. Most rushed them off the phone telling them they were wrong. The press conference would also give them a chance to warn all solo female travelers they needed to be on high alert.

The weight of what they were about to do creased the line on Declan's forehead. "We are about to start a global panic. The only thing I'm worried about is how much the media is going to descend on Edinburgh. They might get in our way."

Kate had worried about that too but the risk of not going public was too great.

CHAPTER 17

Kate and Declan spent most of the morning and well into the afternoon walking from one place to another to check with potential witnesses from Fraser's list. Three people positively identified the same man that Kenneth had seen with Viola. No one had seen the Phantom.

For most of the day, Kate only had one thing she wanted to do. She anxiously waited for Fiona to come into work at Mary King's Close because she wanted to show her the sketches. The woman at the desk had said she'd be in by one.

Kate and Declan stood outside the front door and waited patiently. Her stomach growled so loudly Declan looked down at her. "We'll get lunch as soon as we are done here," he assured her. He patted his own. "I'm hungry too. I wonder if Sam and Fraser are getting anywhere."

Kate wasn't even sure what they had planned for the day. Whatever it was, she hoped they had made more progress than them.

They stood there chatting until Declan tapped Kate's arm to draw her attention. "Fiona is right there."

Kate saw a young woman dressed in period clothing. It took her a moment to realize the young woman was Fiona. "I didn't recognize her with her hair up like that."

Declan pulled the door open and the two of them walked up to the desk and got her attention. "We are hoping you might have a moment to take a look at a few photos."

"Sure," she said, walking around the corner to where they stood. "I'd be happy to look at them. Amy, my co-worker who did the tour with the guy asking those questions, is here. I can show them to her too."

"If you can take us to her now, we can get out of the public's way," Declan said, glancing over his shoulder as tourists walked into the shop. "We can go someplace a little more private to talk."

Fiona guided them out the side door and down the steps they had taken before. While it was dark, it wasn't quite as spooky as it had been when they first saw the close. Kate followed right behind Fiona as they made several rights and lefts.

They ended back in the room where Mable's body had been found. There was a young woman dressed similarly to Fiona lighting two lanterns. "Amy, this is Agent Walsh and Agent James. I mentioned them to you yesterday. They were interested in learning about your interaction with the man who was asking all those questions about the close."

Amy finished lighting the lanterns and hanging them up, which provided more light in the room. When she had everything the way she wanted, Amy walked over to where they stood. "I'd be happy to help. It was terrible what happened to that woman."

Before Kate showed her any of the photos, she wanted to hear what happened directly. "Can you tell me about your interaction with this man?"

Amy spoke slowly and clearly. The incident had stayed with her. "It was about two weeks before the woman was murdered. It was on my last tour of the day and a man was on the tour alone, which wasn't unusual. He kept interrupting me to ask questions about access to the close at night. I explained that wasn't possible but he persisted. He wouldn't stop interrupting me no matter how many times I tried to continue the tour. It was starting to annoy the others. He insisted there must be a way into the close at night. He even joked that kids must break in from time to time. I assured him nothing like that occurred and that we had good security. Eventually, he settled down and the tour was over. When the tour ended, people approached and thanked me. A few gave me tips. I never saw him again but I didn't see him leave either."

"Did he finish the tour with you?" Kate asked.

"I can't be sure now. At the time, I thought he was hanging in the back. I counted people as they left and I was sure the numbers added up. It's possible I counted someone twice."

"Was it possible that he was in here looking around, figuring out a way in?"

"Not that night," Fiona said, interrupting. "As I admitted, it's possible on the night of the murder because I didn't do my walkthrough. That night Amy and I both walked through and made sure no one was here. I know that because that's when she told me about the guy. I stayed behind with her because he made her uncomfortable."

"You said he had a British accent?"

Amy nodded. "He also said he was from London and was here for work. He didn't tell me where he worked or what he did." She wrapped her arms around herself in a hug and sighed. "He gave me a creepy feeling. I can't explain it. We see all kinds of people from all over the world. Some people like history and others like ghost stories. This guy didn't seem to be paying attention to any of it. He was only focused on access. When I pressed him why he wanted to know, he didn't have an answer. It was after that he got quiet and hung back. I had no way of knowing he'd kill a woman down here."

Declan offered her words of comfort. "You couldn't have known. It sounds like you did everything right. You didn't provide him the information he wanted and you did a walkthrough at the end of the night making sure he was gone. You had no way of knowing he'd come back." He stopped and corrected himself. "We don't even know he's the man in question. But you were right to raise a concern about him."

Kate pulled out her phone and handed it to Fiona. "There are three photos of sketches. Let me know if any of them look familiar to you."

"Is one of these men the killer?" she asked with her eyes wide.

"We don't know. We don't know who they are or how they are connected. We are just trying to narrow things down. Let's call them men of interest for now." Kate looked at the girls and she could see by their expressions, they weren't happy with the answer. "It just means they could be witnesses, knew the victims in some capacity, or they might be the killer. We don't know what we don't know."

"I understand," Fiona said and then looked down at the phone. Amy stood over her shoulder. The first man they scrolled past with barely a mention. It was Fiona who pointed to the Phantom. "I saw this man last night at The Mitre. He was in the back having dinner alone. I only remember him because he was having a long conversation with the waiter about the beer selection. He had a loud laugh. I don't know his name though."

Kate avoided looking at Declan who she knew had his gaze focused on her. "Did you happen to see where he went when he left?"

"I left before he did. The staff there might remember him." Fiona furrowed her brow. "You don't think this guy did anything, did you? He didn't seem the type."

Kate wasn't going to get into his infamous backstory. "As I said, we don't know how he's involved. I know you said he was eating alone, but did you see him speaking to anyone other than the waiter?"

"No. He seemed like a regular diner chatting about the beer selection." Fiona scrolled to the last photo. "I don't know either of these other men."

Amy took the phone from her hands and raised it closer to her face.

She studied the photo for several moments. "This could be him. The man I had on the tour had his hair parted differently. He had the same high cheekbones and the eyes look the same."

Kate took the phone back and showed it to Declan. It was the same man that Kenneth indicated was with Viola. "Have you seen him around at all after the tour?"

"I never saw him again." Amy looked at Fiona and she said the same.

Kate thanked them for their help. "I don't think we need anything else. I'll be in touch though if we do. If you think of anything else, give us a call."

"Do you need me to walk you back?" Fiona asked.

"We can find our way," Declan assured her even though Kate didn't feel so certain. When they were away from the room, he asked, "Do you think the Phantom and this guy are working in tandem?"

"Both of them killing the women?"

"It's happened before in other cases. It's rare but it's happened." Declan guided them back through the maze to the front door. He waved to the woman behind the desk and then held the door open for Kate as they walked back onto the street. "We need lunch."

Kate didn't feel like eating but her body had other plans. "Let's go to The Mitre and we can speak to the staff. I find it hard to believe the Phantom is going out like this and interacting with people."

Declan smirked at that. "He's got to eat, Kate. Have you ever wondered what the Phantom does when he's not committing art heists?"

Kate didn't want to admit how much she thought about every facet of the Phantom's life. She played it off. "I assumed he's in his lair plotting his next crime."

"He's not a supervillain like in cartoons," Declan said, still smiling at her.

The pub wasn't crowded at that time of day. Kate assumed they had missed the lunch rush and were far too early for dinner. They walked past the bar and found a table in the back where they could sit and order food. A server came over to them before they even got fully seated and handed them menus and took their drink order.

After ordering a soft drink, Kate asked, "Were you working last night by chance?"

"I work most nights but take an occasional afternoon shift," he said with a smile. "Have you been in here before?" When they said they hadn't, he went through some of the menu items and made suggestions.

Kate had a one-track mind though. She pulled out her phone and scrolled through the photos and showed him the one of the Phantom. "Do you happen to know this man?"

The server bent over to look at Kate's phone and he nodded. "He's been in here a few times."

"Do you know his name?"

The server shook his head. "I don't know him like that but we chatted a bit while I was bringing his food. I talked to him about our beer selection."

"Did he pay with a card or cash?" Declan asked.

The young man straightened up. "I can't share that information."

Declan pulled out his badge and discreetly showed him his credentials. "We are working on the murder investigations of the three women who were killed in the closes. This man is someone we'd like to speak to. Any information you have for us would be helpful."

The young man shifted his eyes toward the bar. "Let me get my manager for you." He started to walk off but Declan called him back and they both ordered.

"We're here for lunch too," Declan said, flashing him a friendly grin. "We just thought we'd take care of two birds with one stone."

When the server walked off, Kate leaned on the table. "I'm not sure the Phantom would be working with a partner murdering women. He has a crew for the heists, but murder? I don't know."

"Maybe this other guy is among that circle, Kate." The server dropped off their drinks and promised the manager would be over shortly. Declan took a sip of his drink and watched the bar area. "As far as I'm concerned, he's a person of interest whether you want to admit it or not."

Kate held her hand up to stop him. She had a dull headache and had no desire to argue with him. "I admit it could be him. I'm only trying to make sense of the two men and their roles in this. Two serial killers working together across Europe and Brazil seems highly unlikely to me."

Declan wasn't going to let the point go. "Is it possible they are one-upping each other? One of them kills and then the other follows with another murder, upping the risk and the thrill with each one."

That was more likely to Kate but still, she had a hard time thinking that was what was happening. She started to respond when a man appeared at the side of the table. He had a printed page in his hand and asked to see their badges. When he was satisfied with their credentials and Declan's suggestion to call Chief Inspector Fraser if they needed more proof, the manager confirmed he'd seen Declan on television.

"I have no problem sharing information with you if you think it's going to help stop this guy," he said and then looked between them. "I have to admit though, this is more curious by the second. Declan isn't all that common of a name, at least that I've heard." He turned to Kate. "Now that I've heard your last name, this is even more strange."

"What do you mean?" Kate asked with confusion in her voice. She wasn't sure what he meant.

He lay the piece of paper on the table. "The man who was in here paid with a credit card on all three transactions. The name listed is Declan Walsh."

She and Declan lunged for the sheet of paper to see it for themselves. Declan was quicker than her though. He brought the paper to his face and cursed loudly. Then he handed it over to her.

Kate scanned down the transactions to the name on the credit card. Right there in black and white – Declan Walsh. It seemed the Phantom had *borrowed* their names.

"Who is this guy?" the manager asked. "Is he the killer?"

Red had fanned up Declan's neck and face. "He's an international art thief known as the Phantom and a suspect in this murder investigation."

Kate opened her mouth to correct him but saw the rage burning behind his eyes. She needed him to calm down before he publicly said something he couldn't walk back. The Phantom was mocking them and it was pushing Declan over the edge.

She turned to the manager. "Thank you for providing the information. We can take it from here."

He tapped once on the table. "Come back anytime. I'd be happy to help in any way I can."

When the manager was gone, Kate looked over at him. "Calm down. You look like you're ready to have a stroke."

Declan bore his gaze into her. "I'm going to take pleasure in putting a bullet in his head."

She knew he meant every word. Kate also knew from this moment forward, she was going to be hard-pressed to get Declan to see anyone else as a suspect.

CHAPTER 18

Kate, Declan, Fraser, and Sam argued for nearly thirty minutes before the press conference about whether or not to turn the sketches over to the media. Without more information about these men's involvement, Kate thought it was reckless and might push them further underground.

Declan and Fraser thought it was the only way to get the public's help.

In the end, Kate and Sam won out only because Declan wasn't sure what he was legally going to say related to their involvement. He might have called the Phantom a suspect with the manager of The Mitre, but he knew better than to do that in the media. The last thing the FBI wanted was a lawsuit. Kate was glad he backed down because she didn't want to have to get Spade involved. She knew he would have sided with her and it was akin to running to Mom during a fight.

Kate stood back from the crowd and watched the podium over the sea of reporters. The press conference was taking place right in front of St. Giles Cathedral. It was a formidable backdrop for the announcement.

"This is quite the spectacle," a voice said from behind her.

Kate turned her head to see Billy standing right beside her. "I didn't realize you'd be here."

"I am a journalist." When Kate didn't respond, Billy shrugged as if he didn't care one way or the other. "Fraser came to see me again. He thought I knew more than I told you yesterday. He even speculated I might be involved. I'm not involved if you were going to ask. I told you everything I knew. If I were involved, I wouldn't have contacted you in the way that I did."

Kate looked over at him. "It was the way you contacted us that alerted our suspicions. Fraser is a good cop. He's just making sure to cover all his bases."

Billy let the subject drop. "He asked about my tactics to get witness statements."

"You said you had journalists on the ground who did that for you."

"It was more than law enforcement was willing to do."

From his tone, Kate sensed he was itching for a fight. "What is it you want, Billy? You've shared information with us and helped the investigation significantly. I'm not sure what more I can do for you. I told you I'd be in touch with information or additional questions."

"I don't want anything now but the time may come when I do. Are you going to be willing, Agent Walsh?"

Kate pulled back from him. "You're being creepy and cryptic and the FBI doesn't work that way. If you need something, state it outright. If you have more information to share, tell us. We are doing the best we can to stop this guy. I'm not going to play games with you though."

"I see," he said, stepping back.

The press conference started and all eyes were on Declan as he stepped to the podium and started to detail what they knew about the cases in Scotland so far.

"He's a handsome man. Don't you think, Agent Walsh?"

"Agent James?" Kate asked, not sure who he was referencing. When Billy nodded, she laughed. "He did very well with women when we were in training."

"That isn't what I asked. I asked if you thought he was handsome."

"He's my partner," Kate said and left it at that. She knew her voice was constrained in a way it shouldn't be in front of him.

"Things happen with partners all the time."

Kate didn't say a word, retreating into silence as Declan delivered the news that the murder cases in Scotland were connected to what they believed was a global case with victims spanning across Europe and Brazil and victims of all nationalities.

As Declan handled the flurry of media questions, Billy stepped closer to her and whispered right in her ear, "How long have you two been sleeping together?"

Kate turned to him. "What did you say?"

He smiled like a Cheshire cat. "You heard me, Agent Walsh. How long have you and your handsome partner been shagging, banging…." He winked and rattled off a few more euphemisms until Kate held her hand up and told him that was enough.

She was about to deny his allegation when she saw the familiar profile of a man move through the crowd behind them. Kate turned back to Declan but there was no way she was going to be able to signal to him. Billy's mouth was still moving in his lewd accusations but all Kate focused on was pushing her way through the throngs of onlookers to get to the person she thought she saw.

"Excuse me. Excuse me," Kate shouted as she bumped and jostled the people behind her. "FBI. Let me through," she shouted again when the people didn't move. Finally, two men saw what was happening and parted the sea of people for her. One of them asked if she needed help as she ran past him into more open ground. She waved him off and kept going.

Kate looked up the street, cursed loudly to herself and lowered her head. *Did she see him or were her eyes playing tricks on her?* She didn't know.

When Kate raised her head again, he was there only one block up about to turn right on one of the connecting side streets. Kate didn't hesitate this time. She pumped her legs in a sprint to get to him. She zigged and zagged through people, which caused people to shout at her to slow down and watch where she was going. He turned back to see what was going on and their eyes met. It was only for a fraction of a second, but recognition took hold.

He knew she was after him and he knew who she was.

Kate couldn't be sure but it appeared to her he shook his head once before turning right and disappearing. She wasn't deterred.

Kate made it to the block he had turned down and was stopped again as the crowd coming toward her grew even more dense. She walked quickly apologizing as she went, all the while scanning the crowd for him.

Kate couldn't even shout the man's name. She didn't know it. As Kate shoved past a family taking up the wide berth of the sidewalk, he turned back once again. When he spotted her this time, he took off in a run. Kate followed suit and now a chase was on. Only there wasn't anywhere for him to go. The sidewalks swarmed with people and the traffic on the roads prevented him from crossing again. He aimed straight down the road and so did Kate. She couldn't close the gap between them though. She had never seen someone run so fast.

He disappeared behind buildings as traffic forced Kate to stop on the sidewalk and wait for the cars to pass. She bounced from one foot to the other impatient but stuck. When the traffic freed her, she jetted out into the road at full speed, following in his same path. Greyfriars Kirkyard. She had to choose between going left or right. She chose right and ran directly down the path, narrowly missing an older woman and her daughter who shouted at her to stop running.

Kate yelled an apology as she ran to the crest of a small hill and looked out at the sea of graves. At the far end of the cemetery, she saw a flash of movement. Kate sucked in a breath of air and pushed herself as she ran down the slope of the cemetery. She tucked low and looked through the rows of graves to where she thought she had seen movement. There was no one there.

Kate stepped off the main path and onto the grass. "I just want to talk!" she shouted. "Please, I need to speak with you."

The man stepped out from behind a large mausoleum back up the hill to her left. He peered down at her. "You know I can't talk to you."

Kate turned and looked at him. She took a step to walk toward him and he stepped back. It was clear if she tried to pursue he'd run again. She could have taken out her gun and ordered him to the ground, but she wasn't going to test Police Scotland's good will allowing them to carry. Besides, the cemetery was full of tourists. She couldn't start this case causing an international incident. Kate knew he wasn't going to be taken in without a fight. She did the next best thing.

Kate held her hands up in a gesture of peace. "All I want to know is if you killed those American women because I don't think you did."

When he spoke his voice was strong and clear. "I've never killed a woman in my life nor would I ever. Even when I had the chance to kill you, I let you live."

Kate might pay for it later but she believed him. "Do you know it looks like you're the one who's killing them? You're a person of interest. Twenty-five women are dead and you were in every one of those cities. You were seen with at least one of the women. Witnesses gave statements and there is a composite sketch of you."

He looked to the side as people milled around the graves not far from them. He turned back to Kate. "It's why I'm here, Agent Walsh."

"Do you know who's doing this?"

He stared at her and remained still.

"If you know who it is, tell me. We have more resources than you have."

"I don't know," he said with a ton of frustration. "He killed someone close to me and left me a message. There were already so many dead by the time I knew."

"Was Amelia your girlfriend?" Kate asked, trying to remember if that was the victim he was seen with in Paris. "You argued at dinner."

"She wasn't my girlfriend. She was a friend's daughter." He looked at Kate with an expression she couldn't read. He was tired. She could tell that much. "I have to avenge Amelia's murder."

Kate didn't bother telling him that wasn't the way. "Why is he after you?"

"I honestly don't know. It was only after Amelia that I found out he was targeting me. He left me a message near her body and then contacted me after her murder. He told me where she was and the message was there."

"What was the message?"

"He told me about the other murders. He's obsessed with me, Agent Walsh. He wants me to take the fall for him."

"You've been tracking him?" Kate asked, thinking back to what Jax said about his crew getting frustrated with him because he hadn't pulled any recent jobs.

"Since Amelia's murder. It's all I've been able to focus on. Amelia was already dead when we were on that rooftop. That's why I couldn't let you take me in."

Kate shook her head. "That's not the only reason you couldn't let me take you in. You're a thief. You've stolen hundreds of millions of dollars in art and antiquities. You've been a ghost. They call you the Phantom. You thought no one would ever catch you and you want to continue as you have been. That's why you didn't let me take you in."

He told her she was wrong. "Some things are more important. I promised I'd take care of Amelia and I broke that promise. She was targeted and murdered because of me. There's an honor among thieves, Agent Walsh. I have to kill him."

Kate could feel her time was running short with him. "Do you know anything about how he's finding his victims or anything you can tell me to stop him?"

"I wish I knew," he said and pulled his cap lower over his forehead. "I wish I knew because I would have used it to stop him. He's been one step ahead of me this whole time. If the time comes, I can prove I wasn't here in Scotland for the first murder. I have to go." He looked behind him, probably for a way out. Then he turned back to Kate. "Please don't follow me. I know you're just doing your job. Let me do mine."

Kate didn't get a chance to say anything else. He turned from her and took off running.

This time she didn't chase him.

CHAPTER 19

Kate wasn't sure how long she remained in the cemetery. She knew she had to get back to Declan because the press conference had to be over by now. Kate checked her phone but there had been no calls from him.

She'd have a lot to explain when she got back, mostly why she let the Phantom slip through her fingers one more time. There was no way she could have taken him in on her own. Kate had no reason to shoot him and the international scandal it would cause shooting an unarmed suspect in Scotland wasn't something they had time to deal with now. The Phantom was only a person of interest in the case. They wouldn't even have enough evidence to hold him.

Kate left the cemetery and walked the same streets back to St. Giles. The throngs of people had dispersed and there was no one left other than the media and Declan, Fraser, and Sam still at the podium. Kate stepped behind one of the journalists and caught Declan's attention.

She nodded her head to the side to get him to wrap things up. She didn't see Billy and she didn't want another run-in with him. Even a denial on her part would be met with skepticism. That's how the gossip rags worked. He could publish a story if he wanted and then Kate and Declan would have to address the fallout, if there was any. He had baited her, but thankfully, she didn't have time to address it.

Kate hung back while Declan answered a few final questions from the media then left Fraser and Sam at the podium. He jogged past a few reporters and directly to where Kate stood. "I thought that went well. Of course, now that it's out there even more media is going to show up here."

Kate nodded barely listening to him. Her mind was still in the cemetery with the Phantom. "Can we take a few minutes away from Sam and Fraser to talk?"

Declan touched her arm. "Are you okay, Kate? You don't look like yourself."

"I'm fine," she assured him. "We just need to talk."

"Okay." He jogged back to the podium and said something to Fraser and Sam that made them turn in Kate's direction. They waved and she waved back. After a few more minutes of conversation, Declan rejoined Kate. "Let's find a pub and chat."

Kate shook her head. "Let's go back to the apartment to talk. We need somewhere private."

Declan looked at her wide-eyed but agreed. They walked to the apartment and climbed the stairs in near silence. It was only after they were inside and Declan sat down on the couch that he looked up at her expectantly. "What's going on, Kate? You're starting to worry me."

She sat down on the edge of the couch with him. There was no way to cushion the news. "While you were giving the press conference, I saw the Phantom."

"What?" Declan said as he inched to the edge of the couch. "Where is he?"

Kate was careful with her words. "He got away, Declan. There wasn't much I could do. I was alone. I couldn't catch up to him and I have no reasonable legal reason to shoot at him, certainly not with all the bystanders around."

Declan relaxed and put a hand on her shoulder. "It's okay. If you couldn't catch him, you couldn't catch him. He took you hostage before so it's good you fell back. We know for sure he's here now."

Kate moved out of his grasp. "That's not exactly how it went down. I cornered him in a cemetery. I spoke to him."

Declan squinted at her. "What do you mean you spoke to him?"

Kate recounted chasing him down the street and into the cemetery. She explained how far apart in distance they were. "If I had made a move toward him, he would have run. I made a calculated decision to try to get him to speak to me."

"I'll reserve judgment until you tell me more," Declan said and shifted on the couch. He turned his knees away from her. "What did you talk about?"

Kate knew he was angry and trying to make sense of it. "He said he's being framed." Declan went to argue and Kate asked him to stop and let her explain. "He said he knew Amelia and that's why he was having dinner with her. He didn't tell me what they argued about but he said the killer targeted her. He told me the killer told him where to find her body and then left him a message at the scene. He said he was told there were other victims and that he was being framed. He's been trying to find the killer ever since. As far as we know, the killer was silent before killing here in Scotland and the Phantom has been hunting him. He said he has to avenge Amelia's death."

Declan absorbed the information. His chest rose and fell with each deep breath he took. It was hard for Kate to remain quiet and patient while he processed what she told him. She knew if she pushed, he might not be as reasonable as he would with time.

Kate got up from the couch and went to the kitchen to get a glass of water. She was surprised when she turned from the faucet to see him standing there.

"If you had been able to bring him in, would you have?"

"Of course, Declan. He's wanted on countless other crimes. He's a criminal, but I believed him. He said if the time comes, he can prove he wasn't in Scotland for the first murder."

Declan's eyes got wide. "Where was he?"

"He didn't say." Kate saw the skeptical look on his face. She conceded, "I didn't know what else to do. If I went after him, he would have run. I don't think that I could have tackled him and gotten him into cuffs myself. I didn't have a legal reason to shoot him."

"I understand all of that, Kate. That's not my hesitancy."

"Then what is?" Kate asked even though she knew. He didn't like the fact that she believed what he was telling her. They shared a look that said it all. "I'm being objective," she said, trying to reassure him.

"He doesn't fit your profile. I think you might be overlooking him."

Kate held her hands up in defense. "I understand why it looks that way. I want him in prison as much as you do, Declan. I know you'll tell me he's a professional con man and that's how he's pulled off the majority of his heists. His face…" Kate didn't know how to explain the look on the Phantom's face. "It was akin to speaking to the family of a victim. There was tiredness and pain in his eyes. I believe he knew Amelia and he's blaming himself for not keeping her safe. I also believe he's risking exposing himself to find the man responsible."

Declan conceded that. "He is taking a risk being here, especially out in the open. I realize only a handful of people even know who he is, but he had to have seen the news report and know we are here. If he was trying to hide from us, I assume he would have been more careful."

Kate was glad he could see at least a little wiggle room where the Phantom might not be the one responsible. "He said he told a friend he'd watch out for Amelia. I assume he knew her parents. If that's true, then there might be something in her background to give us a clue to the Phantom's identity. We can also go through his past heists and see if there is anyone who might want to seek revenge."

The corner of Declan's lip turned up in amusement. "That's going to be a long list. Think about how much he's stolen over the years. If the killer isn't the Phantom and someone is seeking revenge on him, then it must be about more than a stolen painting. He would have had to anger a real psychopath for them to resort to this. How can we be sure the killer isn't playing a game with him, trying to outdo his crimes?"

Kate hadn't considered that angle. "Are you saying the killer read about the Phantom in the papers and is trying to outdo him? How'd he know where the Phantom is going to strike next? As I said, these crimes are planned. The killer would have to have some insider knowledge about the Phantom and he's called that for a reason."

"Maybe it's one of his crew," Declan suggested. "Is it possible the killer is someone close to the Phantom and he isn't even aware?"

"Anything's possible at this point." Kate sunk back into the couch, her mind trying to recall every detail of the interaction – the man's facial expressions, the words he chose to use, and the inflection in his tone. What he didn't say was almost as important as what he did.

"Your mind is spinning, Katie," Declan said, drawing her attention. "I can see it on your face."

"He said he didn't know who it was, but they left him a message near Amelia's body. They had to have known he was in Paris and connected to Amelia. He knows the killer, even if he doesn't realize it."

Declan looked more positive than he had before. "Then we have avenues for investigation. If it's not the Phantom, then the person is in some way connected to him. It would make sense why we have different composite photos. We can't forget though it was the Phantom who was seen arguing with the victim."

"The fight could have been about anything. Maybe the Phantom didn't want her alone in Paris. If he was a surrogate parent for her, that's what families do – they bicker with one another sometimes. Maybe that's all the witness saw."

Declan nodded agreeing with what she speculated. "Did the Phantom know about the other murders at that point?"

"No," Kate said with emphasis. She repeated what she had already told him. She wasn't sure if Declan didn't understand or if he was trying to trip her up. "He said he knew *after* Amelia's murder. He received a message that she had been killed and where to find her body. The Phantom said there was a message with her body about the other murders. That's when he went back and noticed the dates matched."

"Then the killer must know the Phantom or his real identity."

"That's right," Kate said as some of the pieces started to fit together. "But now we are in a situation of having to look for two men whose identities are anyone's guess."

"We have to explore Amelia's background. If the Phantom knew her parents, then maybe there is something in their background that will lead us to him and the killer."

Kate recalled from the file that Amelia's parents had passed. She explained that to Declan. "There might be other family members to speak to. There was mention of a sister. If Amelia knew the Phantom, then so did the sister." When it looked like Declan was satisfied with the outcome of that, she grew quiet.

"Is there something more?"

Kate wrapped her arms around her middle. "Billy knows about us."

"Knows what?"

"That we…" Kate trailed off not sure what to say. Billy had accused them of sleeping together, which they hadn't. She might as well say what he said because she didn't have another way to explain it. "Billy asked me how long we've been sleeping together."

It surprised Kate when he smiled. "I guess the chemistry between us is palpable to everyone around us because Sam asked me if we were involved."

"That's not okay," Kate said, growing worried she had said or done something inappropriate. "I've never acted like that. Have I?"

Declan shook his head. "We are close, Kate. Even if we didn't have an interest in each other more than just being partners, people would ask. We have a close friendship. We have chemistry that's obvious to people. I don't think it's a big deal."

Kate didn't agree. "What if Billy prints something in his paper? He could derail us."

"He runs a gossip rag. Even if he wrote something, I don't think he could do much damage. If you're worried about it, let's get in front of it and address it with him and tell Spade." Declan sat back on the couch and kicked an ankle up on his opposite knee. "I don't think this is something we need to get worked up about."

"We'd have to lie to Spade." Kate stared over at him wondering if he wanted to bother lying to Spade or if he was fine with the truth – which might effectively end their working partnership. "I don't want a different partner, Declan."

"Agreed." He seemed to consider the options. Then he shrugged. "Let's address it with Billy and explain we have been friends and partners for a long time. If he's not going to let it go, then we address it with Spade and tell him it's nonsense." He must have caught the worried expression still on her face. "If it makes you feel better, I told Sam we were just friends and have been for a very long time."

Kate expelled a breath. "We don't need the added complication on this case."

"Would you be embarrassed if people knew about us?"

"Of course not. It could be a distraction for other people," Kate said it and meant it.

He locked his gaze on her. "When the time comes, I'm going to want everyone to know. I'm not hiding or lurking in the shadows."

Kate smiled and agreed – she caught that he had said *when* the time comes instead of *if*.

CHAPTER 20

Before going to see Billy later that evening, Kate had spent some time learning the TravelShip app. It was a lead they had to run to ground, even if it was something Kate didn't want to do. They decided Kate would chat with the men in the app, give them the number to a burner phone they always had on hand, and then would meet up with them at a neutral location while wired with video and audio. Kate had never used a dating app and it felt foreign to her. She didn't understand how people dated from the platforms. It seemed like such an odd way to meet people.

Even though she had swiped to show interest in a few men she thought might be the killer, no one had matched with her yet. During the cab ride over to Billy's, she complained about how strange it was to look for dates on an app.

Declan glanced over at her. "You haven't dated much, Kate. You had your college boyfriend, the guy you dated for like a year in grad school, and then some casual flings while on the job. It's not like you ever invested time in *actually* dating."

Kate didn't need to be reminded of her lack of a long-term relationship. What Declan said was true though. Men had never been her priority. "Do you call what you did in your twenties dating?"

"Now, now. Let's not fight about that all over again." Declan puffed out his chest and laughed.

Kate didn't want to remember that time in his life. It made her jealous all over again. "How did you and Lauren meet?" She couldn't remember how Declan had met his ex-wife, only that the first time Kate had met her had been a disaster. Casual drinks and dinner had turned into a tense exchange between the two women. At the time, Kate hadn't understood it. She had been perfectly nice to Lauren. Later, Declan said she was jealous of Kate.

When Declan didn't respond because he was looking at his phone, Kate asked him again.

"At a bar," he said finally not taking his eyes away from whatever he was reading. "I was out for my brother's birthday and she was there with her friends. She approached me and then followed me around all night." He looked over at Kate. "The irony of the whole thing is I told her I was an FBI agent and that relationships are hard in my line of work, but she pursued it right to marriage. Then after we got married, she expected my career to change."

Kate knew that part. She had warned Declan early on about it.

"Is there a reason you're asking?"

Kate shook her head. "Just making conversation. What's got your attention on your phone?"

Declan showed her the email from Sam. "He was able to go through Amelia's file and gather as much information about her past as possible. The sister he interviewed is willing to speak to us. He also did a deep dive into her parents and sent us everything he found. We'll have a lot to go through after this. He emailed some of it but said he would run us over files when we get back."

"What about the tip line? Did he say anything about that?"

"Fraser and Sam are going through some initial leads to see if there is anything of value. They said the lines have been swamped and they pulled in additional staff. You know most of it's not going to pan out to be anything."

That's the way it went with tip lines. There was a mountain of data and usually one good lead buried among it all. Now that the world knew the cases were connected, they had put pressure on the countries with cases and hoped their local law enforcement would be forced to share more information. Even Spade was having trouble accessing it all. It was Billy's information they had been relying on so far, and now Kate was going to confront him. She didn't like the dynamics of it.

The cab stopped in front of the shop and Declan paid via the app. They had a car at their disposal if they wanted it but neither of them felt like navigating the narrow Edinburgh streets unless they had to.

The shop flashed a closed sign in the window. Kate stepped back and angled her head up and noted the light on in Billy's apartment. "He's home or left his lights on."

Declan approached the door and found it unlocked. "Maybe safety isn't the issue here that it is at home." He pulled open the door and put his hand along the wall to find a light switch. It was a futile effort though. He ascended the stairs in the dark with Kate right behind him.

When they reached the landing, the commotion on the other side of the door stopped them cold. Declan toed open the slightly ajar door. "There's someone in there trashing the place."

Kate leaned into him. "What's the plan?"

"I'm going in," he said evenly as the sound of crashing boxes and what sounded like a table being overturned echoed into the hallway. "Stop right there and turn around slowly." He paused for a moment and then burst through the doorway. He shouted again for the person to stop, to no avail.

Once fully in the room, Kate took in the carnage – boxes opened and their contents dumped on the floor, upturned tables, and Billy's desk laid on its side. Kate wasn't sure where to step but she didn't have time to decide because Declan shouted to her as he disappeared down a short hallway.

Kate moved swiftly through the trashed living room and office area. She still had no idea who Declan had commanded to stop. The person was out of sight by the time Kate made it into the room, and she didn't think Billy would do this to his place.

Kate made it to the bedroom as Declan climbed out the window. She rushed right after him and joined him on the aging fire escape. It swayed when she added her weight to it. A dark-haired man quickly descended the ladder below, shaking and bouncing the entire platform.

Declan started his descent. Kate did the same, following after him, hoping the whole thing wouldn't give way. The ladder didn't go all the way to the ground and they were forced to drop. Declan hit hard but picked himself up and ran.

By the time Kate righted herself, she saw the man for only seconds before he disappeared around the corner. Declan pointed down the alley where he wanted Kate to go and he went in the other direction.

Kate made her way down the alley not sure what she was looking for as she looked behind trash cans and tried opening the few doors to no avail. She stood looking down the alley toward the main road when a hand closed around her mouth and strong arms dragged her back. Kate elbowed the person's stomach and kicked a foot into their knee.

He didn't let her go until they were farther down the alley.

"Settle down. I'm not going to hurt you," the familiar voice said. As Kate relaxed her body, he let her go. "Twice in one day, Agent Walsh. This is certainly a pleasure."

Kate spun around to face the Phantom. "What are you doing?" she said with anger in her voice. "I need to go after my partner. He might be in danger."

"Who are you chasing?"

"I don't know. We got here and someone was trashing the place,"

Kate said, gesturing toward the building. She wasn't sure why she was explaining anything. She put her hand to her hip as if she were about to draw her gun. "What are you doing here?"

"No need for the gun, Kate. Don't you know they don't take too kindly to those around here. I'm surprised they let you have it."

"We aren't on a first name basis." Kate didn't unholster her weapon. She could fight him here in the alleyway, but he seemed to be one step ahead of them. "I'm going to ask you one more time. What are you doing here?"

"I heard a sleazy publisher lives here and might know something about the killer. I came to speak to him, but you and Declan got here before me."

"You don't know who was up there then trashing the place?"

He shook his head. "I know less than you do."

Kate zeroed in on his eyes, making sure to keep long steady eye contact with him. "I need to take you in."

The Phantom shook his head. "That's not going to happen. I don't want to have to hurt you in the process." He pointed to her chest and then back at his. "This time, you and me, we're on the same side. You need to stay out of my way though."

Kate was tired of referring to him as the Phantom. "Give me a name – something besides the Phantom. It's a stupid name to keep calling a man."

A slow smirk spread across his face.

She knew why. "Not Declan Walsh either. We know about that alias."

"Did you like it?" He reached out and tucked a strand of her hair behind her ear. "Do you think we'll ever be friends?"

Kate swatted his hand away. "We aren't friends. I need to take you in for formal questioning." She said the words but made no move to arrest him. There was a part of her that simply didn't want to and she knew she wasn't going to be able to physically do it. It wasn't that he was so much bigger than her, but he was stronger – much stronger than anyone she'd ever met. She was more curious than defeated.

"You're disappointing me." He frowned playfully. "You can call me Leo. I agree with you that the Phantom sounds silly. I never liked the moniker but the papers called me it and it stuck. Tell Declan I'm sorry for borrowing his first name. I thought you'd enjoy the joke." He looked past her. "Just as easily as I got you, so could the killer. Please be safe. This man will kill you if he gets the chance and he will take pleasure in it."

As he backed up down the alley, Kate called after him. "Did you see Billy?"

He held his arms open wide. "As I said you know more than me. You better go and make sure he's still alive."

"What were you going to do if we hadn't shown up?" Kate asked, ignoring her instinct to try to wrestle the man to the ground and take him in.

He raised his eyes toward the building. "I was going to find out what Billy knew. There was chatter on the street that he's been following the cases from the start. If I heard that, maybe the killer did too."

Kate didn't mention having Billy's evidence. She pleaded with him one more time to come in for formal questioning.

"Until we meet again," he said in response and took off running down the alley.

Kate had no idea where Declan went and could only hope he was safe. She was reminded of Leo's words about Billy's safety and ran back to the front of the building and climbed the stairs again. She pushed open the half-closed door and called his name.

"Billy, it's Agent Walsh. Are you in here?" She heard whimpering sounds coming from farther inside the living room. "Billy, are you here?"

"Agent Walsh," the man said as his voice cracked. Amid a pile of papers and upturned boxes, he lifted his hand out from the pile. "Please, help me."

Kate rushed to the man's aid, pulling off the papers and boxes on top of him. "Take it slowly." She got him into a sitting position. There was blood coming from the front and back of his head. "Do you know the man who did this to you?"

"He was wearing a mask. I couldn't see his face." Bill's eyes rolled and he swayed. "He threw me to the ground when I answered. He told me he needed everything I had on the killer. I told him it was all with the cops. He didn't believe me, Agent Walsh. He said he was going to kill me."

"You're going to be okay." Kate went to the small kitchen off the living room and grabbed a few dish towels to stop his bleeding. While she did that, she also called the emergency number to get an ambulance there. Billy needed to go to the hospital to be checked. She was sure he was going to need at least a few stitches. She returned with the towels and gave him one to hold to his forehead while she applied pressure to the wound on the back of his head.

"Do you have anything left you didn't tell us about earlier?" Kate saw the hesitation in his eyes. "Billy, what do you have? Fraser thought you might have something more."

"I convinced him I didn't." Billy took a deep breath then let it out slowly. "There's a safe built into the floor near my bed. You'll find photos there. One of the journalists in my network took a photo of the man he believed to be the killer in Paris. It's grainy and hard to see. He believed the killer saw him taking the photo. He's been in hiding since."

"He knew someone photographed him?"

"I should have told you while you were here."

Kate didn't get a chance to ask anything else because seconds later,

Declan showed up at the front door covered in dirt and out of breath.

CHAPTER 21

Declan took in the scene with Kate on the floor, seemingly unaware she was holding a rag to the back of Billy's head, and rushed to her. He bent down to her level. "Are you all right? You disappeared on me. I kept chasing him hoping you'd catch up but you never did." He looked her over with concern and only relaxed when he realized she was not injured.

"I'm fine," Kate reassured him and told him to sit and catch his breath. "We can talk about what happened later." She hoped the look on her face communicated she didn't want to discuss it in front of Billy.

Declan did as Kate suggested. "I couldn't catch him, Kate. I tried but he was faster than me and he knew the streets better. Man, can he run. How did he know Billy had information?"

Kate wanted to know the same thing. They turned their attention to Billy. "Well?"

He winced. "I might have told a few people that the FBI was working with me to find the killer."

"We are not working *with* you," Declan said, raising his voice. "You shouldn't have told anyone anything. Do you realize you were only putting yourself in danger?"

"I know that now." Billy pulled the rag from his forehead and saw the blood. He put the cloth right back. "I didn't think the killer would find out and hunt me down. Speaking of that, why are both of you here? Fraser's visit wasn't enough?"

Kate scolded him like a child. "Considering you withheld evidence when we were here and then again with him, no it wasn't enough. It was also a good thing we showed up when we did. You might not have made it out alive."

"Withheld evidence?" Declan asked.

When Kate explained about the photos in his bedroom, Declan demanded the combination to unlock the safe and then left the room. When they were alone, Kate said, "That's not why we are here. We came to speak to you about what you said to me earlier at the press conference."

Billy swallowed hard. "About you sleeping with your partner?"

"That." Kate pinned her gaze on him. "Agent James and I are not romantically involved. We have been partners and friends for a long time. We have a certain comfort between us that I can understand why you might pick it up as chemistry but it's not. There is nothing unprofessional happening between us and you can't print otherwise."

Billy bit his lip and looked up at Kate. "It's already gone to the printer and is on the website."

Kate ripped the rag from the back of his head making him wince in pain. "What do you mean it's already gone to the printer?" she asked through a tense jaw.

"I wrote the story this afternoon. It was the last story I needed for this week's edition. It will be out in the morning." He tried to turn his head to his desk but could only manage to look over with his eyes. "You can see it on my website if you want. It's a great story – lots of tension, lust, and a little romance."

Kate felt the anger cresting the surface. "There is no tension, lust, or romance, Billy. You could ruin our careers. You can't print something that isn't true."

"Actually, I can. I only hinted that you *could be* involved and let the photo speak for me."

"Photo?"

"The two of you looked cozy over dinner last night. I had a photographer follow you and he got some great shots. The one over dinner though. You can't beat it."

Kate's breathing grew uneven as she spent the energy to physically hold herself back from ripping off the man's head. They were so wrapped up in the case they had never noticed a photographer, but then again, every tourist on the street had their camera phone up taking photos night and day. "I can't believe you'd do something like this to us in the middle of this investigation. It's a distraction we don't need."

"But it's a story that will sell papers. A kind of will they, won't they kind of thing."

"This is our lives!" Kate shouted as the ambulance sirens grew closer. "Is there any way to stop this?"

Billy looked right at her in defiance. "Not even if I wanted to, and I don't want to."

Kate stood and threw the bloody rag down on the floor with him. "What is the website address?"

Billy told her and then added, "I'm sorry if this hurts the case."

"You're not sorry." She left him there in a heap on the floor and went to find Declan. She found him standing next to the bed with the carpet pulled back and a board pried out of the floor. He held several photos in his hand. "I assume you found them."

Declan handed them to her. "Fraser was right, he knew more than he was telling us. These photos look like the man in the other sketch, not the Phantom. I'm not sure what country this is. I'm not seeing any landmarks I know. The face of the man is visible from the side. I can only assume the woman he's with is one of the victims."

"Leo," Kate said to Declan's confusion. She might as well get this out of the way right now. "I asked the Phantom what we should call him besides that stupid nickname and he told me Leo."

Declan didn't understand. "You saw him again?"

"He sort of grabbed me and pulled me into the alleyway. He said the word on the street was that Billy had evidence about the killer's identity. He was on his way to Billy's house when he saw us go in."

"You let him get away again?" His voice was a mix of disbelief and confusion.

"He's not the killer, Declan. Besides, there's no way I can bring him in alone."

"That's not true," Declan said evenly, giving her a look of concern. "I don't even know what to say to you right now."

Kate didn't know what to say either. She wasn't acting like herself and was making irrational decisions she wouldn't have made a year ago. Maybe she was softening, but more likely, her instinct told her to focus on the real threat and deal with Leo later. Kate raised her eyes to Declan and then looked away. She didn't like how he was looking at her with a mix of concern and anger.

Kate ignored him and lowered her head to look at the photos. She recognized not only the country but the city. "It's Porto, Portugal. I recognize the view and the restaurant." Kate wasn't sure if this was a victim or not. They hadn't received all the photos yet. There was one thing that was obvious though. He was changing his appearance. "He has his hair parted differently and a goatee. You can recognize through the eyes and nose it's the same man."

"Where did Billy get these?"

"He said a photographer but let's go ask him."

They walked back out into the living room as the paramedics were loading him onto a stretcher. Kate flashed her badge and asked for a moment with Billy. One paramedic protested but Kate stood in his way. "Billy, where did you get these photos?"

"I told you a photographer. He was taking photos of the city. He didn't realize it until about a month after the victim's murder he might have a photo of the killer."

"Did you share it with law enforcement in Porto?"

"I told you I tried but they wouldn't take it seriously. The photographer tried as well. They brushed him off and said the victim was robbed and murdered. They looked at the photos and dismissed them right away."

"Why?" Declan asked, stepping to Kate's side. "Why would any cop see a photo of a victim on the night she was murdered with someone and not pursue it?"

"You'll have to ask them," Billy said with his voice growing weaker. "I told you I've been doing everything I can to get someone to take me seriously."

Kate waved the photos at him. "Why did you keep these?"

Billy closed his eyes. "In case he turns out to be the killer, I'd have something for a story."

"Take him," Kate said to the paramedics. She had another issue to address while they were standing in Billy's apartment. She turned back to Declan. "Billy ran the story about us in the paper. He said it's online too."

"Great. That's just perfect." Declan brushed past her and headed for the door. He turned back once. "You can tell Spade about it when you tell him you let the Phantom get away twice and now you're on a first name basis with him. You've lost all objectivity, Kate."

He left Kate standing there amid the mess. She looked around at all the papers and photos and upturned boxes. She thought she might be able to find the photos of Declan and her, but she thought better of even trying to look. Kate assumed they'd be digital anyway.

By the time they made it back to their apartment, Kate and Declan had sat in tense silence longer than they ever had in the whole history of their friendship. Kate wasn't sure there was anything she could say or do to get Declan not to be angry with her. Conflicting emotions bubbled up inside her, making her uncertain if she had made the right choice.

Once inside, Kate went straight to the kitchen to call Spade while Declan took a shower. The phone rang a few times before he answered.

She didn't even get to say hello before he started right in. "Kate, I was speaking to our counterpoint in Spain. I'm not having much luck getting the information you need. Many of these cases have been listed as closed and they are not interested in reopening them."

"They were listed as closed with no perpetrator ever arrested or convicted?" Kate asked, trying to make sense of it.

"That's correct," Spade said, his voice tight. No one ever said no to Spade, so Kate was sure his frustration was at an all-time high. "What have you found with the information you have?"

"We've zeroed in on two suspects – one really and the other is a suspect from an old case." Kate proceeded to detail all the information from the investigation up to their current point. She left out Billy's story about them. "I've spoken with the Phantom twice, once in the graveyard and the second time in an alleyway. I know, sir, I should have brought him in. I didn't think I could manage it on my own. When I spoke to him his story made sense, and I don't have enough to arrest him on this case. As far as his past crimes…"

Spade had a way of cutting through all the clutter of a situation. "Is it fair to say you think you'd have more luck stopping this killer with Leo out there helping you?"

"I'm not sure helping us is the right way to put it. This has been going on for so long and there's so little evidence that having someone of equal criminal caliber after the same killer doesn't seem like it would hurt much."

Spade remained quiet for several moments. "What if he finds him first? He'll kill him, no?"

"He'll kill him. I don't think this killer will be taken alive." That was the truth at the heart of the matter. "I can't say why. I'm not even sure I understand myself, but I feel like Leo might benefit us in some way."

"You're certain he's not the killer?"

Kate knew her job depended on the answer. Any mistake would cost her reputation. In the end, she had to go with not just her gut but the logic of the case. "I'm sure he's not the killer, Spade." She quickly added, "But it also doesn't mean we aren't making headway on finding out Leo's real identity to make it easier to bring him in later."

Spade weighed the information as he asked a few more questions. "Are you considering him an asset or informant then? Is that what you're doing?"

They did it in mob and drug trafficking cases all the time. "He doesn't want to share much information with us, but what he has shared has certainly helped the case so far. We have new leads to follow and it's clear the killer is in some way connected to him. Leo is also connected to one of the victims and we are exploring that avenue. It might bring us right to the killer."

"What does Declan think?"

Kate looked from her phone toward the doorway to see Declan standing there with a towel wrapped around his middle, dripping water on the floor. She gestured with her hand for him to speak.

Declan took a few steps into the kitchen and stared at the phone. He raised his eyes to her and back at the phone. "I didn't agree at first, Spade. He's a wanted global criminal. But after listening to Kate's reasoning, I do agree with her. I think if we can treat him like an asset, then Kate's interaction with him is justified. Otherwise, I see no reason not to bring him in."

"Okay then," Spade said calmly. "The Phantom or the man that's calling himself Leo is considered an FBI asset on this case. Watch your step though. You're in delicate territory here especially being in the United Kingdom. I'm sure that won't be their viewpoint."

"I'll handle that, Spade. I've developed a good rapport with Sam and Fraser. I think for this investigation, we'll be in the clear," Declan assured and then gave Kate a knowing look. "We have something else to tell you."

Kate stumbled over her words as she told him. "Billy has written a story about us for his gossip paper. It's already online. I've not looked at it yet, but he is speculating that Declan and I are..."

"Romantically connected," Declan said.

"Are you?"

"No, sir." Declan gave Kate a little smile. He was lying because he knew she wouldn't be able to. He was much more adept at defying authority. He'd done it for most of his career. "As you know, I've been staying with Kate through my divorce and we are good friends. That's all."

"Were you involved in the past?" Spade asked and before they could answer, he continued. "There were rumors when you two were in the academy. I had some concerns when I partnered the two of you, but I wagered you'd make good partners or kill each other. I was happy when it worked out. Have you ever been involved romantically?"

"No," Declan said with a conviction in his voice Kate wouldn't have been able to have.

"Then don't worry about a gossip paper," Spade said, having the good sense not to ask if they might in the future. "Call me if you need anything else." He hung up.

Kate had the feeling Spade didn't want to know. "Thanks for supporting me about Leo."

"That's what good partners do, Kate. Even if I don't necessarily agree, I can concede you might be right on this one." He pointed to her computer. "You should look up Billy's story."

"I'll do it in the morning. I want one more night of not knowing what's splashed over a gossip paper about us." Kate stood from the table, looked over at him, and laughed. "You're dripping water all over the floor."

"Is that all you have to say about me in a towel," he teased and then pulled her in for a hug.

Kate rested her head on his damp chest happy they were over what could have been a huge fight. He still trusted her judgment and that was all that mattered.

CHAPTER 22

The next morning, Kate sat at the kitchen table with her laptop, knowing what she had to do. She still hadn't summoned up the nerve to look at Billy's website. Not knowing was somehow easier. Declan hadn't looked at it either. He left early that morning to chase down a few leads with Sam while Kate focused on Amelia's background and her connection to Leo.

Kate had put it off for far too long. She typed in the website address and the page popped up immediately. The first thing dead center was the headline – *Dashing FBI Couple Hunting the Close Killer, Is There Still Time for Romance?*

Kate groaned as she scrolled past it to the photos of them having dinner in Whiskey Bar. There were four photos in all. The most telling was the one where Declan had reached his hand across the table and held hers. It had only lasted a moment during the conversation – the intimate gestures between them so commonplace now. Captured here though, it looked far more romantic than it had been in the moment.

What was most striking was seeing the two of them from a distance the way a casual onlooker might have. She couldn't deny they looked like a couple very much in sync with each other and in love. The photographer had captured the way Declan often looked at her. It was a mix of friendship and….she struggled to find the word. Kate sat back trying to process the look on his face.

Adoration. That was all that came to Kate's mind. If she had doubted his feelings for her before now, seeing this photo she couldn't doubt them any longer. She was surprised by the look on her face. She looked at him with a mix of wonder, amusement, and love. She had to admit it to herself because she was seeing it firsthand. She loved him and he loved her. What kind of love was still up for grabs, but he was right to be hesitant. Their friendship and partnership had to remain intact no matter what else happened between them.

Kate didn't know what she would ever do without him and that scared her more than anything. She scrolled past the photos and read the article. It was full of speculation about the nature of their relationship. It walked right up to the line of libel but didn't cross it. Billy never came right out and said they were in a relationship or had compromised the investigation. He never said they had been intimate. He certainly made it look that way with the headline and the photos. The rest was gossip and speculation. It wasn't nearly as bad as she thought it would be. It was out there and there'd be questions, but they'd survive it.

Setting that aside, Kate focused on more important matters. She pulled the top file from the stack and opened it. Kate went through the information Sam had sent Declan the previous day about Amelia's case. She had been traveling alone to Paris to celebrate her birthday. None of her friends were able to travel with her so she had taken the train from London to Paris for the week. She had several sights she had wanted to see and was crossing items off her bucket list.

One of her friends had given a formal statement to Sam that indicated Amelia was using the TravelShip app to date in Paris. She thought the trip would be romantic with someone. She had matched a man and they had two dates in two nights. Amelia had told her friend how happy she was and how much fun she was having. She did complain that her uncle had wanted to meet for dinner and she was worried he had been following her around Paris worried for her safety. She had laughed it off with her friend in text and then never confirmed whether she had met up with him.

Kate assumed the man she called her uncle was Leo. She dug deeper until she found the information about Amelia's parents – Sylvia and Jordan DeBecker. Sylvia had died of cancer when Amelia was eight. She had a sister and the two girls had been raised by their father. She went to school locally in London and then a Swiss boarding school followed by her education at Cambridge. Amelia had graduated from Cambridge a few months before she went on the trip to Paris. She was twenty-two at the time of her death and the youngest victim among the twenty-five.

Jordan had passed away from a heart attack two years before Amelia graduated university.

Kate scanned the documents looking for more information about him. When she found what she was after, Kate pulled back in surprise.

Jordan had given Amelia the best education money could buy, which is why it was so surprising his profession was listed as a baker with a small shop in London's East End. He may have saved for her education, but it was more likely he got financial help from someone wealthy.

Kate had been expecting Amelia's father to be involved in a high-stakes career or one that might have put him in the middle of international criminal behavior or intrigue. Something that would have put him on the same path in life as Leo. She had expected fancy boarding schools and a good backstory. Instead, she found humble beginnings. Sam noted in the file the bakery had been in the DeBecker family for generations.

The file could only tell Kate so much. She needed to speak to the sister. Kate flipped through the pages until she came to Tara's information. Sam had set up a video chat appointment for them and it was nearly time.

Kate got herself connected and then placed the call. Tara engaged and came to life on the screen. "Thanks for agreeing to speak with me. I'm so sorry for your loss," she said at the start.

Tara looked relieved to see Kate. "I'm glad something is being done about this. Investigator Harris has been wonderful, but he could only get so far. I saw on the news Amelia's murder is connected to many others. It's terrible what's happening."

Kate sympathized with her. "It says in the file that you're a year older than Amelia. Were you close growing up?"

Tara nodded and offered a sad smile. "After our mother passed away, Amelia and I were all we had. Our family worked so much to provide for us. Our whole lives revolved around the bakery. Amelia and I took care of each other."

"That must have been hard," Kate said, thinking back on the loss of her mother. She asked a few more questions about their childhood, which all seemed normal. Their father, Jordan, seemed to be an exceptional parent who did everything he could for his daughters. "Can you tell me about Amelia's trip to Paris?"

"It was spur of the moment," Tara said with a little laugh. "Amelia was impulsive in that way. She had been saving and saving for something special and she wanted to travel. She didn't do much to celebrate her graduation so when her birthday rolled around, she wanted her friends to go with her but everyone had plans. I told her she should wait. She said no, that it's a short train ride from London and she'd be fine on her own. It would be an adventure. She had found a reasonably priced hotel and had all the things she wanted to see mapped out. For the most part, it was a great trip until it wasn't. Amelia checked in with me frequently, texting photos of the things she was seeing. It had been going well."

Kate glanced down at her statement. "You and one of her friends indicated Amelia told you she was talking to a guy on an app and you were concerned."

"That's right." Tara shifted in her seat and adjusted her laptop screen. "Amelia and her boyfriend had broken up a few months prior and she was restless. I don't know when she downloaded the app or started talking to the guy in Paris, but she seemed to be interested in him. I was happy she was happy. I was concerned too. She was in another country alone and none of us had met him. I'm convinced he killed her."

Kate was convinced of that too. "Do you know anything about him?"

"I know a few things now," Tara said and held her phone up to the screen. It was a photo of a man. "This isn't a real photo. I mean it's a real guy but he's a model. This is the photo he had on the app and shared with my sister. She sent it to me then and I thought there was something odd about it. He was a little too perfect. She said in person he didn't look so perfect. She said he was older, more rugged, and rough around the edges, but he looked enough like the photo she didn't question it."

"Is there a chance this might be a photo from when he was younger?"

Tara shrugged her shoulders. "This photo is of a model in his twenties, which is the other issue. Amelia said he wouldn't tell her how old he was but she assumed in his forties. That was the other thing that bothered me. What was this forty-something-year-old man doing dating my twenty-two-year-old sister? I understand age is sometimes not a big deal but she had only just graduated. She barely had a life or any experience. I didn't like it and I told her that."

Kate wouldn't have liked it either and it would have been a big red flag for her. The information helped her though because she was right about the man's age. "She saw him more than once?"

"There were two dates before the night of the murder and she was supposed to meet up with him again that night."

Kate asked Tara to text the photo to her so she'd have it for reference when she was using the app. "Did she tell you his name?"

"She wouldn't tell me. I was so annoyed I called our uncle for help. He was in Paris and said he'd have dinner with her and sort it out."

She had opened the door and made it easier for Kate. "Who is your uncle?"

"Leo Lamiere. We've always called him Uncle Leo. He's not my biological uncle. He has known my family since he was fifteen. My grandfather took him in and cared for him. He was close to my father."

Kate leaned into her laptop. "I don't understand."

Tara explained, "I only know the story my father told me. When he was fifteen years old, he was alone in a park and got jumped by a group of boys. Out of nowhere comes this other kid racing across the park who stepped in to save my dad. It wasn't the first time my father had seen him in the park. After that incident, they became friends. My grandfather realized this kid was homeless. I guess my grandfather felt bad and took him in."

Kate wasn't sure she believed what she was hearing. "What did he say about his background?"

"He wouldn't say much. My grandfather didn't push it, assuming the kid had a bad childhood or there was abuse or something. He had a terrible scar on the back of his head. Leo said his father had caused it."

The story matched what Jax had told her about the Phantom. "Was he from London?"

"No. He said he was from the countryside outside of Paris. He spoke French and English fluently."

"Was he the same age as your father?" Kate had done the math and Jordan DeBecker would have been forty-eight this year had he been alive.

"There abouts. Leo's background was always murky. My father said they knew not to ask a lot of questions." Tara sighed. "Honestly, Agent

Walsh, Leo is such a good man and has been so good to my family, his past doesn't matter. He saved my father and then later, gave my father money to keep the bakery open and even paid for us to go to school."

"What does he do for work?"

"Something in finance." Tara grew suspicious as Kate assumed she might. "Is there a concern about Uncle Leo?"

Kate wasn't sure how to explain it. "He was seen with your sister at a restaurant on the night she was murdered. There was some question early on about his involvement."

Tara pulled back and shook her head furiously. "He would never hurt Amelia. He's been a surrogate parent to us since my father's death. I still run the bakery and no matter what I need he's there for us. He never married or had a family of his own, but he's been there for us. He's our family."

"Does he travel a lot?"

Tara paused then. "I don't want to discuss this anymore. It sounds like you believe he is responsible for something he isn't. I'm not going to help you arrest the wrong person."

Kate held her hand up to stop her from leaving. "It's not that at all. I'm simply trying to rule him out. Someone identified him as a potential suspect and I'm trying to understand what might be a coincidence. I do not believe your uncle is responsible for Amelia's murder." She said that honestly and didn't have to lie to Tara.

It took Tara a moment before she responded. "He's traveled his whole career. He went off to university on a scholarship and has not been based in London since then. Before you ask me where he lives full-time, I don't know. I don't know much about his work either. Amelia and I used to joke that maybe he was a spy. He could be for all I know. The one thing I do know is he didn't have anything to do with my sister's murder. He called me that night and told me he spoke to Amelia but they argued and she wouldn't listen to him. She was going to continue seeing the guy."

"What about anyone else in Leo's life? Has anyone been asking around about him? Anyone that would want revenge on him?"

"My father led a very simple life. I can count on one hand the number of times he left London. There was no one. As for Uncle Leo, I have no idea. He shows up when we need him, but otherwise, his life is separate from ours."

Kate said she understood. "Is there anything about your sister or the trip to Paris you think I should know?"

"Nothing I can think of right now." Tara leaned into her laptop and looked at Kate directly. "Please find out who did this to my sister and stop them. They have killed so many. My sister deserved to live her life. She had everything in front of her."

Kate swallowed the emotion that welled up in her throat. "I promise I will do everything I can to find him and stop him."

CHAPTER 23

After the call with Tara, Kate spent some time searching the internet for Leo Lamiere. Just as she had suspected, she came back with nothing that tied back to the Phantom. Kate couldn't help but feel for him given his background. She wondered how much of what he told the DeBeckers was real. It might have all been made up.

She couldn't focus on him all day though. There was other work to be done.

Next up was a call to Sebastian Thomas, who was Mable's editor at the travel magazine. She was the last victim in Paris and the most recent over all. It was nearing eleven in the morning in Scotland. She did the math to see what time it would be in New York. She wasn't sure he'd be in the office yet, but he had told her he was there sometimes as early as four.

Sebastian answered on the second ring, slightly out of breath and flustered.

Kate introduced herself and said she could call back at a better time if needed.

"No. I'm sorry. There's just a lot going on."

"This early?"

"This place runs twenty-four hours a day."

Kate gave him a moment to catch his breath and get situated. "I understand Mable was in Scotland on an assignment."

"She was writing a travel guide for solo female travelers about the United Kingdom. She was headed to Wales after Scotland. I can't believe she's gone," he said as sadness tinged his voice. "Mable was one of the best we had here at the magazine."

"Was she in contact with you while she was traveling?"

"Not much but we spoke the day before she died. She said she had met someone who was going to be able to give her some access to some of the best sights in Edinburgh."

"Was it a tour guide or a local?"

"I'm not sure, to be honest with you. It sounded to me like it was someone with special access so maybe a tour guide. The day I spoke to her she said he was going to take her to a few places and then she was going to meet up with him again the next day."

Kate was sure this was the killer. "Did she tell you his name?"

Sebastian clicked his tongue. "If she told me, I don't remember it. She didn't usually mention things like that. But that's what Mable did best. She'd go to a new location, meet the locals, and get a real flavor of the city. Then she'd turn in a stellar article that would go viral. As I said, there's no way I can replace her."

"What about dating? Was she meeting any men while she was here?"

"Mable didn't date," Sebastian said with a chuckle. "She was all about work. She said she didn't have time for men. It was too much of a compromise and she wasn't interested."

"What about a fling? Didn't she get lonely traveling all the time?"

"No and no. I asked her about it, even encouraged it, thinking it might spice up an article or two. Not that she needed it, but I thought it couldn't hurt. Mable was burned in a relationship in her twenties and said she just didn't have interest in it. She was doing what she wanted to do." Sebastian sighed dramatically. "And she died doing it. I wish I knew more, but I don't. Mable didn't share a lot until the article came in. She poured everything into that."

Kate asked him a few more questions and then let him go. The man knew nothing of value. Kate assumed Mable wasn't telling him everything about her romantic life. She had the note to indicate she was going on a date. It didn't mean she went but she was trying to meet people.

Next, Kate made a quick call to the hospital to check on Billy's condition. They had kept him overnight to assess for a concussion. The nurse wouldn't give her any details only that he'd be discharged later that day. Kate assumed he was fine. She wasn't going to waste any energy worrying about him when he had brought the attack on himself. Thinking about Billy only annoyed her and she hoped she'd never have to see him again.

She got up from the table and went to the sink. The electric kettle called to her. She grabbed it from its holder and turned on the tap. She filled the kettle to the line with water, set it back down, and flipped the switch. While it was heating, she rooted around in the cabinet and found some tea and cookies Declan had bought at the shop across the street.

Kate pulled her cardigan tighter around her and considered the case. They had so few leads and even the ones they had weren't leading anywhere. They needed just one solid one that they could run to ground. Kate knew if there was one, there'd be more. Eventually, the whole case would unravel. The whistle of the kettle drew her attention back to the present. She poured the steaming hot water into the cup and carried it and the cookies over to the table.

Kate focused her attention on the TravelShip app. She wondered if the killer had been watching her and would know her real identity. She'd have to risk it because they didn't have another option. Kate wasn't going to let one of the other officers with Police Scotland do this for them. If someone was going to risk their life with this killer, it was going to be her. She had a weird calm come over her wondering if Leo would be watching out for her. She wished she had a way to contact him, but she assumed he'd be in touch with her if needed. He'd never be an official asset with the FBI, but it was Spade's way of giving his approval.

Kate set the tea and cookies down on the table and went to the living room and grabbed a blanket off the couch. She carried it back to the kitchen and wrapped it around her as she snuggled back into the pillows in the large window seat. She sipped her tea as she opened the app.

Kate worked a little more on her profile, making it enticing to the killer. She added some details about her travel and what she was hoping to see in Scotland. When she was done with the content, she studied her photo. Declan was right that it looked different enough that it was plausible someone wouldn't recognize her.

Kate set the search parameters from twenty-five- to fifty-year-old men in the Edinburgh area. She set the distance from her as only five miles. The only downside was they had to match with her to allow them to text back and forth in the app.

Kate wasn't sure how long she sat there, scrolling through the profiles. She swiped on a few more that looked like they might fit the killer's details. She was hoping she'd see a photo like the one Tara had sent of the man Amelia had been seeing. Kate hadn't stumbled across that yet.

During the press conference, Declan had skirted around the issue of how the Close Killer was meeting his victims, avoiding saying the name of the app. Kate was sure once that was out there, he'd stop using it. With so few leads, they didn't want to diminish their chances further.

Kate studied the photos of each of the men, carefully studying their eyes, forehead, and nose to see if they looked familiar. It was clear given the varying descriptions of the killer, how he looked in the video Sam provided, and the photo Billy provided he was changing up his appearance. None of the evidence showed him from the front except for the sketches.

Given he had been killing for more than a decade and his connection to Leo, Kate assumed he'd be in his forties. She scrolled past a few men before swiping to indicate her interest in two who could fit the description. It was hard to tell with the photos provided. She did not come across the model photo though. Nothing was ever going to be that easy. She found another man who fit the age range and had a similar appearance. He had the same build and facial features. Kate pulled up the rest of the profile and noted that he worked in the hospitality industry, which could fit, and he was a world traveler. He wasn't looking for anything serious – anything from friendship to a casual fling. Kate swiped to indicate interest and hoped for the best. She continued her search for a few more minutes until her phone started to ring and Declan's face popped up on her screen.

Before she could even say hello, Declan delivered the bad news. "We have another body, Kate. Not far from the back of St. Giles Cathedral. She was in a dumpster in Old Fishmarket Close. I believe she was probably killed last night. I don't think she was there while we were giving the press conference. I figured you'd want to see the scene before they take the body away."

Words caught in Kate's throat. This woman was killed as a direct response to the press conference. The Close Killer had stayed and left them a message. That much was clear with how close he left the body to St. Giles where Declan had connected more than a decade of his crimes. They all knew the possibility was real that he'd do something like this in response.

Kate hadn't anticipated it would be this soon. "I'll be right there."

"You'll need directions. This one isn't easy to find." Declan gave her detailed directions on how to find the close and then how to find them once she was there.

Kate ended the call and went to put on warmer clothes. The rain had started that morning and showed no signs of letting up. When she was ready, she pulled the hood of her rain jacket over her head, went down the spiral staircase again, and hit the street. Kate assumed there might be fewer people on the Royal Mile given the weather but the crowds bustled back and forth on the sidewalk as they had every other day.

Kate turned left at the street Declan told her and then another right. She walked for a few blocks and then found the entrance to the close. The stone pavement didn't make for easy walking. She passed a couple sharing an umbrella with their heads bent together saying what a shame it was what was happening in the city. She turned away from them and walked right into a mother pushing a stroller near the entrance to the close.

"There's been an incident in the close. It's closed for foot traffic today." She lowered her voice. "They found another body. This used to be such a safe place."

Kate didn't know how to address her fears because she had every reason to be afraid. "FBI," Kate said. "I've been called to the scene."

"Another American?" the woman asked.

"I don't know. I didn't get many details. My partner is there now."

"I hope you can stop him," she said as she pushed her child away from death.

Kate watched her walk off with her head bent low as she told her daughter where they were going next. She had a pang of regret for not choosing another path in life. Instead of heading to the scene of another murder, Kate could be pushing her child in a stroller toward a warm coffee shop where she didn't have to think about serial killers and the horrific things people did to one another.

Kate pulled her hood further over her head and proceeded on. She flashed her badge at the uniformed cops standing guard and was let through without fuss. Kate walked a few more feet and then spotted Declan, Sam, and Fraser standing by a large green bin marked for recycling.

"You find it okay?" Sam asked as Kate approached.

"Only with Declan's directions. What do we have?" Kate gestured toward the bin and Fraser lifted the lid. Kate stood on tip toes and peered inside. There was the half-dressed body of a woman. She was wearing only a bra and her pants had been unbuttoned. She was missing her socks and shoes. She had bruising around her neck and on her hands, indicating to Kate she had fought him. The scene was much different than the others in the case.

"Are we sure this is the same killer?"

"There's a note, Kate. It was pinned to her bra strap."

Kate stepped back from the bin and took the evidence bag from Fraser. She could see the writing clearly – black ink on white paper. The killer didn't do anything to try to disguise his writing.

No one will ever stop me. I will kill until the blood lust inside of me dies. You couldn't stop my other crimes and you can't stop me now.

Fraser pointed at the note. "That's a confession from the Phantom. He's admitting it and taunting us. How do we stop him?"

Kate looked over at Declan. She could tell by his expression that he hadn't told them anything about their discussion with Spade. "This isn't the Phantom," she started as Fraser protested. "This isn't the time or place to discuss it. Let's wrap up the scene here, get the medical examiner out to remove the body, and we can go back and discuss."

"Why can't you face the truth, Kate?" Fraser barked at her.

"Not here. Not now." Kate turned away from him and headed back down the close the way she had come in. She could feel their eyes burning a hole in her back. She'd tell them but not standing in the rain over the remains of a young woman.

CHAPTER 24

L ater, back in the conference room of the police station, Fraser looked at her with disgust. "Help me understand how the FBI is letting an international criminal get away right under their noses." He had already pounded his fist down on the table once and screamed at Kate. She had never seen a colleague so angry to the point of being red-faced and out of breath. If she had thought Declan was angry with her, it was mild in comparison.

After they left the scene, they went back to the police station to the basement war room to regroup. As soon as they got in the room, Fraser demanded to know why Kate was so sure this wasn't the work of the Phantom. She had detailed her interactions with him to date, leaving nothing out including his request to be called Leo. She admitted speaking to him about the case, connecting with Amelia's sister, Tara, and finding out more about Leo's background. Sam and Fraser had the same response that Declan had – that nothing Leo told anyone could be trusted.

Kate didn't disagree but that still didn't mean she believed he was guilty of these murders.

Sam seemed to be more level-tempered about it. "Kate, you believe the killer is connected to Leo and you hope that together with his help we'll bring him in. Is that what I'm hearing?"

Kate hadn't said the worst part aloud yet. "He wants revenge for

Amelia's murder. Leo believes she was killed because of him. We are better off with Leo out there hunting for him too. Given the nature of these murders and how long they have been going on, the FBI is willing to gamble with Leo, for now."

"Twenty countries, Kate," Fraser barked. "That's how many countries Leo is wanted in for art and antiquity theft. He's got a bounty on his head – wanted dead or alive in many of those countries. You've seen him twice and let him walk."

Declan pushed back from the table, scraping the chair legs on the floor. "We are wasting time on this. You've been brought up to speed. If you see him, Fraser, you can attempt to arrest him and bring him in. Does that make you feel better?"

Fraser folded his arms across his chest. "Are you certain Leo isn't the killer?"

"I'd stake my whole career on it," Kate said, looking up at him. "I know we have not worked together before, but I don't make blind decisions or take big risks. This is a calculated decision and I hope you can respect that. When the time comes, I hope I'm the one who can bring Leo in. He got away from me in Paris and I don't like this situation any more than you do. Trust me, Fraser, I want Leo brought to justice. Right now, I want to stop this killer more."

With that done and out of the way, they focused on the recent case. Sam briefed them all on the details he'd learned so far. "Brianna Hughes was thirty years old and traveling alone from New York City where she has lived nearly all of her life except for four years of college in upstate New York. She's been in Scotland for more than a week, staying at a rental on Victoria Street. She was found without her cellphone but her wallet and keys were in her pocket. We have not searched the rental apartment yet. I figured the FBI would want the first crack at that."

"We'll head there after we finish here," Declan said. "Do we know anything about her final hours last night?"

Sam posted Brianna's photo on the board with the other victims. He wrote her biographical information under it. Then he turned to face them. "She toured Edinburgh Castle during the afternoon, had dinner at a restaurant on Princess Street, and then stopped in the shop below her apartment. We only know that because the shop owner talked to her for a few minutes and said she remembered Brianna saying she was going upstairs and would be in for the night. With the rain and the cold, she said she was tired and calling it a night."

"We don't know what made her leave," Declan said more statement than a question. "I can't imagine anyone going out last night to meet in that close. She wouldn't be walking through there for anything."

Declan was right about that. The main difference this time was Old Fishmarket Close wasn't near any tourist attractions and it was harder to find than the others. There weren't any bars or anything else that might have been the draw. That left Kate with only one conclusion. "They could have met someplace else and he led her to the close where he killed her. It's not that far from St. Giles and that area is well-lit. He might have met her there."

"With the press conference yesterday announcing this killer was on the loose, do you think she met someone she didn't know last night?" Sam asked. It was a valid question assuming Brianna had seen the press conference.

Kate walked up to the board. There were so many sweet trusting faces looking back at her. "Brianna was from New York City. She knew not to trust people. It's engrained when you live in that kind of environment. She must have trusted whoever called her. That's what this killer is doing. He's presenting as someone these women can trust. He's presenting as someone with access and knowledge of the area. For him to get this many women to go with him, he's coming across as someone mild-mannered. There are no red flags until it's too late."

"There have never been signs of force," Sam echoed what Kate said. "None of the victims was kidnapped. They all went with him willingly."

"That's right," she said, turning to face them. "Even in the grainy video from Paris. Amelia went with him willingly. She made the first move kissing him. She was comfortable with him. He's blending in and coming across like a safe person to be around." Kate looked over at Declan. "We need to get over to her apartment and go through her things."

"I have some family I can follow up with," Sam said. He'd been the one who had made the death notification with Declan earlier. Brianna had enough information in her wallet that they had been able to track her family down in New York and make the call. "When I spoke to her father earlier, he said her sister was willing to speak to me. That's who Brianna had been in contact with the most during the trip. I can see if she knows anything."

"I want to get back out there to see if we have any witnesses who might have seen her with a man last night or even earlier in the day yesterday," Fraser said. Kate was glad he was willing to take on that role. He was more likely than any of them to have local trust to get the information.

Declan walked over to where Kate stood. "Before we go, Sam and I had an interesting interaction with a man at one of the travel tour shops early this morning. He matches the description including his background and how much he bounces from one country to another. We had a few minutes with him before he left for a tour. We asked if he'd heard about the murders or picked up any chatter about it. He said he'd heard it but didn't know much of anything."

"Did you believe him?" Kate asked.

Declan shook his head. "It was an awkward time to speak to him. The driver of the van was there with him and tourists were arriving for the tour. He had to check them in. He denied knowing about the murders at first and when we pressed him on that, he changed his story. Who hasn't heard about it? Of course, he knew. He said he only meant that he didn't know anything about the women who were killed and didn't know anything about the murders."

"I didn't like his whole demeanor," Sam said, drawing their attention. "He's from outside of London. When we talked to him more, he said he's traveled all over for years. He's always worked in the travel industry and he liked it. While he was affable, there seemed to be a flip to his personality when we pressed him about the murders. He played it cool though at the end."

"How did you leave it with him?" Fraser asked and then quickly added, "We can get employment records if we need them. I can ask around while he's still on the tour."

Kate didn't want to arouse suspicion just yet. "If you can ask about him informally that would be helpful. I don't want him to know he might be on our radar. If you can get information without pointing at him as a person of interest, that would work."

Fraser offered a curt nod. "I know someone who I can speak to off the record."

"Perfect," Kate said with a smile. She wasn't sure if she was going to be able to repair her relationship with Fraser. It was clear he didn't like her or trust her. "I appreciate whatever information you can get. You have good instincts. You were right about Billy having that additional information." Declan had brought them the photos earlier that morning.

Fraser moved toward the door and then stopped. "Why did you two go back there last night?"

There was no point hiding. Kate was sure everyone had already seen the cover of the magazine. "When I was at the press conference, Billy asked me how long Declan and I had been romantically involved.

I was concerned he was going to run a story about it. I hoped we could talk him out of it and tell him that we're just friends and partners."

Fraser smirked. "That's not what the photos showed."

"The photos are deceiving. The dinner wasn't nearly as intimate as it looked," Kate said knowing it was a lame defense.

"Not for me to judge," Fraser said, his tone softening. "It's good you went back because Billy might not be alive now. I still don't trust him."

"I don't think any of us do," Declan said and Sam agreed. "I appreciate the information he gathered while law enforcement was looking the other way. He wants the story though."

Kate agreed with that. "I think at the end of the day he wishes he was a legitimate journalist and maybe sees the cases as his way in."

They talked for a few more minutes and then went their separate ways. Once they were out on the street and walking toward the apartment Brianna rented, Declan looked over at Kate. "That didn't go nearly as badly as I thought it would."

Kate wasn't sure that was true. "I thought Fraser was going to have a stroke. I've never seen someone so angry with me. Even when I was a kid and in trouble with my parents, I'd never been yelled at like that. Sam seemed to take it in stride."

"There's a lot more riding on this for Fraser. These cases are happening in his jurisdiction. Leo is running around in his jurisdiction while the FBI agents he asked for help are letting an international criminal wanted by twenty countries run free. I think if the situation were flipped, you'd be blowing a gasket too."

"That's a measured and reasonable response." Kate smiled up at him. She thought about what he said and took it to heart. "I get so focused on the goal I forget about people's feelings. I end up expecting everyone to go with my flow."

"You're not good with feelings, Kate. You're entrenched in logic and building the case. That's all you see and that's one of the reasons you're so good at what you do. I do think that's why Spade partnered us together though."

"What do you mean?" Kate wasn't going to remind him no one else would partner with him given his rogue ways.

Without missing a beat, he said, "I bring you balance. I'm hotheaded and passionate. I can argue the wrong point until I'm blue in the face, but that makes me able to see why others do that as well. You can check my faults but I can also check yours. That's why Spade partnered us together. Fraser is angry now but I'll smooth it over with him."

It occurred to Kate this wasn't the first time he had to do that for them. "Have you done that on other cases?"

Declan shrugged. "Once or twice." He pointed up at the five-story building. The exterior of the first three floors was painted a bright blue and then the top two floors were brick. The whole cobblestone street was that way. It was lined with shops and residences above.

As they stood mid-way on the street that curved to the bottom, Kate took in the sights. "I bet this is a well-photographed street." She saw something curious at the bend. "Is that man in a cape holding a wand?"

Declan turned his head and raised an eyebrow. "It's the Potter Trail Tour. This street was one of the inspirations for Diagon Alley." There was a little childlike glee in his voice.

Kate knew the series but had never read it. To match his tone, Declan had a curious smile on his face. She laughed. "Declan James, have you read the books?"

"All of them – twice," he said proudly. "I was hoping we could take the tour if we have some time before we have to head back."

"You never fail to surprise me."

"I like to keep a little mystery."

"Let's go see what we can uncover about Brianna. Then maybe I'll buy you a wand at the wand shop before we head back."

Declan's eyes lit up as he stared down the road. "There's a wand shop?"

"Focus please," Kate said and pulled open the door to the stairs that led to the apartment.

CHAPTER 25

Declan unlocked the door to the apartment with the key Sam had provided him from the landlord. A pair of boots lay on their side at the doorway as if Brianna had kicked them off and left them where they fell. A living room lamp still glowed and the curtains had been pulled tightly closed.

A cellphone was in the middle of the coffee table next to a mug.

"She left her phone when she went out," Kate said, walking over to it. She peered into the mug at what looked like tea that was no longer hot. "It looks like she left in a hurry."

"Her coat is in the closet too, Kate." Declan stood with his back to her, looking in the front hall closet. "She didn't have a coat on when we found her and there wasn't one at the scene. It was cold and rainy last night. Why would she leave without her coat or her phone?"

The door creaked open behind them and both spun around to look. "Can we help you?" he asked the young woman standing in the doorway.

"Do you know where Brianna is? She didn't come home last night." A woman, who didn't look more than twenty-five to Kate, peered around Declan into the apartment. "I'm Laura. Brianna and I didn't know each other long, we had only met a few days ago. But seeing as we were both traveling alone from the states, we bonded over our travels. I'm worried about her. She left late to meet someone and said she'd be right back. I didn't know who to call when she didn't come home last night."

Kate let Declan keep searching the apartment while she went to talk to Laura. "Are you staying in the building?"

"Just across the hall. I heard you talking and thought Brianna might be back." She looked up at Kate with big eyes.

Kate flashed her badge and introduced them. "If it's okay with you, we can go back to your apartment to talk. You might be able to help us."

Laura said it was fine. It was clear by the sad look on her face she knew something had happened to her new friend. Once they were inside her apartment, she sat on the couch with her hands between her knees. She leaned forward. "I've been scared since the announcement that there's a serial killer. I've been thinking of cutting my trip short. My mom said she'd pay the difference for me to change my flight."

"You said you're traveling alone?" Kate asked, taking a seat across from her as she looked around the small but well-kept apartment. When Laura said she was, Kate added, "It's not a bad idea if you go home. It's not safe here in Edinburgh. If you stay, you shouldn't trust anyone. Do you understand?"

Laura took a deep breath and sighed. "This is my first solo trip. I wasn't sure if I'd be happy traveling alone, but I have been having a good time. Brianna and I had lunch together a few times and I met one of her friends. You're right though. I think I'm going to go back home early." She turned her head to look right at Kate. "Please tell me what's happened. I have such a bad feeling."

Kate lowered her voice. "I'm sorry to tell you this. Brianna was murdered last night and she was found in Old Fishmarket Close. You said she went out late last night. Do you know why?"

Tears formed in Laura's eyes. "She had left her wallet in a pub and was going to get it back."

That explained why she didn't bring her phone or her coat. "What pub?"

Laura corrected herself. "She left it in a pub and a guy she had gone out with a few times had found it. They had gone to dinner earlier in the evening up on Princess Street. She told me she wasn't even aware she had lost her wallet. She thought it was still in her bag. When he called her, she went to her bag and checked and sure enough her wallet was gone. Brianna figured she had left it on the table. After dinner, he said he was going to stay and meet some friends and she wanted to get back home. She assumed after she left he noticed it and then called her after meeting his friends. Maybe he hoped she'd come back looking for it."

It all made sense to Kate. Any woman traveling on their own would have been lured out of their apartment to meet someone they knew to retrieve their wallet, which probably had all of their cash and credit cards, not to mention identification. Brianna had been found with her wallet in her pants pocket. "Did you happen to meet this guy?"

Laura nodded. "I had dinner with him and Brianna once. He seemed like a nice enough guy."

Kate inched forward on the chair. "You saw him. Do you know his name?"

"His name is Rob Knox but he usually goes by Knox."

Kate wanted to leap out of her skin but tried to remain calm and steady so she didn't frighten Laura, not yet anyway. "Do you know where they met?"

"It was on one of the walking tours in the city. He was on the tour too and they struck up a conversation."

"Did he run the tour or was he a participant?"

"A participant. He said he was in Edinburgh with friends. I don't think Brianna met his friends though and he was alone on the tour."

"Where was he from?"

Laura paused for a moment to recollect. "Somewhere in England. It wasn't London, although he said he had lived there at some point. I don't remember exactly."

"Did Laura ever comment on his name? Robert Knox is a fairly famous name here in Edinburgh for being connected to a series of murders back in the city's history."

Laura pulled back in surprise and grimaced. "I didn't know that. He introduced himself to her as Knox. After the tour, he said his first name was Rob. I'm not sure she made the connection." Her eyes got big and she bit her bottom lip. "Are you saying Knox killed Laura?"

"Yes. That's what I believe," Kate said forcefully. "Don't ever see him again. Understand?" She waited until Laura said she did. "Do you know how to reach him?"

"I don't even think I was supposed to meet him when I did," Laura explained as she wrung her hands. "I happened to be in the same pub Brianna and Knox were in two nights ago and Brianna asked me to join them." Laura sat back and stared off past Kate. "At the time, it didn't seem like Knox wanted me there. I heard him tell Brianna he wanted to be alone with her. She had already asked me though. It was uncomfortable at first and I considered going back to my table. Once I sat down, he was talkative and funny. A real charmer. I understood why Brianna liked him."

Kate wondered if that night was when Knox had planned to kill her. Maybe Laura interrupted the plan. This was the first time Kate was aware that someone other than the victim had this much interaction with him. "What did Knox look like? Age? Hair?"

"I have a photo of him," Laura said, surprising Kate. She walked to the small kitchen off the living room and came back with her cellphone. "Brianna wanted me to take a photo of her and Knox. I could tell he was uncomfortable having his photo taken. After I took it, he asked to see my phone. I thought he was just going to look at the photo. I didn't realize until after dinner that the photo was gone. Brianna had asked me to text it to her but I couldn't find it. I only realized this morning that he deleted it but didn't remove it from my photo trash. I restored the photo and kept it. I don't know why but something told me it might be important." Laura held the phone out to Kate and scrolled with her thumb to the right photo. "The lighting in the pub wasn't great."

Kate lowered her head to look at it. The man calling himself Knox now had lighter hair, nearly blond, and lighter brown eyes. He had a blue Henley shirt with the sleeves shoved up to reveal his thick forearms dusted in dark hair and a few braided bracelets on his wrist. In the photo, Brianna also had the same style bracelets on her wrist. Kate raised her head to Laura. "Did Brianna wear these bracelets often?"

"All the time. She had a real kind of Bohemian vibe about her. She liked that Knox had the same style. That's what she noticed right away about him. They bonded over those same silly bracelets."

He was mirroring the victim to breed familiarity. "What else did you learn about him?"

"He said he was thirty-three but he looked a bit older to me. He said he's worked all kinds of jobs. Mostly construction but he's also worked in the travel industry. Brianna said he was smarter than he sometimes came across. We talked about that the other night. There were a few weird things she noticed about him – discrepancies if you want to call it that."

It was exactly the kind of information Kate needed. "What were they?"

"The age for one. As I said, he had told us he was thirty-three but when we were talking about when movies came out, he was off on how old he would have been. We thought that was weird, but neither of us called him out on it. Brianna thought maybe he was trying to seem younger like our age. When he first met Brianna, he told her that he didn't get to travel much and that's why he was willing to go on a tour even when his friends didn't. Another day, he told her he traveled all the time and loved solo travel like she did. It was small things like that. Brianna said she wasn't going to keep in contact with him when she went back but it was okay for now."

"Do you know if they were intimate?"

"He was up here to her apartment a few times. He never spent the night. They fooled around a little but it never led to sex."

"Was it Brianna who slowed things down?"

Laura shook her head. "Knox didn't want to which also seemed weird to us. Normally, it's the guy who's pushing for it and we set the pace. This time he was the one putting on the brakes."

Kate could only assume it meant he didn't want to leave DNA evidence behind. "Did he tell you where he was staying or how to reach him? I'm looking for anything that can help me find him."

"I only know so much because Brianna shared it with me. I only met him one time. He even asked Brianna if she talked to me about him. She told him no." Laura looked right at Kate. "That's probably a good thing if he's the one who killed her. He didn't seem like a killer."

"They never do," Kate said and asked Laura to send her the photo. "I want you to pack your things and come with me. I don't want to leave you here alone."

Laura gasped as she sucked in a breath. "Do you think I'm in danger?"

Kate wasn't going to downplay it for her. Fear was good. "I think you could be in a lot of danger. We believe the man calling himself Knox has killed twenty-six women across several countries. You are the first person we have found who has met him and lived. We haven't had many witnesses. I want to ensure you get back home safely."

"Are you sure he killed Brianna?" Laura asked still not sure. Kate knew she was in shock and it was hard for those who had met killers to reconcile the duality of them. "Brianna was smart. I find it hard to believe she would have been duped."

"I'm sure, Laura," Kate responded evenly "He's gotten away with it for so long because he is charming and doesn't seem the type." Kate stood and handed the phone back, giving Laura her phone number, and waited while she texted the photo. When Kate received it, she said, "I need to go next door and speak to my partner. When we are done, we will escort you out when you're ready."

"Where am I going?"

"We'll figure it out." Kate watched as Laura stood and looked around the space. "I know this feels overwhelming. You're going to be okay. We will make sure of that." Kate headed toward the door and turned back once. "I'm sorry about your friend. I know how hard it is to lose someone."

Laura steadied herself. "You're probably going to think this is crazy. I'm willing to try to get him to meet me if you think it would help. You can use me as bait."

Kate had already considered it. If Laura had been emotionally stronger, she might have even said yes. "It's not a good idea. He's too unpredictable and I'm not sure we can keep you safe in that situation. It's brave that you'd want to help us that way, but my only focus is keeping you safe."

Laura's shoulders relaxed. "I appreciate that. I offered and then immediately regretted it. I'd be too scared."

"It's okay," Kate reassured. "Leave it to us to stop him."

CHAPTER 26

Kate went back to Brianna's apartment and found Declan going through a cellphone. He held it up. "It had a passcode but I tried her birthday. It's a treasure trove of information."

Kate approached with news of her own. She pulled up the photo Laura had sent. "He's going by the name Rob Knox and he met the victim on one of the walking tours. We have one scheduled tonight so maybe we can get information."

Declan peered over at her. "We have a photo of him?" He took the phone from her and stared down at it. "It's not the guy at the tour company Sam and I spoke to this morning, but they are similar."

"It might be him, Declan. I have a feeling he's changing up his appearance. I also believe he's mirroring his victims. It's a way for him to gain trust."

"Explain what you mean."

Kate searched for the easiest explanation. "We often see mirroring with people who have narcissistic personality disorder. When they meet someone new, they will mirror the other person. If someone is interested in hiking, then so is the narcissist. If their target likes bar hopping and karaoke, then they do too. It's a way to quickly build common bonds between them and the other person. It also helps to lower the defenses of the other person. If you like something and the other person does too, well, you think of yourself as a good person so they must be too."

Declan handed her back the phone. "How far in advance do you think he's getting to know them to be able to mirror them?"

"It doesn't need time," Kate explained and searched for a concrete example for him. "Let's say we meet at a bar and in conversation, you tell me you like to hike. I could then say I like to hike too. If I'm smart, I'm not going to mirror you on something I know nothing about. But you'd be surprised how people lie."

"Do they get caught?"

"Often." Kate hitched her thumb over her shoulder in the direction of Laura's apartment. "Laura and Brianna thought he was lying about his age. Brianna noticed other discrepancies too. It's easy to overlook some of these things early on because we all try to impress people to be liked. If I like you and I'm attracted to you and notice you fib about a few insignificant things, I might overlook it."

When Declan understood, Kate explained everything Laura had told her about her interaction with Brianna and Knox. "He wouldn't have sex with her, Declan."

"Some condition may be impacting his ability to perform," he suggested but didn't look convinced.

"It could be that. He might have also ritualized sex and isn't able to get aroused without the violence. More than likely, I think he didn't want to leave any DNA evidence behind. Do we know if Brianna had her hands and face wiped down like the other victims?"

"We don't know officially yet, but her hands were too clean for being in a dumpster. I assume they were washed off." Declan showed her the string of text messages he had found on Brianna's cellphone. "He was pursuing her hard. There were a few times he tried to get her to meet him out late and she declined. She asked him to come over but he declined. I think she was making it harder to kill her than the others, which is why he disposed of her the way he did. There was more anger and violence in last night's murder than we saw with the other scenes."

"Laura said Brianna assumed she left her wallet behind at the pub. I think he took it and held onto it to lure her outside. Maybe once he got her out, he convinced her to go for a walk with him or said her wallet was back where he was staying. Either way, he said something to make her go with him. How far is Old Fishmarket Close from here?"

"Less than a half mile." Declan pointed in the direction. "It wouldn't have taken them long to walk the distance. Do you think she would have gone with him?"

"I don't see any other way it would have happened." Kate had run through a few scenarios in her mind, but this was the only one that added up. "I don't think she'd be happy about it. I know I wouldn't if I were her. She was stuck though. He had her wallet with everything she needed. I don't think she would have refused him at that point. Given he hadn't been sexually aggressive with her and turned her down, I don't think she would have feared for her safety at that point. She'd been alone with him before last night."

Declan shook his head in disgust. "He set the perfect stage for murder."

Kate shook her head. "He made a mistake this time. He left Laura alive. It's why I told Laura to pack her things. We need to make sure she's on the first flight out of here."

"We're sending her back home instead of keeping her safe here?" Declan asked with another question lingering unsaid. Kate gestured for him to ask what he wanted to know. "I figured we might need her. She might know more than she's telling us or Fraser might want to formally interview her."

"She told me everything she knows, Declan. She asked if she could be bait for us to draw him out." Kate saw the way his eyes lit up at the idea. "She's not strong enough. This is her first solo trip away from home. Once we announced there was a serial killer, Laura called her mom to ask if she should come back home. I'm not using her as bait."

"Fair enough," Declan said without argument. "Let me call Fraser and make sure he doesn't want to interview her and then we can get her to the airport."

Kate wasn't sure what Fraser would ask that she hadn't already. In the vein of playing nice though, Declan was right to call him. She waited while he made the call and explained to Fraser what they had uncovered. Relief washed over her when Declan gave her a thumbs-up and then ended the call.

"He's fine with us taking her to the airport. There's one thing we might want to do first. Fraser was able to connect with the tour company about the guy Sam and I spoke to this morning and he's got his employment records. His name is Carter Hill and he started work only a month before the first murder. He is from Leeds, England, and lists several tour companies as past employers including in some of the countries where there have been murders. The timelines don't match up but he could have lied. Fraser's contact said he didn't check any of the references. He called a few but no one got back to him. He said the guy seemed knowledgeable and personable and has been great with the tours. He checked his driving record and criminal history and found no issues."

If Laura could positively identify the guy, then they would be one step closer to making an arrest. Kate wanted to see the text messages again. "Is there a text from last night about her wallet?"

Declan pulled up the call log for Kate. "No texts. But there is a private number that called her at close to eleven. I assume that's the call about her wallet. He was smart enough not to have that in writing."

Kate cursed and rolled her eyes toward the ceiling. They couldn't catch a break anywhere. "Even if Laura positively identifies him, there is no evidence he had Brianna's wallet and lured her out last night. All Laura will be able to confirm is that he was the man Brianna was seeing."

Declan sighed and frowned. "He's not leaving any evidence, Kate. He might have slipped up with Brianna but there's still nothing linking him to the murder."

"He still introduced himself as Knox to Brianna and Laura. If she's able to identify him as the same guy, then we at least have that." Kate knew it wasn't anything and not even enough for an arrest. She was desperate for anything she could hold onto at that point.

Before going to get Laura, Kate tried to call the number that had been texting Brianna but the phone just rang and rang. There was no voicemail or anything. She had assumed it would have already been disconnected. She wasn't sure there was much they could do with it but she saved the phone number in her phone. She left the apartment and headed over to Laura's. She knocked once and pushed the door open.

"I'm just about ready," Laura called from inside the apartment.

Kate followed the sound of her voice to the bedroom and stood in the doorway. "I know you were hoping to help us, Laura. There is one thing we'd like before we take you to the airport."

"Anything," she said as she folded the last shirt and put it in her suitcase.

"My partner Agent James spoke to someone this morning we'd like you to meet. We want you to see if it's Knox. When you see him, I need you to study his face because my assumption is Knox is changing up his appearance. We have conflicting reports about what he looks like and you're the only one we have who has interacted with him. As far as I know, you're the only one who has heard his voice."

Laura turned to Kate with a worried expression on her face. "Will I have to talk to him?"

"It would be helpful if you did. This way we can see how he reacts to you. You'll be with us though. Nothing will happen to you and then we will take you to the airport and wait until you are safely on a flight."

"I haven't been able to change my ticket yet."

"It's okay. Agent James and I will take care of that for you." It was clear Laura was uncertain about all of it. Kate walked over closer to her. "Laura, we want to help you. That's why we are here in Scotland. To help figure out who killed all these women. We are not going to do anything to put you in danger."

Laura nodded. "I can leave my things here and get them on the way back."

The walk to the tour office took less than ten minutes. In that time, Declan had been able to get Laura to laugh. He regaled her with funny stories about his travel misadventures and assured her this would probably be the worst travel experience she ever had and now it would be out of the way.

They got to the tour office as a few of the tour buses were pulling back in for the day. Fraser had let them know when Carter Hill should be returning and they timed it perfectly.

Kate didn't want to give him any chance to slip away.

Declan pointed out the white sixteen-seater van and then stopped walking when he realized Laura had stopped a few feet behind them. He turned to her as she tensed up. "You can do this, Laura. I'm going to be right there with you."

Kate kept her eye on the front of the van as someone with a tour company sweatshirt exited. He stood by the side as the passengers piled out one by one. People shook his hand and handed him tips as they said their goodbyes. From what Kate could hear, everyone enjoyed the tour.

"Since you've met him, Declan, we'll hang back until you introduce us," Kate said and walked back to Laura. She took the young woman's hand and reassured her again. "Do you see him up there? If you think it's Knox, I want you to squeeze my hand twice to let me know. You don't even have to say it aloud." They could only see the back of his head from where they stood. He hadn't turned around yet.

Laura leaned to the side to get a better look at him. "He's got the same height and build as Knox. Different hair color."

Declan waited until some of the crowd dispersed and then approached him. "Carter," he called out and extended his hand. "Agent James. I'm with my partner Agent Walsh and we have a few more questions for you. We also have a young woman with us we'd like you to meet."

"I'm ready," Laura said and walked toward him still holding Kate's hand.

Carter turned to the side just as Kate and Laura approached. He had a wide smile and dark eyes. "As I told you before, Agent James, I don't have any information to help you. I'm sorry about what happened to those women but I don't know anything about it."

That didn't deter Declan. "Where were you last night, Carter?"

"I was in my apartment asleep by ten. I had to be here this morning at six to get ready for this tour. I live over near Stockbridge Market in New Town."

Kate waited for Laura to squeeze her hand but nothing happened. She turned to her. "Anything?" she whispered.

Laura continued to study his face. "I don't think it's him," she said so quietly Kate was barely able to hear her.

Carter turned to Laura and extended his hand. She took his hand in hers. "It's nice to meet you. I'm not sure why they wanted you to meet me but I don't think we've met before."

"We haven't," Laura said and then she got a bit more brave. "I thought you might have been dating my neighbor. We all had dinner once.

Did you know Brianna?"

"I don't know anyone by that name." Carter turned to look at Declan. "If that's all, I need to finish up for the day. My girlfriend and I have dinner plans."

Declan looked over at Kate but she didn't have any questions. Not here on the street anyway. Kate had studied his face in the brief time they spoke. She didn't get the sense it was Knox. She did have a question though. "You meet a lot of people on these tours. Have you had any solo male travelers? He might be going by the name of Knox."

Carter thought for a moment then shook his head. "Doesn't sound familiar to me, but I meet a lot of people. I don't remember everyone's names. You might want to check the office to see if we had anyone register with that name." He said goodbye to Laura and Kate and then left. He didn't seem to like Declan very much which made Kate wonder about their earlier interaction.

As Kate stepped back on the sidewalk, a man bumped right into her from behind. "I'm sorry, miss," he said as he gripped her by the shoulder and slipped a note into her hand. He had his jacket collar pulled high and a cap pulled low over his forehead. He moved fast and was gone before Kate even had time to register what had happened. She felt the paper in her hand and slipped it into her pocket before anyone noticed.

"Should we get out of here and get Laura to the airport?" Kate asked.

Laura smiled for the first time. "I'll be happy to get back home."

Declan heard them but his eyes were focused on Carter as he walked away.

CHAPTER 27

After Kate and Declan made sure Laura was safely on her flight and the plane had taken off, they went back to their apartment before they had to get ready for the tour they were taking later that evening. They both breathed a sigh of relief to be back and be able to rest for a few minutes.

Kate was mostly relieved to know Laura was safe. The airline had been more than accommodating, changing her flight without an additional charge. They allowed Kate and Declan to wait at the gate until it was time for boarding.

Laura had called her mother from the airport and explained the situation. By the time she boarded the flight, everyone was relieved she was heading home and within ten hours would be back in the United States.

Because they had been around so many people at the airport, Kate hadn't had a chance to address Declan's concerns about Carter or the note. She slipped off her shoes at the door, shrugged off her coat, and tossed it on a nearby chair.

She sank into the couch, calling him over. "I know you weren't convinced about Carter. Let's talk about your concerns."

Declan tossed his coat on top of hers and joined her on the couch. "There's something about him that's rubbing me the wrong way. I'm not convinced he's the killer. I believe Laura didn't recognize him. He matches closely. I guess I got hung up on him a little because we have no other suspects."

Kate rubbed the back of his neck where he held most of his tension. "If it's something more than that, tell me. I'm happy to go back and interview him again without Laura. I didn't press him as hard as I might have if she hadn't been there. Finding out if she recognized him seemed more important than anything else."

Declan leaned into her touch and rested his hand on her leg. "I didn't think we could do much more with her there. Fraser told me his contact at the tour office didn't think Carter was the type to kill anyone. He said he's mild-mannered and was always willing to take on extra work. The only issue they said was sometimes he didn't do a great job cleaning up after a tour group. But he told Fraser that happened with many of the guides. We can revisit it if we need to. For now, I think we need to move on."

Kate nudged his pocket. "You got a text while we were at the airport."

Declan pulled out his phone. "It was Sam. None of the leads he was running down panned out. He said he spoke to the pathologist and Brianna's hands were wiped down as well as her face. They followed your tip about the wallet exchange, but the wallet didn't have any fingerprints other than hers. It was cold last night and they speculated the killer wore gloves. We don't have anything, Kate. Twenty-six women dead over more than a decade. Nothing. Not one shred of evidence. Did we do the right thing by sending Laura home? She could have called Knox and asked to meet."

Kate had turned it over in her mind several times. "We had no way to guarantee her safety. Our only choice was to get her out of Edinburgh. You saw how timid she was having a conversation with Carter. Could you imagine her being sent in alone?"

"No. You're right." Declan sighed, leaned into her, and closed his eyes. "It's better she is back with her family. I wouldn't want to have to worry about her too."

The note burned hot against her thigh. She was surprised Declan hadn't asked about it. It was only when they had reached the airport that Kate said she had to go to the bathroom. When she was alone, she read the note. It was from Leo asking her to meet alone at midnight in the cemetery where they first talked. Kate had a mix of fear with excitement.

She rested her hand on top of Declan's. "I have to tell you something and don't want you to freak out."

He looked over at her with a half-hearted smile. "You're pregnant?" he said with a laugh.

If he was trying to induce a heart attack she couldn't think of a better way. Kate couldn't help but notice how oddly calm he was asking the question. "Do you remember when we were talking to Carter and a man bumped into me?"

"Yeah, it was Leo," Declan said without missing a beat. "I saw him coming, Kate. We locked eyes. He hesitated for a moment probably wondering if I was going to pounce on him. When he realized I wasn't going to do anything, he brushed past you. I assume he slipped you a note because he didn't need to get that close otherwise. He had a wide berth on the sidewalk. I've been wondering how long it was going to take you before you told me about it."

Kate sat back with her mouth slightly open. "I had no idea you were even paying attention to him."

"Kate," he said with a shake of his head. "I notice everything about you. I'm always going to keep you safe. If I had thought you were in danger, I would have stopped him. I saw him coming and knew by the look on his face he wanted to get your attention."

Kate pulled the note from her pocket. "We have his handwriting, that's if we believe he wrote it. He had gloves when he handed it to me, so I don't think we can get prints from it."

"I don't care about any of that," Declan said, surprising her. "Once Spade was on board with this, I gave it more thought. If he can help us stop this killer, then I'm willing to let his crimes go for now. We'll have our chance at him again. So…" he said with a pause, "what does the note say?"

Kate unfolded the paper and handed it to Declan. "He wants me to meet him at midnight at the Greyfriars Kirkyard near the Sir George Mackenzie mausoleum. Luckily, our tour tonight will take us into the cemetery and we can find the grave. He wants me to come alone. What should we do? Should we tell Sam and Fraser?"

Declan considered for a moment. "I don't think we should tell them. Sam would understand but Fraser might see it as an opportunity to bring him in. It would be a huge score for Police Scotland. I understand why he'd want to. Heck, I'd want to. I think you and Spade are right though, he might lead us to the killer."

"You'll come with me?" Kate asked, relieved by his answer.

"Out of sight. I'm sure Leo will know I'm there." Declan grew quiet and looked over at her. "You know this is one of the tactics the killer uses. Luring the victim out late at night. Have you considered that?"

Kate nodded but didn't want to believe it. "His story about Amelia checked out, Declan. She was like a daughter to him. Her sister, Tara, confirmed she was involved with another guy and she asked Leo to meet with Amelia in Paris to talk some sense into her. That alone tells me I can trust him – for as much as I can trust an international criminal. He's never been known to be irrationally violent. Even when he's robbed a place. He tied up the guards or drugged them but never killed them. He's never harmed a homeowner when he goes after a private collection. He threatened to kill me on the rooftop in Paris, but he did everything he could to not kill me. He doesn't fit the profile."

"I trust you. You're just going to have to trust me to be there tonight even if you can't see me."

Kate trusted Declan with her life. They only had a little bit of time before meeting the tour group that night at seven. She wanted to talk through the case a little before they left. "I think there are three cases among them all that tell me the most."

"Which ones?"

Kate leaned into him as she spoke. "Amelia in Paris. She is the youngest victim and the one that doesn't fit the rest. We know she was specifically targeted because of her connection to Leo. Then Mable in Edinburgh because she was a writer and savvy. She wouldn't have been lured away easily. It also showed us he scouted a location ahead of time. That indicated how much planning he's been putting into these murders. Then there's Brianna. Laura told me how much he mirrored Brianna early on and the time he spent with her. Once he's fixated on a victim, it seems he carries it through no matter what gets in his way, even if he needs to get creative like stealing her wallet. I think Brianna was next regardless of our investigation. I thought at first it might have been because of us, but it sounded like he's been trying to kill her all week. This would make four victims, two in a short period. He's escalating and taking risks."

"Does it tell you any more about his profile?"

"You mean besides what we already know in the photo?" When Declan confirmed, she laid it out. "White male and fits into European society well. He's probably affluent by birth or acquired the skills to fake it. He has money and he's well-read but he's also good at playing down social status. He can mirror to blend in. But his memory is slipping. Laura said Brianna caught him in a few lies. He's probably not as sharp as he once was or there's been so many murders he's starting to confuse them all. They also said he looked older than his stated age. I'd guess he'd have to be mid to late forties."

"That would knock out Carter Hill. He turned thirty-five last week,"

Declan said. "I didn't stop to consider that would mean he would have committed his first series of homicides when he was only twenty-five."

Kate knew some killers started that young or even younger. "He's on the list but I don't think it's him."

"Me either at this point." Declan checked his watch. "We need to get ready to go."

Kate wasn't ready to get up yet. "Has there been any fallout from what Billy published? I haven't heard anything from anyone other than Fraser. Have you heard from anyone back home?"

Declan tipped his head back and laughed. "Kate, no one I know is reading British tabloids. It's not like they are going to show up in grocery stores and newsstands back home. Billy probably doesn't even have a wide circulation. We'll be replaced on his homepage within a few days. Is it really so bad for people to think we are together?"

"Not at all," Kate said a little too quickly. She ducked her head and blushed as he turned his head toward her. "I don't want it to get in the way of doing our job. I don't want anyone to think we aren't on top of things because of what's going on with us personally. I know it's not distracting, but others may think we aren't fully in the game."

"Sam asked me if it was distracting working with you."

"Distracting?"

"Because of our chemistry together or maybe it's because you're attractive." Before Declan could say anything else, Kate's phone rang.

She didn't recognize the number or the country code. "Hello," she said with hesitation in her voice.

"Stop hunting me," the deep male voice said on the other end of the phone. "You're never going to find me and you're just making me angry. What did you do with Laura? I went to find her and she was gone. Where is she, Kate? Where are you hiding her?"

Kate pointed to the phone and then put the call on speaker, hoping he didn't notice. "Laura isn't your concern. She's safe and you're not going to be able to get to her. She has no idea you're the one who killed Brianna. She said she found it hard to believe, Knox." Kate paused as she said his name, waiting for his reaction. "That is what you like to be called, right?"

He didn't respond to that. "I'm telling you to back off. I had the chance to kill you once and I didn't take it. Don't you remember the rooftop, Kate? I could have killed you then."

Kate knew he was trying to mimic Leo. She scrambled to find something that only the two of them would know. "I didn't think you'd remember our time on the rooftop."

"I remember everything – how you feel and smell." His breathing became uneven. "I think I might kill you after all, just for the fun of it. I'm going to suck the breath from you, Kate, as I choke the life out of you. Your last breath will become my own. I will possess you."

A shiver ran down Kate's back. It was a long time since a killer's words had caused such a fearful reaction in her. He was truly a madman. "Do you remember your complaint about American women, Knox?"

"I've said a lot of things."

"No. You'd remember this. You said it several times to me on the rooftop. If you remember our time together, then you remember this." Kate pressed him for the information. She wasn't sure Leo would even remember. She was only trying to prove to him and possibly to herself there was no way this was Leo, even though she knew he could fake any accent he wanted. It was one of the skills the Phantom was known to possess.

"You're trying to trick me with your games, Kate. I will not fall for it."

"I've already won, Knox. I'm going to win again when I stop you for good."

He laughed then, a high-pitched shriek. "You're never going to stop me. I'm everywhere and I'm nowhere. You let Laura get away from me. You're going to pay for that."

The call ended.

Kate pulled back the phone and stared at it. She immediately called the number but it went to a mechanical voicemail. She knew if she tried to trace the number it wouldn't get her anywhere. He'd have thought of everything and it was easy enough to block the data or reroute it. He didn't even need that many tech skills.

Declan gripped Kate's arm as all the color drained from his face. "Kate, are you okay?"

"I'm fine," she said, lying to herself as much as she did to him. "We are going to find him and kill him if we have to." She knew then her earlier assessment was right – they'd never take him alive.

CHAPTER 28

Old Town Edinburgh had a much different vibe at night than it did during the day. Kate felt transported back in time and her eyes played tricks on her. Every shadow and dark alley came alive in the dark, making her normally steady nerves prickle with anticipation.

The killer's call and threats didn't help matters any.

"You're tense, Kate," Declan said beside her as they crossed the street to the side of St. Giles Cathedral. A crowd of about twenty people had gathered around the small tree that sprouted from the sidewalk. Declan grabbed her hand as they crossed the street. "Maybe people will think we are a couple and won't remember they saw me on television giving devastating news."

He had on a Boston Red Sox cap pulled low over his forehead and had changed into jeans and a flannel shirt under his jacket. Kate had changed clothes too, opting for a heavy sweater and jeans. She had pulled a gray knit hat over her ears. She hoped no one would recognize them. They had passed several reporters giving nighttime updates and none of them even turned their way.

Kate had made the reservation online and then found the woman in the crowd with her cellphone out checking people in. Kate assumed this was Vivian. She stood about five-five, had wide hips, and a round pleasant face. Her Scottish accent was thick but not so much that anyone would have trouble understanding her. She flashed a wide grin when Kate gave their names.

"I heard you might want to ask me some questions. If you could wait until the tour is over, I made sure to leave time," Vivian said. Kate thanked her, both for leaving time for them to talk and not outing them to the rest of the group.

The last thing Kate had wanted from the others was to be peppered with questions and disrupt the tour. Blending in was the only thing they had hoped to accomplish. Kate and Declan stepped back from the crowd and found a spot leaning up against the brick wall. They could see everyone as they gathered and had a clear view of Vivian. She was organized and moved efficiently. She waited until exactly seven and then called for anyone who had not checked in with her to do so. No one moved toward her, but they all looked around at each other.

"We are just waiting for Logan MacInnes to join us. He guides another tour but has graciously said he'd cover my tours during my upcoming holiday vacation." Vivian looked up the road and waved. "There he is now."

The crowd turned to see a man heading toward them. He picked up the pace and slowly jogged toward the crowd. When he arrived, he took a bow and flashed a toothy smile. He had broad shoulders and a tuff of red curly hair sticking out from under a scally cap and a full red beard. He had a steady build like one of the men she'd seen in a video once of Scottish men competing in the Highland games.

"I'm so happy you're all here tonight. It's going to be a cold one, but we are going to keep a good pace so that should warm you up. At the end, we'll stop the tour at a pub and you can all get a drink," Logan said with a thick Scottish accent, thicker than Vivian's.

Kate had to focus to catch what he was saying.

Vivian started the tour with a brief historical overview of Old Town and St. Giles Cathedral, which was built in 1124 by King David I. Kate had a hard time wrapping her mind around the history she stood beside. It was close to nine hundred years ago. She thought the history surrounding her in Boston was old but this was centuries upon centuries older. It was hard to fathom it was all still standing.

The group moved slowly along with Vivian who was pointing out stones near the western door of St. Giles. She spoke loudly above the crowd. "This stone mosaic heart is called the Heart of Midlothian and marks the location of the entrance to Edinburgh's Old Tolbooth which was demolished in 1817. If you see any locals spitting on it, it's a sign of good luck. The tradition has changed in meaning over the years. People used to spit on it out of disdain for the executions that took place within the Old Tolbooth. You'll see, Edinburgh is a city of rich history and architectural gems but steeped in violence. You'll be encountering more than a few spirits tonight."

Declan gripped Kate's hand a little harder and she leaned into him. "You can't be afraid," she said with a laugh. "You're supposed to be protecting me."

"Not from ghosts I'm not. You're on your own with them." He leaned over and kissed her on the forehead.

An older woman and her husband caught their eyes. She smiled over at him. "I remember being young and in love."

Kate wasn't sure what to say but Declan smiled back at her. "How long have you been married?"

"Fifty years. We are on an anniversary trip."

Kate couldn't quite place the accent. German or Dutch most likely. They congratulated the couple and then focused on the history lesson. Vivian pointed toward the front of the church and asked them to follow her. The website said the tour was not for people with mobility issues and that made sense now. Kate wasn't someone who thought she walked slowly but Vivian's pace was next level. Probably because she walked the same route so much. Between the stairs, the hills over stone ground, and the cold, Kate kept her head lowered and watched the ground as she walked. The last thing she wanted to do was fall flat on her back or break an ankle.

They went down a steep staircase, then down a hill, and around the corner. Vivian gave them a history lesson as they went. Logan had mingled among the crowd and was asking people where they were from and why they were in Edinburgh. He cracked a few jokes and kept the crowd lively and talking. Kate thought he was perfect in his job.

When he got to them, he tipped his cap to them. "Vivian told me you'd be joining us tonight. I can stick around after the tour is over too if you'd like. It's great to have you here."

"Where are you from in Scotland?" Kate asked.

"Up north in Inverness. Have you had the chance to see anything other than Edinburgh?"

"No," Kate said, wishing work wasn't the reason they were there. "We won't have time to go anywhere the case doesn't take us. So far, it's been focused on Edinburgh."

"Maybe once you solve it, you can take a trip up north. It's a beautiful train ride."

"Maybe," Declan said and then the two of them chatted for a few minutes about Scotland's landscape.

While Declan was engaged in conversation, Kate focused her attention on Vivian who was telling them the history of the South Street Vaults, which they were about to enter. Kate tried to get her bearings as she knew Old Fishmarket Close had to be nearby. The layout of the roads and the crowd of buildings sometimes made it difficult to know exactly where they were or in what direction they'd need to go. Declan didn't seem to have any trouble with the navigation. For his first time being in Edinburgh, he seemed to already know the lay of the land.

They filed into the vaults one by one behind Vivian with Logan taking up the rear. Kate couldn't see a thing so she pulled out her phone like others were doing and used the flashlight app. Vivian explained how the vaults once formed the arch chambers of South Bridge, which was completed in 1788. For close to 30 years after that, the vaults were used to house taverns, workshops for cobblers, and storage space for merchants. In later years, the vaults were overrun with the homeless, sick and dying, and people engaged in criminal activity.

Given the cold damp conditions of the vaults, most of the businesses left by the 1820s and only the poorest in the city remained until close to the 1860s when the vaults were completely abandoned. Kate focused harder when Vivian started telling the stories about Burke and Hare and how it was speculated they found some of their victims down in the vaults. She asked if anyone had heard the story of Burke and Hare and only a few people raised their hands.

Kate hung in the back with Declan. She turned to Logan who was right near her. "Vivian does an excellent job of storytelling. I can see why this tour is so popular."

He smiled broadly. "She's one of the best."

"Have you been a tour guide here long?"

"A little more than a year. I was with another tour group before that. I have a knack for remembering facts and can tell a good story too." He winked at Kate and then moved on to mingle with some of the other guests. Kate wondered what tours he gave in the city. There had been many to choose from but Vivian only provided this one.

They followed the crowd through the vaults. Vivian moved them from one cavernous room to another, walking up wooden stairs that looked more recent than the vaults. They had to duck low in a few of the doorways and, for a stretch, Declan had to walk with his head lowered so he didn't hit it on the stone ceiling.

They followed Vivian out to the night air and then down one street and another and another. There were so many twists and turns, up flights of stairs and down others, that by the time they reached Greyfriars Kirkyard, Kate needed to catch her breath.

Vivian spent nearly a full thirty minutes giving the history of the cemetery and walking them to important gravestones, pointing out names that were familiar to them all. She gave a brief history of the school next door and then took them to what was known as the Black Mausoleum that housed the supposed malevolent Mackenzie poltergeist. It was in the part of the cemetery that had once been used as an overcrowded prison called Covenanter's Prison. Vivian explained as people stood in the vault they were often attacked and came away with burning scratches. Some people felt dizzy or nauseated.

Kate and Declan joined everyone else standing in the mausoleum. Neither Vivian nor Logan joined them. Vivian explained she'd been scratched one too many times. Nothing happened to Kate while she stood there and it didn't feel particularly creepy to her. She was getting anxious to speak to Vivian and wondered if Leo was there now lurking somewhere in the cemetery waiting for their meeting.

Finally, after what felt like longer than fifteen minutes, the tour ended. Kate and Declan walked out of the mausoleum and stood near Logan as Vivian said goodbye to the other guests.

"How can we help you?" Logan asked as they waited.

Declan let go of Kate's hand and turned to him. "Are you familiar with the murders that have taken place in the city?"

"Of course. It's horrible. Edinburgh might have a dark past but we don't have crime like that here usually. It's why people feel so safe."

Declan moved so Vivian could join them. He got right to the point. "We suspect the killer might be taking tours like this to meet single women. Do you have many single men on the tour?"

Vivian and Logan shared a laugh and then she apologized. "We always have single men on these tours flirting and trying to pick up women. I've joked that we aren't that kind of group. It's been an ongoing thing and can sometimes be annoying but mostly it's hilarious to watch. Your assumption that he could be finding victims this way is unfortunately possible. No one stands out if that's what you're asking."

Kate pulled her phone from her pocket. "You'll need to use your flashlight to get a look at this photo. Have you seen this man? This is a recent photo of him within the last week with the most recent victim."

Vivian stared down at it. "He doesn't look familiar to me. She does though. I think she was on one of my tours earlier in the week."

"Do you know if she talked to any men on the tour? We believe this is how they met."

"I don't remember. It was a crowded tour and people were chatting with everyone. I don't remember her talking to anyone specifically," Vivian said and handed the phone to Logan. "You run many more tours than I do. Does he look familiar?"

Logan peered down at the photo and then raised his head to Kate. "You think this man is the killer?"

"He's a person of interest, at least." Kate didn't want to overplay her hand.

Logan stared at the photo longer. "I think he was on one of my tours about a month ago and then again last week. I see so many people I didn't think much of it. You think he's meeting victims this way?"

"We do," Kate said. "We had to register for this tour and give our names, email address, and phone number. Do you think you can go back in your files and look for his contact information?"

"I can try but it's not going to be that easy. I'm not sure which night this was or what tour and we don't have photos matched up with names. I can see what I can do though."

Kate didn't think the killer would be giving real information anyway, so it was a long shot. She thanked them for the information. "If either of you see him, please contact us immediately." She pulled Vivian aside while Logan spoke to Declan. "This man is extremely dangerous. We think he might be changing his appearance. He's going by the name Knox as in Robert Knox."

Vivian recoiled. "That's sick. I'll be on the lookout. If you send me this photo, I'll circulate it around the city to all the tour operators. Can I give them your number if anyone has seen him?"

"Definitely," Kate said and thanked her again. She waved as Vivian and Logan walked off together.

Declan joined her. "He promised he'd be in touch as soon as he could find the information. We've got a couple of hours before we have to be back here. What do you want to do?"

Kate's stomach growled in response. "Let's find a pub, get some dinner, and get warm before I have to face Leo."

CHAPTER 29

At eleven-fifty, Kate entered Greyfriars Kirkyard and went to the left, following the path to Sir George Mackenzie's mausoleum. She had learned a little about the man during the earlier tour but had read much more over dinner. He was an infamous brutal character in Scotland's history. It made sense why there was a violent poltergeist named after him.

George Mackenzie was a lawyer and the Lord Advocate during the rule of Charles II. He earned a reputation as one of the most vicious persecutors of the Covenanters, the people who rose up and signed the National Covenant in 1638. He imprisoned many Covenanters in a section of Greyfriars Kirkyard they had seen during the tour. Mackenzie and his guards tortured the prisoners. They were subjected to starvation, beatings, exposed to the harsh elements, and some were murdered. Often their heads would decorate the spiked gate to terrify and warn the other prisoners not to rise up.

Mackenzie's mausoleum had been desecrated and vandalized many times. It was easy enough to find. It was rounded with a dome on top and four large column pillars. It also had an iron fence around both sides. The doors were accessible although locked. Kate had not walked up to the doors and peered in. Declan had earlier but she wasn't going to press her luck.

Kate stood on the paved path a few feet from the mausoleum. The moon shone bright overhead and the cemetery wasn't as creepy as she thought it might be alone. Mostly, it was serene and might be even more so if she hadn't been waiting to meet up with an international art thief who probably wasn't a serial killer.

His footsteps echoed against the cold night. Kate turned as he approached and he smiled at her. "I'm a bit surprised you showed up."

Kate gestured toward the mausoleum. "You chose a fairly creepy spot to meet. Do you know the history of George Mackenzie?"

"I do," he said looking up at the structure. "The evil that men do, Kate. Throughout history, men who have wielded great power have abused it." Leo looked down at Kate and locked his gaze on her. "Some of us are trying to right some wrongs. It may not seem that way but we are. There are still good men among us." He looked out over the grounds. "I assume we are not alone."

Kate knew he'd suspect. "No one is here that will arrest you if that's what you're wondering. It's only for my protection."

He turned his head toward her. "Protection? You know I'd never hurt you, Kate."

She didn't like him calling her by her first name, but she couldn't exactly insist on the formal now. "We believe this is how the killer is meeting his victims. Getting them to come out to historical sites or bars late at night. We believe the last victim had her wallet stolen and he returned it and murdered her. I had no idea why you called me out here. You can't expect under the circumstances I'd come alone."

Leo stepped back and put his hand up. "I'm sorry. I had no idea that's how he was doing this. Had I known I would have tried to get a message to you another way. Given…" He made a sweeping gesture with his hand.

Kate filled in what he didn't say. "Given you're an international criminal wanted in twenty countries, the dead of night in a cemetery was probably the best bet to meet up with an FBI agent who should be arresting you."

Leo chuckled but admitted nothing. He stepped toward her, but when she stepped back, he stopped. "I mean no harm. I'm curious though. Why aren't you arresting me?"

Kate played her cards. "I thought you might bring value to the investigation. He's targeting you and I hoped you'd lead me to him. I spoke to my boss and he agrees we could use you as an asset on this case." Kate grew brave and took a few steps toward him so she was almost toe to toe. She had to angle her head back to look up at him. "Don't mistake my kindness. There will come a day when I will arrest you and you'll face justice for all the crimes you've committed."

Leo's expression told Kate she didn't stand a chance of that ever happening. He simply raised his shoulders in a half-hearted shrug. "Aren't you supposed to say alleged to have committed? As far as I know, there is no proof I've ever committed a crime."

"Did you forget holding me hostage on the rooftop in Paris?"

His gaze roamed over her. "I don't think I'll ever forget holding you in my arms. I think of it often. Have you thought about it at all?"

"I've replayed you getting away many times over. It kills me now to be so close and not have you in handcuffs." She realized too late that the tone of that sounded sexual.

The smile didn't leave his face. He chuckled to himself.

"Do you remember what you told me about American women then?"

Leo nodded with the smile still on his lips. "That you're too controlling and demanding. I like it on you though, Kate."

She was sure he wasn't the one who called her.

Leo leaned in closer to her. "I'm going to offer you some advice. You can take it or leave it. When you're back in Boston in your brownstone, snuggled up by your fireplace some night, look into the history of the art and artifacts some claim I stole. There have always been questions about where it ends up after I take it. I'll tell you now that if I'm guilty of all they have said, you can rest assured the pieces are back to their rightful owners."

"Are you telling me you're some kind of Robin Hood?"

"Think of me as someone who's righting some wrongs and delivering some long overdue justice."

This was a dance between them Kate wasn't going to continue. Not right now anyway. She wanted to ask how he knew she lived in a brownstone in Boston, but she knew he had probably researched her. "Why did you ask me out here tonight? Have you found some information?"

The sound of the wind in the trees drew both of their attention. Kate knew Declan was out there but she had no idea how close.

Leo looked around too but didn't see anything and focused right back on Kate. "I know you spoke to Tara and learned more about my background."

Kate hoped that wasn't the only reason he had dragged her out here on this cold, windy night. He had to have known she would ask. "I called Tara to learn more about Amelia. It's what a good investigator does. I also learned what you told the DeBeckers. I didn't think it was all true." She let her tone go soft. "Is it true that you were an orphan living on your own?"

It wasn't what Kate had initially thought about him. She had believed him to be well-educated at some of the finest boarding schools in Europe. His taste in art and overall refinement didn't match the story.

Leo hesitated and lowered his eyes away from hers. "I show people what they need to see. Jordan DeBecker was my friend though. That much is true. I was living on my own and we rescued each other. My family was not as poor as he believed them to be. I didn't want anything to do with them."

"Can I ask why?"

He looked back up at her and shook his head. "You already know too much, far more than anyone else knows about me. I will not make it easy for you to catch me. I will never spend a moment in prison, Kate. Understand that. My childhood was confined and controlled by others. I will not go back to that."

Kate knew not to push. "Tara cannot be why you risked sending me a message on the street and wanted to meet out here tonight. Did you want something else?"

Leo widened his stance and folded his arms across his chest. He braced himself against the wind and shielded Kate from some of it too. "It took me a while to figure out who had this much access to knowledge about my schedule and movements. It took me even longer to accept that this must be someone from the inside. I know my team isn't happy with me right now, not since Paris. I've been on this quest to find the killer and stop him. As a result, all other plans have been put on hold. That's angered some people. I have a traitor in my midst. No one knows where I am now, but they are certainly asking. It's put me in a position of trusting no one, not even men I've trusted with my life."

"Where was the last place they knew you to be?"

"Paris but then when Amelia was murdered..." The pain on his face was indescribable to Kate. "I didn't care about anything else. Nothing else was as important as finding who killed her. I think I've narrowed down who among my team has betrayed me. I do not think he could be the killer though so I'm confused."

Jax had told Kate that people weren't happy and were starting to break ranks. He hadn't called her back yet with the information and she didn't want to out Jax. There was one way to expedite this and clear up his confusion. She pulled the phone from her pocket. "We have a photo of him. At least, I believe this to be the killer. He was seen with the last victim. We know from a witness that he thought he had deleted the photo. She was able to retrieve it and show us."

"Is your witness safe?" Leo asked with concern in his voice.

Kate nodded but wouldn't say more. She extended her phone to him, but he didn't take it. "We believe he frequently changes up his appearance and mirrors the victims early on as a way to gain their trust."

"Mirrors?"

"Mimics. We are all guilty of it when we want someone to like us but this killer goes to extremes. He has a broad knowledge base and is quick with research. Either way, he's able to pull off different personalities. He also stole the victim's wallet to meet up with her later and get her alone."

Leo zeroed in on Kate. "What do you mean he stole her wallet?"

"They were at a pub earlier on the night of the murder. Based on witness testimony it seems Brianna was hard to get alone. He went to her apartment but she wouldn't go anywhere else alone with him other than in public. She also went home early most nights. It sounded to me like she made it difficult for him. We believe on the night of the murder he stole her wallet at dinner, acted like he had found it, and lured her out late to retrieve it from him."

There was a flicker of recognition in his eyes. "You said Brianna invited him to her apartment. Did they have sex?"

"No. Brianna told a friend she wanted to but he refused." Kate forced him to take the phone and look at the photo.

Almost as soon as he looked down, his head snapped back up. "Are you sure this is the killer?"

Kate again saw the recognition on his face. "This is the man Brianna was seeing while she was here in Scotland. He introduced himself to our witness as Knox and we know that's a name the killer used. He also fits the description. As I said, we believe he changes his appearance but the height and build are the same."

Leo held Kate's phone in his gloved hand. He stared at the photo and then stumbled back a few feet. He sat down on the curb while still looking at the photo. "I know this man."

Kate's heart raced not sure she had heard him correctly. "Did you say you know him?"

Leo took a breath and looked over at Kate. It took him a few beats to get out the words. "He's my stepbrother."

Questions flooded her. She sat down on the curb with him, close enough their knees were nearly touching. This was the closest she'd been to the man since he had taken her hostage. "What's his name?"

"Markus Lamiere was his name at birth. I have no idea if that's what he's using now."

CHAPTER 30

Kate knew for Leo to tell her about this man, he'd have to disclose information about his past. They shared the same last name. "I know you don't want me to know much about you but we need to stop him, Leo. I need to know everything you do, even if it means sharing things about your past."

He didn't hesitate this time. "For Amelia, I will tell you." Leo handed back her phone and then stared up at the sky. "My mother married his father when I was a small child. I couldn't have been more than five. Markus was three at the time. We moved from my home country to France. We lived right outside of Paris. Lucien Lamiere was a brutal man. I'm not sure why my mother married him. He was wealthy and maybe she thought he could take care of us. We lived in a mansion outside of Paris and had a summer home in the south of France. We traveled around the globe frequently and he taught me all about art, music, and history. I went to the finest schools and had everything I could have ever wanted, except for safety and love."

"Is that why you left?"

"My mother died when I was ten and Lucien wanted to mold me after him. He did for a while and then the violence escalated." Leo reached up and touched the back of his head but offered Kate no explanation. "After I left, I still heard from Markus. Lucien never came to look for me. I suspect he was glad to be rid of me."

"You kept his name," Kate said, not sure she would have.

"I used his name to open doors. A name has little meaning to me. I've been called many things. It was never the name my mother gave me. That's the one no one knows."

Kate had already suspected that. "After you left, did you go to London?"

"Not at first. I traveled around. Pickpocketed and begged on the street. I stole things to be able to eat." He took a breath, steadying himself. It was clear to Kate the memories were not pleasant. "I'm ashamed of how I lived at that time but I was a child. What other choice did I have? It was only when I met Jordan in London I felt like I had a home and real family."

"Tara said you rescued Jordan."

Leo expelled a breath then sucked in another. "I saved him from a few bullies but it was him and his father who saved me. If I had stayed with Lucien, one of us would have surely killed the other."

Kate believed what he said as she could hear the conviction in his voice and see the way his hands tensed as he spoke. "What happened to Markus after you left?"

"It took him a few years to find me and even then it was coincidence. He had been on a school trip in London and he spotted me on the street with Jordan. I told Jordan to go home and I'd catch up with him later. Markus was almost eighteen then and he was as brutal as his father. He bragged that day about the animals he had killed and the power that brought him. He seemed to take real pleasure in it."

That was certainly an early marker of a budding serial killer. "When did he leave home?"

Leo told Kate he didn't understand. "He never did. Markus went to Oxford and then moved right back to France to live with his father. He's never worked a real job in his life. Then again, he doesn't have to. Lucien died about a decade ago and left him hundreds of millions of dollars."

"A decade ago?" Kate asked, interrupting him.

Leo looked over at her, sensing her tone. "Ten or eleven years. Why?"

"The murders started ten years ago. Lucien's death could have been the stressor that set him off. Do you know anything about his romantic life? How was Markus with women?"

Leo grew quiet causing Kate to wonder if he was trying to recall a memory or delay answering the question. After a few moments, he explained, "As Markus got older, particularly when he was at Oxford, he told me stories. He said he could get any woman he wanted. He's never had a significant relationship that I'm aware of. He was open about his exploits with women, but I can't say that I believed all of them were true. I assumed they weren't. He often spoke of violence combined with sex. He told me about seeing prostitutes because they'd let him be rough. He talked about violent pornography and that it was getting more difficult for him to find enjoyment in what he called boring sex. I don't know if he told me these things to shock me or if he was trying to get me to normalize it for him. I told him more than once he needed to seek help."

"Did he ever tell you specifics?" She saw the confusion on his face and she reframed. "What kind of violent acts got him off?"

Leo squinted at her. "Do you want to know?"

"Don't be squeamish with me. I've heard it all."

Leo didn't look comfortable telling her. "I haven't thought about this in a long time. Years ago, I begged him not to tell me anymore until he got some help. You may think of me as nothing more than a criminal, but I've never once harmed a woman." Leo looked over at her and raised his hand to brush the hair away from her face. "I wouldn't have hurt you on that rooftop, Kate. I was only trying to get away and had to scare you into not doing something stupid."

His hand left her face before she had a chance to brush it away. "I'm not accusing you of hurting women, Leo. Just tell me what Markus told you. Often, a serial killer will test out his fantasies long before the first murder is ever committed. What did he tell you?"

This time Leo got right to the point. "He mentioned wanting to strangle a woman to watch the breath go out of her. This was twenty years ago, Kate. It's not something I've thought about in a long time." He looked away from her. "I didn't talk to him often and when I did, I wished we hadn't spoken at all. There was always something off about him I could never quite put my finger on. We haven't been in touch since he told me Lucien died."

"Do you believe he could do something like this?"

"Yes," he said quietly not hesitating. His tone was tinged with frustration. "I don't know why I didn't immediately think of him when this started. I should have known."

"It's not an easy thing to know. We don't want to think anyone we know is capable of something like this." Kate had so many questions but she tried to stick with the most important. "You had some recognition on your face when I mentioned stealing the wallet. Why was that?"

"It reminded me of a story Markus told me when he was in school. He'd often take something from a girl and then say he found it to win favor over her. Be the hero. It was a trick he had used several times and was proud of. I thought of him when you told me about the victim's wallet. It sounded like something he would do."

Kate wasn't surprised to hear that. "I think he might be changing his appearance. Is that something he'd be capable of doing?"

Leo stared down at Kate's phone again. "The one thing Lucien taught us was how to blend into every environment and every social class. Markus always had a flair for the dramatic. He's tried out different accents before. He'd always try to mimic mine even when I worked hard to sound more French like him and Lucien. But yes, these kinds of chameleon lessons were something Lucien instilled in us. He said it was important in business and life. It's how I could go from being the stepson of a millionaire to a kid living on the street and lying about being an orphan."

"You didn't lie," Kate said, feeling a little bad for him. "Was he jealous of your relationship with Lucien?"

Leo leaned back on his hands and stared up at the sky. "It wasn't like that. It didn't matter how much time Lucien spent with me or the nice things he did, it was always made clear to me who was his *real* son. There was no mistaking that. If anything, Markus seemed jealous that I got out. He told me he hated his father for all the reasons I did. When I left, he wanted me to take him and I wouldn't. I couldn't. I knew Lucien would come after us. I knew if I left alone, I'd break free. I had to make a choice."

Kate didn't blame him for that. She probably would have done the same thing if she had been in his situation. "What about your schedule? Would he have access?" These were just minor details now. It certainly sounded like Markus could be the killer. All the early hallmarks of psychopathy were there.

"I don't know how he'd get that information unless he was getting it from someone on the inside of my business." Leo grew quiet for a few moments and Kate let him process whatever was on his mind. "When I said initially I thought it was someone on the inside, maybe they are just sharing my schedule with Markus. Although, I don't know how they connected."

Kate knew there were always ways. "Could he have hacked a phone or computer?"

Leo turned his head to fully look at her. "I don't put much in writing," he said, sending more of a message with the way he looked at her. Putting things in writing could be evidence.

"Got it," Kate said. "If this is Markus, how—"

"There is no *if*," Leo said, his voice commanding. He stood from the ground and held his hand out for her. Kate hesitated but took it and let him pull her to her feet. When they were both upright, he said, "That photo you showed me is Markus. He has aged but it looks like he's trying to play himself off as younger. He's there with one of the victims. Someone is seeking revenge on me. He's fulfilling some sick demented lust he has for violence and murder while trying to pin the crimes on me."

Kate didn't know how to ask this without making him incriminate himself. She wasn't even sure if it mattered. "Does Markus know about your business – the truth of it?"

It wasn't a lighthearted moment but Leo chuckled. "Let's say Markus knew what I was doing years ago and he asked to join me. I told him no several times."

"Why?"

Leo focused his attention out across the cemetery. There wasn't much light even from the moon and the stars. "For several reasons. His father was the one who sparked the drive in me and Markus is too much like his father."

That didn't make a lot of sense to Kate. She let him continue uninterrupted.

"Markus was always obsessive-compulsive over something one minute and reckless the next. He was prone to losing his temper and wrecking everything in his path. I can't have that kind of unpredictability." He looked down at Kate and they made steady eye contact. "Markus is all about power and wealth. He didn't have the same mission as me."

"Mission?" Kate asked but Leo refused to say more. She went to the murders. "When this first started, did you think it could be Markus?"

"Never once," Leo said, cursing his stupidity. "I was so blinded by rage after Amelia's death, I wasn't thinking straight. All I wanted was to kill the person responsible. I didn't slow down and consider everything."

"Did he know the DeBeckers?"

"I didn't tell him but he found out about them after I saw him in London. I thought for sure he'd go back and tell his father where I was and maybe he did. Lucien never contacted me and Markus never outed me to Jordan or his father. He could have shown up at the bakery and destroyed the life I had. He never did."

Kate had many questions still but one was the most important. "How do we stop him?"

"I need to contact him and tell him I know."

"Will that drive him away from here?"

"It might, Kate. I don't know what else we can do."

Kate was surprised he thought of them as a team. "I don't think it's a *we* situation. Knowing his identity now, the FBI and local law enforcement can handle it from here. You still need to figure out who is giving your personal information away." She knew she had Jax in her back pocket and the chance to find out more about Leo was there.

They'd be one step closer to arresting him when the time came. Kate ignored the niggling of guilt that crept up at the thought of arresting him. Kate worried that she'd compromised herself as Declan thought she might.

"Maybe there's a way I can draw him out and the FBI arrest him," Leo said but the insincerity in his voice didn't escape her.

"You don't want him arrested. You want to kill him," she said evenly. When he didn't respond, Kate said, "You don't need to do that. You shouldn't do that because I can't ensure you'd get away with a murder like that."

"It wouldn't be murder," Leo said without any trace of remorse. "I'd be doing everyone a favor. I'm regretting not doing it sooner."

Kate knew Declan must be getting restless waiting for them. She had no idea the conversation would go this long. "Give us a chance to do our jobs."

Leo gave a curt nod but made no promises. "Where is your partner? I'm surprised he didn't tackle me when I passed the note to you earlier. He looked like he wanted to."

"Agent James is out there somewhere watching us." She turned and looked up at him and the way the shadows played with the features on his face. Another time or place, she might have been interested in him. The way she had been in Paris at the café. "He wasn't happy about my decision to speak to you and not arrest you when I had the chance."

"You never had a chance," he teased. "When you explore the art I'm accused of stealing, you'll wish that we weren't on the opposite sides of the law." He reached out and turned her chin to face him. Kate didn't brush him off. "You're going to have a hard time wanting to arrest me if the time comes."

Kate was already feeling that. She stepped out of his touch. "Let's not give Declan any reason to shoot you."

"I saw the gossip paper. Is it true that you're involved?" Leo asked with his eyebrows arched. "It makes sense. Who else are you going to date?"

"It's not true," Kate responded but the answer sounded hollow.

"It wouldn't be a bad thing if it was true, Kate. Don't let a chance at love pass you by. It's probably my biggest regret in life. I always wanted to fall in love."

Before Kate could respond, he stepped back into the shadows with the promise to contact her again if he found Markus. She was left standing there watching him walk away. A jumble of emotions bubbled up inside her and she was surprised by the wetness of tears on her cheek. She harshly wiped her eyes and stalked off towards the entrance of the cemetery, assuming Declan would show himself.

CHAPTER 31

"Markus Lamiere is the killer," Kate said and then repeated it twice to Sam and Fraser who looked confused by her sudden announcement. They had gathered in the conference room at the police station to go over the evidence they had uncovered the night before. They sat at the table and each gave their update.

Kate had saved her update for last. She and Declan had decided that would be best.

After her meeting with Leo, Declan met her at the gates of the cemetery. When she explained what she learned, Declan had been surprised Leo had given up the information so easily.

By the time they made it back to their apartment, neither of them had any doubt about Markus.

They had stayed up late researching information about Lucien and Markus Lamiere. She had been surprised by the wealth of information online about them. The only missing information was a photo of Markus. That seemed to have been scrubbed from the internet.

Kate read the lengthy obituary for Lucien and she checked the dates against the first murders. His death was six months before the day of the first murder. Kate assumed that had been the pivotal moment in Markus's life. With his father dead, he either felt free to kill or the stress of his father's demise had sent him over the edge. Kate couldn't be sure.

With the information she had been able to find, Kate put together a timeline of Markus's life from the time he was young to his days at Oxford. After that, the information was absent. He attended one of the most prestigious schools in the world and then disappeared. He was mentioned in Lucien's obituary as the man's son but no other details were provided. Kate knew from Leo that Markus was the sole beneficiary of his father's estate and that was worth in the hundreds of millions.

They had called Spade and updated him about the finding. He assured Kate and Declan he'd put the best of their team on the search to find out everything they could.

Kate and Declan finally went to bed at two in the morning, slept for a few hours, and were back at it by eight that morning. Neither Sam nor Fraser had much of an update to give. All the leads they had explored yesterday hadn't panned out – which was another nail in Markus's coffin.

Kate had waited until everyone else was done before she explained how Leo had slipped her a note and asked her to meet him alone the previous night in Greyfriars Kirkyard. She had watched Fraser's reaction to the news. He looked away once when she was talking, glancing down at his phone and then back up again. He didn't seem to have any reaction to the situation. That was the best Kate could have hoped for.

"Was the meeting fruitful?" Sam had asked, looking between Kate and Declan. He had seemed fine with Leo's help from the start. As he had put it, sometimes one sacrifice must be made for another. Stolen art, no matter how much it was worth, wasn't worth more than human life.

With her tone calm and even, Kate explained, "Leo identified the man with Brianna in the photo we have. His name is Markus Lamiere and he is Leo's stepbrother." Sam and Fraser stared at her for a few beats as they absorbed and processed the information. She repeated the name twice more.

Even if Fraser didn't like it, he couldn't deny the results it produced. "Are you serious? We have the name of the killer?" He sat up a little straighter in the chair.

"Not just the name but some background on him," Declan said, echoing Kate's tone of accomplishment. "We were also able to gather more information about Leo for when the time comes to arrest him. He was forthcoming with information with Kate that we might not have otherwise been able to obtain."

Kate gave them the overview of Leo's early life with his mother, the abuse he suffered at Lucien's hand, and then fleeing to London. She explained the relationship between Leo and Markus and all the details she had learned about his life.

"It sounded to me like Markus showed early signs of being a budding serial killer. He suffered abuse in his childhood, he killed animals for fun, and he expressed sexual desires related to violence. He also told Leo once that he fantasized about strangling a woman and watching the breath leave her body. He articulated these murders more than twenty years ago. Markus also has the financial means to roam from country to country. Leo said he's never held a job. This leaves him time to focus solely on hunting women. He was raised to be well-read and adaptable. If he isn't the killer, this is certainly the best lead we have to date."

Sam and Fraser asked Kate a few questions and she responded as best she could. The one question they both came back to was how to find him. Sam asked, "Is it safe to assume he's not going by Markus Lamiere?"

Kate thought that was a safe assumption. "We know he's going by Knox with some of the women. Because we don't have all the case information from other countries, we can't say for sure that's what he uses every time. We know he's changing his appearance and we can only assume he's not going by his given name. He has money so he could get a new passport off the black market and change bank accounts and such. That would be easy enough to do but he might be cocky enough to think he doesn't need to do that. I think we should take some time today to canvass Edinburgh and speak to hotel staff, pubs, and shops and see if anyone has seen him based on the photo we have. We can also mention his name. I don't think we should go to the media with it quite yet."

It sounded like a good idea to everyone. "I can look more into his background. I have a contact at Oxford and can inquire about his time there," Sam volunteered. "You never know he might have told some of his classmates about his plans without really telling them. Much like he told his sexual perversion to his stepbrother."

Kate thanked him. "The more information we have about his past the better."

"What about his home in Paris?" Fraser asked.

Declan said he had that. "I'm going to run down some of those leads today. I've made some initial calls this morning and I'm waiting to hear back. There was a law firm mentioned in his father's obituary. I assumed his estate might have been set up through them. They should be able to provide us with some information with some pressure applied."

"The French are tough," Fraser said with a sigh. "If you run into roadblocks there, let me know. I might have a contact or two that can help. In the meantime, I'll work with some of the shop owners I know to circulate the photo we have and get some people keeping an eye out."

Kate had one concern about that. "We don't want them to post the photo publicly or go to the media with it or his name yet."

"Understood. Given the circumstance, I think people will be more than willing to help however we ask them to help. We have the Christmas market starting this weekend and we are starting to get into a more heavy tourist time. Shops are already complaining that sales numbers are down from the previous year. If I can make them feel like they are helping us, they'll do whatever we ask."

It sounded to Kate like they had a solid plan for the day. "In the meantime, as we are running down those leads, I've had some hits off the TravelShip app that I'm going to explore. If I get lucky, I might connect directly with Markus that way. I'm also waiting for information about who could be feeding details to Markus about Leo's schedule. We can't rule out that this killer has an accomplice."

Fraser squinted his eyes and a worry line creased his forehead. "Kate, I want you to be careful with the app. I don't think you should meet anyone without all of us out there watching. He called you last night and threatened you. He might know exactly what you're doing."

Kate agreed with him and appreciated his concern. "I'll only be talking to them within the app for now. I'm fairly certain I can rule out a few matches on conversation alone. If I feel like anyone I'm speaking to is Markus or calls himself Knox, we can decide how we'll handle that. I won't do anything without the rest of you."

"I'm not saying the app isn't a good idea," he reiterated. "We want to make sure you're safe. Do you have any idea what Leo is going to do now? Will he back off? Will he allow us to use him to draw his stepbrother in?"

Kate and Declan had considered all of those questions last night. "Given Markus seems to be wanting to frame Leo for these crimes, I don't think he'll meet with him. I also think we'd be hard-pressed to get Leo to come close enough to risk being arrested."

Fraser raised an eyebrow. "He's been willing to meet with you."

"I seem to have built rapport with him. I think it's because he took me hostage and didn't hurt me in the process. He believes we have formed a kind of odd bond. The first time I saw him here, I couldn't arrest him. I didn't want to draw my weapon in the cemetery because there were tourists around and because of your gun policies here. I didn't think it was wise. From that, he thinks we are a team in this."

Fraser seemed to understand. "Do you think he will be an ongoing issue in this case?"

Define issue is what Kate wanted to say. Instead, she explained, "My biggest concern with Leo is that he will go after Markus on his own. If we have any chance of taking him in alive, then we need to get to him before Leo does."

"Sounds like either way it's a win," Sam said much to Fraser's chagrin. "I understand you don't want suspects being shot in Scotland by a civilian. It's not a good look, but you have to admit taking out this killer anyway possible is a win for Scotland and all of Europe."

"I'll concede that."

After the discussion died down, Fraser and Sam got up to leave with their plan for the day. Sam said he was going back to his hotel to make some calls and start the Oxford research. Fraser was going to hit the streets and start going shop to shop. Kate texted each of them the photo so they'd all have a copy.

When Kate and Declan were left alone in the room, he looked over at her. "That went better than I expected."

Kate could tell there was something more he wanted to say. He'd had the same look on his face since last night. She had noticed him a few times looking at her with this same expression of confusion and concern. "Declan, you've been dancing around something since we met at the gates of the cemetery. What do you want to know? Just ask me."

"It's silly, Kate. At least, I hope I'm being silly."

She had no idea what he was talking about. "Since when do we hide things from each other? You're concerned about something. Tell me what it is."

"Fine." He sat up straighter in the chair and focused on her. "Kate, I think you've been emotionally compromised by Leo. I thought you were being reckless with him for the sake of solving these murders. After watching the two of you last night, there was an intimacy between you."

"Intimacy?" Kate asked, her voice betraying her and rising an octave. "Are you suggesting I'm attracted to him?"

"I hadn't been until you just said that." He stared at her until Kate told him she wasn't attracted to him. She didn't sound convincing even to herself. Declan bypassed it and continued. "You're allowing him to breach the professional wall you normally have with people. He's calling you by your first name. He touched your hair. You sat so close to him I wondered if you were going to sit on his lap."

"Don't be ridiculous, Declan. It was cold last night. When he sat down on the curb, I sat next to him. I'm trying to build rapport with him. I don't like that he called me by my first name and that he knows where I live. I just..."

"He knows where you live?" Declan asked loudly, interrupting and not hiding his shock. "Why does he know where you live?"

"I don't know. I assume after our encounter in Paris, he might have researched me. I don't know if he knows the street address, but he referenced me being home in my brownstone in Boston." She went on even though Declan was staring at her as if she'd just admitted killing someone. "As per him touching my hair and the rest of it, yes, I've breached some professional barriers in this situation. He's an international criminal, Declan. The playbook is out the window. I can't force him to call me Agent Walsh and bark at him every time he says or does something I don't like. I'm trying desperately to get him to trust me and gain information from him."

"It's more than that, Kate, and we both know it. You're feeling bad for the guy. You heard his abuse and orphan story, which we don't even know is true, and you're feeling bad for him." Declan stared right at her and asked a question she'd been asking herself. "When the time comes, are you going to be able to set all of this aside and arrest him knowing he'll spend the rest of his life in prison?"

"Have I ever not done my job?"

"That's not an answer."

Declan was right, she had been compromised. She wasn't sure how it happened or why but she felt a pull toward Leo she couldn't explain. She had gone through a range of emotions trying to diagnose herself for her strange behavior. Kate came up blank. She had chalked it up to Stockholm syndrome. She had bonded with her captor during a high-stress situation and now she was having to rely on him to solve this case. A bond had been formed. But there was no way she was going to admit that to Declan.

Before he could respond to her question, her cellphone rang. She pulled it from her pocket and stared at the screen. Declan wasn't going to be happy about this call either. "It's Jax. He might have some information about who is betraying Leo from the inside."

"I'll leave," Declan said and stood. He looked over at Kate one last time while she answered the call. He shook his head in disgust as he walked out the door.

Kate knew he was upset but she couldn't deal with it right now. She had more important things to focus on if they were going to stop this killer.

CHAPTER 32

"Kate, where are you? I'm here in Edinburgh," Jax said as Kate answered the phone.

"I told you not to come, Jax. This isn't a good time." She looked toward the door wondering if Declan was standing on the other side or if he had gone for a walk. "I can't see you."

Jax wasn't going to take no for an answer. "You have to see me, Kate. I have information for you. I thought it would be better to deliver it in person. I'm at a hotel." He gave her the address. It wasn't far from her on the Royal Mile. "Can you meet me soon?"

Kate stalled, not sure what to tell him. She needed the information but she knew what he'd be expecting if she went to his hotel room. They had danced this dance before. They easily fell into bed every time they saw one another, but things had changed for Kate. Even if they were not seeing eye to eye right now, her feelings for Declan hadn't changed and anything with Jax would be a betrayal of that. Even going to his hotel room alone would only escalate the issues brewing with Declan.

Her decision had been made. "I can't meet with you at your hotel, Jax. Let's meet at a pub and we can discuss the information you have or you can come to the police station and meet with Declan and me."

"Kate," he said drawing out her name. "We haven't seen each other and I just thought…"

"I know what you thought, which is why I cannot meet you at the hotel." Kate dropped her voice low. "I'm involved with someone and we can't continue that part of our relationship."

"Who are you involved with?" Jax's tone was one of disbelief. He had known Kate for years and knew her work had kept her so busy that she didn't have time for dating. When Kate didn't respond right away, Jax guessed. "Is it Declan? Did the two of you finally decide to break all that sexual tension and do something about your weird relationship?"

Kate didn't know what to tell him. Obviously, he hadn't seen Billy's gossip magazine story about them. "I can't discuss this with you, Jax. I told you not to come here. If there's something related to the case you want to discuss, I can meet you at a pub. We can catch up over lunch."

Jax grumbled words Kate didn't understand. He cleared his throat. "I guess if lunch is all I'm going to get, I'll have to settle for it. The information I have will be valuable to your case, so I need to get it to you one way or another. I'd prefer not to have to see Declan. You know there is tension there."

Kate watched the door for his appearance. "I can meet you without Declan. That's not a problem. I'll text you the name of the pub and the time." She paused and turned her back to the door and dropped her voice low. "I appreciate your help, Jax. I'm sorry things have changed."

"Not as sorry as I am," he said before ending the call.

It seemed Kate was angering everyone. When she turned back around, Declan was standing in the doorway with a question on his face. Kate didn't want an argument. "Don't look at me like that. I'm not meeting him at his hotel. We are meeting at a pub. I'll get the information he has, have a quick lunch, and leave."

"Are you going alone?"

Kate sighed. She got up from the table and took a few steps toward him. "Would you like to come with me? You and Jax don't get along and I figured it was best if we avoided a confrontation. I have nothing to hide, so if you'd like to come along to meet with him, you can."

Declan smirked and ran a hand over his head. "I don't want to see him. I don't want you to see him either. I don't know why he couldn't give you the information over the phone." He paused for a beat. "Actually, strike that. I know why he didn't. I don't want you to *want* to see him."

Kate reached for his hand and he allowed her to take it. "I only want to see him long enough to get the information that could help solve this case. Jax and I are in the past – the long ago past when I didn't even think you were interested in me like that."

"I was always interested in you," he said with conviction. "You weren't interested in me."

Kate squeezed his hand harder. "If you hadn't been such a player back then, things might have been different. My only focus right now is hoping Jax isn't wasting my time, but we both know he has access into Leo's world. He helped last time and he might be able to help now."

Declan pulled her in for a hug and kissed the top of her head. "I didn't say I didn't trust you. I don't trust him." He breathed her in and then expelled an audible breath. "I feel like we've had a lot of tension on this case."

"Well, you accused me of being compromised by Leo." Kate pulled away from him and let her hand linger on his chest. "You better be careful with your accusations or I might get ideas in my head and ditch this FBI life for a life of international intrigue with Leo." Kate couldn't do anything but joke about it because what Declan had said was true. Saying it aloud sounded ridiculous. "When we finally take him down, I'll let you slap the cuffs on him."

Declan rolled his eyes at her and sat down at the conference table. "Bring me back lunch."

Kate promised to return with food for him. She walked the distance to the pub keeping an eye on her surroundings and the people passing by. Most were in coats, hats, and gloves. She tried to look at each of the faces of the men who passed. Kate assumed Markus must be hiding in plain sight and hoped she'd be able to recognize him when the time came.

Kate entered the pub and stopped close to the doorway to scan around the room to look for him. In the back of the pub facing the doorway sat Jax Talbert. He had the same chiseled jawline, dark hair that was a little too long, and a permanent grin plastered on his face like he was always in on the joke. Talbert stood closer to six-four and looked like he'd been spending serious time in the gym lifting weights. He had a way of living that always brought him right up to the line of illegality and too occasionally crowding it – not that he'd ever admit it. He had a rakish quality about him that drew Kate in time after time.

She squared her shoulders and walked through the pub to the table. "I'm glad you were willing to meet me here. Do you have the information?"

He laughed as his gaze roamed over her. "Just that like no kiss or lunch first? I feel used, Kate. I'm not a wham bam thank you ma'am kind of guy. If I'm remembering correctly, and you know I am, you like a little foreplay first." He rested his thick forearms on the table. "Actually, it all depends on your mood. I recall a time when..."

"Don't recall a time," Kate said sharply as her cheeks warmed. She pulled out the chair and sat. "Come on, Jax. I told you I'm not in the same place I was in Paris or even a few years ago when we met. I can't fall into bed with you. Please respect that."

Jax watched her. "You're in love."

Kate shook her head not because she wasn't but because there was a part of her that hadn't even admitted that to herself. She was still trying to stop herself from having deep romantic feelings for Declan.

"Love or not, I'm not going to betray someone important to me for a few minutes of passion with you."

Jax clutched his chest and groaned. "Kate, come on. It was more than a few minutes. I last longer than that. Don't speak those lies about me." That alone broke the tension between them. Jax laughed and that got Kate laughing too. "It is good to see you, even if you are only going to allow me lunch. Just know if you ever change your mind, I'm only a phone call away."

That's all it ever really was between them – a lot of phone calls and passionate sex when they could meet up. Emotions hadn't played too much of a part in the affair. Kate had to admit it was good to see him too. She had an easy rapport with Jax. There was none of the tension and complication she felt with Declan.

"I'm glad we got a chance to reconnect," she admitted easily. "Let's order lunch and then you can tell me why you're here. It better be more compelling than wanting me naked in your bed."

"Don't flirt with me." He hid his smile behind the menu but his eyes crinkled in the corner and Kate could tell that even if he wasn't going to get what he wanted from her, Jax was still going to help the case.

When they finished ordering, Jax leaned on the table. He glanced around and lowered his voice. "I only know him by Dimitar. He's Bulgarian and has been working with The Phantom since the start. He's tired of playing second fiddle and doesn't like a lot of the decisions that have been made recently. He wants out but he's going to bring the whole thing down with him when he goes. Whatever the Phantom is doing has set Dimitar on edge. It's opening up a power vacuum that Dimitar is willing to fill. I got word he's willing to speak to the FBI."

Kate had to walk a fine line with what she was able to tell Jax about the case and Leo. "Someone who has been working with the Phantom has been providing his schedule to the killer. Do you think that person could be Dimitar?"

"I assume if anyone knows his schedule, it would be him. He's taken over in the Phantom's absence." Jax paused for a moment and chose his words carefully. "I don't know if Dimitar has taken over because the Phantom put him there or because he rose to that height with the Phantom being gone. Since Paris, the man has been missing in action, Kate. Even when he was physically present, he wasn't himself. They don't know if he's lost his edge or if something more is going on. Is he still a suspect?"

That much Kate could disclose. "He's not the killer. Not only does he not fit the profile, but the information we uncovered suggests that the killer is targeting these women and killing them in lockstep with the Phantom's schedule to make it look like he's the one responsible. His motive is two-fold. Not only is he getting sexual pleasure from these crimes, but he's also seeking revenge on the Phantom."

Jax whistled loudly. "You've figured out that much. Do you know who it is?"

"We have some idea." She saw the question on his face. The man's name was already public to some but the connection back to Leo might never be made public. "His name, at least at birth, is Markus Lamiere. He's French and his father was a powerful and wealthy man. When the father died, Markus inherited all the money. We believe he's able to blend into any environment, change up his appearance, and with some of the victims, he's going by the name of Robbie Knox."

"Does that name mean anything?"

Kate told him the history of the name here in Scotland. "It's a sick connection but one that is probably giving him a laugh."

Jax cursed the evils that men do. "What is his connection to the Phantom?"

Kate couldn't disclose that. "We believe they had some association early in the Phantom's life. But as you know what's true or not about the Phantom remains to be seen. I don't know if the person sharing the Phantom's schedule is aware of what's being done with it or if they are an accomplice."

The server dropped off their food and glanced at Kate. She had overheard what Kate said but didn't react to it. Kate hoped the young woman wouldn't repeat what she had heard. When she walked away from the table, Jax continued. "From what I've heard, Dimitar isn't happy and hasn't been for a long time. If he thought he was working with someone to bring the Phantom down, I can see him doing that."

"This has been going on for more than a decade."

"Dimitar and the Phantom have worked together longer than that. He's willing to speak to you. If he isn't the guy, then maybe he can tell you who is."

Jax pulled a piece of paper from his shirt pocket and slid it over to Kate. "This is his number. He won't meet face to face. He'll speak to you though."

Kate wanted to tell Jax about meeting Leo but couldn't. She settled for a lingering question instead. "Have you ever heard any rumors about the Phantom and why he steals what he does? Is there a particular history behind the art he's taken?"

Jax popped a French fry in his mouth. "You heard about the Nazi lure?"

"Nazi?" Kate asked her tone indicating surprise. "I've never heard any rumors about the Phantom other than he is a master thief and prolific in his methods. There is also very little record of the art he's stolen. No one knows where it ends up."

"All of that is true," Jax said, taking a few bites of his fish. He washed it down with his beer. "There was a story that went around a long time ago that the Phantom was stealing back works of art that were stolen by the Nazis during WWII and giving them back to their rightful owners. The Nazis were prolific art thieves in their own right. While some of the art has been returned through governments, there are still more than thirty thousand pieces of art still missing from that time. The legend is the Phantom is settling the score. He's stolen other art to fund this work."

Kate's mouth hung open. "Could there be any truth to it?"

Jax sat back and appraised her. "Do you want to know what I think?"

Kate nodded a little too enthusiastically. He caught the look on her face and he cocked his head to the side in a question. "Come on, Jax, the man took me hostage. He could have killed me while he had the chance. I didn't get the sense from him that he's the bad guy he's been made out to be. If the legend is true, it confirms my instinct about him."

Jax made her wait several moments before he responded. Even taking a long sip of his beer. "I think it's true, Kate. I had contact with one man in Austria who was searching for three paintings his grandfather once had. One of the paintings was hanging in the Louvre. I put some feelers out and that painting was stolen within a year of my conversation with him and returned to his family. He came home from work one day and found it hanging in his living room. It had a short note in the corner that read: *Back home where it belongs.* About a month later, I heard a rumor the Phantom had stolen that painting. It's one of the crimes associated with him."

"It's hard to believe," she said but it wasn't having spent time with Leo.

"People aren't all good or all bad, Kate. Life is a lot of grey."

"I'm starting to see that." They finished the rest of their lunch catching up with each other. Kate ordered Declan's lunch and the two went their separate ways. She watched him walk off, grateful that he had shown up in person even if it had made things awkward with Declan.

CHAPTER 33

When Kate arrived back at the police station, she found Declan hunched over his computer having a conversation with someone over video chat. She quietly put his lunch on the table near him and pulled out a chair. She had decided for the sake of their relationship not to tell him about Jax's flirting and proposition.

She watched him across the table as he worked. There was a time when Declan was so difficult to work with and went rogue so often that no one wanted to be his partner. It had been in the early days when he hadn't had control of his temper, he was drinking far too much, and he made decisions in his own best interest and not in the best interest of the team. Kate wondered exactly when those roles had reversed. Now she was the one going rogue and convincing him to go along. *But was it rogue?* That was the question she kept coming back to.

Declan wrapped up the call and then closed the lid of his laptop. "You're back sooner than I thought you'd be. How was the meeting?"

"I told you I was only going to meet with him for the information."

"Did it end up needing to be in person or something he could have given you over the phone?"

Kate knew he was going to ask that question and there was no point in lying. "He could have told me. We're old friends, Declan. I'm not here often and he wanted to see me."

Declan sidestepped asking for details and went straight to the information. "What did he have for us?"

"A man by the name of Dimitar. He has stepped in while Leo has been gone. He has been dissatisfied with Leo for a long time and is willing to speak to us. I assume he's trying to fully take over and with Leo in prison that would be possible."

Declan considered that. "He'd never be willing to testify if that's the case."

Kate had considered it on the way back to the police station. "All I want to focus on right now is whether he knows who is sharing the man's schedule. If he wants to share information about Leo that's all the better. Prosecution we can worry about later." She pointed to his laptop. "What did you find out about Markus?"

Declan looked down at the notes. "The law firm wouldn't speak to me on the record. It took a few tries but I finally got one lawyer who I promised to keep off the record who told me that Markus was running his father's estate. I have an address for him, but I was told he's never there. He travels quite extensively for business. When I pressed him about the business, he wouldn't say. I got the sense he didn't know. He said that Markus is a weird guy and the law firm had threatened to drop him as a client. When I asked why, he wouldn't say. I even went as far as to mention Markus might be a person of interest in these murders and he told me he wouldn't be surprised."

"That's a condemnation if I ever heard one. I can't imagine anyone agreeing someone could be a serial killer if they hadn't already engaged in some strange behavior." Declan had garnered more information from the law firm than Kate would have thought. "Did you call the house where he lives?"

"I did," Declan said. "I asked to speak with Markus and was told he wasn't there. This confirms he uses that name at his home in France.

I spoke with the house manager and was told he wasn't sure when Markus would be back. He was gone and only occasionally showed up. He'd be there for a few days and then gone again. That's not to say he doesn't use an alias in places where he isn't known."

"Did you ask if they keep a schedule?"

"They do not, unfortunately. I don't think they'd share it with me anyway. I tried to ask a few other questions about his behavior, but that's when the house manager shut down. He said he couldn't speak about his boss and that was that. He hung up before I could ask anything further."

"Sounds like he might have some idea about him." Kate considered the limited options they had. "Do you think there's any way the French would allow us to search the residence?"

Declan shook his head. "I was speaking to a prosecutor when you came in. He said there is no way based on the information we currently have. While France doesn't have the same kind of search warrant provisions we have, it's still unlikely we'd get authorization, particularly because the police there never identified a suspect in their cases. They aren't going to let us come in and search the home of a prestigious family in France."

Kate sat down across from him. "I know Lucien Lamiere was wealthy, but what do you mean prestigious?"

"The prosecutor I spoke to knew the family," Declan said evenly. When he saw the look of surprise on Kate's face, he said, "Lucien Lamiere was philanthropic, sat on several high-profile boards, and made quite the name for himself. He was heavily involved in the arts and with a few schools. He made a real splash on the society circuit. I asked about his marriage and children. I was told there was a wife a long time ago but she died. He speculated that there were two sons but the woman's son went to live with relatives and Lucien's son is Markus. If that other son is Leo then we just confirmed something he told us."

"We can't be sure though," Kate said now surprising Declan. "I haven't been so taken in by him that I fully believe everything he tells me. It was a nice story, but it doesn't mean it's true. He could have known Markus another way and still used the last name for access. Did he remember the woman or the son's name?"

"Elena was the second wife to Lucien. He couldn't remember a last name but it's more than we had. I'm sure we can find more in the records. We have to assume Leo isn't his real first name."

"It might have been something Lucien called him or one of his many aliases." Kate had never thought that was the man's name. She had assumed he lied to her. She had something else on her mind though. "Bulgaria sided with Germany in World War II, right?"

Declan squinted at her and smiled. "Since when do I know much about history? What does it matter?"

Kate knew he was lying. She was pretty sure he had taken many history classes at Boston College. He might have played dumb occasionally but Declan had been an excellent student. He had to be to get into the FBI Academy. "Nothing important right now."

He watched her for a few more seconds, knowing she was keeping something from him. "They were part of the Axis powers with Germany." Declan paused to see if she'd respond and then he shrugged when she didn't explain. "None of this helps us locate Markus. I think it was important that we confirmed what Leo said. That's one more step in the process. He knows the man whether he was his stepbrother or not. There is a connection there. Give Dimitar a call and see what he says."

Kate had no idea where Dimitar was in the world, so there was no way to calculate a time difference. Either he answered or he didn't. She punched the numbers into her cellphone and listened while it rang. It went on for so long that she thought there was no voicemail and no one would answer. Kate was just about to hang up when a deep male voice gave a guttural grunt instead of a hello. Kate asked for Dimitar and the man grunted a yes.

Kate introduced herself and Declan. "I was told you were willing to speak to me about the man known globally as the Phantom."

"Yes," he said giving nothing else.

"What is it you can tell me about him?"

"What do I get in exchange?"

Kate wasn't authorized to give him anything, especially if she wasn't arresting him. That's the only way they would barter with him. "We aren't offering you anything. You've been allowed to have this conversation with us in anonymity, but unless you are turning yourself in for the crimes you've both committed, there is nothing we can offer you."

"Then I'll tell you nothing and handle it on my own."

"Handle what?" Kate asked her concern notching up.

"The Phantom has had his time. He's done it his way and now it's my time. I will get rid of him if he stands in my way."

Declan cleared his throat. "You can't threaten to kill someone while on the phone with the FBI." Kate glanced up at him and Declan shrugged. They knew nothing they would say would matter to the man.

As expected, Dimitar only laughed. "You cannot stop me just as you could not stop him. He's so self-righteous and noble. His time is over."

Kate tried a different tactic. "He took me hostage in Paris. Do you remember that?"

Dimitar dared to laugh. "You know so little for an FBI agent. I wanted to kill you and he wouldn't let me. I saw you on the street and it was my idea to take you hostage. I said you were our ticket out. I was going to kill you at the end but he got to you first. Even when you were on that rooftop, I had a clean shot and he kept blocking you with his body. That's how soft he has become – a fool. He can no longer run this operation."

Kate and Declan shared a look. She was alive because Leo had protected her. Even taking her hostage might have been an act of protection. He had told her the truth. "It's clear you're not going to help us, Dimitar. I only have one question. Have you or anyone else shared the Phantom's schedule – what countries he's gone to and when? This is important for another case we have."

Dimitar was silent for the first time on the other end of the phone. Gone was the bravado that he'd once had. "What does this have to do with anything?" He asked a question he already knew the answer to. Kate could hear it in his tone. He'd been surprised by the question.

Declan leaned toward the phone. "I'm going to take your silence as a yes. I'm also going to take your silence and the hesitation in your question to indicate that you know what is being done with the Phantom's schedule." Declan raised his eyes to Kate. "I guess that's one way to get rid of him."

"How do you know that it's not him killing those women? I told you he's gotten unstable. He's not making rational decisions."

Kate felt loyalty to Leo now that she knew he had protected her. "We know he did not kill those women. We also know now by your admission that you are an accomplice to these crimes. Trust me, Dimitar, I'm going to find you and arrest you."

He laughed a deep guttural growl. "I could have killed you before and I can do it again. Find the Phantom and arrest him. Get him out of my way and the murder will stop. I will take care of the killer myself."

"We asked for information and you refused to give it," Declan reminded him. "You've also admitted again to knowing the killer. Who is it?"

Dimitar fell into silence again. For an international criminal, he wasn't as smart as Kate thought he'd be. She pressed him. "Dimitar, we have enough evidence to arrest you and put you in prison for the rest of your life. If you want to have any bartering chance when I find you, it's best to help me now."

"Leo Lamiere. You find him and you'll have found the Phantom."

"What about the killer?" Kate asked but the call had already ended.

Declan pointed at the phone. "His story doesn't make any sense, Kate."

"What do you mean?"

"If he's been helping Markus for a decade, then he's not recently frustrated with Leo. This hatred has been simmering for a long time."

"I agree with that. I need to discuss it with Leo and see what he thinks."

"Do you have a way to contact him?"

"He said he'd find me." Kate worried about what might happen in the meantime. She also wondered, if Dimitar was that frustrated and had played such a long game, why he just didn't kill Leo and save himself all the trouble. There were too many missing pieces for it to make sense. She said that to Declan.

"You need to speak to Jax," Declan said, stunning Kate into silence. He stood from the table. "Hear me out, Kate. He connected us to Dimitar. He told you information about Leo being missing in action and that his crew was getting frustrated. He knows more than he's telling you and has been holding back for a long time. When it was art at stake, we could let it slide. Now real lives are in danger."

Kate took an audible breath. She knew he was right. She also knew this was the time to come clean with everything she knew. "We can talk to him. There's something I need to tell you first. I didn't tell you everything Jax told me."

"That was obvious by your out-of-context World War II question." Declan didn't sit back down. He gestured for her to get on with it.

"Jax said part of the legend of the Phantom is that he's stealing stolen

Nazi art and returning it to the rightful owners. He's stolen other art to fund this work. Jax told me a story about a man who had his family's artwork returned to him and the Phantom received nothing in return. Now hearing Leo held me hostage to protect me from Dimitar, I don't know what to think about it all. The person we thought the Phantom was is much more complicated than when we first got involved in that case."

Declan seemed to take the information and Kate's admission in stride. "This is all the more reason we need to speak to Jax. He's in that world, Kate. He knows far more than we do. Did you mention the name Markus Lamiere when you met him the first time?"

Kate shook her head. "I didn't say anything. I wasn't sure how much information I should share. I didn't tell him about meeting Leo either. He was still calling him the Phantom."

"I don't think we should mention we have a communication channel with Leo. I do think we need to see how Jax reacts to Markus Lamiere."

Kate got up from the table. "Try to go easy on him when we get there. I don't think he's hiding anything purposefully."

"We'll see how he reacts," Declan said with a mischievous smile. "If I have to rough him up, then that's what happens."

Kate sighed and closed her eyes. This was not going to go well.

CHAPTER 34

Kate had to text Jax to get his room number. All she told him was that she had a few more questions and that she'd be there soon. He seemed far too excited about her visit.

"Did you tell him I was coming with you?" Declan asked as they entered the hotel and headed for the elevator.

"No. I didn't think he'd see us."

"Good. I do love a surprise." Declan looked over at her. "Plus, he's probably getting himself all worked up thinking you're going to sleep with him. I'm going to be excited to see his disappointment." Declan stepped into the elevator with a smug grin on his face and hit the button for the sixth floor.

Kate knew before they got to Jax she had to be honest with Declan. "Jax asked me why I wasn't going to sleep with him. I told him I was involved with someone and I'd never be disrespectful like that."

Declan shifted his eyes toward her. "You told him you were involved with someone?"

Kate turned her body to his. "I figured since you told me what you wanted the other night that we were involved. You didn't exactly ask me on a date or anything but you know…" It was hard for her to say the words. This was about as close as she was going to get to telling him how she felt about him.

"Involved," he said, repeating her word. "I can live with that." He bumped his hip into her side and smiled down at her. "Just remember you said it first."

Kate's cheeks warmed. "Let's focus on work. Try not to scare Jax. I think he's a little afraid of you."

Declan shrugged. "He should be, especially if he ever tries to sleep with you again."

"Settle down." Kate wasn't sure how she felt about his little jealous streak. Half the time she thought he was kidding, but he'd always been this way with her. It didn't bother her and he wasn't controlling about it. He was just good at expressing his displeasure with something.

By the time they made it down the hall to Jax's room, they had game faces on and were ready to get down to business. Declan was going to take the lead. He knocked once on the door and Jax called that he was coming.

A moment later, Jax pulled open the door with a bright smile on his face that quickly fell to a look of confusion and then one of disappointment. "I didn't know you'd be joining us, Declan." He didn't miss a beat though. Jax stepped out of the way to let them in and gestured toward the small sitting room to the left. "Kate, you said you had some questions. Were you able to speak to Dimitar?"

Kate could hear the edge in his tone. He wasn't happy to see Declan, but he wasn't going to show him that. Kate knew she'd hear about it later. "That's why we're here, Jax. I spoke to him and he was useless. He seemed to be under the impression we'd be offering something for the information. He ended up telling us the Phantom's name, which we already knew."

Jax didn't hide his surprise. "You already knew the Phantom's name?"

"Kate's been in contact with him and has spoken to him a few times," Declan said as he sat.

Kate offered Jax a half-hearted shrug. "You know there are things about investigations I can't share."

"That's a pretty big secret, Kate. I can't believe you've met him. No one has except for a few members of the Curators."

Kate got the sense Leo wasn't living as low profile as most people thought he was. His superpower was living among society and blending in. "We had to rule him out of these murders. All signs pointed to him. He's been missing in action because he's been tracking this killer too. He's not why we're here though."

Before Jax could respond, Declan locked his gaze on him. The two men held steady eye contact, neither looking away. "We need to know how you know Dimitar. He's now a subject of our investigation."

"Subject? You think he's killing these women?"

Declan didn't mince words. "We believe he's an accomplice to the killer, ensuring it looks like the Phantom is the one responsible. We need to understand what else you may know about him and the Curators. You can start with your connection to Dimitar and how you got his phone number."

Jax looked at Kate. "Do I need a lawyer? Is this an interrogation?" His tone might have been tinged with concern but his body language betrayed him. Jax sat on the arm of the oversized chair like he didn't have a care in the world.

Declan noticed it too. "If you haven't done anything wrong, you don't need a lawyer. We are trying to understand what you know about Dimitar?"

Jax turned his attention away from Declan. "Kate, I swear to you, I didn't even know Dimitar's name until you asked me what information I could find. You came to me, remember? I called a few contacts for someone who'd be willing to speak to you. I'm feeling a bit blindsided. I thought I was helping you."

"You were helping us," Kate said, trying to hide the pity she felt for him. She had indeed gotten him into this mess. "We aren't discounting that, Jax. You've been in the art world a long time, but I know because of our relationship you might not tell me everything. I know you haven't wanted to put me in an awkward situation. Things have changed. This isn't about art anymore. Women are being murdered and have been for more than a decade. We must stop this killer. I need to know what you know."

Jax shook his head and stumbled over his words. "Kate, please. I don't know anything about it. What is it you think I know?" He looked between Kate and Declan and it was clear the level of seriousness he was facing. He relaxed his body as if it deflated. "I know a guy not in the Curators who has on occasion helped them sell what they have stolen. He had contact with someone who gave up Dimitar's first name or the name he was using. I don't even know if that's his name, Kate. You have to believe that. I'm not in any way directly connected to these people. I don't know any more than that. I told you all I know is rumors. I had heard rumblings the Phantom was missing in action and they were getting tired of it. Some were breaking ranks. I didn't know any more than that."

Declan didn't let up. "What about Markus Lamiere? Do you know him?"

There was a flicker of recognition in Jax's eyes. "From Paris?"

Declan shared a look with Kate and then focused on Jax. "Yes, from Paris. How do you know him?"

"I've sold him some art. His father was a client of mine toward the end of his life and then his son took over the estate. I brokered several deals – all legal," he stressed the last word. "What does he have to do with anything?"

"Have you met him in person?" Kate asked, drawing his attention to her.

"A handful of times."

"What does he look like?"

"He's about five-foot-eleven, medium build, dark hair, and brown eyes. He's not unattractive but he's not going to command a room either."

Declan pressed him. "What about his demeanor?"

Jax seemed to be catching on to it now. "He's like his father – arrogant and entitled and prone to fits of rage when he doesn't get his way." Jax frowned at Kate in confusion, pleading for more information with just a look. "What does this have to do with the case? How does Markus fit in?"

"We believe the killer is Markus Lamiere," Declan said without missing a beat. "Do you have his phone number? I need you to contact him."

Jax stood from the chair, his agitation on full display. "What do you mean Markus is the killer? If that's true, I want nothing to do with him. I'm not going to call him."

"You're going to call him," Declan said standing. He took a few steps toward Jax who backed up. "If you think he'd be willing to meet with you, we can bring him into custody. We are not able to find him. This may be a way."

Jax furiously shook his head. "You can't send me out there alone to meet a killer."

Kate said his name once and then twice, softer the second time. "We aren't going to put you in any danger. We will be there watching you. You don't need to do anything other than have the conversation you normally have. We need to draw him out. Call or text him, whatever way you normally communicate. Tell him you might have something he'd be interested in and see if he's willing to meet. Ask him where he is and then tell him you're in London and see what he says. If he shows up, you're not even going to have to sit with him for five minutes, we will swoop in, and arrest him."

Even though that's what Kate wanted to do, she knew because he left no evidence behind that they had nothing more than a photo of him with the victim. That was the only real evidence they had connecting him to the case. They had nothing but grainy images and a sketch from an eyewitness. It was a poor circumstantial case at best.

"Call him right now," Declan urged. He advanced on Jax and stood toe to toe with him. "We aren't playing around, Jax. We will keep you safe."

"No," Jax said, looking over at Kate. "I'm not going to risk my life for this."

Declan pulled out his phone and showed Jax a photo. "Look at her, Jax. That's what he did to the last victim. Do you want to be responsible for this happening to someone else? You alone have the power to help us catch him. Don't wimp out now."

Kate could see Declan's rough approach wasn't working. She touched Declan's arm and pulled him back. She stepped in between them. "Jax, listen to me. We are doing everything we can to stop him. He has been killing across Europe and Brazil for a decade. He's showing no signs of stopping. You have to help us. All we need you to do is set up a meeting and signal that it's him when he shows up. You can do that. I know you can."

Declan waited for Jax to respond and when he didn't, he asked, "When was the last time you spoke to him?"

"A couple of months ago. He had asked me to keep my eye out for some Chinese pottery from the Ming Dynasty. His father had an extensive collection and he was hoping to find more."

"Did you ever find it?"

"Not yet." Jax swallowed hard and looked around the room but didn't seem to focus on anything. "I've been checking auctions and private collectors but so far nothing has come up that would be of interest to him."

"He's waiting for your call then," Declan said evenly. "It sounds to me like that's the perfect cover for you. You give him a call and tell him you found a few pieces he'd be interested in. Tell him it's a delicate matter and you need to meet him in person to discuss it."

Jax rubbed his hands together nervously and then wiped them down his thighs. "I can do that. Where should I tell him to meet?"

"Ask him where he is and tell him you're in London but that you're heading north for another meeting. Just see what he says. If we have to apprehend him in London that's what we'll do. We will meet him wherever he wants to." Declan looked to Kate for confirmation and she nodded.

Kate touched his arm. "We want to make this as easy as possible for you. We don't even need you to wear a wire or anything like that. We need him to show up and that's it."

Jax didn't respond to Kate. His expression was one of shock but resignation. He left the room explaining he needed to get his cellphone.

When he was gone, Declan looked over at her. "Do you think he's going to be okay?"

Kate wasn't sure. She'd never seen Jax anything other than confident and too sure of himself, bordering on arrogance. "It either works or it doesn't."

Jax came back carrying his phone. "Do you want me to do this on speakerphone so you can listen in?"

Declan pointed to the coffee table. "Put it down there and call him. We'll stay quiet. Remember you've spoken to him countless times before. The only goal is to get him in person as quickly as he's willing to meet. Apply a little pressure if you have to."

Jax hit the speakerphone button as the phone started to ring. He put the phone where Declan told him as the call engaged. A man with a posh British accent gave a cheery hello. "Hi Markus, it's Jax. I have some news on the Ming pottery you've been seeking."

"Excellent news. How long before you can acquire it?"

"I can get it to you within the week but there's a catch. It's a sale by a private owner and he has some documents he wants the buyer to sign. You know how picky some of these sellers can be. Anyway, I'm here in London but heading north soon. Is there any chance you can meet up today or tomorrow? We're on a tight deadline and the items will go quickly."

There was no hesitation in the response. "I'm in Edinburgh. Is there any chance you're headed this way? I can come south if you need me to."

"I can be there this evening. What do you say eight o'clock?" They went back and forth briefly about where to meet before deciding on a pub a few blocks off the Royal Mile. By the time the call ended, Jax had beads of sweat forming on his brow. He looked up at Kate and Declan. "I hope you know what you're doing because that didn't sound like a serial killer to me."

Without missing a beat, Kate said, "That's exactly why he's been getting away with this for so long. Let's get you ready for tonight."

CHAPTER 35

At a quarter to eight that night, Kate watched from a nearby park bench as Jax moved toward the pub. There were a few plainclothes officers inside waiting for him, and Sam, Fraser, and Declan were positioned outside of the pub. The last thing they wanted was for Markus to see any of them and be spooked.

Once Jax took his seat, Kate had a perfect view of him through a large window near his table. He had chosen it purposefully. They had scoped out the pub earlier and ran through the plan with him. They had not alerted the staff inside of the pub about what was going to happen because the fewer people who knew the better and the less chance Markus could be alerted. They had no idea who he knew in the city. Kate assumed he'd been there for some time and had probably gotten to know a handful of people.

She checked the time on her phone. Markus had four minutes to get there if he was going to make it on time. Kate had given Jax a pep talk on their walk to the pub earlier. Declan had told her to go alone with him and psych him up for it. She had expected Jax to be angry with her and an argument to ensue when they were alone, but he correctly sensed the gravity of the situation.

Once they saw the pub and he had a better lay of the land, they walked around the nearby park together where Kate was sitting now. Jax had promised her he'd do everything he could to help. He had been embarrassed that he had to be talked into the task and apologized for his cowardice. Kate let him off the hook, explaining she was sorry she had dragged him into the case. Their relationship for what it was had been repaired by the end of the walk.

Jax sat at the table staring down at the menu and would glance up when someone passed by his table. He licked his lips a few times and took generous sips of water.

"What are we watching?" Leo said as he came around to the front of the bench. He sat down next to her uninvited. "Do you think it's safe for you to be sitting out here alone?"

Kate wanted to say she was surprised to see him but she wasn't. She assumed he had been watching her. "Do you know that man in the pub?" she asked, gesturing toward the window.

Leo leaned forward and stared across the grass. "Jax Talbert. He's an art and antiquities dealer. Why are you watching him?"

Kate didn't see any reason not to tell Leo the plan. "It turns out Jax has worked for Markus, and Lucien before his death. He called Markus tonight and told him he came across some Ming pottery. Jax lied and said there was some paperwork Markus had to sign for the private collector before the purchase could be made."

Leo cracked a smile and the corners of his eyes crinkled up. "It's a good ruse but Markus isn't going to fall for it."

Kate turned her head to him. "How do you know?"

"He's smarter than that."

"He told Jax he was in Edinburgh. Jax said he'd meet with him anywhere from here to London. He'd have no way of knowing it's a setup." Kate studied his face. The cemetery had been dark but the streetlight wasn't far from where they were sitting and she could see his face more clearly now. Kate hated to admit it but he was a handsome man. She had thought that the first time she saw his face at the café in Paris before he took her hostage. "There are cops all around us, Leo. You're taking a risk by being here."

"No one is paying attention to me. I look like some complication on a bench near you. Besides, from where they are positioned, I'm not sure they can see us talking. All eyes are on poor Jax in there. I'm surprised he has the stomach for such a thing."

Kate thought back to Jax's initial reaction. "Do you know him?"

"The art dealing world is small, Kate. Jax knows me as another art dealer – Leo Lamiere. He does not know me as the Phantom."

"I mentioned Markus Lamiere and he never connected the two of you."

"He wouldn't. It's a common enough name and has opened doors for me. I use Lucien's name when it suits me and the situation. I've never connected the dots for Jax."

Kate turned to him not hiding the surprise on her face. "You're not hiding away in some cave and then creeping out at night to steal art? They called you the Phantom for a reason."

Leo had a good belly chuckle. "Is that what you thought? That I'm spending my life hiding away?" He shook his head. "I have legitimate work. I've had a lifetime of traction out of this identity. I'm going to have to make a change after this is all over."

"Leo is not your birth name?" Kate asked, even though she had already assumed it wasn't.

"No. I don't use that name and haven't for a long time. Jordan and his family knew me as Leo. I said I had no last name. Sometime later, I started using Lamiere. I might have hated Lucien but as I said his name opened doors for me." Leo stared straight ahead. "It doesn't look like he's going to show, Kate. I'm telling you Markus isn't stupid. Look how long he's been getting away with this. I'm sure he's tied Jax back to you."

"To me personally?" Kate asked, the inflection in her tone giving her away.

"That guy?" Leo asked with a laugh. "Kate, please tell me you have not been with him. I might lose all respect for you." He lowered his head and angled it so she could see that he was teasing her.

"It was a fling," Kate admitted, even though she wasn't sure why. She found herself having a tingle of feeling for Leo she shouldn't.

"Even a fling wasn't the best choice, but I guess I can let it slide." Leo sat back on the bench and stretched his arms out wide, his hand resting near her shoulder. "What's your favorite painting?"

Kate didn't have refined taste in art the way she was sure he did. She was almost embarrassed to say. "I know it's a little cliché but I've always loved *Café Terrace at Night* by Van Gogh. I had a poster of it when I was in college. I could stare at it for hours imagining myself at the table watching the world go by."

"It's a serene image. I can imagine you there too."

Kate focused her attention back on Jax and then checked her phone.

"I told you, Kate. He's not coming."

Kate texted Declan that she would meet him when she was done. She explained Leo had shown up and she was going to tell him about Dimitar. Kate knew just by telling him that he'd hang around and wait for her. He might be able to see her from his position.

"I haven't found out much of anything, Kate," Leo said, drawing her attention away from her phone. "I spoke to the staff at the Lamiere estate but they have no idea where he is. I had a contact dig around in Markus's banking information and credit card and there's been no activity. I'm assuming he's traveling under a fake passport and has other financial resources in whatever name he's using."

Kate put her phone in her pocket. "You were able to do all of that? We don't have enough for any kind of warrant. Even if we got the information by other means, it wouldn't stand up in court."

Leo brushed her hair off her shoulder and she didn't stop him. "I told you before he's not going to court. Markus wouldn't be able to stand one day in prison. He's going to make you kill him if it comes to taking him in. Even if you manage to arrest him, he'll kill himself once he's on the inside. He's not built for confinement." He sighed long and deep. "Neither of us are."

Kate ignored the implication. "I found out who's sharing your schedule."

Leo turned sharply to her. "Who is it?"

She angled her body so they were facing each other. "I assume I wasn't given his real name. Maybe you'll know the alias. He called himself Dimitar." Kate watched his face for recognition but none came. "Maybe it will help if I told you the man I spoke to admitted to wanting to kidnap and kill me in Paris. He said you kidnapped me to keep me safe, and on the rooftop you kept putting your body in front of mine so he wouldn't shoot me."

"He told you all that," Leo said and cleared his throat.

"Is it true?" Kate watched him closely. When he didn't respond, she told him the rest. "He said he's been trying to get you out of the way for a long time. It sounded like this wasn't the first thing he tried. I don't know how he got hooked up with Markus. I believe he's an accomplice in these murders. He knew what was going on and wanted you to take the fall for it. I don't think he meant for it to take quite this long. I don't understand why he'd be so patient if he wanted you gone. I'm missing something I was hoping you'd clear up for me."

Leo sat straighter on the bench and turned away from her. "His name isn't Dimitar. I know who you're talking about though."

"Will you tell me his name? I need to bring him in."

"That's not how it works. You'll never catch him. I have to handle that on my own."

"He's going to try to kill you."

"I'm sure he will try but I'll get to him first."

"You can't tell me you're going to kill someone, Leo," Kate said, trying to control her breath. She could tell he was more hurt by the news than he was angry. "Who is he to you?"

"Someone I took in who had nowhere else to go. I knew he wasn't happy. I told him more than once he could go. He didn't owe me anything. The only caveat was he wouldn't reveal anything about…"

"The Curators," Kate said, finishing his sentence. When Leo didn't respond, she said, "He told me your name is Leo Lamiere. He was still trying to convince me you killed the women. He tried to barter information for money or favors. He didn't want to give up any information for free."

"He wouldn't, Kate. Not out of any loyalty to me but because he's a psychopath." Leo turned to her then. "Look at me, Kate."

Their eyes met in a steady stare. "You have to be careful. The man who calls himself Dimitar is far more dangerous than Markus could think of being. I thought I had him contained but I see I don't. Maybe I never did and I was deluding myself. I have more of a mess to clean up than I initially thought."

"You don't have to do this on your own, Leo. Let the FBI handle it. Give us a name and we'll bring him in."

"You won't be able to, Kate. If I thought you could safely get to him, I'd gladly turn him over to you. This is a choice I made a long time ago and it's come back to bite me now."

"How did you meet?" Kate wasn't sure what to ask. She wanted to keep him talking in the hopes of finding out something she could use to find him.

Leo pulled his cap lower over his forehead. "He was young, running the streets, hurting people, and I thought I could reform him. I sent him to school and thought an education might help. I thought structure might help. When none of that worked, I let him work with me to keep him close. I thought I could contain the rage that burned inside him. He hasn't been playing the long game with Markus, Kate.

He's an accomplice fulfilling some sick fantasy in these murders. I think he's using Markus as much as Markus is using him. He wants power and to dominate people. I wouldn't be surprised if Markus is sharing the details of the murders with him. I honestly thought I had him contained. Now I know he's been playing me the whole time."

Kate wasn't surprised by the news. "How do we stop them? If I don't know who Dimitar is or where I can find him, I can't stop him. If Markus doesn't show up here now, I don't know how we stop him. You haven't had much luck finding Markus. He can't run forever. Have you tried to call him?"

"Over and over again. I haven't said anything about the murders in the hopes he'd meet with me. Nothing has worked. I assume he knows we know he's committing these murders." Leo looked back at the pub. Slowly, he inched forward and pointed. "Jax isn't alone. There's someone at the table with him."

Kate peered over at the pub. Jax had his head down reading from a piece of paper. The man sitting across from him had a hat on, the hood of his sweatshirt up, and his arms resting on the table. She watched as Jax's features turned from confusion to fear.

He dropped the paper and stood up abruptly, knocking over his chair. All at once, four plainclothes cops rushed the table. Kate turned back to Leo but the space where he once sat was empty. She left her position in a run toward the pub and got to the door as Declan and Sam walked the hooded man out of the bar.

"It's not Markus, Kate. He sent someone with a message," Declan said as he stopped in front of her. He reached up and tugged the man's hood off to reveal someone who didn't look like the photo of Markus. Kate studied his face and reached her hand out to touch it. She felt his short blond hair and tugged on it once to make sure it wasn't a wig and felt the contours of his face.

"I'm not him, lady," the man shouted at her in a Scottish accent so thick Kate had to focus to understand him. "I told them some guy paid me to bring a note to that guy in there. You can't arrest me for that. I didn't even read the note."

"We're going to interview him," Sam said and then hitched his thumb over his shoulder. "You better go in and talk to Jax. He's freaking out about the note."

Kate looked up at Declan with her eyes wide in a question.

"Go in, Kate. We got him into this. I can take care of this guy," Declan said as he pushed the man forward. He continued to shout that he'd done nothing wrong and they had no reason to hold him. That may be true but he wasn't going anywhere until he was properly interviewed.

Kate trusted Fraser, Sam, and Declan to do that. She walked into the pub to find Jax sitting in a chair surrounded by the four cops. They parted to the side as she approached.

Jax's eyes were wide and full of fear. With a shaky hand, he gave her the note. "He's going to kill me, Kate."

Kate lowered her head, unfolded the piece of paper, and read it as she absorbed Jax's fear. *You betrayed me and now you must die.*

CHAPTER 36

Kate waited as Jax raced around his hotel room, throwing his clothes and other personal items into his suitcase. She felt badly that this was how it went down. "Jax, I don't think he's going to kill you. We can always put you in protective custody until the case is over. We can make sure you're safe."

"No," he said sharply not looking at her. "You got me into this mess and I don't trust you or that idiot partner of yours to keep me safe."

Kate knew there was no point defending Declan or herself. Jax was rightly afraid and angry that he had helped the FBI.

Jax muttered to himself as he threw his unfolded clothes into the suitcase. He ripped shirts off hangers and chucked them in along with shoes and a belt. He went into the bathroom. "I came up here to see you, Kate. I missed you. I know that we haven't been able to have a normal relationship over the years with your travel and mine, but I honestly thought one day we'd get together. Now, you're telling me you're in love with someone else and then you try to get me killed. I mean simply breaking up with me would have done it. I didn't need to die."

Kate bit her lip as she listened to him rant. It wasn't a funny situation but she had never heard him go on and on like that. She had no idea that he had felt anything for her except friendship and occasional lust, which is how she would have summoned up her feelings for him. "I don't know what to say, Jax. We had fun with each other. I didn't know you felt that way. I figured you'd have found someone else by now."

"There's been lots of someone elses, Kate." He came out of the bathroom with a handful of toiletries that he dumped unceremoniously into his suitcase. Then he put his hands on his hips and turned to her. "You're infuriating."

There were no right words to say, so Kate stayed silent.

Jax looked over at her. "I almost loved you. Do you know that?" When Kate shook her head, he said it again. "Had we been able to spend a little more time together, date like normal people, I would have fallen in love with you."

"I'm sorry, Jax. I had no idea you felt that way about me."

"You're sweetly oblivious like that." He came over to her and took her hands in his and kissed her on the forehead. "I hope whatever man you're dumping me for is worth it."

"I'm hardly dumping you. We didn't have a thing for either of us to dump the other." Kate leaned against him then released his hands and hugged him. "For what it's worth, had things been different, I might have fallen in love with you too."

He groaned. "That's like a knife to the heart. If this guy ever does anything to hurt you or doesn't treat you how he should, call me. I'm pathetic enough to come running back." He kissed her again on the top of her head and then pushed himself away from her. "I mean it, Kate. One call and I'll come to you no matter where you are in the world."

"Where are you going?" Kate asked as he went back to his suitcase and zipped it closed.

"I have a few things I need to finish in London and then I'm getting out of Europe. I don't know where I'll go but..." He looked over at her and shrugged. "Now that we aren't going to be a thing, I have no reason to lie. I have a passport and credit cards under an alias I can use in times like this. I can get away for a time. I'll let you know where I am and you can tell me when he's captured or dead and I can return to my normal life."

Kate wasn't surprised by the passport or the credit cards. In his business, he ran across criminals and ruthless characters all the time. "I'll call you as soon as I know anything. Do you want an escort? I can send someone with you."

Jax shook his head as he pulled his suitcase up. He went over to her, kissed her again this time on the lips, and pulled her into him. "Please be safe. I know you know what you're doing and I know Declan will protect you. For Markus to turn on me like this, he's out of his mind."

"I am sorry I got you involved."

"I don't regret it, Kate. There's little good I do in the world. If I had been able to help you catch him, it would have been worth it. You have to stop him." He wheeled his suitcase toward the door as Kate walked with him. They made it down the elevator and outside where a cab was waiting for him.

Kate stood at the side of the car as he put his suitcase inside.

He turned back to her before getting in. "I don't want to be dramatic and act like I'm never going to see you again because I'm sure I will. I also know the idiot you're involved with is Declan." He held his hand up when she tried to deny it. "Kate, it's obvious just watching the two of you interact. So go figure out what's between you once and for all. When it all blows up, and we both know it will, let's give ourselves time to figure out what's between us."

Kate wasn't going to argue with him. In truth, she worried it was all going to blow up between Declan and her too. She wasn't going to admit that to Jax though. "I'll call you as soon as I know Markus is apprehended."

He got in the car, shut the door, and she waved to him once as the driver sped forward.

Alone on the street at night outside of the hotel, Kate stood there on the sidewalk for a moment. She pulled her jacket tighter around her knowing that evil lurked not far from her. She wondered if Markus or even Leo was watching her now.

Kate felt a mix of emotions about not feeling more conflicted about Leo's threats about killing the man who had called himself Dimitar. Kate knew in his world it was kill or be killed. If Dimitar was as bad as Leo had described and truly an accomplice to these murders, maybe it wasn't such a bad idea that he was taken out by any means possible. She knew even admitting that to herself meant that she was getting jaded in her job. She was a federal officer who had taken an oath to serve and protect. She shouldn't be thinking or worse hoping that Leo did the job for them.

Kate stood watching the cars and the foot traffic for a few minutes longer. She wasn't sure if she should go back to the police station or meet Declan at the apartment. Kate pulled her phone from her pocket as someone called her name.

"Agent Walsh, how are you doing this fine evening?"

Kate turned to see Logan approaching. "I'm well. How are you? Tours over?"

"Just finished one and walking to get a late dinner." He looked around the area. "Where is your partner?"

"He's wrapping up a few things and will be along shortly," Kate said absently as she checked her phone.

"I was going to call you but hadn't had a chance to see Vivian to get your phone number. I think I might have found a few names for you in our tour records. The office is closed now but I can get them to you tomorrow evening when I'm back from a tour. Would that work?"

Kate glanced up at him. "That would be great. I'm sure either Agent James or I will have a chance to get them from you. I appreciate your help with this."

He tipped his cap to her. "Anything to help you and this great city. We want to make sure all our visitors feel safe and have a wonderful experience. I'll be seeing you. Have a lovely night."

Kate watched him walk away and then focused her attention back on her phone. She finally had a few matches and initial messages from men on the TravelShip app.

One of them from a man calling himself Knox.

Kate's heart raced and she held her phone like it was burning her hand. She looked both ways before crossing the street and turned in the direction of the police station. She walked as quickly as she could, dodging people as she went.

Kate walked right into Declan. He gripped her arms to steady her. "What's the rush, Kate?"

She wanted to tell him but she wanted to know about the witness they were interviewing. "Did you get any information from him?"

"Nothing. He was sitting in a park about a half mile from the pub. A man approached him and paid him to deliver the note to Jax. That was it. The guy needed the money. He described Markus. When we showed him the photo, he positively identified him. I don't know how Markus got tipped off but he did. It wasn't anything that Jax did. He was perfect on the call." Declan looked across the street in the direction of the hotel. "Has he left?"

"He said he's going back to London and then will go somewhere else until we tell him the coast is clear."

Declan had a concerned look on his face. "He didn't want police protection?"

"No," Kate said definitively. "We got him into the mess and he didn't trust us to keep him safe."

He sighed loudly and ran a hand through his hair. "We still have nothing, Kate. This guy is still out there, one step ahead of us. He's probably lined up his next victim already."

Kate handed him her phone. "Check the TravelShip app. I finally got a hit from Knox. He's not using a photo in his profile, but he signed off the communication with Knox."

Declan took the phone and lowered his head to read the message. "He's got to know it's us, Kate. After what just happened with Jax, don't you think he knows you by now?"

Kate would think so but the photo didn't look like her. She had changed her age and her hair was different as well as her makeup. It had been good enough for an in person undercover gig. "I don't know. Does that photo look like me?"

Declan raised his head and smiled at her. "It's hard for me to tell because I know it's you." He pointed to the closest pub. "Let's try something and see." Before Kate could stop him, he walked into the pub and right up to the first man he saw. He stuck the phone in front of him and asked, "Does this woman look like the woman standing next to me?"

The man looked down at the photo, over at Kate, and then back down at the photo. "Maybe her sister." He handed the phone back to Declan.

Declan walked up to four more men and none of them could identify Kate as the woman in the photo. She trailed behind him humoring him and then when he went to another group of men, she grabbed a table and ordered them both a beer. She also ordered two orders of fish and chips. She was suddenly ravenous and wanted to eat even if it was going on ten at night.

Finally defeated, Declan came back to the table and sat down. He handed the phone back to her. "I guess no one knows it's you. After the threat to Jax, and the killer's phone call to you, I'm not sure I like the idea of you interacting with him. I'm sure even if the photos don't look the same, he must know its you on some level, Kate. I don't think he's going to fall for it."

Kate didn't like the idea of interacting with Markus either. If he knew it was her, she'd have the protection she needed but it might be enough to draw him out. If he didn't know, the same would apply and she'd have the element of surprise. "If he's focused on me, maybe there won't be another victim."

"What are you going to say?"

Kate opened the chat message Knox had started and responded. "I'm going to be friendly and flirty and a little forward. I'm telling him I don't like chatting and would much rather meet up for a drink at a local pub if he has the time." She glanced up at him. "Do you think that will scare him off?"

Declan shook his head. "If he knows it's you, he'll know what you're doing. If he doesn't and he's searching for his next victim, he'll want to meet. Either way you can't lose."

Kate didn't hesitate. She typed the message as she planned with Declan's blessing. It had been a long time since she'd had to be flirty and sweet and seem interested in a stranger. She showed him the message and he approved. Kate hit send and set her phone down next to her, practically holding her breath while she waited for a response.

In the meantime, when the server brought them beer and told them their food should be out soon, Declan thanked her and then looked over at Kate. "We're eating?"

"Aren't you hungry?"

"I was hungry about four hours ago. Now I'm starving," he said, reaching out and taking a sip of beer. "You don't normally take charge like this though."

Kate didn't know what he meant. "I take charge during cases all the time."

"Dinner isn't about the case."

"Are you complaining?" she asked with her eyes wide. She was feeling like maybe she had done something wrong. He wasn't usually one to complain.

Declan took another sip of his beer. "Not at all. You decided and I like it. What am I eating for dinner?"

"Fish and chips. Same as me." Kate leaned her arms on the table and watched him. Her emotions were a swirling mix making her feel uncharacteristically anxious. It's possible it was all about having matched with Knox on the app, but Declan was the one in front of her. "Jax figured out that it was you and he thinks it's going to blow up on us."

The corner of Declan's lip turned up in a smile. "Do we care what Jax thinks?"

Kate shook her head. "I think we need to talk about what happens when it does blow up."

"Maybe it won't, Kate. Maybe we can live happily ever after."

Kate laughed and was grateful for Declan's optimistic attitude. There was still much to talk about though, even if this wasn't the best time. "I don't believe in fairytales. Even if we get together and don't break up, there are going to be rough patches that we'll have to navigate differently than most couples because our lives are literally in each other's hands and we are already living together." Before he could respond, she added, "I don't want you to move out."

Declan took another sip of his beer and watched her over the rim of the glass. "I can't afford to move out. I could go live with one of my criminal brothers in South Boston. I don't think the FBI is going to like that."

Kate was on the verge of telling him he couldn't do that when her phone chimed. She picked it up and read the message. "He took the bait, Declan. He wants to meet tomorrow night at nine."

They exchanged a look across the table, knowing Kate was about to meet with one of the most prolific serial killers to have ever killed across Europe.

CHAPTER 37

The next day was a flurry of activity. Kate and Declan spent the morning checking in with Spade about the case, going over the cases again with Sam and Fraser, and planning for Kate's date with Knox. Nearly all of them were in disbelief that Kate could be speaking to the real Knox.

After dinner the night before, she had messaged Knox in the app quite late into the evening. Kate did a good job of pretending to be a tourist in Edinburgh for the first time. She talked about her extensive travels to other cities in Europe.

When Knox pressed her about what she did for work, Kate fell back to her standard lie of history teacher. She said she was taking time off because she was contemplating going back to school to get her PhD. Kate hadn't been expecting Knox to be so knowledgeable about American history, so it was good she had picked something where she had a depth of knowledge. It allowed him to mirror her and show off.

Kate shouldn't have been surprised by his conversational skills and his general knowledge base. If Knox was truly Markus, as they all believed, he was well educated at the best schools. As Leo had told her, Lucien had spent the time to educate them about a number of subjects.

Kate tried in different ways to try to figure out if it was Markus. She had asked about his upbringing, schooling, family, and siblings.

She tried to build a timeline of where he had traveled. At the end of the conversation, after they said goodnight, Kate went back through the messages and found Knox said nothing incriminating. There was nothing to tie him back to Markus or any of the other cases. This man's story was well rehearsed and solid.

The next morning when Kate and Declan arrived in the basement conference room, Sam and Fraser were frustrated by the lack of progress and were happy to hear that Kate had made a connection with Knox through the app.

They were worried about the logistics of the meeting and wondered if it would go bust like it had with Jax. The more they talked about it the more Sam and Declan were convinced that Knox was messing with them yet again and wouldn't show.

Fraser had been optimistic like Kate. Halfway through the day though, even he started to worry that it might not happen. None of them wanted to talk about the long-term plan if the killer wasn't caught in Edinburgh. All of them knew he'd leave and repeat the pattern in another city.

There could be many more victims to come.

Kate felt the weight of the case riding on her shoulders. By three o'clock that afternoon with no more leads to run down, they were ready to take a break. Kate needed to go back to the apartment and shower and change for later that night. She also needed to eat something, which she hadn't done all day because her stomach had been churning.

As she was gathering her things, Sam stopped her. "Kate, are you sure you want to do this?"

She raised her eyes to him. "It's our only option. We don't even have any more leads left."

"We can sit at Markus's house and wait. He's got to come back at some point."

Kate knew that would do no good. She had accepted the harsh reality of the situation that morning. She had not spoken it aloud yet. Kate sat down at the conference table and looked at the three of them. "The way I see it, we have a two-fold problem. We got lucky when Leo was able to identify Markus from that photo, but that's all we have. Does a Markus Lamiere exist? Yes, we know where he lives. We have some information on his background. A handful of people have confirmed he has some strange ways about him. He isn't home and he told Jax that he'd meet him in Edinburgh. Between the four of us, we have canvassed all we can, and can't find him. We have to assume he's also using an alias and has the passport and credit cards to match. Because we are in Scotland, he wouldn't even need a passport to come up from London, so there's something else we can't confirm. We can't locate him despite our best efforts."

Sam nodded along with her as she spoke. "We know that, Kate. What's the second problem?"

"We have no real evidence tying Markus to any of the murders. Sure, there are a few circumstantial things and Billy was able to get some sketches from witnesses. Even that evidence is shaky and he's an unreliable witness. It's multi-layered and the sketches didn't come from witnesses interviewed by law enforcement. There's no record of these witnesses or chain of custody. All we have as far as evidence in the cases here in Scotland are one witness who saw Markus with one of the victims and that photo. It's barely even circumstantial evidence."

Kate took a breath and looked at the three of them waiting to see if they'd connect the dots. When they didn't, she went on. "Let's talk then about where most of the information about Markus has come from – the man known as the Phantom. I mean thank God for him because without him, we wouldn't even have a name. We can't sideline the reality though. He's an international criminal wanted in twenty countries. Even if we can somehow manage to arrest him and

I convince him to testify, what does he really know? He has a story about a stepbrother who is trying to set him up for murder. Leo has lied his entire life. I don't even know what's true or not about him. He has massive credibility issues. Put him on the stand compared to Markus Lamiere, son of the great Lucien Lamiere, who was a wealthy, well-respected part of Paris society. We don't have a chance. We don't even have enough evidence to get a search warrant."

Declan widened his stance and folded his arms over his chest. "We know all this, Kate. It sounds to me like you've got something else on your mind."

Kate knew as soon as the words were out of her mouth, they'd all object. She had to tell them or they'd move in too quickly tonight. "It's likely if I'm messaging with Markus, he knows it's me. He called me and I'm sure he knows my identity even if I proved the photo in the app doesn't look like me. He will be expecting this kind of setup. We have to let him believe we are this desperate. I know he wants to kill me. He told me so. I have to let him attack me," she said keeping steady eye contact with Declan. "I have to play the victim right up to the point where he tries to murder me and only then can you move in and take him."

"Absolutely not," Fraser said and looked at Declan. "You cannot let her do that. What if we can't get to her in time?"

Declan didn't flinch and didn't look away from her. "Kate, you know what you're saying. You're going to allow him to take you away from our surveillance points. You're going to end up alone with him and you're going to allow him to put his hands on you. You're going to have to be intimate with him up to the point he snaps and tries to kill you. You understand that, right?"

"This is madness," Fraser shouted when he couldn't get Declan or Kate to look at him. He turned to Sam. "Please talk some sense into them."

Kate broke eye contact with Declan only long enough to look at Sam. "You know this is the only way. You know it is. If we can get him to act out the same ritual he's done in every other case, then we can tie all the cases here in Scotland together. We might never be able to prosecute those other cases, but we'd have him here. We'd know for sure and we'd have him then."

Sam's features were tight. "What if we can't get to you in time?"

"I'll have my gun and I can fight," Kate said, trying not to allow her voice to show how scared she was about the whole plan. It was the only scenario she could figure out that would give them any kind of chance to stop him. She had to sacrifice herself. "I can fight him off long enough for the three of you to rush in."

While Fraser muttered how insane the whole plan was, Sam considered it. After a few beats, he asked, "Are you sure this is the only way?"

"We either catch him here or this will continue for another decade or more. If he truly takes the bait tonight, this is the best way." Kate paused for effect. "It's the only way."

Sam looked over at Declan. "It's your call."

Declan remained quiet for several more moments until the tension rose so high in the air that Fraser left the room. Declan went to the table and sat across from her. "Kate, you know you don't have to do this."

"Yes, I do," she said with unwavering conviction.

"Are you sure? This could cause you lasting trauma. We've had tough cases before." Declan offered her an expression of sympathy. There was an entire unspoken conversation happening between them. He was talking about the case when they were undercover when Kate had been drugged and nearly sexually assaulted. They rarely spoke about it, but Kate knew he didn't think she had processed it properly. He had asked more than once if she wanted to see a therapist beyond the two sessions the FBI made her attend. Declan had never pushed her though when she said she was fine. It didn't mean he didn't hover around her at times.

Kate knew this was asking too much of him. "You'll be there and won't let anything happen to me."

He searched her face and then looked over at Sam. "Everything Kate said is true. We don't have much of an option. I'm in for as long as Kate wants to do this."

With that settled, Declan left with Kate to go back to the apartment before they'd all meet back together later that night. On the walk, they grabbed a late lunch at a pub near their apartment. While they were eating, they laughed and talked about everything and anything other than the case.

Declan told stories of the first year they knew each other while they were still in the FBI Academy. Kate knew he was trying to break the tension hanging over them. She appreciated his efforts to make her laugh and let her know it would be okay, even though neither of them could make that promise.

When they got back to the apartment, Kate said she wanted to lay down for a short nap. Declan said he was going to follow up on a few things in the kitchen and possibly check in with Spade again. Kate didn't want to speak to Spade for fear he might try to talk her out of the plan.

Once in the bedroom, she closed the door a few inches to block out some of the light. She undressed down to the strappy tank top she had on under her sweater and dropped her jeans at the side of the bed. She peeled back the covers and climbed in.

Kate wasn't sure if she'd be able to sleep as the tension knotted across her shoulders. The case had taken a toll not only on her mind but on her body too. She had never been one to nap, not even as a child. Kate knew she had to rest before meeting Knox later that night.

She reached out to the nightstand and checked her phone once to make sure he hadn't messaged her. When she didn't see any messages, Kate closed her eyes to sleep.

She wasn't sure how long she'd been asleep when the bed shifted under Declan's weight. She rolled over on her side to see him standing there, stripped down to his boxer briefs. Even though they had slept together wearing not much more since being in Scotland, the air in the room felt different. The words caught in the back of Kate's throat but she reached over and pulled back the covers for him.

Before getting into bed with her, Declan softly said, "I want to hold you, Kate. I have about an hour before I need to leave and I just want to feel you against me."

"You didn't hear me say no," she said, looking up at him.

Declan slid into the bed next to her and wrapped her in his arms. She rested her head on his chest as he ran his fingers over her shoulder. He shifted their bodies so their legs were entwined. "Are you scared, Kate?"

"I'm not sure scared is the right emotion," she lied. "I want so badly for this case to be over and for us to achieve justice for all the victims. If I thought there was another way to go about it, this wouldn't be what I'd choose. It's better than nothing. I don't want you to worry about me."

"I'm always going to worry about you, Katie. Even when you aren't doing something incredibly stupid and dangerous, I'm going to worry." He said it with enough of a chuckle she couldn't be too angry that he was calling her actions stupid. They lay like that for a long time in silence.

Kate wondered if he had fallen asleep, but when she turned her head to look at him he was staring up at the ceiling. "You said you had an hour before you were leaving. Where are you going?"

"Logan from the tour company called me and said he had some

records for us. It's not far from the pub. I was going to stop there and grab them before I meet with Sam and Fraser. Not that I think there's anything in there that can help us, I'd just rather have the records before you have to sit down with Knox."

Kate realized then she had forgotten to tell Declan about the records. "I saw Logan last night and he said he had them. With everything going on with Jax, it slipped my mind."

Declan rolled Kate to her side until their faces were inches apart. "I don't want to talk about Logan right now."

"What do you want to talk about?"

"I don't want to talk," he said as he kissed her softly. She kissed him back and that only encouraged him. He parted her lips with his tongue and the kiss grew more passionate.

Kate moved her body against his suggestively but his hands remained around her waist. She lost herself in the kiss with only the fleeting thought about how much she enjoyed kissing him and how long she had waited for him to kiss her again after the last time. She pulled back from him and looked him in the eyes. "Do we have time?" she asked, letting the question linger between them.

"Not now and not like this. I honestly just wanted to be near you. I wasn't expecting more," he said, planting a soft chaste kiss on her lips. He rolled to his back and pulled her with him. "I don't want to rush anything with you, especially not the first time."

Kate smiled into his chest. He'd given thought to all of this, maybe even more than she had. She lay there with him trying to let the feeling of being wanted overtake the stressful feelings of what was to come later that night. "We won't rush then. There's plenty of time."

Kate said the words and could only hope that she lived to see tomorrow.

She snuggled closer into him and closed her eyes.

CHAPTER 38

By eight-thirty, Declan still wasn't back from the tour company. Kate paced back and forth down the road from the pub where she was with Sam before meeting Knox. He had put in an earpiece and a small recording device.

"Have you tried his cellphone?" Sam asked as he watched her.

"At least twenty times. This isn't like him at all, especially not right now."

"Maybe he found something at the travel company."

Kate shook her head. "Even if he found something, he wouldn't miss being here now and he would answer his phone. Something is wrong." Kate could feel the deep ache inside her bones that told her something wasn't right with the whole situation. Part of her wanted to bail on the meeting with Knox and go find Declan, but a more rational part of her brain knew that wasn't possible. It was too late and there was too much riding on this meeting.

"Kate, he'll be here," Sam told her again. He could see the stress on her face and kept watching her, probably wondering if she was going to crack. "If you want to call this whole thing off, we can. All you have to do is message Knox and let him know you need to reschedule."

Kate checked her phone one more time. "No. I need to get in there now. I have to believe whatever is keeping Declan has to be vital to the case because he'd never miss something this important." She turned to Sam for him to check the earpiece that was covered by her hair and the small video recording device on the button of her shirt.

Fraser was in position along with a whole team of law enforcement around the pub. They did not have anyone undercover inside the pub because there was nothing for them to do. The whole goal for Kate was to allow herself to be moved someplace else where he would hopefully attempt to attack her.

"I'm ready," Kate said but wanted to scream. Her worry about Declan had turned to frustration quickly.

"I'll be there for you, Kate. Nothing is going to happen to you that you don't allow to happen. We are all here with you," Sam reassured her.

The sound of her heart beating in her ears drowned out Sam's words. She knew everything he was saying was true but that didn't make the situation any easier. All Kate had to do was walk the few blocks up the Royal Mile toward Edinburgh Castle to the pub.

Kate felt all eyes on her as she walked the short distance. She knew cops were flanking both sides of the road all waiting to pounce on Knox as soon as they got the evidence. Kate made her way into the crowded pub and found a table where she could watch the door. She checked her phone one more time and then left it on the table where she could continue to check it and watch the time.

A server came over and Kate said she'd wait to order. There were people all around her laughing and drinking and going about their night like there wasn't a serial killer prowling the area. Kate focused only on the door and drowned out the rest of the noise.

The minutes ticked by quickly at first and then it felt like time stood still. Knox was more than fifteen minutes late. She reached for her phone and checked the app to see if he had messaged her but there was nothing.

"Agent Walsh, I'm so glad I found you," a familiar voice said and pulled out the chair across from her.

She raised her head to see Logan sit down. Kate glanced to her left and then to her right looking for Declan who she had expected to be with him. "Logan, you can't be here right now. I'm waiting for someone."

"Knox. I know," he said and leaned forward on his arms. "Declan came to see me and then Knox showed up. He trashed the tour shop to get the records back and then took Declan."

Kate looked around her waiting for one of the officers to rush to her aid. She was sure someone was listening. "What do you mean he took Declan?"

Logan gulped air down and his hand shook as he spoke. "Declan came into the shop as it was happening. Knox overpowered him and took his gun. Declan tried to get away but Knox attacked him. There was a struggle and Declan was shot. He's wounded and Knox said he would only let him go in exchange for you. He sent me to get you."

Kate put her palms flat on the table. "Where did he take him?"

"Princess Street Garden." Logan looked across the table with pleading eyes. "Agent Walsh, you can't go. He's going to kill you. You can't go."

"I have to go," Kate said, standing. There was no way she was going to sit there and not go after Declan. It made so much sense now why he hadn't shown up or returned her call. Declan had been right – he knew it was her. Kate didn't fully trust Logan but she had no idea what else to do in the moment. "Did he tell you where in Princess Street Garden he was going to be?"

Logan stood with her. "He told me where to take you." He looked around the bar. "Where are the cops? He said if there were cops, he'd kill Declan the moment he saw any."

"I'll go alone," Kate repeated the words in the hopes Sam and Fraser had heard her through the audio. She was surprised she wasn't hearing anything through the earpiece and could only hope that they'd follow her.

As Kate headed toward the front door, Logan pulled her back. "There's an easier way to get there. We can go down into the basement of this pub and out the back alleyway. There's a close that runs to Market Street and then the entrance is just past Waverly Station."

Her spine tingled in a sort of knowing. This is what the killer did but she'd have to follow him. She didn't know Edinburgh well and had no choice but to follow him whichever way he wanted to get there. Kate only hoped Sam and Fraser were listening.

As Kate followed Logan to the back of the bar, dodging people and tables, Kate glanced around at the faces of people hoping to see someone familiar. There was no one. She followed closely behind Logan as they entered a staff-only area of the bar and then descended a sharp staircase. They took a sharp left and then a right before exiting the backway.

The cold air stung her lungs as she moved quickly by Logan's side. He tried to talk her out of going the entire way, begging and pleading with her that there had to be another way.

"Did Knox tell you his real name?" Kate asked as they cut through a small alleyway that looked smaller than any close she'd seen in the city. When Logan didn't respond, she said, "You said you found records of the tour. What name is he using?"

Logan didn't respond to any of it. It was almost like he couldn't hear her. There was no acknowledgment of what she said. Her suspicions continued to grow but this was the plan – allow herself to be led.

They zipped by people in the alleyway. Logan didn't slow down for anything and Kate did her best to keep up with him. She tried to ask the questions again but was still met with silence. When they cleared the close, Kate grew confused. She could see the Walter Scott Memorial straight ahead to the left and knew they were close to the gardens. That must be the real destination as Logan said.

They waited at the light to cross. "What's the name of this road?" Kate asked, hoping if Sam and Fraser weren't seeing a video of her location they'd at least hear the audio.

"Waverly Bridge," he said then picked up his pace. They were practically moving at a run. They passed the entrance to the Christmas markets with the tent lights still aglow. A handful of people were coming out of the sectioned-off area, talking and laughing, oblivious to the two of them.

All Kate could focus on was Declan and what she'd do when she saw him. She wasn't going to exchange herself for him but hoped that she or one of the many cops that should be following her could subdue Knox in the process.

They got to the steep staircase of Princess Street Gardens and Logan turned to her. "Be careful, they can get slippery in this weather."

Between the rain and light snow they had earlier in the day, the steps looked coated and slick. Kate held onto the black iron railing as she followed Logan down. Kate focused ahead but couldn't see much in the dark. She and Declan had not ventured into what was considered New Town Edinburgh because the case hadn't brought them there. "How much farther?"

"It's not far now. Hurry," Logan said practically shouting at her. They hit the sidewalk and Logan picked up his pace. He shoved past a group of young men, one of them calling him a foul name. Logan didn't seem to mind.

Kate apologized to the group as she passed them and then flashed her badge when they started shouting at her. It silenced them and she had to jog to catch up to Logan. He ducked to the left and went down a steep embankment to another sidewalk. Kate slowed her pace and held onto the railing. The ground was made of small uneven rocks that weren't laid out in any kind of grid. They were laid hundreds of years ago but now some of them stuck up higher than the others and were slick with remnants of snow and mud.

Kate glanced up to the main sidewalk but there was no one following them. She craned her neck to look up even higher to the lights of Princess Street filled with shops and restaurants.

"Logan, please tell me where we are going?" It felt to Kate like they were going farther down into the pit of the gardens. The pavement turned to wet, snowy grass and the light diminished the farther they went. On the other side of the gardens, perched high, was Edinburgh Castle. Its lights cast an eerie menacing presence.

Finally, Logan stopped in the middle of the field. He turned to her with his arms open wide. "They were supposed to be right here. I don't understand, Agent Walsh. Where could they be?"

Kate came to a stop in front of him and caught her breath. They were in the dead center of the field and she could only see a few feet in front of her and behind. They were surrounded by darkness. Far off in every direction were lights but she assumed no one could see them.

"This can't be the place," Kate said as soft rain started to fall. They were in the middle of a field with nothing around the immediate vicinity. She spun in every direction looking for any sign of Declan. She turned back to him. "This can't be it, Logan! Where are they?"

"I don't know." He sucked in sharp breaths. "I don't know."

Kate stepped toward him as a slow evil smile spread across his face. She stopped dead in her tracks.

He pulled a gun from his waistband before she could grab hers. "This looks like the perfect place to me, Kate," he said all trace of his Scottish accent gone. He didn't even sound French. He spoke in a crisp English accent he'd probably been perfecting since boarding school.

Kate eyed the gun and she couldn't be sure in the dark, but it looked like their FBI-issued firearm. "Is that Declan's gun?"

He waved it back and forth. "He doesn't need it anymore. He's dead, Kate. I killed him."

Kate's breath caught in her throat. She reached for her gun under her coat but Logan barked for her to stop. He thrust the gun forward and promised to kill her right there if she moved again. Kate put her hands in front of her.

As she watched in horror but not surprise, Logan reached up with one hand and tugged the red beard from his face. Before she could react, he ripped off the hair on top of his head, revealing a shaved head. He then picked at the skin near his chin and peeled off the prosthetic skin from his face.

Kate stood motionless as her mouth dropped open in a silent scream.

"I'd pop out the contacts but that's kind of hard to do one-handed," he said with a laugh. "Oh, I nearly forgot the best part." He reached up under his shirt and pulled off padding he had around his middle that made him look about forty pounds heavier – finally looking like a mix between the man in the photo and a sketch of the man with the shaved head.

When Markus was done, he held his hands wide and took a bow.

When he straightened himself, evil burned in his eyes. Kate had no doubt he'd shoot if she tried to move. Not that she could get much traction under her feet to run.

"You don't have to kill me, Markus," Kate said, taking a step back from him. She would have felt like a fool for not seeing it sooner, but there was no way she could have. His disguise down to his thick Scottish accent had been flawless.

Markus grinned a sick smile. "No, I don't *have* to kill you. I want to." He advanced on her quickly, grabbing her face with one hand and jabbing the gun into her stomach with the other. He mashed his face into hers and stuck his tongue in her mouth, trying to suck the life from her.

Kate pulled back and tried to wrestle free of him.

One thing she knew for sure – she wasn't going to die without a fight.

CHAPTER 39

Kate fought for her life harder than she had ever fought. It was like a tug of war with Kate pulling back and Markus coming forward and then Kate would get some ground and shove him back only for him to be on her again.

With the gun in one hand, Markus couldn't get a good grip on her face or neck. Kate used the complication and the wet muddy grass to her advantage. When he went in for another sucking kiss, Kate clamped her teeth down on his lip. As he yelped back in surprise and pain, Kate knocked the gun from his hand. It went skidding into the darkness.

He howled a curse and drove his body into hers. She slammed back into the ground with such force her head bounced once and then twice, making her see stars and knocking the wind from her.

Markus mounted her, slamming her back down into the ground. "You're not going to beat me. I've been doing this too long to be taken out by someone like you. I killed your partner and I'm going to kill you!" He wrapped his hands around her neck and started to squeeze.

Kate couldn't get any leverage on her back. She tried to get her legs up and her feet to his chest to push him back but he was sitting too far up on her chest. She tried to pry his thumbs back and get her arms in between his to break his hold. None of the hand-to-hand combat moves she knew so instinctively were working. Kate slapped her hip for her gun but found the holster empty.

Kate fought her body which desperately needed air. She tried to slow her heart rate and think, think, think but she couldn't form coherent thoughts in the heat of the moment…what more could she do? She didn't want to die like this.

As she started to lose consciousness, she thought about Declan and what might have been. Memories of their time together floated by like a hazy cloud that at least gave her a second of peace.

Almost as if hearing her thought, a man shouted from the darkness. "He's not dead, Kate!"

A blur whizzed by, releasing the pressure from her body. Kate gasped for breath, short and shallow ones at first. Then she found the energy to push herself to a sitting position and sucked in a deep breath, letting it out. Slowly her breathing returned to normal but the threat wasn't over.

There were sounds of a struggle, grunts and moans, off to her left. Kate reached for her gun at her hip then remembered it was gone. It must have been knocked out when Markus tackled her. She scrambled to her feet.

"Stay back, Kate," the man shouted again.

It was hard to distinguish the voices with the ringing in her ears. Kate didn't stay back. She moved in the direction of the voice and quickly came upon Leo standing over Markus with a gun pointed at his head.

"Leo, no," Kate said weakly but didn't have the energy to say or do much more. "What do you mean Declan isn't dead?" She knew she should be more concerned about the scene in front of her but she remembered he said *he isn't dead* and she needed to know what he meant.

"Declan's not dead. He was knocked unconscious. I overheard the cops up on the road when I was headed down here. They aren't sure where you went. Your audio and video cut off at some point." He said all of this without looking at her. He never took his eyes off Markus. "You need to get out of here, Kate."

"No. Leo. Not like this. I need to take him in," Kate said, searching her body for handcuffs and finding none. Feeling defeated with no gun or cuffs and no ability to physically restrain Markus, she looked down at him. "Why? Why did you do all of this?"

"It's always why with you cops," Markus said with an evil laugh. Even forced to the ground on his knees, he remained arrogant and defiant. "The real question is why not? There was no one to stop me. No one cared about those women. Even the cops didn't do anything."

"People cared, Markus. They had family and friends and people who cared about them." Kate knew there was no point trying to reason with a psychopath and her desire to try never failed to annoy her. She knew they didn't think, reason or process information like normal people did. "You're going to prison for a long time."

Markus tried to stand but Leo ordered him back down. He obeyed the gun pointed at him. "You're forgetting one thing. You have no evidence I did anything wrong. I haven't admitted anything and you don't have any physical evidence. It's your word against mine what happened out here. I have the best lawyers who will convince a jury you're an overzealous FBI agent with an ax to grind. You're not thinking rationally. You've got an international criminal in front of you with a gun pointed at me and you're not doing anything. Don't even pretend you don't know who he is. No one will believe you. Your partner doesn't know who hit him. You have nothing on me."

Kate couldn't argue with him. He was right on all counts. If her audio and visual were down she had no record of what occurred. She turned to Leo. "How did you know where we were?"

Leo didn't answer with words but his eyes drifted to one of the pockets on her jacket. She reached her hand in and came away with a small tracking chip. He had been tracking her movements this whole time. "The alley?" she asked, remembering back to when he had his hands around her.

Leo nodded.

Kate wasn't sure what she was feeling. If Leo hadn't bugged her, she'd be dead now.

Leo nodded his head again and then looked at her with sympathy in his eyes. "I did what I had to do. I knew you'd lead me to the killer."

The rain came down harder now, washing the mud from her face and hair. She rocked on the balls of her feet not sure what to do. She had no idea where her gun went. She had no handcuffs to bring him in. Kate reached into her pocket for her cellphone in the hopes of calling someone but found that gone too.

She looked at Leo with pleading eyes. "Leo, please. Not like this."

"We don't have a choice, Kate."

Kate stood there with the rain coming down watching them. Two international criminals – one far worse than the other in terms of violence and destruction. It was odd to think of Spade in that moment but something he told her a long time ago came back to her. He told her that every FBI agent will come to a point where they have to make decisions that might be morally ambiguous for the greater good. Things weren't always black and white.

Kate didn't feel like a good FBI agent at that moment. She felt helpless and unprepared and had no backup. The decision weighed heavily on her but she heard no reinforcements coming. There was no one out there with her but two criminals.

They were both right.

Even if she could arrest Markus right then and there, he might never even stand trial for what he did. Those who knew him as Logan knew an upstanding member of the community and an excellent tour guide. Those who knew him as Markus weren't talking. They had already tried. The rest of the women who had seen the evil side of him were dead. She had compromised herself with Leo. Even Declan could testify to that.

Kate looked over at Leo who was finally looking at her, studying her carefully. Then she looked down at Markus.

"You can't leave him here with me," Markus said with fear in his voice for the first time. "He'll kill me. You can't leave me here with him!"

He was right. Kate shouldn't leave him there with Leo. He had a choice – either come willingly or die. Kate reached down to try to pull him to his feet. "You're under arrest, Markus." He lunged at her again – his fingernails scraping against her neck and drawing blood.

Markus cursed at her and called her a vile name. "I told you. You're not bringing me in."

Kate's whole body deflated as the last of her energy drained from her. She raised her eyes to Leo one last time pleading with a look. She wanted to ask him if he was sure. But the look on his face told her this was the only way to stop Markus.

It was the only way to keep the world safe from him.

He looked at her with sympathy, knowing the position he had put her in. "I won't do this with you here, Kate. You need to walk away from this clean."

A wry laugh escaped her lips. "It's too late for that." She looked down at Markus then over at Leo for the last time. "Stay here. I'll be right back," she commanded then walked off into the darkness with the rain coming down heavier now.

The wetness on her face was a mix of the rain and her tears.

Kate wasn't sure how far she was from them when she heard the gunshot. She stopped in her tracks and turned back but couldn't see anything. When Kate turned back again and took another step it was like walking into a new reality, one in which she wasn't the same woman who had walked into Princess Street Gardens.

She was leaving a different person – a different kind of FBI agent, one with blood on her hands.

Kate wasn't sure how long she walked before she saw Sam and several other uniformed cops rushing toward her. "He's dead," she said weakly not meeting Sam's eyes.

"Kate," he said, wrapping her in a hug. "We thought you were dead." He stood back from her and looked her over. He touched the scratch on her neck that would be accompanied by bruising later. "You're bleeding."

Kate started to speak but her voice didn't sound like her own. It was monotone and without depth like a person in the aftermath of tragedy dealing with shock – which she supposed she was. "I tried to bring him in but I couldn't. He attacked me and got me to the ground. In the process, he knocked my gun away from me and my handcuffs. He tried to kill me." She paused for a few beats. "He would have killed me but there was someone else out there. He shot him."

"Who shot him, Kate?"

"Leo. He came out of the darkness and pulled him off me. There was a struggle and he shot him," Kate said the first lie among many she was sure would come. What wasn't a lie was what she said next. "If Leo wasn't there, Markus would have killed me. I was nearly dead. If it wasn't for him, I wouldn't be standing here right now."

Sam looked her over. "It's okay, Kate. Where is Logan? After you left the pub with him, we lost all contact with you. All the audio and video was lost."

Kate blinked at him several times, not sure she heard him correctly. They knew nothing. Markus had been right. There was no evidence against him. "There is no Logan. It was Markus in disguise. He lured me out there and then took off his disguise. Declan?"

"He's okay, Kate. Once we heard Logan say Declan had been taken, we sent cops to the tour office and they found him unconscious. He's okay but refused to go to the hospital. He wanted to look for you, but we made him go back to the apartment with another officer. He probably has a concussion. He needs medical care but he's refusing until he gets word from you."

"I lost my phone," she said, glancing back over her shoulder.

Sam yelled to Fraser who was descending the stairs into Princess Street Gardens with more cops. "I'm going to take Kate to the medics and call Declan for her." He gave Fraser a quick update about what had happened.

"I'm so glad you're okay, Kate," Fraser said and put his hand on her arm.

Kate knew she had to be slipping deeper into shock because she couldn't hear anything he said. The constant hum in her ears drowned out everything else. When Fraser was gone, she let herself be led by Sam up the stairs to the medics and a crime scene tech who took photos of her injuries. When they were done, a medic checked her over, put some antibiotic ointment on her scratch, and eventually cleared her. They told her she was in shock and shouldn't be alone.

She felt nothing. All she wanted to do was see Declan.

Kate was forced to give a full statement before they'd release her. She was sure this was one with many more to come. There'd probably be hearings too about the case and she'd have to account for her actions. She wondered if she'd lose her badge – maybe be fired.

Kate wasn't sure if she cared.

Sam helped her down from the back of the ambulance after she gave him her formal statement. "I'll drive you back to your apartment. Declan is waiting for you."

Kate nodded but no words came. She let him guide her to his car and closed the door for her after she got in. She stared out the window at the pouring rain as he drove her the short distance back to the apartment. He told her they'd meet in the morning to debrief.

Kate let herself into the building, slowly climbed the stairs, and told the officer standing at the door he was free to go. He confirmed he'd just been cleared by Fraser to leave but wanted to wait to see if she needed anything. There was nothing she needed from him. The man on the other side of the door was the only one she needed. He left her standing there and descended the stairs.

Kate stood there long enough to shed her wet clothing, shoes, and socks. She stripped down to her wet bra and panties and shivered against the cold.

Kate turned the knob on the door, pushed it open, and stepped inside. She made it as far as the foyer.

"I thought you were dead, Kate," Declan said, standing in the middle of the living room looking no better than she did. He cursed loudly when he saw her naked skin wet and streaked with mud. In one fast movement, he grabbed the throw blanket from the couch and wrapped it around her, pulling her close to him. "I thought you were dead," he said again.

"I thought you were dead too," Kate said, the emotion catching in her throat. She leaned into him and cried, full sobbing tears, releasing all of the stress and fear she had been holding.

Declan held her tighter against him.

She sobbed until there was nothing left. For the first time, Kate felt truly safe.

She pulled back and looked up into his eyes. "I need you. Here. Now. Nothing else matters." She whispered words she had never uttered to another person in her whole life.

CHAPTER 40

I t was all the invitation he needed. Declan took her face in his hands and kissed her gently at first, their lips barely touching. He said her name in a whisper. The kiss quickly grew deeper as neither could contain the heat between them any longer. Kate matched his passion with her own, his arousal evident against her. She pushed the day's events out of her mind and focused only on him.

Kate broke the kiss long enough to drop the blanket from her shoulders and claw at his tee-shirt, pushing it up so she could put her hands on his bare skin. He did the rest tearing it over his head and tossing it in a heap on the floor. She ran her fingertips down his chest and taut stomach. She tickled the tiny trail of hair that went from his navel into the waistband of his jeans. She had seen him shirtless many times but this time was different.

Kate was more aware of the softness of his skin and the firm defined muscle of his chest and stomach. She traced the scar on his shoulder from where he had been shot, thinking briefly of the only other time she had thought she lost him.

Declan allowed her full access. Kate stood on her toes and kissed him again, enjoying the sensations. His kisses were playful at times, ardent at others. He told the whole story of how he felt for her in a kiss. Still, she knew he was holding back, letting her take the lead. It couldn't have been easy for him.

He nuzzled her cheek and nipped playfully at her earlobe, making her shiver. He pulled back and looked her in the eyes as his fingertips traced the contours of her face and then the scratch at her neck. "Are you sure? I don't want to hurt you," he asked, his voice husky.

"I've never been more sure of anything in my life," Kate said and stepped back from him. She paused only a moment to look into his eyes as she unhooked her wet bra letting the straps fall from her shoulders. She held it in front of her for only a moment before dropping it to the floor, her nipples hard under his gaze. She wasn't done though. Kate watched him as he took in every curve of her body as she hooked her fingers into the sides of her panties and shimmied them down her legs to join her bra on the floor.

Kate righted herself and stood before him completely naked. Nervous laughter escaped her lips. Declan wasn't laughing though. His gaze roamed over her body and the intensity of his look told Kate all she needed to know.

This time he didn't wait for her to make a move. He took two steps and backed her into the living room wall possessing her mouth and burying his hands in her damp hair.

Kate attacked his belt and the button of his jeans. She wanted all of him against her naked flesh now. She undid his pants and he broke the kiss long enough to step out of them. Kate pulled him close again and grazed the tip of his erection with her fingers. Declan sucked in a breath but he had other plans.

With nothing standing between them, he lifted her, and Kate wrapped her legs around his body. He buried his face in her breasts, kissing her soft skin. "You have no idea how many times I've imagined this."

Kate rested her head back against the wall, enjoying his lips on her. "Probably not as many times as I've imagined it," she admitted.

Declan groaned in response and carried her to the bedroom. He lay her gently down on the bed moving on top of her in the same move. He kissed her lips again allowing their bodies to meet. "You're perfect, Katie. Perfect," he said as he expelled a breath.

Declan propped himself up on one arm and stared into her face. He looked on the brink of saying something but words never escaped his lips. He smiled at her and then leaned down for another kiss before trailing wet sucking kisses down her body to her hot wet center. He teased her with his lips and tongue, bringing her to the brink and then backing off. Breathlessly, she begged him to both stop and keep going as she squirmed under him.

Then she gave over to the sensations coursing through her and moaned his name in utter bliss.

As her body continued to spasm, Declan moved back up and joined their bodies together for the first time. He leaned down to kiss her as Kate moaned his name mixed with a laugh. He kissed her passionately as he rocked their bodies together.

Through uneven breath, Kate whispered in his ear, "If I had known you were this good, I would have done this a long time ago."

Much later, when they were both satisfied and lying twisted in the sheets, Declan pulled her close to him and traced his fingers over her back. "I thought this might be awkward but it doesn't feel that way."

Kate had thought the same. She had wondered about the aftermath, when lust had been quenched, if she would look at him differently or regret it. She saw him differently but it wasn't regret. Kate just wanted to do it again. "I don't think there could ever be anything awkward between us. We know each other too well."

Declan chuckled. "We know everything and let me tell you I had no idea the passion bubbling under that cold exterior." She nudged him in the side and he laughed. "I'm serious. I thought it would be good but that was..." He had no words and neither did Kate.

She sighed into him. "I need to shower." Her skin was still mud streaked and she wanted to wash away the field and dirt and thoughts of Markus. She didn't want to ruin the mood but they still had work. She propped herself up and looked at him. "We need to talk about what happened."

Declan nodded. "Let's take a shower and then when you're feeling better, we can talk."

"You're joining me?" Kate asked surprised but happy.

Declan followed her into the shower. They soaped and scrubbed and gave themselves over again to the passion that still burned hot between them. If Kate had thought it would dissipate after, she was gladly mistaken.

When Kate was wrapped in a bathrobe and Declan sat beside her on the couch, both sharing the comforter they had stolen from the bed, he told her how he had gone to the tour shop and been attacked as soon as he walked in. It had been as Markus described it. He hit Declan in the back of the head and knocked him unconscious.

"How are you feeling now? We probably should have taken you to the hospital," Kate said, wondering if sex while having a concussion was the best course of action. He seemed fine though.

"I'm okay," he said and took her fingertips and pressed them gently to the knot on the back of his head. "When I came to, my only concern was you. Fraser wouldn't let me go to you. He wouldn't tell me anything. He made me come back here and an officer waited with me when I refused to go for medical treatment. I wanted to get to you but Fraser said you were missing. That's all I knew, Kate. They wouldn't let me get to you. What happened out there?"

Kate recounted what happened at the bar and then what followed later in Princess Street Gardens. "It was so dark, Declan. The farther we got into the field, the less I was able to see even though off in the distance there were lights. Down there in the thick of it, it was impossible to see much around us. When he peeled away his disguise,

I wanted to be angry at myself for not seeing it sooner but his disguise was flawless. There was no way anyone would have been able to tell."

"I didn't see it either, Kate." Declan pulled her closer to him. "What happened?"

Kate described how he attacked her and the struggle that followed. "If Leo hadn't shown up when he did, I'd be dead, Declan. He saved my life – again." She took a breath knowing she was going to have to tell him the truth and that would implicate him if push came to shove.

She couldn't lie to him, not now, not after what they just shared.

"Declan," she said softly. "I let Leo kill him. I knew if I walked away what was going to happen. I told them to wait there because I didn't have my gun or handcuffs or even my phone. When I tried to get Markus to his feet, that's when he went for my neck and I got this scratch. I knew we didn't have the evidence we needed. At that moment, I played judge, jury, and executioner. The only thing I didn't do was pull the trigger. I knew what would happen though."

Hearing the tone of her voice, Declan asked, "Are you feeling guilty, Kate?"

"Of course. I didn't tell Sam the truth. I told them there was a struggle and Leo shot him. I didn't tell them the rest – that there was time to think it through. There was time to do something else."

Declan shook his head. "There was nothing else for you to do. What needed to be done, was done." He didn't waver in his conviction and it was the response Kate assumed she'd get from him. When he felt her body tense, he pulled her closer. "Kate, you did the right thing. Twenty-six murdered women. Someone had to stop him one way or the other. I never thought I'd say this but I owe Leo a thank you for protecting you when I couldn't and for doing what needed to be done."

Kate sighed with some relief but the guilt still hung over her. "What do I do? Do I tell Sam and Fraser what *really* happened? Do I tell

Spade?"

"No," Declan said with conviction in his voice. "We will take this to our graves. There was a struggle and Leo showed up in the nick of time and saved you. That's all anyone ever needs to know. He made sure you were alive and then got away before you could apprehend him. That's the official story from this point forward." They shared a look. It wasn't the first secret between them and it wouldn't be the last. "Do you understand me, Kate? You're not going to tarnish your record, not for a man that would have killed you."

Kate nodded, grateful that Declan would protect her in this way. What she did wasn't illegal, but it wasn't morally just in her mind. Then again, maybe it was. With Leo's action, he assured there would be no more women murdered. She closed her eyes and rested her head against his chest.

Kate had no idea how long they stayed on the couch like that, but when she woke the next morning, she was alone in bed wrapped in the covers. She heard Declan on the phone in the kitchen and smelled bacon and eggs cooking. She lay there longer than she wanted but her body was sore from the fight with Markus.

Kate breathed in and out, accepting what they had discussed the night before.

When Declan ended the call, he walked into the bedroom and sat on the edge of the bed. "I talked to Spade and told him. We need to meet with Fraser and Sam today and go over a few things but then we are cleared through the New Year. Spade told us to travel or do whatever we want to do. He's happy with the resolution, Kate. The official story hit the news this morning. The Close Killer was killed by a good Samaritan during an attack on an FBI agent. There is no mention of the Phantom. Sam said they found Markus in Princess Street Gardens with a gunshot wound to his head. They found your gun and handcuffs but didn't find your phone. We can get you a new one today."

"That's it? Just like that it's over?" Kate asked, not sure how she was feeling.

"It's over, Kate. Trust me, no one is mourning Markus Lamiere. The news coverage is global. Sam and Fraser credited your hard work and said you were resting from the attack but that you'd recover. If there are questions, no one is asking them. What do you want to do? Do you want to stay here or travel somewhere else?"

Kate looked up at him. "What do you want to do?"

"Whatever makes you happy, Katie." His tone was sincere.

Kate sat up in bed, pulling the sheet with her. She tucked it under her arms covering her breasts more for warmth than modesty. Kate knew what she wanted. There was no question in her mind. "I want to go home with you and celebrate Christmas. I want to go to your parents for Christmas dinner and be with your family. I want it to be loud and cheerful and to play with your nieces and nephews. I want a traditional cozy Christmas at home for the first time in years – with you."

"That's what we'll do then." Declan leaned down and kissed her sweetly. "Right now though, you need to come to the kitchen and eat the breakfast I made you."

The day was spent in meetings and case closure. There were no more official statements to be given. But there was endless paperwork and conversations, mostly assuring them she was okay. They thanked Fraser and Sam for their help. Then they made calls to each of the victims' families and explained what had happened to their loved ones. That was the hardest but most satisfying part of the day. They took down the evidence from the boards and boxed up other files.

Kate and Declan thanked Sam and Fraser again for their hard work and dedication on the cases. They left the basement conference room together and on the street outside said their goodbyes.

They walked the Royal Mile one last time before going back to the apartment to pack. Declan had scheduled them on a nighttime flight back to Boston. Kate slept most of the way as Declan watched over her. Each time she woke, she found him staring at her. He'd smile, ask if she was hungry, and hold her hand as she fell back to sleep.

By the time she made it back to Boston, Kate would have thought she'd feel well-rested but she needed more sleep and she needed to be in Declan's arms. When the cab dropped them off, they were already entwined in an embrace. The passion hadn't abated.

They didn't even make it to her bedroom. Kate grabbed him right there on the stairs and when they were done and panting, they laughed at themselves.

A knock at the front door was the only thing that pulled them apart.

Declan pulled his shirt on and tugged on his jeans to answer the door. He pulled it open smiling back at her and then spoke to the delivery guy. "Are you sure? Okay," he said and signed for the package Kate couldn't see.

He looked up the stairs at her as he dragged in a box that stood taller than him and at least four feet wide. "Were you expecting something?"

"No," she said and pulled her shirt over her head and wiggled back into her panties. "What is it?" They worked together to undo the outer box and then unwrapped the bubble wrap. It wasn't until it was fully unwrapped and Declan was holding the object that came up to his chest, Kate stepped back and gasped. Her heart thumped.

Café Terrace at Night by Van Gogh.

Kate reached for the note tucked into the corner of the painting. She tugged the card from the envelope and read the handwritten note aloud. "I wish I could have given you the real thing but you would have only returned it. I know an excellent forger who did this years ago for me. Enjoy it, please. Don't overthink it. Dimitar is taken care of and I'm free. The world is a little safer. I know we'll meet again.

When that time comes, I hope you enjoy the chase as much as I do. Until then, be well and love fiercely, Kate. You deserve it."

Kate raised her eyes to Declan. She was rendered speechless.

Declan broke into a wide grin. "Looks like you made quite the friend, Kate."

"I don't even know what to say. I'm going to feel terrible when I have to arrest him."

"You will arrest him?" Declan asked.

"Of course," Kate said even though she kind of hoped she would never have to. Leo might have been an international criminal but there was far more to him than she ever knew. That was like most people though – a little good, a little bad, and a whole lot of complication.

Kate took a breath and smiled at her complication. "I think life is about to get incredibly interesting."

About the Author

Stacy M. Jones was born and raised in Troy, New York, and currently lives in Little Rock, Arkansas. She is a full-time writer and holds masters' degrees in journalism and in forensic psychology. She currently has three series available for readers: paranormal cozy Harper & Hattie Magical Mystery Series, the hard-boiled PI Riley Sullivan Mystery Series and the FBI Agent Kate Walsh Thriller Series. To access Stacy's Mystery Readers Club with three free novellas, one for each series, visit StacyMJones.com.

You can connect with me on:

- http://www.stacymjones.com
- https://www.facebook.com/StacyMJonesWriter
- https://www.bookbub.com/profile/stacy-m-jones
- https://www.goodreads.com/StacyMJonesWriter

Subscribe to my newsletter:

✉ http://www.stacymjones.com

Also by Stacy M. Jones

Watch for FBI Agent Kate Walsh Book in Early 2024

Access the Free Mystery Readers' Club Starter Library
PI Riley Sullivan Mystery Series novella "The 1922 Club Murder"
FBI Agent Kate Walsh Thriller Series novella "The Curators"
Harper & Hattie Mystery Series novella "Harper's Folly"

Sign up for the starter library along with launch-day pricing and special behind-the-scenes access. Hit subscribe at http://www.stacy mjones.com/

Please leave a review for Close Killer. Reviews help more readers find my books. Thank you!

Other books by Stacy M. Jones by series and order to date:

FBI Agent Kate Walsh Thriller Series
The Curators
The Founders
Miami Ripper
Mad Jack
The Fuse
Dead Senate

PI Riley Sullivan Mystery Series
The 1922 Club Murder
Deadly Sins
The Bone Harvest

Missing Time Murders
We Last Saw Jane
Boston Underground
The Night Game
Harbor Cove Murders
The Drowned Boys
What He Saw

Harper & Hattie Magical Mystery Series - Completed series
Harper's Folly
Saints & Sinners Ball
Secrets to Tell
Rule of Three
The Forever Curse
The Witches Code
The Sinister Sisters
Scandal Knocks Twice
A Treasure Most Deadly